Florissant Girls

Florissant Girls

A NOVEL

———

WILLIAM M. O'BRIEN

Charleston, SC
www.PalmettoPublishing.com

Florissant Girls

First Edition

Hardcover ISBN: 978-1-63837-004-8
Paperback ISBN: 978-1-63837-006-2

In memory of a beloved sister
Susan Margaret [O'Brien] Fischer

Part One

—

Letters from the Basement

1

Jacob lifted his head from his arms that were folded across the top of an old worktable. He sat upright, staring into space. He studied the motes he had disturbed, now at play in the early shaft of morning light. Some were moving upwards, in accord with an obscure purpose, while others swirled downwards; all were in apparent discord with the stern measures of gravity. *How did I come to rest here?*

He glanced over at his twin mattress and shabby box spring pushed into one corner; the snarled, collapsed sheets had a forlorn cast, as if recalling more than one lost body! He had risen in the middle of the night, afraid for a moment he had entered into a nightmare. He had found his way into a sort of catacombs, where spectral figures conducted a strange business; opening and closing huge sliding drawers. He stood aloof watching as people climbed out of these infernal slabs. Now his desk lamp shone down on the opened book he had been reading. There was evidence he had drooled onto the pages of the book, simply entitled *The Idiot*.

He pushed away the novel and reached for a box of stationery. There were letters he needed to write, to stay in touch with certain people. He did not know why he persisted in this activity. In his worst moments he knew these epistles were doing more harm than good; his despair was bleeding onto the handwritten pages. How could this be avoided? His very breathing was fouled in this close, dingy atmosphere. He knew he had to find some way to clear the mind of resentments, but how?

"I need to get into the city," he said aloud. He wanted to talk to some of the people he used to know; before he and Jenny, his girlfriend of seven years, had agreed to call it quits that previous winter.

He thought he might ask the landlady if he could borrow her Volkswagen. Several times Frances had let him do so in the past, after he had first moved into the apartment upstairs. By some curious arrangement she had not charged him rent when he lived in the second story; a furnished space that was, to a man with no income, nothing less than a luxury loft apartment. He had really started to enjoy those times, as embarrassing as this was to admit. He had developed a mystic sense of holding opposite beliefs in balance; he was certain, for instance, that things were bound to improve for him, despite his reckless lethargy. Then the formidable woman found someone to whom she could rent the upstairs loft, and he, the passive mote, was directed to these subterranean quarters.

"She drove me out like I was nobody! Under that damned holy disguise, she's just a mean old witch." He felt his anger tightening around his heart. He had reasoned quite differently just before he had fallen asleep. He had been extolling her generosity, and how lucky he was that she had taken him in, when he was in such dire need of lodging. Then again, why had she gotten so stingy with her car? She didn't even use it, most days, and all he wanted was to go see some people from the old crowd. Jenny's crowd, really; most of the ones who mattered had known each other since grade school. He had always remained something of an outsider, even when playing the grand host at their apartment . . .

"Friends?" The word galled him. His mind pondered the maneuvers used by people to better themselves vis-à-vis others inhabiting the same social circle. The fellowship could appear as histrionic as the animosity of 'professional wrestlers' seen on television. Not so long ago, while reading in the middle of the night, he was overcome by a stark fear, that his thoughts were no longer wholly of his own making. And yet whose thoughts are entirely his own? Where do any thoughts even come from? He was too alone, too often, and there is nothing printed on paper that can act as substitute for other faces, when they are serving as mirrors to reflect upon the viability of your behavior.

"Whatever's been lost, can be gotten again, that is for sure." His mind had adopted a curious habit of beginning monologues, and never finishing them.

He ranged his eyes over the floor as if expecting a small audience to appear. A troop of handsome field mice usually made visits in the middle of the night, happy to dine on scraps he laid out for them. Why act as just another belligerent power? They are the native inhabitants. He was amused by these dialogues, until his real fears crept too close, and he had to imagine himself abiding in the ghastly labyrinth called mental illness.

He began to proof a letter he had started writing to his mother. He soon crumpled the paper and tossed it in the direction of a large cardboard box used for waste paper. There were other crumpled epistles littering the floor. Taking a clean sheet he decided to write to his uncle Julius, who had not written him back since his last note weeks before. Much depended on this affluent uncle, who had implied very emphatically that he would remember him in his will. And he was said to be at death's door; though, he had been holding residence there for some months. The last Jacob heard, he was taking an interest in gardening, with the help of his loyal housekeeper.

There was a sudden rapping on his solitary window, at ground level, set behind an empty rack of shelving units. He knew who it was. One of the neighbors happened to be someone who had attended the same grade school as him. They had been of the same class; and this stranger acted as though they were obligated to become friends. Jacob muttered over the foolishness of trying to make friends at this low ebb in his life.

"Okay, okay," he muttered to himself, going over to peer through the window; noticing how cloudy the panes were under the whorls of dust spun by unaccountable lapses of time. He recognized the compact body of the man leaning over, his hands on his knees, staring in at him; his eyes bugging out insanely. Jacob nodded and the man straightened up and ambled off towards the backyard. Jacob retreated into the heart of his cave, one hand rising to feel the whiskers on his chin. Months earlier he had been tempted to grow a beard, but he was afraid of being mistaken for a common vagrant. How could he ever explain his sojourn, or whatever this was he was doing with himself these days, to anyone else, when it was beyond his own powers of reason?

2

Jacob shucked his pajamas and put on a pair of old jeans, a rumpled, faded Arrow dress shirt, which he left unbuttoned, and slipped into a pair of ancient loafers. He passed through a narrow chamber in the front section of the basement, where the landlady's washer and dryer were located, and climbed a series of small winding stairs leading to a tiny landing at the back door. More steps led up to another landing and her door, and wound back around climbing to the celestial loft upstairs, where some ridiculous bald character had moved in after Jacob had been dislodged.

He fumed again over this past indignity; none of it had been adequately explained to him. He paused, trying to ascertain if Frances was at home or not; her door was closed, but that didn't mean anything. Sometimes she left the door wide open when she was absent. He stepped outside; instantly the mild summer air was a soothing balm on his face.

"Hey Cody, how's it going?"

"Not bad." His neighbor had been standing on the sidewalk, hands in his pockets. They ambled over to an iron table on the patio, set atop the little rise of the tiny back yard. They sat down near an old silver maple tree, ravaged by time, and stately in rustic deportment. The early summer leaves overhead began chanting in a tongue very appealing to mortal senses.

"What do you have planned for today?" Cody asked him, looking steadily ahead, as if he were making a study of the huge sycamore tree that lorded over the crossroads below. He was already dressed in his security guard uniform, even though he didn't have to go into work until later in the afternoon.

"Nothing much." Jacob always felt sheepish explaining himself to this phantom from his childhood, whom he barely remembered. He was certain they had never been friends while he was attending St. Margaret's grade school.

"You're shitting me." Cody exclaimed.

"What?" Jacob was irritated by his excitement.

"Over there, do you see that?"

Jacob looked and saw nothing that meant anything to him.

"Joby's car is gone."

"So?"

"It's been sitting there for over six months. They finally made him move it."

Jacob tried to envision the immobile hulk that had once been such a nuisance to the neighbors; he had reserved judgment, not wishing to act like a stakeholder who belonged in these parts.

Cody settled back as if it were an established custom for them to gather in this manner to take account of matters in their tiny realm. Jacob wondered if it had something to do with the fact both of them were approaching the milestone of being forty years old. One begins to assay the concept of time differently, using a wider lens; and possibly it is natural to feel sympathy for others who also perceive mirages where once dreams had shone in the oasis of a solitary vision.

"You going to the Garden, later on?"

"I don't know." Jacob answered testily. He hated being interrogated by Cody. "Probably." He patronized a Chinese restaurant on Florissant Road, named Chengdu Garden. Several times Cody had seen him in there and had come in to join him, without invitation, sitting at his table just to visit without eating anything himself.

"These are the best days," Cody inhaled a deep breath as if he had not a single care in this world.

Jacob studied the man's nondescript features; he had a quality of appearing familiar to many people at first glance. Jacob watched him soaking up the goodness of the morning as the leaves worked with the sunshine in their magic fibers. It was maddening, his inscrutable acceptance of things, the very model of responsibility and duty. He affected Jacob in a wildly paradoxical fashion. He made him feel the delightful spirits of youth coursing in his veins once more, and also, in a contrarian fashion, his presence seemed to confirm Jacob's worst fears about himself. That he was guilty of forsaking the responsibilities that justify a man's existence.

Jacob asked about Cody's wife, who was a nurse; she was constantly being kept away from her work by a battery of mysterious ailments. Because of these infirmities their finances were apparently in a shambles. They lived in the duplex behind the house where Jacob dwelled, and although he did not know it then, that building was also owned by Frances.

"She's at her mother's with the kids right now. She's okay, I guess. We're hoping to hear from this new doctor pretty soon."

Jacob could not remember every affliction in Cody's life, and was tentative in his questions lest he reveal how poorly he had listened to the litany from day to day. The man had endured many ordeals and yet here he was, rather content, and at his leisure. The fact Cody was a stalwart husband, and father, made Jacob feel worse about his own predicament.

"Man, I could use some coffee," Jacob exclaimed, hoping Cody had some brewing in the duplex.

"I already had mine," Cody said placidly. He was a night watchman at a university in the city and possessed infinite powers of quiet observation. Other watchmen were caught napping on the job; never Cody. He caught the other delinquents, in fact, and after some arcane calculation, which only he was able to comprehend, decided whether to inform against the malefactors, or give them a fair warning. The supervisors at the security company had grown to rely on his infallible intelligence.

"Hey, do you think you could borrow the crone's car today, and let me use it for a short while?" They both looked over at the blue Volkswagen

Beetle, owned by Frances. It was nestled under the overhanging branches of wild shrubbery at the end of the driveway.

"Why don't you ask her for it?"

"She won't let me use it anymore. She's got this idea that, like, I'm not worthy of having custody of her vehicle—"

"It's because you're not paying rent."

No, Jacob thought to himself, it's because I'm not looking for work. "I'm in a tough spot here, but I have some things I have to do. She used to let me borrow it. Now she treats me like a child."

"She's been really good to Sally and me."

"Sure, she thinks the world of *you*. She'd be glad to do anything for you. Come on, why don't you just ask her—"

"No! I can't ask her for it. I don't need it for anything—"

"You could use it to get to work"

"I always take the bus, and Metro Link."

"Wouldn't you rather drive yourself; avoid all that hassle?"

"I don't need to."

"But, I mean, besides the convenience, you'd have more time to spend with your kids. That alone makes it worth while. Doesn't it?"

Cody shook his head in silence.

"Don't you want to get home sooner?" Jacob's voice was strained, a note of embarrassment rang out like feedback from an electric guitar.

They had exchanged harsh, adversarial glances as they spoke. Cody wore his implacable simplicity like armor. He was incontrovertibly his own man. Jacob was starting to believe that underneath his unflappable resolve there was a natural cunning at play. Why else would he be going out of his way to toy with him? He was probably glad to find someone to pity; such a creature can be used to confirm one's superior position.

They both leaned back and looked into the distance, moved again by the motion of leaves and the gentle stirring of early summer airs touching something responsive in the hidden fabric of their beings. Jacob sighed, feeling his frustration subside into the creative instinct that was transforming his despair into personal songs of protest; none of which made any sense to him. His subconscious sampled these tormented strains and put forth grand movements of discontent, the notation of which he could never hope to decipher for his own edification.

"Can you tell me why you need her car?" Cody asked after a moment.

"I need to go to some places in the city. I want to see about some things."

"Can't you take the bus."

Jacob looked at him malevolently. The idea of showing up at his old haunts on foot, or to be seen stepping off a bus, this left him feeling terribly despondent. Was that a gleam of triumph in the man's eye? Since Jacob began reading the Dostoevsky novels he had found in the basement, nothing was accepted at face value anymore. Strange, unknown feelings arose after his scrutiny of these texts. He spent many hours studying the lives of people he knew; trying his hand at that occult sport of attempting to solve the mysteries of human nature. It was not a very profitable enterprise; but he was coming to the realization people were not always aware of the motivations that lay behind their actions.

The dappled sunlight finding its way through the woven foliage danced about them as sprites were once thought to do, when human life was more intimate with the play of the mysteries of life, before Science stole everything for its prosaic lab work. Jacob began to hum the melody of a Neil Young tune he learned to play on his guitar as a teenager. Cody's head swung to the left and fixed on something. Jacob followed his gaze and saw that Frances was advancing up Church Street, passing under the great tulip tree. She jogged right at the corner to cross Maple Avenue at a slant, heading directly for her driveway.

She ascended the little mound of her back yard. She turned to face them. She stood erect, reminding Jacob of one of the cottonwood trees rooted in the marshy ground at the bottom of Adams Avenue, near where it joins Elizabeth. The trunks are chiseled like ornate columns, abandoned by time; preserving somehow the classic grace of forgotten ages.

"Miss Frances," Cody spoke with courtesy.

managed to say, a tinge of unease discernible in his

.alk to you both. Wait one minute." She turned and entered
he.

Th .wo men looked at one another; her desire to speak to both of
them at once, that was unusual, and surely nothing to welcome. They
glanced at one another with doubtful looks, affecting a show of false,
silent bravado.

The forbidding woman had a splendid name, Frances Guinevere
Ambers. Jacob called her the Giantess behind her back, for she seemed to
tower over him. Cody called her Miss Frances in the servile attitude used
by those wild cavaliers who served under the banner of Elizabeth. Frances
had been a nun for many years, and it was said she left her order in the
stormy wake of a sordid parish scandal, somewhere near Baltimore. It was
whispered she had toppled several pillars of the church, much like Samson;
but she was subsequently defrocked, or shall I say deflowered. She lost
her order's official maidenhood; being practically disrobed, and stripped
of many illusions. She lost the witch costume, not to mention the heavy
crosses, and all the other mass-produced jewelry that once adorned her
person. Her present habit called to mind eccentric grandmothers seen in
tarnished silver frames resting on mantles. She was a layperson at the local
parish of St. Margaret's; the attending priests had been less than eager to
accept her into the fold. Her infamous story had gone the rounds, in many
rectories, to shake the faith of the fathers in their docile flocks.

Jacob and Cody stood by the chairs where they had been sitting, as the
leaves overhead were bestirred to a chorus of gentle, Homeric mirth. The
men fell to praising the weather with glaring fervor, resorting to senseless
beatitudes. They looked around with nervous nonchalance, each making a
study of his own feet, and then the sky. They fell silent, as if by some tacit
signal enjoined to make ready for a looming contest. Jacob buttoned up his
shirt, feeling more straitened as he stood behind his chair; mustered again
to await further orders.

3

When Frances came back outside it was clear she would be digging into the earth, tending her gardens, very soon. She wore old men's trousers with a loose peasant blouse that flowed around her sturdy spare frame like drapery. She was shod in a pair of high-top, work boots, clearly visible beneath the rolled cuffs of her pant legs. Her colorful outfit had one final piece, or layer, a faded green vest that was stretched far beyond the original pattern, and clung to her form like the vines often seen woven about the trunks of great trees rising from the underbrush in a forest.

She was known to be careless of her hair, and had not visited a salon since before she took her vows. Now the thick calico strands were drawn back and bunched in a knot on the nape of her neck. Jacob noticed the many loose strands glowing in the sunlight. Her outfit was complemented by a large floppy hat with a wide brim, the strap suspended loosely beneath her firm chin. Those who knew her were aware she preserved a keen affection for Katharine Hepburn; and there is a film in which the venerable actress wears a hat just like this one.

She nodded to the two men, indicating that they should sit down, as she clutched two heavy gloves in one of her large hands. They promptly did so with much scraping of the metal chairs on the concrete pad of the patio. She twisted at the gloves with her free hand, waiting for them to be seated. The swollen purple veins of her hands caught Jacob's eye; reminding him of his mother. He felt a son's random pang of inadequacy at the stark vision trials of the woman who had borne and reared and loved ...... everything.

"What did you want, Miss Frances?" Cody asked politely, looking at Jacob after he spoke, as if petitioning her to please keep his affairs separate from those of the basement tramp, as was only proper.

"Here, let me sit down." It appeared as though she had at first thought of addressing them while standing, but now had second thoughts. She laid her gloves on the open mesh of the table. She leaned forward and clasped her hands together, holding them above the table on which her arms rested.

"Can I just ask you, first, do you think I can borrow your car today?" Jacob had not intended to make such a pathetic appeal, but something about her weary face made him take a chance. She remained utterly impassive. Her dark green eyes began to roam over his features, as one imagines a Roman field officer in charge of the siege engines might have surveyed the breastworks of an earthen stronghold in Germania, or even the great walls of Jerusalem.

"Are you actively looking for work these days?" She posed the question as her hands took up her gloves and tightened her grip until the leather squeaked.

"I've got," he scratched at one bristled cheek with a nervous hand, "I've got some things going." His halting voice quavered in defeated tones. He took a quick peripheral notice of Cody, whose body now shook in derisive appreciation of his comrade's predicament.

"No." She spoke slowly, "I'm afraid not." She laid her gnarled hands flat on the wrought iron. "Now look, here's what I needed to tell you. Well, first, Cody, your wife called me—"

"When?"

"She caught me when I was at the flower shop, earlier. She said she was calling you, but you didn't answer."

"Oh, I wasn't there, I was just over here visiting—"

"You need to go see her. You can use the car. She reached into the huge pocket of the vest she wore and placed the car keys on the table in front of Cody. He placed his hand over the keys and rolled them into his palm. He stood up to go.

"No, wait. Let me talk to you a minute."

Cody sat down again and Jacob stood up, saying, "I need to tend to some business of my own, so I will have to catch you later. I'm sure this can wait."

"No, sit down Jacob."

He did as he was told, not looking at Cody; feeling once again childish and foolish, and helpless in her matronly grip.

"I wanted to tell you both that I am going out of town, for a week or so; and I want you both to watch over the place."

"No problem," Jacob said, anxious to be on his way.

"Where are you going?" Cody asked her.

"I have to visit some people in Baltimore."

"Family?" Cody asked.

"Yes, and others."

Jacob wanted to secure permission to use her kitchen, but he was afraid of being rebuffed in front of Cody yet again. His pride gave forth a piping of sour grapes; no, he wouldn't stoop to begging her for access to her kitchen! And besides, one did not always need to get formal authorization to enjoy the usufruct of necessary things, not if you listened to nineteenth century radicals . . .

"I'm leaving the car in your hands, Cody; to use as you see fit." After saying this she looked meaningfully at Jacob, and he flushed. Cody looked at him as well, with a grand, impartial stare, and that accentuated the sting. Cody had deep brown eyes set close together, and a small, almost pointed nose, and there was something inquisitive ever wrinkling upon his countenance. He belongs to the rodent family, Jacob thought maliciously.

"I'll look after things for you," Cody affirmed proudly, as though to needle Jacob; and the point was taken. Jacob felt a shudder of social inferiority, and to the likes of this insufferable night watchman! Of course, in this setting, what could he expect? Nothing was fair around here; he seethed in his own resentments.

"And keep an eye on Mulligan. I don't really know him that well, as of yet, anyway. So, if you can, just be extra vigilant; watch over the property. I would appreciate that very much."

"No problem," Jacob said, beginning to wonder why the upstairs board-er kept his mountain bike chained to a post in the front section of the base-ment. Who did he fear would try and steal that damned precious Trek bike? The man hardly ever used it. Jacob was dying to give it a test drive. Why not be neighborly, offer it to others for their enjoyment? But the miserable bastard rarely even spoke to anyone. Jacob wondered if he made such a preposterous figure when he had lived upstairs; so certain he was then that he would soon enough be clearing out of the neighborhood altogether . . .

"And quit taking his paper," Frances admonished Jacob.

"What? Did he complain again?"

"It's his paper; he wants you to leave it alone."

"I always put it back. I fold it perfectly and put it right back where it landed!"

"He can tell. He doesn't like having it mussed. Just leave it alone."

"I don't know how he can tell." Jacob was embarrassed at having to defend his misplaced sense of injured pride.

"You can go to the library if you want to read the paper." Cody spoke with miserable innocence. He had once offered to let Jacob read his paper, he just had to ask; a thing Jacob refused to do.

Cody and Frances were both looking at Jacob now, and he had to re-mind himself that he lived in a basement, had no job, nor vehicle, nor phone, nor what might be called prospects. They could see his chest de-flate as he sank back in his chair.

"When are you leaving?" Jacob asked, hoping to bring an end to this dreary conclave.

"On Monday. Cody, I want you to drive me to the airport, and come get me when I get back."

"Sure."

"I'll call you, let you know the times and everything."

"I could do that for you," Jacob offered.

"No, that's fine. Okay then, I want to do a little work around here." She stood up and put her gloves on and went down the steps and circled around on the driveway to the garage doors and used a code to start the electric opener and waited as the door rumbled up before her, and when it was half open she bent over and disappeared into garage.

They had both been watching her and now they looked at each other.

"Do you know anything about this Mulligan character?" Jacob asked. He still entertained the idea of trying to rent the upstairs unit, if he ever landed another job; which, since he wasn't even looking, was improbable, to say the least.

"No, not really. I think he works downtown somewhere, maybe for the government?"

"Are you sure he's paying rent?"

"Oh yeah; that's why she had to put you out. She needs money like anyone else, to keep things going."

"How much does he pay?"

"I can't tell you, that's something I've been told in confidence."

"Oh for crying out loud. Just tell me!"

Cody shook his head.

Jacob felt hopelessly foolish after lighting the fuse on his own petard to launch himself into the ridiculous posture of pleading his own case as a petulant mendicant. It was disconcerting to hear Cody state plain facts that seemed to align in a logical way, and militated against Jacob's efforts to maintain *his* dignity, while Cody remained the imperturbable, respectable one. Well, what did he expect? To them he was hardly more than a beggar now. That was the simple truth of the matter. But he did have prospects; that was what no one seemed to take into consideration! It is true he had not gotten around to settling on his future course of action, but once he came into his inheritance, then he really wanted to do something. At his age, to be thinking about doing something, some day, this was not worthy of him. Oh yes? And what was, exactly?

4

Jacob was walking up South Clay Avenue, passing the old Spencer house on the crest of the hill. There were more large houses further down along both sides of the road, less grandiose. He thought of the things one hopes for, and never achieves, and of the personal treasures obtained, after much toil, and then lost with frightful ease. He paused at the corner, the hill on Adams was always enticing; the tupelo tree forming an archway over the sidewalk would turn to a burning bush of brilliant red in the autumn. He turned the other way onto a sort of open pasture area, preserved for rabbits and men on foot who have forsaken the traffic of more busy routes. The sward descends to a footpath directing one across the railroad tracks, and further along provides access to South Florissant, a main thoroughfare of his earliest childhood.

It had been a few days since Frances had flown off to other realms. His routine had hardly changed, except that he tried to be extra careful in his borrowing of the haughty rentier's *St. Louis Post-Dispatch*. He folded it up very neatly, carefully inserted it back into the plastic bag, and tossed it back onto the driveway. Except, this morning, when he came out to throw the paper back into the driveway, there was Cody, standing outside his backdoor, smoking a cigarette. They stared at each other. Jacob withered under the silent judgment.

"What's your problem?" Jacob flung out at him.

"She told you not to do that." Cody said mildly, waving his little fire stick as a sachem might, to ward off evil spirits.

"He doesn't even know!" He looked cautiously over his shoulder at one of the second-story windows.

"Just go to the library."

"I don't want to have to walk all that way—" He turned his back on Cody and thrust his arm out in a gesture of angry dismissal; which, he knew, only made him look more ridiculous. He skulked back to his cavernous dwelling.

Once settled at his desk he found he was unable to write any letters, and so he turned to his collected edition of Dostoevsky stacked on a homemade shelf. He brushed off a coat of velvety dust before laying a fresh volume on the table, and opening it at random he read the passages presented, as believers were wont to do with scripture. It was intriguing to not know exactly what you were reading; even the names of the characters were changed for unknown reasons. He cared hardly at all about plot developments. He imagined these characters actually lived in his tenement, and he was having to piece together who they were, and why they were in such an uproar about everything. After a while he needed to be outside, moving his limbs like he was going somewhere.

The earth was in flower. His senses cropped at the fragrant grass found everywhere growing rampantly; the aesthetic product never bound in sheaves nor used to fodder the restless herd. His mind was ripe for rumination and took up idle questions concerning the plodding nature of life. Then a passage from one of his texts crept out of someone's lawn; the idea that some people have a gift for seeing something new in the world. They are compelled to destroy some part of the present to replace it with something better, or at least different. So that lawlessness gives birth to higher law. Is that right? He had meant to go back and read the pages again, but instead had decided it was time to get some fresh air. Nothing puts a heart to rest like the sound of unspoiled leaves stirring in the winds.

He began playing a song in his mind, "Mother Nature's Son," as his fingers worked an invisible fret board; then he began improvising lyrics drawn from his present enjoyment of these surroundings.

On another walk he proceeded down Maple, past the school yard, skirting a hill flattened across the top where several basketball courts were enclosed by tall fencing. Sometimes young black men came there on weekends to play. When he had lived upstairs he could watch them from his windows. The competition was fierce; the camaraderie profane and endearing, fully alive with the amateur passions of youth. Beyond the empty courts he fell in with a population of dandelions, rising from the tall grass and blazing like suns in a new galaxy. A gigantic white oak tree caught his attention; leaves astir and shivering, breathing the air as though it were intoxicating to hardwood trees at this time of year. At the tracks he realized how often he was coming upon this junction; would he ever traverse the fields of memory and encounter himself coming from another direction?

He took St. Louis Avenue to the Post Office where he bought stamps. He put the little booklet into his pocket and left the building and continued walking on the same road towards the creek. He had noticed the Post Office was predominantly staffed with black people. It was just beginning to seep into his mind that the federal government had taken the onus upon itself to ameliorate the degrading effects caused by a legacy of white oppression. The nation was able to attest, on paper, that black souls were of equal worth to white souls (even though souls have no color), but in the general community that did not translate into fair and equal housing or labor practices. He had witnessed the discrimination first hand, at work, at job sites, at bars, in living rooms, and bedrooms . . .

Jacob reflected on his season living in the residence upstairs. How that arrangement had come about, much to his benefit, was never really understood. His mother had been involved; she had used his brother Luke to pass the word for him to go see Frances, who had taken him in, with hardly any questions asked. He recalled how he had quaffed a beer while cooking in his spacious kitchen, looking out over the slate roof of the public school across the street, offering bon voyage to a fleet of clouds forever setting sail for other principalities. He had been as content as any fine gentleman of Old Ferdinand had ever been, except that he was a vagrant, burning through his last resources . . .

On Adams he could enjoy the fine art of sidewalk design. The flags climbing over the hill revealed the challenges posed by a setting in the throes of perpetual change. The very old but intact pieces fit snugly to those freshly poured that have suffered as yet no fault nor discoloration. Some plates were smooth, still laying true, while others are tilted and badly off kilter; many are slightly fractured like ancient statues, or aged faces. A few are in need of replacement, completely shattered, as if they had been struck in anger by a wandering prophet. One sees the earth is rough on superficial outpourings that plot the straight and narrow. True meanings can be extracted from these scrolls only in passing, as one reasons in a salutary mood of abstract values. Jacob was quite elated as he crested the highest point and began his descent towards Elizabeth.

"Step on a crack, break your mother's back." He unexpectedly dredged up an old nursery rhyme. He looked down at his feet. At one time he had run along right here, heedlessly stomping on each crack, singing this refrain. How could that be? How is such a terrible song ever composed in the first place? He could not delve into *that* just now . . .

In his march up Elizabeth he recalled the previous spring time when he made a habit of coming this way early in the morning to see hundreds of crows making a grand rendezvous. For days they congregated in the trees each morning, before dispersing to get on with the business of begetting more crows for the glory of their jealous crow deity. Jacob found himself wondering why his mother had so forcibly dissuaded him from moving his belongings back to her house after he quit his job.

"We don't want to keep your things here." She declared, clearly exasperated by his request. She had glanced at his father, who only listened as if thinking about something else; puffing on his pipe, like a modern Solomon, whose silence is appreciated by everyone, especially the child involved.

"What should I do with them?"

"Put them in storage." She said emphatically. "You have savings?" She was beginning to look very distraught.

Yes, he did, but why pay money to store my things? It seemed a waste. He had thought it would be much easier asking his parents for this favor, than one of his brothers. Her attitude made it clear he could not ask any of them; it was a case of being self-sufficient. "One must stand on his own two feet." The axiom had been passed down through the ages in many families including his own. He had never had any argument with such reasoning before, now he was willing to grasp hold of counter arguments, however nonsensical, to defend his dishonor!

That previous winter, when he was living upstairs, just before retiring for the night, he would peer through the windows. The antique panes of glass were rife with tremulous imperfections, which made distant street lights glimmer like stars. It seemed at times he had discovered the depths of untold mysteries. He was having thoughts he had never had before. When he first moved back to his boyhood neighborhood he was never really in despair; now, living in the basement, it was different. He was cognizant of the fact he had come a long way from his previous life in a very short time. He had consoled himself with the idea he could go back anytime he wished. In truth, he understood he would not be able to circle back to those days, not any time soon, not ever.

5

His practice of taking to the sidewalks every day made him a familiar sight, and those who made the effort, found him willing to discuss whatever they had on their minds. He listened to the usual gossip; later dispensing fair portions to other inquisitive neighbors he encountered along his route.

"Mr. Gates, do you have time for a fresh muffin?"

To be called 'Mr.' by these old ladies made him feel like a stage personage. He learned to appreciate gossip taken with fresh baked goods in the early morning hours, when everything seemed clear to him, even his clouded vision. He was accepted as someone who could be trusted to go about freely without a known cause laying behind his movements. They never heard all the secret criticism of the world he was amassing, and which he kept for his own counsel. He was sure to have enough time in his private quarters to thrash out useless theories on the imponderable frailties of the human heart; none of which seemed to have an easy solution. The neighbors concluded that he was between positions.

He enjoyed having neurotic conversations with himself about himself. In the most cordial attitude he afforded himself the benefit of the doubt, in nearly all his failings. One day followed another, and there seemed to be no pressing need to do much more than follow this healthy regimen. He was even getting more letters sent off, some to people who were amazed they were receiving word from him in such a strange manner. He had asked his mother for addresses and she had sent him an abridged version of her Christmas card mailing list; she had typed the list for him and regretted it very soon thereafter. He experimented with transcribing edited dialogues from his texts, as if referring to people he knew, for those people he did know, but not very well, and his mother soon reprimanded him for doing so. He dropped that habit, but was still never sure, as he dropped a letter into the mail slots, if it was bound to raise eyebrows. He knew most people would find his unsolicited letters peculiar, but once he had taken up the pen he could not help himself.

One morning while tramping down Paul Avenue he saw a fox cross-ing an empty lot and entering the leafy fringe along the banks of Moline Creek. It was reassuring, for some reason, to see a wild creature at home in these parts. In no time he was at the corner of Darst and Elizabeth, where the two great elms stood on opposite, diagonal corners. These trees were equal in height and majesty, except that one had lifeless limbs, as if posing in the last ecstasy of some secret dance. The denuded branches clutched only a few shriveled leaves; the last remnants of a memorial wreath. The other tree, on the southeast corner, had a full complement of boisterous leaves, now sonorous in the wind. The mighty branches dipped and waved as he passed beneath. This tree was still working with sunlight; growing while storing energy, and allowing humans to breathe the precious byprod-uct of its labor.

After walking for some hours he engendered a growling hunger. He made his way to Chengdu Garden, on Florissant Road. He took his usual seat in the back, nestling himself by one of the large picture windows.

"Yates!" One of the two brothers, who were the proprietors, accosted him right after he had seated himself. They had gotten his name wrong when he first began to patronize the establishment; he had never found a suitable occasion, nor reason, to correct them. The young man with a shock of straight black hair addressed him with a burst of indecipherable speech that left Jacob free to speak his mind just as rapidly, when his turn came. He could hold forth on any topic he wished, for it was all pro forma courtesy at this point.

"This is my favorite place, my brother." He spoke to the restaurateur with enthusiasm that was not feigned. "If they ever ask you what happened to Gates, tell them he has gone to find America." He tried to remember something else he had read so he could regurgitate it now in his own style. "Some say it is in the past."

"You like special?"

"No, let me look."

"Oh, okay," The man smiled as if this were some elaborate hoax, and he did not mind, too much, indulging such a foolish caprice, since it must be a device by which a good customer wished to save face, in some fashion.

Jacob began to peruse the menu he had read many times, as if looking for hidden symbols, and his scrutiny paid off; he found several tiny dragon emblems he had not noticed before. Most of the items listed were not available on any given day, and the art of dining in this establishment lay in the arcane negotiations one conducted in sign language with one of the brothers. He took his time. They had never encountered such an inscrutable foreign devil before. He would ponder easy questions as if he were a scholar of Confucius; since none of their Mandarin was any more intelligible to him than the Latin gibberish resurrected to celebrate the incomprehensible Catholic mass. Jacob stood proudly on ceremony, handing back the menu while reciting something he had read in one of his texts; knowing he was going to get the daily special.

Jacob leaned close to stare past his own reflection in the window at a parking lot stretching over to the raised embankment of the railroad tracks. The lot used to be a loop for the bus line, and earlier than that it was used for a street car line. As a child he had ridden his bicycle around the unpaved track with much bravado. It had been a worthy obstacle course. One time he had been pedaling around the circle when a bus turned off Florissant Road and began snorting like a monstrous bull, rushing up behind him, having lost its temper at the sight of a boy parading through his territory!

The brute machine had positively groaned, throwing off more black smoke from the upright stacks. It was speeding up! The child had grossly miscalculated, thinking he could outrun the beast, so he turned to cut away from the demon's path, but the bike got caught in the mud tracks made previously by those giant tires. Unable to pedal out of the way he abandoned the bike and ran to safe ground. The beast had swerved to save the tiny bike, out of some mechanical gallantry, but the boy was certain he would not have survived its wrath. Moloch would not deign to spare a mere Halfling of his species! The memory left him feeling a little breathless, as if he were actually becoming a child again, or possibly a mad man. Who can tell the difference?

He began to recollect the first years with Jenny, when they had enjoyed being together, and reveled in that other dimension, called happiness. Could it be, all of that was over for him? The weight of that consideration distorted his ability to think properly. Why should the past prove fatal to his ability to make decisions now? He thought of more letters he ought to write, troubled by the fact these efforts to stay in touch seemed so dishonest. He had been sending them off like clockwork when he lived in the loft, even keeping a log so that he would know when one had been mailed and when it was time to dispatch the next one. That meticulous record-keeping had lapsed and he wasn't even sure when he last sent a letter to his mother. He knew it was overdue. She had sent him money again just last week, and he hadn't sent a note to thank her yet.

"She must be pretty sick of me thanking her for things like that," he thought.

One of the proprietors brought his food and spoke to him without any laughter so he nodded his head and smiled with a closed mouth. He had learned in discussions with other patrons that the brothers were enrolled in the Engineering program at Washington University. The vital energy of the two enterprising young men put him to shame. Then he thought of what an inscrutable fellow his neighbor Cody was; and looking up he saw him entering the restaurant. He remembered Cody had mentioned he would be taking some time off from work.

"What are you having?" Cody asked him as he seated himself.

"I'm not sure."

"They ordered for you?"

"Yeah. Whatever was left on the road last night."

"Yeah."

"Hey man, why don't you let me use the car?"

"I *can't*"

"Come on Cody."

He shook his head, looking down at the table. "Can't do it"

"You mean you won't. She'd never know. You're just being a jerk."

His head kicked up and he looked directly at Jacob. "What if she asks me? What am I supposed to say to her then?"

Jacob shook his head, looking down at his plate. Cody's implacable nature, when clad in plates of such rectitude, was a hard thing to run up against.

"Hey, did you see O.J.?" Cody exclaimed.

"O.J.?"

"The football player."

"Yeah, but I mean, is he around here?"

"No," Cody began laughing. "He's on TV; on every station."

"I don't have a TV; you know that."

"He's out in LA somewhere, in a white Bronco, with a hundred cop cars following him."

"A hundred cop cars?" His voice richly phrased his incredulity.

"Helicopters are giving live feeds to the TV stations."

"What?"

"They think he killed his wife. No, I guess it's his ex-wife? I'm not sure."

"A crime of passion."

"I guess so. It's on every channel."

"It's still on?"

"It was when I left my place. I got tired of watching a car driving slowly down the highway. It's like this really insane parade. People are cheering him on from the overpasses."

"What's going to happen?"

"They'll catch him."

Jacob exhaled a blast of disdainful air. "Yeah, I know that, but, do you think he's like, going to make a last stand, or something?"

"Nobody knows. You want to go watch it?"

"I'll wait to read the newspaper." They exchanged an uncomfortable look; for a moment they had seemed to be conversing like true friends, and now it was back to being unlikely acquaintances who tolerated each other.

Jacob recalled other famous people who had ended up in crime stories after doing an unthinkable act. The neuroscientists are baffled. Pastors have no answers, but are willing to soothe the congregation, expecting tips for their service. The cops resort to that rare solvent, scandalous dark humor.

"Do you really need to use the car?"

Jacob noticed Cody appeared sympathetic; but he retained the bearing of a presiding magistrate.

"No, not really."

"Do you want *me* to drive you somewhere?" His face lit up with the glow of inspired thought.

Jacob cocked his head, considering this might be the answer; but then Cody would be there observing him as he tried to gather intelligence about Jenny, and the old crowd, and how his absence was being interpreted by them.

"No, it's not something I need to do right now."

One of the brothers came and took away his plate and the other one followed up with a towel to clean off the table top as Jacob and Cody raised their arms to allow him access to all the surface area. Cody and Jacob made ready to leave.

"What are you going to do now?" Cody asked him.

"Pay my bill." He wished to offer an ironic echo of Cody's earlier reply to his question about the police chase.

"After that?"

"I don't know." It was more than a little irritating for a poor man of leisure to be asked all the time what he was going to do next. He thought of attempting again to convince Cody to let him borrow the car. Maybe he could go back to visit his former place of employment, see how the old work gang was doing. He had gotten close with some of them, and they weren't returning his letters. During his time there they had gathered infrequently after work to relax and trash whomever was not there, and to complain of management, which he had been a part of, until the change of ownership. Going there would feel strange. He'd left on such bad terms, really; at least with the old bastard who purchased the place from his uncle. He would not want to see Jacob anywhere near the premises.

"Sally thinks you're grieving."

"What?" He was startled by this impertinent intrusion into his nebulous griefs. It felt like an accusation. "Grieving over what?"

"From your breakup."

"No one died, for crying out loud." Jacob said, his anger bubbling up and almost choking his words. This was none of their business. Was he talking to Frances about him?

"How long were you two together?"

"Seven years." As he said this his stomach clenched. "Cody, I can't talk to you about that right now."

"No problem. We'll see you then." He hardly ever affected to have been slighted by Jacob, which was integral to his eccentricity.

"Sure, later. I think I'll walk some more." He only heard it after he had said it, the irony; this was his only avocation now. Stating the fact only heightened the sense of how ridiculous his present life must appear to others.

"I better go call Sally and see about the kids."

"Say, are you going to be around later?"

"Yeah, I think so. Why?"

"Do you want to come over for a beer?"

Cody knew from past experience that such an invitation meant he was supposed to pillage his icebox and bring beer over to the patio.

"I'll buy some beer," Jacob stated. He noted Cody's guarded acquiescence.

"Okay, then. I'll see you later."

"Later, man."

Cody set off walking towards the train trestle, passing underneath as though entering a tunnel, going through and past the red brick building old enough to be listed in the quaint historical register of a people utterly new to this fertile land. On the other side of Church Street stood the bank building, one of the first buildings erected in the municipality of Ferdinand. The stonework has a classical design, showing off its inalienable purpose with an ageless facade. Jacob went the other way, in devotion to the creeds underlying old sidewalks.

Going to see Jenny's crowd would be awkward; not for them! They would obtain a good joke to pass around. He could picture the scene. What are you doing these days? Living underground, with a small circle of philosophers; field mice, actually. Going to see his uncle would be awful, for many reasons. Going home to see his mother would be fraught with filial torments; hearing that trembly introit of organ tones as he faced the anguish in her eyes. Well, it didn't matter; he wasn't going anywhere. He had no vehicle. His thoughts could go far off, but his feet cleaved to the sidewalks of Ferdinand. He did not know why, but for some reason there was no dread in holding fast to these purlieus of his past; his regressive steps almost seemed foreordained.

6

Later that day Jacob and Cody sat on the patio, leaning back in their chairs at the iron table. A half dozen empty beer cans rested on the table. A large bowl contained nothing but the salty glitter left from a bag of potato chips. They might have been ancient lords returned from the hunt, tired of feasting, ready for dancers and jesters. They might have been two even more ancient tribesmen, reclining near the carcass of a slain beast they had roasted over a fire, clubs laying at rest beside them, partaking of their fraternity in silence, as they marked time by the stars.

Jacob had inquired about Sally and the kids. He had listened attentively, letting himself imagine the actual experiences they must be going through in their lives. They made an attempt to speak of politics, but neither had much interest in the topic. They marveled over rumors stating the Los Angeles Rams were moving their team to St. Louis. They got a little carried away as they swapped stories about the old Cardiac Cardinals (now wearing jerseys for a tribe in the desert). They grew animated recalling that incredible Monday Night game when the Cardinals beat the Cowboys 38 to *zero*! In those days the mere mention of America's Team always put the Cardinals' franchise on a war footing, much as the Pawnee served as sacred enemies for the Osage.

Shortly after these evocations of a glory that never was, and having no way to foresee the coming of Kurt Warner, nor believe a prophecy of such wonders, they lapsed again into silence, staring at things not to be seen.

Jacob reached out and crumpled an empty beer can. Cody suggested they buy another six pack, and volunteered the use of the landlady's bug. Jacob laughed instantly, which caused Cody to laugh even louder. They proceeded to St. John's Liquor Store on the corner of Florissant and Paul. Cody recalled standing outside the entrance as a teen, waiting to accost adults to convince one of them to be a sport and buy beer for him and his pals.

The store was drawing steady traffic; white men and black men passing by each other, in full comity regarding the incontestable rights of men to practice the rites of Bacchus in their own way. Jacob selected the Schlitz brand, malt liquor, no less. They proceeded back on Paul and swung around, dipping under the railroad tracks, maneuvering through the tight underpass, and were lifted up along the curved spine of Elizabeth, making way at the spanking pace of twenty-five miles per hour.

"I like to do the speed limit to piss people off," Cody exclaimed.

"Fuck 'em." Said Jacob, admiring the priestly procession of sycamores. The sinuous road unwound itself before them. On both sides the trees spread leafy limbs overhead, giving one a continual sense of coming fresh upon a picturesque scene.

"Let's take a grand tour of the old neighborhood." Jacob brayed.

"It ain't the old neighborhood to me," Cody responded.

Jacob learned that Cody had never lived anyplace else. Once, shortly after Sally and Cody became serious, she had suggested they might want to consider moving out of the region altogether. This caused Cody to open up to her in a way she had never observed before. He spoke of his childhood, of the people he knew, of his mother; of the fact that everyone cannot take flight for other places just because things are changing, and new people are arriving. Jacob was coming to understand this about Cody; he was protective of his past experiences as if they were part of this suburban landscape. It was important for him to bear witness to what had occurred in these haunts, and how he had changed, and why it all mattered. It kept him grounded, and possibly a little bit unbearable to many.

They began to mock each other as they drove onto the campus of McDermott High.

"Remember how we used to smoke out at the trees?" Jacob asked. "They couldn't stop us, without going full Gestapo, so they made it a policy that was where we had to smoke!"

Cody informed Jacob he had dropped out sophomore year. They moved on to discuss a wide range of extracurricular activities that took place in those long lost seasons of the now mythical past. And then everything became oddly coterminous for a moment, and the trudge into adulthood was shorn of its disenchantment. They swapped stories about bedding women; most of what was said was technically true, the staging was enhanced, as was deemed necessary. Some of these tales reflected poorly on themselves now; so they sacrificed the legends to generate the pleasure of honest laughter.

All of a sudden Cody began poking fun at his wife's idiosyncrasies; it was done in a way that made it clear to Jacob their conjugal bond was durable. He remembered when he felt that way about Jenny and himself; how they acted in a contrarian fashion out of hubris and pride. It grew quiet again. In a chastened mood they agreed they probably shouldn't be drinking in the car, which was no problem, since all the beer was gone. Songs of the chase ebbed back into quiet eddies in their bloodstreams. The sportive fates enjoined them to make a stop at Jack in the Box, exactly where the McDermott students once stole away in their days of exalted truancy.

Not wanting to make a mess in the car, they devoured their succulent tacos on the lower level of St. Margaret's, while sitting on the bleachers. They gazed out at the field, remembering the carnival rides set up at the end of every school year. Cody had more memories of those carnivals than Jacob, who had attended only a few in those golden years when he was old enough to have full governance of his own movements. These memories were as precious as anything else he treasured in his memory. They did not remember even knowing one another in those days; except for the fact of belonging to the same herd of wayfarers making steady passage through the same hallways and rooms. There were no mutual memories, and yet a common enthusiasm bubbled forth, like the musical phrasing of a nearby cataract, lost to the eye in the surrounding woodlands.

Jacob turned to glance up at the Grotto where the Madonna was stationed in her yellow brick enclosure. She bore the same downcast demeanor; her power being vast sufferance. At her feet lay several epochs; swatches of crumbly, fissured asphalt, and a few remnants of the broken tablets of the original concrete; and everywhere, the natural weedy growth that patiently despoils the effects of human idolatry.

"Let's get back." Cody said. "I need to check in."

After driving home, Cody entered his house to use the bathroom and to call his wife; upon coming back outside he sat down on the patio. Jacob came out of his basement with his guitar and sat there, tuning the instrument. The cool shade had risen everywhere like a tide. The leaves at the top of trees had been set aglow by the last sunlight. One felt a tenor of gentle currents in the creeping night, and deep stirrings moved in the depths provided by the shade. The air brushing the face was more instructive than all the sermons ever published.

Jacob began playing individual parts of various songs. He was oblivious to any sense of an audience. "Why don't you play something all the way through?" He was chided by Cody.

"I'm just getting started. I haven't tried to really play in a long while." So saying, he began a song and found himself instantly in the arms of this sweet old discipline that never abandons a faithful servant, however negligent that person has become.

"You're pretty good with that thing." Cody said after a while.

"You think so?"

"Yeah, it sounds good to me. That was Neil Young, right?"

"My version of 'Out on the Weekend,' from *Harvest*."

"Oh yeah; that, and *After the Goldrush*; you had to have those two albums."

"Do you still have them?"

"Oh yeah. But I play CDs now."

"I cut my teeth on that stuff. He's an original."

Jacob began playing an instrumental piece called "Henry." It came back to him in that strange affinity that gives a musician the feeling of being in a trance that is more vivid and reflective of himself than the play of mere consciousness normally allows. He played the simple arrangement through without mishap, and stopped at the end feeling refreshed after this renewal of musical companionship.

"What was that? I feel like I should know it."

"That's the little intro piece they play right before 'Maggie May'; on the album *Every Picture Tells a Story*."

"Oh yeah, I still have that album on vinyl. I can't play those anymore. Oh, what a song *that* was. It really takes me back."

"It's always been one of my favorites. That whole album, really. You know, Cody, our generation had a brilliant sound track; we were lucky in that, at least."

"No doubt about it."

Jacob set the guitar carefully in one of the empty chairs as if giving it a seat of its own, so that it might look up through the foliage and sample primal melodies. Jacob liked to look at the handsome instrument, to enjoy the physical appearance of the object that for so long had been an indispensable part of his emotional existence. He was once told by a superior musician that one owns his instrument only to the degree that he is devoted to its proper use.

The guitarist who said this to him was rather peevish at the time. He had asked Jacob to come by and hear his band play, and afterwards they settled down to talk business. He wanted to know if Jacob would like to join their band. Jacob had declined, saying he was probably not band material.

"I play for myself." He had responded.

"Well, if you ever get tired of playing with yourself, let us know."

Jacob smiled. "What defines proper use?" He challenged him.

"Why, I suppose you have to find that out for yourself, don't you?"

"Were you ever in a band?" Cody asked him.

"What? No. I never went electric. I used to play a lot more often, though; I mean, more seriously. I've gotten rusty."

"For every thing there is a season."

Very well said, Jacob thought. He reached out and took back his guitar, not able to leave it there on such a precarious pedestal. He sought to play a semblance of 'Turn! Turn! Turn!'; a song the Byrds made into a smash hit. He was not very successful. He clutched his guitar, leaving the strings alone; listening to his surroundings. They both paid attention to the flutter at the top of the trees as the last sunlight was dwindling into mere glimmers. They had reached a point where nothing needed to be said anymore, so they looked around in a spell of lethargic contentment.

"How come you don't have a car?" Cody broke the whispery silence.

"Well, in my previous job I had a company vehicle, a really nice truck, all tricked out. Like I told you, I worked for my uncle, and it was a great job; and then he sold the company and everything went to shit. A sad tale, my friend."

"So what are you doing here, anyway?" Cody persisted. "Is this like a midlife crisis, or something?"

"Is that what it looks like to you?"

"I don't know. I don't even know what the hell those are supposed to be. When I was just a little kid my old man took off and never came back—was that supposed to be one? I doubt I'm going to get to have one myself. It seems like another one of those things they reserve for the assholes. There aren't enough of them to go around, so some of us are bound to come up short."

Jacob laughed at this superb example of Cody's stealthy wit.

"Did they fire you?" Cody asked.

"No. I quit." He glanced up through the many tiers of darkened breathless leaves above the table. "After my uncle sold the business everything changed. They took away some of my authority, and the word went round they were going to take away the truck. I started acting like a jackass. I would have gotten fired, the way things were going; so I just said, fuck it." He had never shared that honest rendition with anyone before, not even himself.

"And Jenny? Was that when you two broke up?"

"Right before I quit, it was around the same time. Hey, losing the truck and the girl, that's pretty good midlife crisis material." He began strumming his guitar. "Oh, life done me so bad. I had to walk, and there wasn't any dough, and no where to go. No rolling at all, I never got stoned. I had no truck, I was flat broke. It got sad; it was no joke." He was voicing his words in parody of a country song. "Maybe I should get a repertoire together, go on the road, cut an album. Do you think Frances will let me take the bug to Branson? My tour will be called, 'Singing the Midlife Crisis Blues.' What do you think?"

"What if this uncle doesn't die for a while?"

Jacob studied Cody's face; it was devoid of malice. He was asking sincerely, do you believe you have a good footing on these shifting sands beneath your feet?

"I'm not really thinking about it that much anymore. I can't explain where I'm at right now. I feel like I'm going in circles. What's holding me to anything? What's at the center of things? You know?"

"I almost forgot." Cody tapped his forehead with a palm. "Frances said she might let Gregory move in here."

"Gregory?"

"The guy she brought back with her from Baltimore."

"I didn't know she had—"

"I thought she told you."

"Where is she going to put him?"

"Not sure, but wait, I heard something about him from a cop I know. He was living around here somewhere, and I think she may have been paying his rent, but anyway, he was up at the Ferguson Lounge and he got into a fight."

"That can be a rough place."

"This cop I know, he said this other cop, who walked in after the fight, told him when he came in, the first thing he sees is these two guys rolling around on the floor. And this Gregory dude, he's up at the bar trying to order another beer, after laying them out." Cody began chuckling. "The bartender, who called the cops, he's just staring at him, not sure what he's supposed to do."

"Oh, well, that's great. That means she's going to throw me out and let some maniac stay in the basement."

"Yeah, I wouldn't mess with the dude."

Jacob shook his head in dismay. "What's the next lowest rung, after the basement? Living in the ground?"

"Could you move home?"

"Home?" Jacob mused out loud. The awful scene came back to him; of how his mother discouraged him from moving back home after he quit his job. He had parted ways with Jenny, rather gallantly, letting her keep the apartment. Although, truth be told, he was soon to be unemployed, and could no longer afford to pay the rent. He wondered how in the hell *she* was able to continue paying the rent? He had driven by the place and noticed her car several times, while driving the borrowed Volkswagen—how long ago that pathetic reconnaissance mission seemed to him now.

"To your parents. You said they live in West County?"

"Yeah. No, I haven't thought of moving there."

"You could go there if you had to go there, right?"

"If I had to, I suppose."

"Things could be worse."

Jacob laughed. Cody had suffered and endured as much as anybody else he knew, and none of it seemed to have marred the aplomb of his personality.

"Yes, it could be a lot worse." Jacob echoed the worthy proverb.

"Is that why you want to borrow the car? To go see your uncle."

"No, he's being well cared for . . . he has this woman he keeps around, a sort of housekeeper. I don't want to go see him just yet. Last time I saw him he told me not to pester him for no reason." Jacob exhaled a poignant gust of air, shaking his head, as if in wonderment at the perverse stubbornness of the human spirit. "He's always been a tough old bird. He hates being in this condition, unable to do hardly anything he loves anymore."

"Well, in the future, you can use the car if you need to; just let me know and I'll borrow it, and we can work out a way to get it to you. She doesn't need to know."

"No, that's okay. You'd have to go and tell her, anyway."

"I might not."

Jacob laughed. "You know you would."

"Probably."

"It doesn't matter. I . . . I don't know. I feel like I've got all these things I need to figure out, and I don't have the energy to do anything, except for drifting along like a derelict."

"Hey, there's another song for the tour. Mommas, don't let your babies grow up to be North County derelicts."

Jacob laughed. "I like it, and I won't be giving you credit for that one either." Cody had a fairly good singing voice, surely as good as his own. "I should get started on that play list, so I can take it on the road."

"I wouldn't worry. Things will work out."

Jacob smiled, glancing at Cody, who lived in a tiny box, but whose visage was now quite serene. His eyes swept across the embers flaring out on the western horizon. He was quietly taking in all that was unseen in the gloom. All of this was to him as homelands once were to the ancients; a hallowed place where the local gods inhabited features of the landscape. The religious instinct resided in things close at hand that a living spirit could reach out and touch. There was nothing more fearsome or holy than the worst and the best as it was experienced each day in the relentless play of natural elements.

"Yeah, things will work out." He repeated the words as though reciting a new charm, the power of which he really does want to believe in, regardless of his mind's recalcitrance. It was Cody's singular, untouchable creed. He had no choice; he had to hope for better things, as he labored for his family in the face of implacable odds, against which he squared himself, standing his ground. Maybe it was a good way for him to start over. Maybe one had to pray first; then, when the strength of belief came from much devoted practice, one could act in faith, and become the practicing devotee he was meant to be. Maybe the wheel of life was an exercise wheel, something to be spun continuously under our feet to make us stronger . . .

7

At first light the walls of his lair shrank back to an earthly scale. His abode was not a vast netherworld after all. In the dead of night he had rolled over to see again the furtive creatures on the floor standing up, paws raised, staring up at him with shiny eyes. He wondered, after another deluge, would a liberal race of mice be praying to giant slugs that were said to have once existed in underground temples?

Jacob disembarked from his twin mattress and set about his morning ritual. He repaired to a bathroom facility, the likes of which you might expect to find below decks on a sunken ship, after it has been hauled from the depths, and left to dry out for a generation. After washing he moved over to a little 'kitchen' area where he had his hot plate and an old coffee pot, which Cody had recently loaned to him. He made coffee and while the aroma filled the room he sat at his desk and pored over a passage in one of his texts. He was intrigued by the personalities. He enjoyed the Russian author's passionate intensity; the fervor of his skeptical view of all the standard explanations for human conduct.

After a while he set aside the ponderous book and began writing a letter to his fraternal uncle. It took him an inordinate amount of time to finish, considering the brevity of his final message. He was spending more time on his letters now, but feeling no better about them afterwards. So many versions had been fed to the rejection box before settling on the one he finally sealed in an envelope. Wasn't that proof of his insincerity?

He may as well be writing campaign speeches for some party hack coming out of his rotten stews, to once more cajole the blessings from an ignorant electorate, so he might secure another term of corrupt practices. At least he had staved off the temptation to insert provocative quotations stolen from his underground books.

He no longer had any idea what to say to Julius, the poor wreck of a man, whom he had worked for with such pride. He wished him well, he asked if he wanted him to get him anything, even though they both knew he had no means to get him anything of any worth. He was really just asking if he wanted him to come by and see him. His uncle was aware of his circumstances. He had written to him rather tediously of his bizarre new life when he was living upstairs, and feeling as though he were embarking on a new adventure. Now it was just that he doubted everything he had ever done. He couldn't very well put that down in a letter.

He showered and shaved and dressed in clean clothes. He used the washer and dryer in the basement, which belonged to Frances, and she was sure to harass him for not buying his own detergent. The renter upstairs also used her machines and he bought his own soap and sometimes Jacob stole from his stores and was inevitably reprimanded by Frances. It was proving to be a poor business, collecting resentments against a benefactor. He was slowly depleting his savings, despite the meager stipends from his mother. He assumed these disbursements were unknown to the other members of the family; but he was wrong, of course, and he knew it. Certain things you wanted to believe so badly you managed to muster the practical credulity that allowed you to face yourself in the mirror. Once you turned away it was lost again. It was like doing magic tricks for your own amusement.

One of his curious talents was an uncanny ability to become happy for no reason. The euphoric quality of good weather bolstered him, as did the sonorous chanting of trees, or the simple hymns sung by songbirds, and certainly he had grown to appreciate the trenchant comedy of squirrels. When he had lived upstairs in the loft they perched in the maple tree, staring at him, on occasion emitting chortles, as though he were a droll character featured on a popular sitcom. Now he was sitting on the patio, and they were in the maple, looking down, and snickering.

He was glad to give them the pleasure. He stared at a new flotilla of clouds coming to anchor over his private lagoon of blue sky. His eyes dropped to admire a local grand seigneur, the great sycamore tree on the corner of Church and Maple, bearing two mighty arms upwards, as if holding up this corner of the world. Just then Cody and Sally came out of their duplex and approached him from across their driveway.

"What are you doing?" Cody asked him.

"Nothing. Hi Sally, how are you doing?" Jacob asked. Her small oval face was compressed around her large luminous eyes. She was very thin, and appeared to be awfully frail.

"I'm good." She spoke in her quiet, steady voice; she reserved the right to speak of her tribulations only with loved ones. Her demeanor bespoke a delicate, sensitive nature, resigned to its role of meekness and homespun dignity. Jacob wondered if it would have been thus, had she not been given such grievous medical crosses to bear. "Pretty soon I will be able to go back to work." She sounded quite pleased.

"That's great!" Jacob said. He knew how important this was to her. He looked at Cody, who was watching his wife closely. The first encounters between Jacob and Sally had not gone so well; he then being wrapped so tightly inside his own guilt shrouds, he was unable to fully appreciate the plight of anyone else. Her forbearance was instructive; but still, it made him feel a little inadequate.

Frances came out and sat down at the table, hardly looking at Jacob. She had come out to talk to Sally, and as they all sat down Jacob realized his presence was not welcome. These people had a long history together and could only speak openly to one another on certain matters in private. He was about to take his leave when Frances said to him,

"Your mother called, she said your brother is coming by to see you later this afternoon."

"Which one?"

"Gosh. Let me think . . . We talked about them all." She bit her lip, flustered. "Isn't that funny? I can't remember. Well, one of them. So, make sure you're here, later in the afternoon." She looked away from him and turned happily towards Sally. Her fondness for the woman washed as bright lights across her craggy face.

"Sure," Jacob said softly, seeing that none of them was paying attention to him anymore. "I've got things to do." He stood up clutching several letters that needed to be mailed.

"Jacob?" Frances called after him as he headed for the post office.

"Yes." He turned and stood still.

"Can you buy me a book of stamps?"

"Sure." His penury nipped at his pride. He thought to himself, "I'm like a spoiled child to them. I must be taught to share."

He headed out to Church Street, turning right and walking up the hill, then he turned right again onto Clay, climbing that small rise, passing by the empty Spencer mansion. He swept his eyes over the front yard, and the two large white oaks at opposite ends of the plot. In the back of the property there was a tennis court. He had a vague remembrance of watching a squad of older boys playing street hockey on that court, slapping around an orange plastic puck, which had been cut open to insert coins to add ballast so it would slide better on the pavement. He remembered one time the older Spencer girls had come out to watch; immediately the boys began checking much more fiercely, and before long they were using profanity and exchanging verbal threats. He had longed to take his place on that tournament ground someday . . .

He paused on the sidewalk to view the carriage house directly behind the house, used as a garage in modern times. It was perched on the edge of the estate. Around that corner the land fell away to other yards, stretching out to Church Street and down to Elizabeth Avenue. There was a For Sale sign planted in the front yard. He proceeded to the Post Office and afterwards strode up to Wabash Park, where he sat at a picnic table under a large pin oak to watch the people in the public pool. A grassy hill enfolded two sides of the pool and he could look down at the bright turquoise water flashing seductively in the late morning sun. All the clean youthful bodies of various hues were of one single race, called humans, thrashing about in this strange, chlorinated medium. He imagined a colony of highly evolved sea urchins, who served to enlighten the state by devoting themselves ex-clusively to the mystic art of play.

When he was a boy his mother made Luke take him here to his swim-ming lessons. Luke would sit at a table on the hill reading one of his car magazines, sneaking long, lascivious glances at the young female instruc-tors who strode about with authority, wearing spotless swim suits. After the lessons were over they would eat bologna sandwiches and potato chips. Luke bought a bottle of Coke for himself and a root beer for Jacob, a nec-tar after his exertions. They explored the shoreline of the lake, feeding scraps of food to the fish and ducks. There had been a small natural area just off the parking lot with parts of the ground beaten smooth by many scrambling feet, and a tangle of brush enclosing a copse of willow trees that spread their branches over the greenish depths. One day they discovered that someone had left a plastic bread bag in the water and it had become a bladder with several fish hovering inside. He put his hand into the water and snatched the bag by the mouth, hauling it up dripping before his eyes.

Luke leaned in to have a look at the catch. He smiled in a genuine way Jacob enjoyed even in remembrance.

"Let's take them home!" Jacob said.

"You don't want these fish," Luke said. "They'll just end up dying. You'll have to bury them in the back yard in a couple of days. Is that what you want? Go on, put 'em back." Jacob was on record by then for having lost a few wild 'pets' that he had captured by ingenious means, but which did not take to living under his rule in captivity.

However, the boy refused to relinquish his prizes so quickly. He had to admire these incredible fish, undisturbed inside the factitious chamber, as oblivious of Jacob's world as he was of theirs. What must it be like to dwell in a separate dimension altogether? He slipped the bag back into the lake and pulled it up by the sealed end, removing a deflated piece of slimy plastic. He had watched, but did not see, how the fish vanished into the vastness of their world. He flung the collapsed bag onto the shore, and Luke scolded him for littering, using profanity, which Jacob would emulate later in similar circumstances.

Jacob was standing in the same place, except now the ground was paved right up to the lake's edge. No slippery mud, no tangles of vegetation, no spawn of small, glittering fish to be seen loitering about to greet magic urchins. He trudged back on Florissant Road, making for Church Street; in a short time he was in his den reading, then he was sitting on the patio once more. A brother was coming to see him. No doubt on a mission to talk some sense into him.

He began to think of Jenny, living in their old apartment without him. They had had a great deal of fun there. The Loop was on the edge of the city's western frontier; one of those locales that enticed people from the entire region. It was probably the best café venue in the metropolitan area. There was a constant stream of promiscuous life, offering fantastic contrasts, which induced fresh excitement to invade the stagnant heart. Many expectant people came to merge into the secret promise that comes alive in that convergence of the electric dusk with the rising shadow empire of voluptuous night. There was always that heightened awareness of the larger community, the sense of collective needs not easily addressed; the presence of those mystic desires of the individuals to be known to one another for unknown reasons. To be as fellow strangers who are in league, as explorers sent to the same darkling spell of time, having but one script, the unexpurgated catalogue of human desires.

For most of their time together Jacob and Jenny had been happy; making their apartment into a friendly stopover for people coming to the Loop. What did all that pleasure amount to now? What did it profit a man, all this pursuit of happiness, when it somehow leads one directly into the haunted basement of his own heart, in search of all he has never known? He experienced a sharp, twisting stab of pitiless remorse, remembering how he had been forced to walk about in a disemboweled state, after he had found it necessary to exorcise his feeling for Jenny. Now he faced the unknown without that confidence he once possessed. He could see that it was necessary to start over again, but he feared he had not the fortitude, nor power of will, to bring about that sort of regeneration.

8

He was keeping vigil on the patio when a white truck bounded into the driveway. Jacob heard the creaking suspension before he recognized that it was Luke who had come, with his wife Loretta. From the passenger side she was looking at Jacob with a pathetic smile. Her long lustrous dark hair was falling down around her face onto her shoulders. Luke climbed out of the truck and walked up the steps and stood there. Jacob remained seated.

"This is a nice setup you've got here," Luke said in a congenial voice that almost masked his sarcastic intent.

"It's a great neighborhood," Jacob replied, feeling an increase in tension.

"I know that as well as you, I guess." Luke put his hand on the back of a chair as if considering whether or not he should sit down.

"What are the charges?"

"What?"

"Like at the beginning of *Apocalypse Now*."

Luke snorted, nodding. "That was a great movie."

"Hi Loretta!" Jacob yelled, raising his arm and waving lightly with one arm extended. She smiled genuinely and returned his greeting in a quiet voice.

"Come on," Luke said, "Why don't you take a ride with us."

"Oh shit, now I'm in *The Godfather*?"

Luke made a face of annoyance. Jacob thought to himself, okay, no laughing matter. I get it.

"For real, you're not having me committed, are you? I think I have a right to an attorney."

"Can you afford one?"

"No."

"Then come on, let's go."

"Is this your truck?"

Luke remained silent.

"It's a classic."

"Come on."

Loretta scooted over and Jacob climbed into the cab, feeling apprehensive. Jacob considered that just to put him at ease, before dropping the hammer, Luke might be taking him out for a nice dinner.

"Have you guys eaten yet?" Jacob asked. "There's this great Chinese—"

"I want to show you something." Luke said, looking sideways at Loretta. They backed out of the driveway and proceeded out to Church Street, turning right, going up the hill.

"Where are we going?" Jacob asked.

"The Spencer's house is for sale."

"I know, I walk by there all the time."

"You want to take a look inside?"

"Are you guys thinking of buying it?"

"Yeah, right." Luke scoffed.

"It would be great to live there, wouldn't it?" Jacob launched into another reverie, as was his custom now.

"You think so?" Luke asked. Loretta laughed as if sharing a joke with herself. She had this low musical laugh that she seldom allowed the world to hear. Jenny had never gotten on very well with her, and had once called her humorless.

"The realtor is supposed to be here," Luke said.

"She's the owner," Loretta corrected.

"She's the realtor, and the owner."

"You know, somebody could live in The Joint, if they wanted to rent the place out." Jacob offered.

Luke seemed startled. "Yeah, maybe. Do you want to be a squatter now?"

Jacob didn't say anything.

"We never called it The Joint, that I can remember; that came later." Luke responded after a moment.

"Luke's been telling me some pretty wild tales about that place." Loretta said.

"I think I went one time, and the party had already broken up." Jacob said. "That was just about over by then, I think."

"No, I don't think so," Luke said. "They kept it going for quite a while, from what I heard. It would get shut down, and then it would start up again. I mean, *all* the Spencer kids were pretty wild."

"*They* were pretty wild?" Loretta teased her husband for having the temerity to refer to others as having been wild. She had heard him confess to countless hair-raising adventures that made for quite the riotous chronicle of his youth. After he began telling her the truth about his service in Vietnam she wished he had never done so, and clung the more tenaciously to the naughty suburban tales of his youth.

Luke recalled a period when the eldest of the Spencer boys had salvaged an old, short school bus, which he decorated in lurid colors after reading *The Electric Kool-Aid Acid Test*. The flamboyant vehicle, adorned with its own hippie coat of arms, was known throughout the region. The local police turned a blind eye, knowing to whom it belonged.

Sweeping into the driveway spur that ran up to the side door they parked behind a Cadillac Brougham. They let their eyes rove over the grounds. There was a brick wall separating the side yard from the back yard, adorned with two little arches at opposite ends, which allowed passage for vehicles and pedestrians. For years the house had been a social fixture of Ferdinand, evoking those cheery family scenes consecrated in movies such as "Meet Me in St. Louis." It had once been that sort of place. Now it was a relic of the myth we preserve in our hearts to keep from having to excavate truths of the social structure that are too disturbing to bear scrutiny. The house was still sitting on the highest ground in the surrounding landscape. I have surveyed the plot myself. I have even consulted topographical maps to verify that it is not just a trick of someone's memory.

A smartly dressed buxom woman appeared in the doorway and waved for them to come up the stairs. Beatrice was a widow who had come into a real estate business when her older husband was felled by cardiac arrest. She had been his third wife and a lot of people who used to treat her in a rather shabby fashion now seemed to believe it was time to mend fences. She was investing in the town, and she was passionate about making use of this venerable house. In her fresh blossoming high school years she had attended a few of the open houses held there every December. She had never forgotten the feeling of moving about in that rare atmosphere of social splendor.

She gave them a tour, as if intent on showing them every nook and cranny of the three-story, Tudor edifice. Jacob had no idea why they were there. None paid much attention to the dusty floors and discolored walls, rather floating through the interior mansion of their own imaginations. There were stately hallways on two floors. A wide elegant staircase swirled up from the first floor, winding to a sumptuous landing, before doubling back and ascending again in another sweeping flight to the second floor. There was a more discreet, auxiliary stairway, once used by the servants. Beatrice studied Jacob as she shared these intimate details of the house.

"All of that was from a different era," she said significantly. Her late husband had become a stingy drudge, a social horror, one who loved his privacy at home. He wanted his wife to stay there also, ready to audit his complaints of the people he had no desire any longer to go and see. Why bother? He questioned her motives; 'Just to be seen? To let everyone know you're still part of that crowd.' She now had the power to arrange her own 'crowds,' just as she wished, and she found it was more stimulating than anything else she had ever done.

On one of the trips up the stairs they all stopped to exclaim over the studio photographs of the Spencer children, arranged on the wall, flowing upwards on the same incline as the steps.

"I'm not sure what to do with these. I can't seem to take them down." Beatrice explained. Luke stationed himself before one of the photographs; the young woman's hair swept around her pretty face and curled up above her shoulders.

"Who's that?" Loretta asked him, coming close and jabbing an elbow into his ribs. He emitted a sheepish laugh.

A few steps further down Jacob stood in front of the portrait of the daughter named Deborah. She had been in his class at St. Margaret's. He had only indistinct memories of her, but clearly recalled being boyishly smitten when he was in the fifth grade. She carried herself about in the gloss of superior cultivation; on her youthful features shone a rare beauty as elusive as grace. She remained forever aloof as an utterly fascinating creature of purest longing.

"Matthew dated this one," Luke said, having moved up a few more steps.

"Really?" Jacob said, moving up next to his brother to look more closely at the young woman's visage.

Luke regaled them with a story that sounded like it was taken from a movie they had all seen. They laughed and fell into separate swoons of nostalgia. They strolled along the generous hallway on the second floor; large bedrooms enfiladed off both sides. Luke began talking about the son who had been his friend for a while. After the Gates family moved out of Ferdinand to a smaller house farther north, all Jacob's nascent friendships fell away, but it had been different for his brothers. They had been old enough to stay in touch, and Luke spoke now of some of these aboriginal friendships that were still intact, and of others that were only exhibits in the apocryphal halls of legend.

The Spencer boys had all gone to St. Paul's, a storied prep school notorious for granting well-bred scions the liberty to raise hell and then come out of it with a valuable diploma and names perfectly unsullied. The Jesuit priests juggled these ticklish affairs like court eunuchs, handling the boys, the parents, and the law enforcement officials with the dexterity formerly used to cozen favors out of wary kings by paying outlandish homage to their spoiled queens.

"So, you're an electrician, right?" Beatrice questioned Luke.

"That's right, Beatrice."

"Everyone calls me Bitty—I know, like in 'Old Bitty'—but I'm not that old, I swear I'm not!" She actually appeared younger than her age; and personal confidence clearly enhanced her appeal.

"Are you getting many offers on the house?" Loretta asked, wanting to verify what she'd heard from a sister-in-law about why they had come here.

"The truth is, I'm buying the place myself. It needs a ton of work, but once it is restored . . . I think of what it could be, you know? I want to recapture what it once was." Her face was radiant. "That's the idea that attracts me." She had stepped into the mirrored halls of her own romance. They gaped at her handsome, earthy, blush-frosted face.

"Well, thank you for letting us take a look inside," Luke said, somewhat confused regarding his mother's vague instructions about taking Jacob to see this woman.

"Oh, that's fine. And one more thing. Let me see now, you're Jacob, right?" She had turned to look at him rather intently.

"Yes." He answered, somewhat puzzled; this had been established upon their arrival. She seemed ready to say something more to explain her studious attention. But she simply stared at him a moment longer; as if taking his measure; one imagines Isabella sizing up Columbus right before letting him take her ships on his portentous voyage.

Loretta seemed anxious to wrap things up. She moved closer to Luke and put an arm around his back and locked her hand on his waist.

"Thanks again," Luke said. "So you can call . . ."

"Don't you want to see the carriage house?"

"Sure." Jacob said at once, fearful of leaving, remembering that his brother had yet to lecture him about his untenable situation.

They climbed the stairs. Jacob looked out the windows.

"You said you came here?" Luke asked Jacob.

"Once or twice." He was wondering, was it empty one time when he came? They surveyed the barren room, the walls nearly devoid of any decoration and stained badly with the rich pigments of decay, sloping up to the ratty ceiling. The wooden floor was resinous with the rot and residue of ancient bacchanals.

"It's hard to believe they let it go on for so long." Luke mused. One might ask the same of the author behind the human story, which is allowed to continue on this earth after all that has happened. Possibly it affirms that a worthy quest provides its own glory in advance to ensure continuance of the noble experiment.

Luke looked out one of the windows on the back wall. He could see the thread of Elizabeth Avenue winding past the many tall sycamore trees stretching along its length for several blocks. The past was strangely solicitous for a moment, and he felt a surge of emotion impeding the trajectory of his present life. He looked back at Jacob, as if overcome by vague sympathies.

"We had epic games out there," he said softly. They left The Joint and came out through the garage and stood together on the driveway. Beatrice shook Luke's hand and nodded to Jacob and Loretta.

"We certainly have some things to talk about," she said earnestly, looking at Luke. "Well, I have to scoot. We'll talk soon!"

She went up the drive in her professional haste, heels tapping out the brittle tempo of her determined march.

"What was that about?" Jacob asked. "She sure seemed in a hurry to get out of here."

"What do you mean? She just gave us the grand tour."

"But what did that mean, 'something to talk about?' She was acting kind of funny, wasn't she? I mean, she wasn't showing us the house to sell it to us. Do you think she's afraid I might try to break in to steal something? Did you see how she was looking at me?"

"Maybe we should steal some of those portraits." Luke said.

"Let's do it!" Jacob expressed a boyish avidity for selective pilfering.

"Stop it, you two." Loretta reproached them. "You can tell she really wants to put this place to good use."

"Put it to use? What does that mean? Is she opening a bordello?" Jacob was eager to prolong the jocular mood, wishing to forestall scrutiny of his current mode of living.

Luke crooked his mouth to censure the timing of his brother's risqué humor.

"Mom talked to someone about letting you see it." Luke explained, clarifying nothing.

"Mom did? Why would she want me—?"

"We wanted to see it," Loretta explained, not suppressing her conspiratorial pleasure. "Didn't you enjoy seeing the famous Spencer house?"

"Yeah, it was cool to see it."

"Is she good friends with your mom?" Loretta asked.

"I don't think so." Jacob answered as Luke and Loretta continued to stare at one another, somewhat dubiously.

"If the house isn't for sale, why would she want people tramping through it." Jacob felt exasperated, not sure why Luke was involved in any of this.

"You can tell she likes showing it off. It's her pet project." Luke spoke with renewed fervor. "She's going to put money into it, I know that much. We could get some work out of it."

"Oh, I see. But it just seemed like she had something else in mind, though." Jacob said.

"What do you mean, brother? Like what?" Now Luke was clearly playing with him.

"How should I know? You're the one who's talked to Mom about something to do with me, that you're not sharing with me now."

Luke began laughing in his arrogant, chuckling manner as if everything to do with human affairs was too comical for him to take any single incident too seriously. Jacob observed his brother, knowing he could never force an answer out of him, especially when he was highly amused by the officious curiosity of others.

"Was there another reason why you came to see me?" Jacob asked pointedly.

Luke looked sharply at him, his humorous mood vanished. "Come on, I'll give you a lift back to your place."

"I can walk from here." Jacob said, wanting to get away; resentment bubbling up from the sewers of his mind.

"Come on, get in."

Jacob climbed into in the truck, settling into resignation again. "How long have you had this thing?"

"Just got it."

They drove back to Jacob's place and Luke parked on the street. He got out of the truck and Jacob looked at him suspiciously.

"Let's talk."

Here it comes, Jacob thought. Luke was not usually the one commissioned to enforce family norms, but for some reason he had been chosen for this task. Too bad they haven't given up on me, Jacob thought, then they would have to let me sink to my own level.

"Let's go up here," Jacob said, leading the way up the two tumbled flights of back steps, between a short stretch of level walk, leading to the iron table. They both sat down and Luke appeared rather uncomfortable. Jacob heaved a great sigh, bracing himself for the worst; wanting to scream at his inquisitor, just spit it out! He saw Loretta walking away, going up Maple, as if fleeing the scene of an impending disaster. He stared after her.

"Where's she going?"

Luke did not acknowledge his question.

"Just tell me. Did Mom send you to talk to me? Time to pay people back? What is it?"

"No. Well, sort of, but no. Here." He held out his hand with the truck keys.

"What's this?" Jacob reached out tentatively to take what was being offered.

"Keys to the truck. It's yours."

"You came here to give me this truck?"

"Yeah."

"Whose idea was this?"

"I may have suggested it; but we all went in on it."

"All of you?"

"Yeah. That's what I'm supposed to be saying, but it was mostly Mark who paid for it." Mark was a maintenance superintendent at a manufacturing facility and did rather well for himself.

"Oh." Jacob held the keys in his palm, hefting another weight for the scales of his unworthiness.

"We know you need wheels to get back on your feet. You're on my insurance plan."

"On yours?"

"So try not to roll the thing on Florissant Road or anything, okay?"

Jacob remained silent, looking down at his hands.

"I don't want to get on your case, Jacob; but shit, you're starting to worry Mom."

"I know." He wanted to say something more, but he couldn't bring himself to violate their fraternal custom, which called for reticence when nothing more purposeful could be adduced.

Looking at Luke it occurred to him that he was the one who most resembled their dad in appearance. When they were younger it had always been Matthew who favored him to an uncanny degree; until after Henry's accident, and the ensuing ordeals. Everyone still spoke as though it were Matthew who bore the closest resemblance to their dad in his physical features, but this was no longer true. In personality, Matthew was most like the younger Henry C. Gates, the congenial, popular fellow, possessing the same gregarious traits as their father. However, Luke's visage bore indelible signs of some deep harrowing; subtle delineations glimpsed only on occasion, as something veiled in smoke becoming clear for an instant.

"Everyone wants what is best for you."

"I don't know what to tell you. I've been out of sorts—"

"Jacob, you have to come to the house for Father's Day."

Jacob sighed. The truck is a bribe? No, it was more than that, but he was reminded rather jarringly that his behavior was effecting other lives.

"I'll be there."

"Good. And quit sending those damned letters to people you hardly even know. What is that about?"

The look on his brother's face made Jacob laugh. "Hey, thank everyone for the truck. How much do I owe—" His voice was grinding to a halt before he was interrupted.

"Don't worry about it."

"Well," he started to say he ought to know how much money he owed each person and explain that he fully intended to pay everyone back; but was that true? He wasn't acting like he cared about any of that, so why would he want to say it now?

Luke didn't wait to see if anything more was going to be said. He stood up and began walking slowly down the steps to the driveway.

"How are you getting home?" Jacob called to him.

Then he saw Loretta in her car coming down Maple, crossing Church and coming up to the driveway. He watched Luke get in the passenger side door, and kept his eyes on the car as it turned around and drove out of sight. It struck him suddenly: she had hidden her car because they were not sure they were going to give him the truck! They had to see him first, observe him, let him prove himself to them? So, he had passed the test? What grade had they assigned him? To whom was the final report to be handed over? Mom . . .

He repaired to his basement quarters and took a seat at his desk. He tried to read for a while but it was impossible, his mind was thinking of Luke's recent behavior. He had come to offer gifts, smoke the peace pipe, obtain the pledge that treaties were going to be upheld. It made Jacob feel much better, and worse. He started to feel miserable, until he accepted and appreciated the fact he had his own vehicle! He could go into the city any time he wanted.

He selected from the shelves a volume he had not touched yet, and there were many uncut pages. One of the charms he found in these old books was the need to use a blade of some sort to slice through the virgin sheaves. He read very slowly, as some masters have enjoined, falling into a spell of intense consciousness. The pages excited his mind to recall many past events of his life, that now seemed like dreams. These memories were strangely dynamic, as if he could almost see into what might have been during certain poignant moments. He became lost in himself, ranging about in unchartered territory.

He was looking at his own and other lives in a way he had never really done before. He attempted to recapitulate what he knew of Luke's early development. He had graduated from McDermott High in '67; his graduation party lasted till morning. Later that year he was a soldier fighting in the hill battles around Dak To in the central highlands of Vietnam. He was decorated, and after he came home that ribbon seemed to eat into his chest when other men wanted to speak about his martial exploits over beers. Jacob had watched it happen, and he had never talked to anyone about it. He could see on his brother's face his inability to deflect something he wanted to disown, and over time the visage grew more gaunt and mirthless. The hard cheerfulness he had seen so often as a boy, as Luke teased, tyrannized, protected, helped and instructed him, had dwindled down to a precious reserve. Jacob remembered gatherings at the house when their father would call for Luke to come and meet someone, in those first months, after he came home.

"Luke, come here!"

His paternal hand would go up to his son's shoulder and sneak onto his neck for a hearty clasp of manly pride.

"Here's my war hero," proclaimed the father, who himself had been shuttled around the South Pacific in choice assignments during the Second World War. He was fond of saying, "Mostly we sat on our asses and waited for something to happen."

Jacob remembered Luke's face, sensing more than seeing his distress; but no one else seemed to notice. Everyone appeared to be very happy while Luke's face underwent some deformation under the press of hidden anguish brought back from the bush.

After his release from the Army Luke became a union electrician and began to frequent bars on the east side that stayed open all night. If that topic came up at family gatherings their mom would say, "Please talk about something else!" His one constant in life was that he always loved to go fishing. He did not care about the laws governing private property; if there were a productive bass lake in a remote location he took pride in trespassing to gain access. His standard joke: 'I found another pond in the bush.' He called all rural folks Charlie. This activity frequently got him into trouble, and he found his way down to the Lake of the Ozarks in the middle of Missouri, a veritable Mecca for bass fishermen. After a time he ran into a local sheriff in a diner who struck up a conversation with him. Certain questions led to his war service and it had seemed natural, for the first time, to talk freely of those matters. The sheriff had served in World War Two, seeing action in the Hürtgen Forest, and he also had been decorated. It was years before either man knew this fact about the other.

The sheriff invited Luke home to his house for supper and there he met his daughter, Loretta. His fishing vacation became a permanent re-settlement, as he found a job working on a construction site. It was in his blood and he was motivated and he became a crew leader before long. The sheriff had loaned him his personal truck and said it was granted on one condition, he had to come over for dinner a couple times a week. This proviso was unnecessary since Luke practically lived there as it was. They played horse shoes out in the back yard, which was more of a field, and stretched back into a rocky forest where they sometimes took a .22 rifle and shot squirrels which Loretta cooked after they had cleaned them for her.

"I'm sick of us hanging around here," she said to Luke one day.

"Okay. What do you want to do?"

"I want to move to St. Louis."

"Oh." He still wasn't sure what was going on. He thought life was quite good, other than the fact he did not get to fish nearly as often as he would have liked, but it never seemed to bother him, not that he thought about it that much.

"With you!"

He nodded as she fell into his chest and looked up at him.

"Well?" She demanded.

"You mean get married?"

"Yes!"

"Does Marion know?"

"Yes!"

Marion was the sheriff. The mother had died some years back, and Loretta was very tired of being her father's cook, and friend, and on-duty nurse when he drank too much, and spoke to her about how much he had loved her mother. She wished he would give a chance to the three or four women who were constantly trying to get him to go off with them to social venues where they might conjure again the arts needed to persuade a man to abandon the fiefs of barren liberty. Many had sought to drag him to church, where they might set his mind right, to no avail; but then there was one, who asked if she could go fishing with him. Despite the fact they did precious little serious fishing that day, they did discuss many topics dear to the sheriff's heart. They ended up in a church, after a decent interval, exchanging vows. All that happened a short while after Loretta moved to St. Louis as Luke's fiancée. Marion was happy to invite the married couple to come back to the lake to attend his wedding. He made Luke his best man.

Jacob remembered that Loretta gave birth to a child shortly after their wedding anniversary, and it was a boy; he had contracted a blood disorder. Little Henry died when he was eight months old and the devastation was beyond words. He could see Luke's face, as if it were yesterday; that fatal acquiescence to suffering sown into his whole bearing.

"He lived longer in the womb," Luke once said to Jacob while they were staring at a camp fire; they had gone on an overnight fishing trip, and the topic of children had come up. He had not really been speaking to Jacob in that moment, but giving audience to his own demons. In Luke's ensuing silence then, Jacob now, many years later, could feel the pain, and imagine how Luke was fighting its destructive power. He felt very lucky to have such good brothers, and did not want to ask himself if he deserved them, or god forbid, what he would deserve, should he fail to straighten himself out in time.

9

There was no way to avoid going to his parents' house for Father's Day. Only his mother could offer a pardon; and she could not do so without many acts of contrition on his part beforehand. He arrived early.

"Did you come in your truck," She asked eagerly.

"Yes. Thanks Mom." He could not look directly at her. She hovered by his side. His father shuffled into the living room.

"You're the first one here," He said, leaning on his cane, now used mostly for ceremonial occasions. "Do you want a beer?"

"That would be good." He began walking towards the kitchen to go out the back door to the enclosed porch where several large coolers were stocked with cold beverages. He felt a twinge of embarrassment at the idea of drinking and making merry, as if nothing had changed. Turning towards his dad he said, "Well, happy Father's Day."

"Thank you, son." His dad turned slowly as though executing a laborious procedure. His wife had come up and put her hand on her husband's back as they stared at him. He began losing his nerve under this pitiable attention. He was a poor enough prodigal. There was no Russian widow to taunt him with her gold, and his failure to become a leading man worthy of her hand . . .

He looked out at the lush back yard. They had purchased the dilapidated house in west county before the land rush began in earnest; all the older brothers had worked diligently to restore the building. Jacob acted as a laborer, not a true craftsman. The mother had actually found and selected the house, but it was the father who liked to remind everyone that it had been a fortuitous move. They had earned substantial equity that would serve them well in their declining years. Unless a certain wayward son continued to nibble away at the unrealized principal.

"I'm glad you came," His mother said, leaning towards him. Her smile was painfully affecting, as if she were bearing his sorrows, as mothers are sometimes wont to do, as is their prerogative, by the very design of life.

"I wouldn't miss this." He said awkwardly.

"How is everything in Ferdinand?"

"It's going pretty good." He replied as if it were a normal thing to say, but he felt utterly fatuous. It seemed absurd of her to be asking about that which made no sense to him or anyone else.

He later assumed a bluff posture before his three older brothers. They came with their wives, and all their children, even the older ones, who came with their spouses and children. It was a packed house. He strained to participate in the various conversations, while taking note of the dominant motifs involved in the public levity. Despite all their problems everyone was doing his and her part, and now was the time to make light of all difficulties in the name of tribal fellowship. He felt out of place. His mere presence upset the balance of the group.

As it grew late he was visited by a wretched thought, that he was being a very lousy representative for his sister Johanna. Someone made a comment about a photograph of her and him at their First Communion and he heard the word 'doll'; although he did not know if it had actually been uttered. The family had doted on them when they were young, and he had heard Johanna being called 'a little doll' so often he sometimes referred to her as 'the doll' in his memories of her. He feared everyone cherished her ethereal presence as a meditation upon the glories of what might have been. That had not happened in a long time, that feeling of oppression, as thoughts of her life's forfeiture closed too loudly around him. So much of what was said seemed, in his mind, to be about her. He kept placing her into the context of everything that was happening in the present, unable to disburden himself from a vast sense of remorse over his continual failings.

He finally made a faltering excuse for having to take his leave, addressing his mother in the kitchen. She bestowed upon him her precious, ruinous, pietà compassion. Using a thief's audacity he bolted while everyone else was outside conducting one last swarm about the paterfamilias. It pained him to think none of them would be surprised by his sudden dash; most would be relieved, some moved to pity. It had been worse than he expected, but he found release in a song played on KSHE, that old reliable station; de facto Congregatio de Propaganda Fide of his generation. He enjoyed hearing them play a live version of "Not Fade Away" by the Grateful Dead, from the iconic Skull & Roses album. He managed to soar upwards on the harmonic resonance of the electric strings that helped to define a generation that tore down idols left and right (and then later helped to put many of them back in place).

His flight did not even last till the end of the song. Exiting onto Florissant Road he drove as if he had no particular destination in mind. He had a sudden urge to buy a pack of cigarettes; a bad habit he had gotten rid of long ago. Jenny never had quit smoking. He stopped at a little convenience store, not sure if he was going to buy cigarettes or not. He decided to purchase a can of beer, something to wash away the bad taste of the aborted buzz left back at the party.

"Gates?"

Jacob turned around, holding a Schlitz Tall Boy in the air as if it were a totem; the natural love child of that great peacemaker called Fat Man. It took him a second to recognize who had called out his name.

"Hey, Robert." He greeted an acquaintance he'd known since high school. He had never been a friend. He had played on the football team. He had slick hair and was wearing an odd assortment of clothing, like the caricature of a salesman seen on a TV show. He was buying cigarettes and he waited for Jacob to buy his beer and they went outside together.

"It's been a long time."

"Yeah," Jacob replied.

"I'm on my way home. Father's Day." Robert said, not alluding to the fact he was returning to the home front belatedly after a costly spree on a gambling boat.

Jacob mentioned that he was just coming from a family event himself. "Can I have one of those?"

"Sure." Robert shook the pack until several of the paper cylinders were extended outward for easy extraction. "Take as many as you want."

"No, just the one. I quit." Jacob smiled feebly.

"I know what you mean." Robert said as he held out his lighter.

"Thanks." He felt pretty foolish cadging a cigarette. They smoked while looking around as though trying to remember how this ritual was supposed to go.

"What are you doing these days?"

"I'm between jobs right now."

"No problem." Robert said, somewhat gravely. They both nodded; saying nothing more for a moment.

"I was just heading home now, so—"

"Where do you live?"

"Over by Vogt school."

"So you live here, now?"

"Yeah." Jacob was at a loss. What more could he say? "Back in the old neighborhood again."

"You lived here before?"

"Till right after the fifth grade."

"Ah, well it's changed a lot."

Jacob kept silent, not wishing to engage him on this subject.

"Well, I own Ferdinand Motors. I bought it a couple of years back."

"Really?"

Robert put his hand on the hood of a 7-series BMW and struck a pose.

"That thing is yours?"

"This is me," he replied, patting the black metal.

"Sweet." Jacob said, admiring the vehicle. I'm in that truck over there." He nodded towards the old pedestrian vehicle.

"Nice truck." Robert seemed sincere in his nonsensical admiration.

"Say, can I bum one more smoke?"

"Sure, take a few."

"No, no. Thanks."

Robert looked at Jacob's can of beer as if he were wondering if he was going to open it and take a gulp. Seeing that he was not going to do so, his eyes narrowed.

"Well, enjoy the day, man." Robert said and turned towards his car.

"You too."

Jacob started his truck and left the parking lot in a state of bewilderment. Now he was begging cigarettes like a vagrant! He remembered that Robert had been one of those car fanatics; always buying and selling cars as a teenager. Now he owned a used car lot. Jacob wondered what his own youth might have foretold. His one lasting passion was kept isolated in a very restricted musical keep. He was seen as being rather aloof; trying too hard to be an acolyte of Dylan. Then going away to college he had discarded that persona, learning how to party on a larger stage, becoming more social, a truly fulsome character, who appreciated the fun of courting the sportive ladies who inhabit dorm rooms; until the official grading system drove him off the campus.

A Beatles' song came on the radio so he motored around the neighborhood. For some reason he pulled into the upper parking lot at St. Margaret's and parked at the far end, near a retaining wall. A narrow road descended from the upper parking lot to the lower level where there was a ball field. On the other side of the drive there had once been a huge oak tree. As a boy he would sit there under the tree, after school hours, looking down on the field below.

He sipped from his beer and began smoking his last cigarette. He held it up and observed the tobacco smoldering like a tiny extinguished torch. It tasted more harsh than the earlier one and he crushed it out in the ashtray. His revulsion reminded him of how he had finally quit smoking. He sipped at his beer, sweeping his eyes over the three levels of the church and school grounds. He glanced over at the middle level, on the edge of which the Virgin Mary was ensconced in her hard shell.

He had a strange thought, incited by something he'd read in one of his texts, at the end of which, the ruined hero finds himself unhappy because he cannot properly blame himself, as his society has done. It leads him to wonder if he can ever find redemption if he doesn't have any belief in the improvement of one's moral substance. The author was buried somewhere on the other side of the world, entombed in his stories; his ideas are still germinal seeds, bred for all soils. He had delved into the substratum of human behavior, where his eloquent refutations of hope seemed to stand out in stark clarity. And yet, turning about, he would always in the end leap into the arms of those ancient stage managers, who devised fictive human shapes, and resplendent celestial forms, to breathe life into visionary dreams. One was supposed to find comfort in shopworn fables?

Jacob moved to sit on the hill where the oak once stood. The hill sweeping down to the ball field looked so much smaller than his memory had foreseen. There, in his absence, his class took possession of this field for their medieval tournaments. The nuns dawdled over their lunches before coming down to police the mayhem wrought by seventh and eighth grade boys. Jacob never made it to the lower level, having transferred to a public school after the fifth grade. His first day he got into a fight over a girl. They didn't have separate levels there. He had found this girl to be quite pretty, and she had smiled at him like he was her dearest friend. It suddenly made no sense to let his shyness prevent him from speaking to her. She stared unabashedly with her beautiful, unguarded eyes. She giggled at something he said about a teacher, and something flashed at him through her exotic lashes . . .

Then he was surrounded and being interrogated by several other boys. They began mocking him. Someone shoved him from behind. He did not know then how all that fury got coiled up inside him, but in that moment it erupted. He found himself battering one of the boys who had stepped forward to push at his shoulder. Luke had instructed him on what to do in this situation. Don't wait, once you know you're going to get into it. Strike first, if you have to; if they're putting their hands on you. The boy was dazed after one blow, after the second he fell down, and Jacob stood over him and was hauled away by an adult. He never talked to the girl again, at least not until years later, and by then they had decided to forget about the incident.

Jacob heard a party of people up by the Grotto. He looked at them a moment, and then heaved himself off the ground and went to his truck and drove away. He might have remained there at the base of the vanished oak, pondering his life, for an unconscionable amount of time, if those other people had not appeared. Those odors emanating from the ground had induced reveries of marvelous clarity to smother his senses, as he was flung into the past. For just a moment he was unseated from the fatalism holding him in thrall to forces beyond his comprehension.

10

As soon as Frances learned of his truck she accosted him; would he mind picking up several saplings and miscellaneous landscaping materials from a nursery. Somewhat annoyed, he tried to put her off; but she was tenacious, and he had no basis for refusing her request. He was clearly beholden to her.

"Thank you so much, Jacob," she said, after coercing his consent.

"She can't always treat me like her servant," he muttered to himself.

Something about her methods raised his hackles, and she somehow used that emotional distress to rout his defenses. So, he ended up in the yard acting as her assistant gardener. He dug holes so she could plant a few dogwoods. He cut and bundled branches she had pruned from trees and put them into large trash bags. He raked dead leaves out of flower beds and laid down fresh mulch; and afterwards he sat down in the shade with her and chatted over a meal of delicious chicken-salad sandwiches. He found himself fielding a barrage of questions, swatting at them like swarming insects. Was she gathering materials to write *The Decline and Fall of Brother Jacob*? Then she was talking about herself and he mulled over his own dissatisfaction in the mild umbrage of several aged trees.

She's trying to get the particulars of my resume so she can push me in the direction of gainful employment; then she will start charging me rent. She knows everyone in town, and if I'm not careful she'll arrange to have me serve as an indentured servant at some shit job before I even know what happened. There's probably not anything I can do about it either. She'll enlist the help of Mom. How well do they know each other, I wonder? It would almost be better if she gave me an ultimatum: pay rent, or get out! Then where would I go?

He resolved to pay a visit to Marlow's Pub, a favorite haunt of his old gang. He considered going early on a Wednesday afternoon; anxious to avoid seeing too many of the old crowd at once. During the off-hours he might encounter only those celebrants not currently in the work force; who know precisely why everything in the world is fucked up. None of these folks is ever responsible for his own failures, and there is always room for another disciple wanting to learn how to assign blame elsewhere.

Jacob walked in the front door and did not see anyone he knew. Then a man at the bar called out to him, so he went over and sat next to him. It was John Sutten, one of the characters who had come along in recent times; no one had vouched for him. He was one of the indigenous people of Dog Town, one of those seedy, urban fiefdoms constricted over time by the python growth of surrounding thoroughfares, and the concomitant squeeze on property values. During St. Paddy's Day swarms of inebriates take to these streets to honor that most universal of solvents, which holds the power to absolve humans of their misery for an evening.

"What's up, my man!" John addressed him as a comrade returned to the front lines for regular duty.

"Hey." Jacob addressed the bartender; ordering a draft beer.

"Long time, man."

"Yeah, I've been, well, I don't know what I've been doing"

"I got you there. I'm doing the same thing." The native laughed in a husky manner. He sported long unkempt hair, and a week's worth of whiskers that clung stubbornly to his hollow cheeks. His dark mahogany eyes glittered between shielded slits. "It's all good. It's all good."

They quaffed from their beers, exchanging news about people they knew in common. John merely frequented many of the same taverns. He didn't know that much about any of their actual lives. And Jacob's knowledge of the group was no longer current. He was hardly different from this other character. They resorted to inane clichés, as if pronouncing abstruse verities that had escaped all the wise men since Socrates. He felt himself getting caught up in the spurious camaraderie that breeds like bacteria in these haunts.

"Have you seen Jenny around much?" Jacob asked directly.

"Oh man." John turned to look at him with a serious mien, betraying he had heard about their break up. "Yeah, that's right."

Jacob was thinking, what's right?

"Yeah, you and her."

Jacob shook his head impassively, as a way of requesting more information on the topic raised; thinking to himself, please try and say something intelligible.

"Sorry man, sorry, I was just . . ."

"Hey, no big deal, I was just curious."

"She's pretty much with that one dude."

"That one dude?"

"The Easy Rider guy."

Jacob shook his head more vigorously. "What guy is that? She's going out with a biker now?"

"No way. You don't remember the guy? That yuppie biker dude?"

Jacob was stunned; he had no idea who he was talking about.

"Yeah, they wear all the leather duds and shit. Everything's brand new." John was warming to the subject; he was the closest thing to an expert on this subject presently available. "Me, I don't like those fully dressed hogs. It's an old man's bike, that's what I say."

Jacob wasn't listening. Is this why I came? he wondered, just to hear it said out loud that she was with another man. I knew that, didn't I? The real reason was to find out who it was. He never knew the identity of the other guy. Wasn't that strange?

"So, where you working now?" John asked him, a crooked leer bending across his lips.

"Oh, I'm running a small job out in West County."

"Yeah, who with?"

"I'm actually in Ferdinand, right now."

"No shit, in North County?" Jacob recognized at once that having to change his story hardly changed the man's affected credulity. It was a practical virtue; one highly coveted by paladins of the afternoon buzz.

"Yeah, I'm doing some landscaping work now."

"Hey, that's cool, man. Whatever it takes. Anyway you can get a little scratch, right?" John began nodding, staring at him and smiling, with an eerie exposure of his toothy mouth that put Jacob in mind of a crocodile taking up his position at the edge of a river shoreline. Jacob became thoroughly dejected, raising his glass to his own reflection in the mirror behind the bar. Glad you came, Jakey?

He was on the verge of giving this guy a message to relay to Jenny, should he happen to see her; and realized at once how stupid that would be, to enlist him as his ambassador. He looked up at the big clock on the wall. There was a sign right under it touting the wisdom of making any time a good time for drinking. The ethos espoused by beer commercials adorned the surrounding walls for the patrons who had no other heraldry to sustain them.

"You should stick around, I'm sure more people will be showing up." He had seen that Jacob was anxious to leave, maybe inferring also that he wanted to get out before too many more people did show up. "Let's have one more, come on. What have you got to lose?"

Jacob ordered another beer, and John asked him if he could possibly get him one too. "Things are pretty tight right now. The old lady's just about got me on an allowance. I'm not shitting you. But it ain't so bad, not really. She's pretty steady. You know what I mean?"

Jacob bought two beers; leaving his untouched, he excused himself abruptly, saying he had a contractor he needed to see about a project. John smiled knowingly, his eyes snatching at the prize of an extra beer. His visage was a forlorn mask of lurid cheer; like a faulty neon sign, with dead letters, flashing ironic signals over a lonely storefront.

"Don't work too hard." John quoted from his book of common prayer.

"Not to worry." Jacob answered, his morale now like a dead thing he had to drag behind him on a leash, in violation of innumerable social conventions, and health ordinances, not to mention common decency.

He found himself driving the short distance to Forest Park, and there taking a seat at the Boat House. There were several empty tables in the back near a rusty chain-link fence that swept around the grounds. A cluster of river birch trees were just outside the fence and the colors of the bark and the play of leaves in the breeze made the vacant space rather pleasant. A young woman came out and took his order for a beer and in a moment he felt quite at ease. If you were going to partake of dissipation, this was how to enjoy the process! There were not a lot of families bustling about to shame the solitary tipplers, as the place had fallen on hard times. The concession was in need of renovation, and it was just a matter of time. The park itself was one of the city's treasures; the demand for quality services at this franchise would be answered in good time.

In size alone this park dwarfs Central Park in New York, and in the matter of naturalistic, rustic charms, and various other amenities, there is simply no comparison. This grand dame of parks, born in 1876, and christened, so to speak, at the 1904 World's Fair, has become a teeming habitat for the romantic notions an advanced society is incapable of casting into the toxic landfills of progress. There must be a public sanctuary where primary virtues are protected from the inexorable drive to fashion new worlds made by hands; something to balance the works done in steel, concrete, brick, and glass. The jealous fertility gods demand an egalitarian place of their own, set aside to temper the monomania used by rugged individuals to scale the heights of social class in order to gratify personal ambitions.

Here, one finds his own Walden Pond. Here the earth's austere benevolence is administered by pious cultivators for the public good. There are elaborate trails that pass through the woods and wind about miniscule prairies and circle about numerous ball fields that ring with the cries of adults at play. Numerous hills are crowned with mature trees that lord over their brilliant, thriving courts of indigenous flora. The landscape has been scripted for use by adopting a studious attitude towards the regulation of nature's laissez-faire temperament. The original patrician passion for golf is here extended to all so as to confuse the matter beyond recognition. There are amphitheaters, museums, greenhouses, open fields for lolling in the grass, and many ponds to support herons and kingfishers and all their prey. A picturesque artificial river winds through verdant tracts to sing of all things kept alive in the wild. The original watercourse lays underground, a slimy concrete habitat of great service to the rats, for whom we act as grudging, liberal benefactors.

There is still evidence, in the many monumental relics, of the past glory of a city that once aspired to glitter in the eyes of the world. Seen atop a hill to his left Jacob admired the attractive World's Fair Pavilion, and the long rolling hills, interrupted by broad, green terraces, coming down to the road. He and Jenny had disported there many times. This whole park had been like one huge back yard for them. He looked out over the pond, and at the few paddle boats making their way in splendid laziness, going nowhere slowly and coming back again to disembark upon the land of scheduled time. His eyes rose up over the copse of trees on the far shore, and beyond, to rest on the statue of Saint Louis, the crusader, astraddle his warhorse. A very Catholic breed of king. He would have been at home at St. Margaret's, at the time when Jacob was a child, with his extensive brood of children. He holds up his sword in a gesture of peace and order. Let there be peace, just as we prescribe, or else! The shabby city has gone past its ambition to rank among the finest cities of the land. It now lives in seclusion, dawdling over manuals that teach bourgeois manners to timid souls afraid to unseal the just deeds of Madam Clio. Not all the past sins can be buried in the landscape like the axle of a great wheel . . .

He ordered another beer and bantered with the young woman who brought it out to him. He adopted a role, intimating that he had some time to kill, before going forth once more to meet his obligations. What a laugh. He knows he must learn his place, and the limitations thereof; and he resents it, and knows he cannot possibly let it be seen that he does, or else an even more stringent sentence will be decreed. Is self-banishment an actual possibility? Why had he come here? To loiter in the dreadful past, as though wishing to steal only the good portions and parcels; to somehow sanctify a sense of place, that now feels as if it is no longer his to enjoy? What am I doing? How long can one ask himself such questions? What happens when you stop?

He left a generous tip and his glass half full of sudsy amber fluid, having decided he had lost the privilege to such an indulgence on a sunny day. It was an obscure sensation, but it nonetheless felt good to imagine he was taking even these paltry steps towards salvation. Maybe it was hopeless to expect much of anything from the world. He must learn to be in the world, enjoying the natural realm, without expecting to be a part of all that other business concerning social status. Was that realistic? How would that even work? He needed to be on good terms with his own people; he still owed them that effort, he needed to merit their approval by virtue of his own, his own . . . what?

11

Opening one of his volumes at random he sought to lose himself in one of those soul-searching exchanges constantly breaking out between the overwrought characters. He swam about in the turbulence of their contrasting visions. They were forever pitted against each other, and themselves, and the world; unable to bring harmony to the formulation of their stated beliefs, or the repudiation of all beliefs, for that matter.

He began to reflect upon the recent trip back into the family circle. What a debacle it had been. Being a passive observer lets you see too starkly into the selfish wheels grinding beneath the ceremonies of innocence. As a spectator one has nothing to offer the group, except for heretical critiques. Such persons must be relegated to a subordinate role; in every rebuff and insulting quip, made to suffer a perverse, gradual decay of social relevance. In the process depleting his vital stores of confidence . . .

Now he had to move again, and so his present life, as ridiculous as it had seemed, obtained the favor of nostalgia. He vowed that he did not want to walk these streets anymore, if he was only going to lose them again. He did nonetheless, feeling especially unworthy when confronting the trees; his most loyal companions! Anger flooded his heart and left behind the spiteful sewage. He became sullen, calculating how much more time he might have before he would have to move out of the basement.

Frances said she had information on another place where he might take up residence. He was resigned to letting her determine his fate. He could not help but think of his father, who had comported himself rather well on Father's Day. He knows his place; a position secured after much loss, and agony. Knowing one's place, that was an achievement to be sought after; all he needed was a roof over his head. One morning he walked to the City Hall on Church Street to buy a newspaper from the machine out by the sidewalk. He brought it back and sat on the patio reading. In Rwanda genocide was taking place in broad daylight; monitored by the world press with chilling reserve. The armies of Western powers rested, their economies did not miss a beat; every gross domestic product was geared to operate in fiscal comity.

In a short while Frances came out of the house and walked over to him, sitting down and taking her time to compose herself.

"So, Jacob?"

"Yes?" He looked up at her as if he were in a school room and she still wore her old black habit, with the heavy cross on a chain, that fitted her person like a knight's mace, and which she was licensed to use on incorrigible schoolboys.

"Tell me, do you want to stay in Ferdinand?"

He had not expected to be quizzed on such things. "Yes, I do." He spoke without reflection. For a second he thought maybe that buffoon Mulligan was being extradited for past crimes, and she was going to offer him the luxury suite upstairs. To be in the loft again! It was too good to be true. "Why do you ask?"

"You may be able to stay at the Spencer house."

"The Spencer house?"

"Yes. Beatrice is having, oh, she is having all kinds of thoughts these days. I don't know myself if it is such a good idea. She doesn't know if she wants to have her own salon, or make it into a bed and breakfast, or what."

"What's any of that got to do with me?"

"For now, she just wants to have someone staying on site, to keep it from being vacant. And to help in the upkeep and maintenance, and such."

"What did you say she wants to do with the place?"

"Well, that's her problem. What to do with the place. My lord she doesn't have any clear idea herself, and I told her, well, it's not like she . . . never mind. I do think she may be someone you ought to talk to, while you can."

"You think I should talk to her?"

"Yes! She's up there right now. Go up there and see her."

"Oh."

Once more thrown into the arms of chance by others. He walked along the side of the house to the grassy expanse of Allen Place, and proceeded straight towards the old Spencer house. Beatrice was standing at the side entrance by the driveway waiting for him. She was dressed casually in jeans and a blouse, wearing flat, comfortable shoes. She wore very little makeup.

"Why don't we take a stroll," she suggested. "I am trying to figure out what to do with all of this; now that it's mine!" Her voice was lyrical as she swept her arm out in a extravagant gesture, inviting Jacob to survey her duchy. "This place has so much potential, don't you think?"

"Sure."

They found themselves sauntering about the grounds. Beatrice burbled over prospective landscaping projects. They circled the house and as they started to go around again Jacob spoke up.

"Frances told me I ought to talk to you."

"About doing some work for me?"

"Yeah, and that you might be letting, you might have . . ."

"What?"

"Rooms available?"

She stopped walking to shake her head doubtfully. "You mean to rent?"

The word rent struck him as holy scripture is said to affront Satan's general staff. He blushed. He wasn't sure what he'd been led to believe by Frances now that he went over it in a more objective light.

"To rent?" He seemed to be impossibly confused by the concept.

"Yes, possibly. You could rent out several rooms. Is that what Frances said to you?"

"She just said I ought to come talk to you." Now he was shaking his head at her in his bewilderment.

"By the way, did you say you used to go up in The Joint, when you were in high school?"

"Yes."

"I was never a part of all that, but I went to the open house the family gave every year, during the Christmas holidays. I went several times. Oh, it was grand."

"Yeah?"

"Do you remember those?"

"No."

"Well, it was pretty exclusive, really. Not that they refused anyone, that I know of, but it was formal. Very chic affairs. Oh, they were just wonderful. It was like something out of the past. Wearing long gloves; it was just full of romance."

"It must have been something."

"Now, do all your brothers do construction work?"

"They do, I mean, they all have. They are not all doing that work currently. Why?"

"Oh, I was just wondering. I am not sure yet what to do with this place. I want to keep it as true to its old . . ." She drew in a deep breath, and exhaled her speechless excitement. "I think it should be preserved, for Ferdinand; maintained with the idea of adding permanence to its charm. Do you understand?"

He nodded because she had lost him in her ardent effusions.

"I am thinking of making it into a bed and breakfast."

"Yeah, sure." He nodded agreeably. "I think that would be a good thing to have around here." He actually thought the location was terrible, and recalled reading that such places failed more often than new restaurants. It actually made no sense.

"I suppose you could be the groundskeeper!" She reached out to touch him on the arm, as though to assure him he was not imagining his good fortune. She leaned closer and peered intently at him. She was the chatelaine, bestowing noblesse oblige upon a simple townsman (or, town simpleton: he wasn't sure which part he was supposed to play). In her gracious manner he inferred he might aspire to become the first steward.

"Okay." He had a vague notion he was passing muster.

"What do you think?"

"It might work." He managed to say.

"Well, that's one idea anyway. There's so much that can be done with this place. It could be an attractive venue used as a gathering place, a sort of meeting house. Do you see?"

"Yes," he nodded, not having any idea what she was talking about. He glanced up at the dormer windows on the garage roof. Was she intending to offer him that space?

"You are single, is that correct?"

He could not help looking at her face with alarm.

"Forgive me for prying, but I just wanted to know. I mean, if you are going to be on the premises. You understand?"

He thought he did, but he wasn't sure. She was sampling various offerings of bliss which she'd brought to life from her own ineffable visions. The hubris was pulsing from her eyes. Every belief was rendered equal in such a trance. They both became somewhat embarrassed and looked away together and began walking to resume a redundant tour of the grounds. He was relieved to hear her warbling once more about the past glory of the Spencer house.

"So you will think about it, then?" She was holding out her firm hand to be shaken.

He performed the ritual, as he had done many times, but like many rote customs, the act can seem all of a sudden rather peculiar. He was bewildered by her mania for the meaning of this one house. As he walked away he turned once to look back at her and found that she was standing very still, her arms folded, staring up at the building. It was no longer a structure housing the echoes of past lives, but the busy nursery of *her* imperishable dreams.

Later in the day Jacob was feeling restless, sitting on the patio. Upon seeing Cody he called out to ask him if he wanted to go to the Chengdu Garden. Sally was presently staying at the duplex with him along with the the children, and after a consultation he was informed they had concurred. Sally asked him how it had gone with Beatrice. It soon became evident that anything Jacob had confided to Cody was familiar to his wife. They enjoyed a communal feast. The Chengdu brothers always encouraged people to share their meals; since they were not proficient at bringing the entrées out at the same time, they directed the diners to partake of whatever dish was there on the table. It was not a bad scheme for adding spice to the most primal of all human activities.

"So you think Frances asked Beatrice to let you become her grounds-keeper?" Sally asked him, keeping an eye on her children, who had disembarked from the table to engage in single combats with chop sticks. The shrill histrionics made for an unwitting spoof of the way politicians wage holy wars in public over rich spoils they will apportion in private.

"Yes, sort of, but I'm not sure why."

"She may have suggested it." Cody said. "But you know, Beatrice would not take you in if she didn't think you were going to work out for her. But you're saying you think she has some crazy attachment to the house?"

"Her face lit up whenever she spoke of the old days. Do you remember the Spencers holding open house during the holidays?"

"I've heard about that, but not really."

"You never went to any of them?"

"Come on. Did your family?"

"I don't know . . ."

"You all have your own memories of the place, though, don't you?" Sally asked, after reaching out and hauling in her son by his wrist and chastising him for not listening to her. "Don't get too wild!" She admonished him as he broke free, raising his stick over his head to assail his sister once more.

"We just went there. It drew us like Stonehenge drew the Druids." Cody said.

"What are you talking about? What do you know about the Druids?" Jacob challenged him.

"They built Stonehenge."

"What does that have to do with anything?"

"I saw something on TV about it. Why do you think they assembled all those rocks there?"

"To keep track of the seasons, right?"

"Yeah, but why right there?"

"Maybe something happened there at one time."

"Or it was just a convenient place, an open field behind a shuttered bowling alley that was handy."

"Are you guys ready?" Sally was growing weary of watching the children and listening to these two men discussing ridiculous subjects. She wished to call her mother to make arrangements for staying with her later in the week. Leaving the restaurant they walked as a troop through the old downtown section of Ferdinand, then under the railroad trestle, before turning at the corner to walk up Church Street. It was always a happy sight to see the hill rolling upwards, past the homes and trees, towards Elizabeth and that suggestion of enchanted woodlands beyond, birthplace of so many fairy tales.

"Well, good luck in your new digs." Cody said to him outside his duplex. Sally and the children had gone inside.

"Well neighbor, it's going to be pretty weird, living up there all alone."

"More weird than living in a basement?"

Jacob laughed.

"You may as well enjoy living in the big house for a change."

"Yeah." Jacob stood motionless, his mind was elsewhere.

"You want a beer? I may have some left—"

"No."

"Something on your mind?"

"I feel like I'm losing people."

"Like who?"

"I don't know. People I once knew. Worse than that, I think I'm becoming one of those people nobody likes."

"Well, fuck 'em." After delivering that emphatic dictum, Cody swung about and strolled to his door and disappeared into his home.

Jacob turned away from his dwelling, sweeping around the side of the house and out to Maple Street. He walked beyond the Vogt School playgrounds, cutting through the large back lot and strode up the grassy sward and crossed Clay to get back to Mount Adams. He climbed the rise and plunged down the path on the other side, coming out on the level area at the bottom, passing by two huge cottonwoods. He imagined these lords of the vegetable kingdom regarded him with a certain measure of respect, as a glad fellow who was on the right track. He continued up Elizabeth on the sidewalk as the mystic sycamores flung over him their ghostly arms. An imaginary companion trooped beside him; the happy child he had been in the fifth grade. It suddenly made perfect sense to him that he would be staying in Ferdinand; it almost felt as if that was all that mattered to him now. He had no idea why that should be so important. He was content to be treading along the sidewalks; not having to worry about where he might lay his head. He felt the instinctive goodness of not needing to know the provenance of ordinary mysteries, to still enjoy the nourishment of human sentiment. In this state he was touching upon infinite treasures stored in our teeming universe.

Part Two

—

The Empty Mansion

12

On occasion one's buried faith heaves out of the earth, showing cracks; doubt has riven the foundation. We then question that base material manufactured by human thought, or blame the deficiency on the impurity of the organic substance itself. One may resort to the conjuring tricks of organized religion, or the opaque tenets of philosophy, or take solace in the parables found in ancient scrolls. One even strives to gain knowledge from stories of anguished souls who have gone before, and suffered, just as we, seeking truth in life's continuity.

Perhaps in the end, every search comes back to one's starting position; who can say? I only pluck at these metaphysical strings to draw attention to the fact Jacob did not move into the big house as a happy man, although it might have looked that way to the casual observer. Suffice it to say, he did not leave all his spectral torments behind in the confines of that infernal basement, where even the local field mice had cause to question his sanity. Something had changed, on the inside, and so the perceived world appeared to be changing around him as well. He was breathing in that fresh agency of incontestable mysteries, instead of feeling desperate to know the unknowable, and constantly being suffocated by his ego's exhaust. He was reworking his beliefs while maintaining good relations with those he cared about most, and you do not make that sort of passage merely on a conscious level.

He began taking walks at dusk, when the magic dust of sunset would gather around him as if he were a lightning bug about to set himself aglow. He wanted to glance across front lawns at the houses, their lights still burning, pushing something outward to merge into the leafy, trilling gloom. He could not help feeling like a cicada lord in his stewardship of these earthen verities. Ownership did not matter to the man becoming as the boy he once had been in these his first homelands. He also liked to walk around the block right after getting out of bed of a morning; his awakened senses feasting on every aspect of the dewy morning. Many of the old, sleepy, disheveled houses stood aloof, brooding upon lost privilege and imagined grandeur. Such structures become as memorable characters found in old stories; personages every succeeding generation refuses to abandon.

As he moved forward he studied the sidewalks as if he were poring over scrolls discovered at Qumran; he cherished the sermons etched on these concrete slabs. They filled him with childish wonder. The sycamores on Elizabeth, infallible presbyters, welcomed him with austere reservations. They could not be bothered with all of his trivial concerns, holding up their crooked arms to the firmament; taking sustenance from the contemplation of higher prophecies. He was taking the measure of forms at play in the void of his own cosmos, in the glowing silence finding his way to his own song.

13

One day Beatrice came by early and found him outside collecting dead sticks fallen from the trees. He bundled them up and put them out at the curb; saving some for kindling, should the need arise for a bonfire. She was attired in a smart business ensemble, holding a steaming paper cup of coffee. He answered her questions regarding chores he had accomplished for her around the grounds and in the house.

"Well, that's good." She began to take her leave.

"Let me show you something." He decided to mention another of his ideas.

"Can it wait?" She paused a few seconds before she decided to follow him around to the area behind the garage complex.

"Here." He pointed down into a sort of leafy pit, which had long before been the open courtyard in front of the stalls underneath the carriage house. "I think we ought to clear all that out."

"Hmm." She began holding her coffee cup close to her mouth, taking tiny sips.

"You're not going to leave this wildlife habitat here, are you?"

"No, you're right. Clearing it out would be a good thing."

"It's such a nice piece of ground you have there."

"Maybe you could get some estimates for the work."

"No, I meant that I could start chopping away at it. We've got the tools. I've got the time."

"Oh, yes, that's a good idea. Keep up the good work!"

He watched her walking to her car beyond the archway; her heels tapping an exotic cadence on the driveway. He then spent several hours hacking at the shrubs and tearing away vines and digging out the roots of small trees and large bushes. He spooked a nest of harmless garter snakes and watched the richly-dressed serpents slithering around in provocative movements. He stood still to listen to a boisterous chorus of cicadas. He decided to rest for a while in the shade of a maple tree that was on the other side of the pit from the hill. He sat on the concrete retaining wall, munching into a ripe apple, feeling good there was sufficient work laid out for him to perform. It would take a while to clear the ground sufficiently so that something useful for guests could be made of the area.

Later in the afternoon he walked down Allen Place to see what Cody was doing. He found him on the patio drinking a Coke. He took a seat at the table.

"You look like you've been working some." Cody said.

"Clearing out the brush behind the old stables."

"Does she tell you anything about what she wants to do with that place?"

"All the time. It keeps changing. I don't think she knows, really. She's sort of giddy with ideas."

"I can't figure out what you are supposed to be in this scheme."

"Yeah, it's a good question. Who is Jacob Henryevich?"

"Whatever, dude. But you're like, the groundskeeper, right?"

"That's Chief Groundskeeper, to you, watchman. Do you have any beer on the premises?"

"No, Frances might. She buys beer for Gregory. But you can't go in there."

"Why not?"

"Man—"

"Oh, don't worry, I'm not going to disturb the brute. Where is he?"

"He's down in the basement."

"He's down there now?"

"I think so. It's pretty weird, he doesn't come out a lot."

"You know, I was wanting to get my books out of there."

"Your books?"

"Well, not mine, but I found them down there, just rotting . . . I don't think anybody wants them. I'm sure he has no use for them. I think I'll just collect them now. Can you help me?"

"You bring them outside, and I'll help you take them up to your place."

"What are you afraid of?"

"I'm not afraid! I just don't like being around that guy. He's not all there." Cody tapped a finger on his temple. "Frances is trying to help him get on his feet, I guess. He doesn't need the two of us crowding him. That's his space now, you have to respect that."

Jacob pondered Cody's impassioned speech. His logic had no flaws, yet he could not resist making the attempt to recover his seminal texts.

"I'll just see if he minds. I doubt he wants them."

"What are they, books of the damned?"

Jacob laughed in a wry manner, twisting his upper body to look back as he made his way towards his old quarters.

"Hey! Gregory? You in there?" Jacob stood at the opening leading into the interior dwelling. He heard guttural sounds and put his head in and stepped forward a short distance. Upon seeing a Rembrandt portrait come to life, standing over the familiar worktable, turning to face him, Jacob entered his old shadow world cautiously.

"Who are you?" Gregory demanded. His person was a rumpled array of old clothing and rough demeanor.

"I'm Jacob. I know Frances."

"What do you want?"

"I was wanting to take these books, here. If you don't want them."

Gregory looked at the books neatly stacked in the upright position on the shelves. He appeared to be suspicious and befuddled.

"You've read all these?"

"No, I just glance at them, now and again."

"This is my book. Frances gave it to me." Gregory leaned over the table and put his hand on a large, leather-bound Bible. His long thick black hair was both ruffled up and matted down like the fur on a bear emerging from hibernation.

"Do you read that book a lot?" Jacob asked him.

"I try to. Not all of it. Some of it doesn't make any sense."

"Jump to the end."

"The end?"

"Here," Jacob walked over and leafed to the last gospel. "I used to glance at these pages when I was younger."

"I know about the New Testament." Gregory bristled. They both stood there looking at the passage where Jacob had place his finger at random. "But to all who received him, who believed in his name, he gave power to become children of God." Jacob leaned closer to the page, suddenly intrigued; then he noticed how Gregory was staring at him, somewhat ominously. He straightened up and suggested he might just take the other books then, if he didn't mind.

"There are mice down here." Gregory said flatly. His face indicated he was making an announcement that might affect Jacob rather badly.

"I know. Sorry about that; I used to feed them."

"You fed them?"

"I lived down here before you."

"You did?"

Jacob found himself under intense scrutiny. Gregory's haggard face changed from a menacing frown to a look of innocent puzzlement. Jacob felt a sympathetic pang, wondering how far apart they were. He thought of how the dregs of society live in a different world than the 'best people' who jostle about in polite circles, where status had religious significance. Justice and mercy for the downtrodden have little importance other than serving as deterrence against disorder; and giving merely a way to dress one's prestige in costly costumes. *Life is competition. Returneth the harsh slave master his talents, strike off on your own . . .*

He recalled from one text a character's recurrent dream of a baby, upon which the world has turned its back. A theme of life's innocence, and brutal human indifference. Adults can also be as helpless babes, he thought, inspired by a recent vision of degraded creatures that once had vibrant wings, which have become bent, torn and frayed along the edges, who are lost in life. They emerged from the earth to feel the first sunlight, and the intoxication of being lifted off into the air to whirl over the trees on musical wings. To live, to sing, to mate, and then to die. But some are battered fresh from the womb, and have no recourse but to go back into the ground as uncompleted things.

"Is Frances your friend?" He was asked in a voice that seemed to echo inside his own head.

"Yes, I guess so. She puts me to work, anyway." He tried to make light of the tension collecting in the dim room.

"She always puts people to work."

"She's a good woman." Jacob wanted to get out of there.

"She's a very good woman." Gregory stated emphatically, as if he doubted Jacob's sincerity.

Jacob nodded in agreement, looking at the wide blood-shot eyes that peered at him with incongruous intensity from under a shock of wild hair. He felt the heat coming out of a private inferno and turned his attention to the books.

"I'll have to make a couple trips to get all of them," Jacob said as he stacked four of the books in his hands. Gregory pitched in and grabbed the rest of the books and carried them outside. Cody greeted them and agreed to help Jacob carry the books to his new digs. Gregory stood there, in an old shirt with his name sewn into the fabric over his heart, watching them, as if expecting other instructions.

"Thanks Gregory," Jacob said. "Remember to feed those mice. And clean up after them."

"Yeah." Gregory seemed to come out of a reverie. "I think I will. Cute little devils."

"You have to be good to God's little creatures."

"The little creatures." The man echoed.

Cody and Jacob began the trek up grassy Allen Place towards the Spencer house.

"What the heck were you talking about, feeding the mice?"

"Nothing, that's just underground talk. You wouldn't understand."

"Something only derelicts know about?"

"Children of the earth, Cody; and actually, we prefer to be called lords of the earth."

"You're sure it's not mad dogs of Ferdinand?"

"Oh ye of little understanding."

"Man, these things are heavy." Cody exclaimed as his load of old books shifted in his arms.

"Be careful of those sheaves, you carry a great harvest there."

Cody began laughing from the resonant cauldron of his belly. "Jakey, you're a trip. You don't care what people think, do you?"

"I'm just trying to learn the songs of this earth. I'm practicing new measures all the time."

"That's what I'm talking about! Nobody talks that way, unless they're touched in the head!"

"Well, I'm pretty sure I've been touched."

"And cracked!"

"You know, watchman, not everything can be seen from your watch-tower. How does it feel? To be completely grown. A dog without a bone."

"To have no phone in your home."

"Beware fool, there's no one to call."

And they were off, testing each other on the actual lyrics, and making up silly derivations of songs composed by the magus known to us as Dylan.

14

He was happy working outside. He enjoyed listening to the breezes soughing in the grass at dusk, when he sat upon the richly fragrant ground. At night he stared into the Milky Way with reverence. He slept as in a restorative tomb; his cares were like seeds sown in good ground.

Then it was Monday, after the Fourth of July weekend; a cool front had come down from the north, charging the air with poignant mnemonic devices. His head swam upstream against the current to spawn memories. Jacob marveled over the weather's affect. His moods were acutely sensitive to the palpable touch of the external world. Stirring autumnal notes swirled around him as he walked the perimeter of his estate. Abruptly that arrangement ceased, and it was torrid summer again.

He had gone to his parents for the fourth, and Luke and Loretta came by; everyone else was absent; out of town, or doing other things. Luke had chided him at first about his protracted vagabondage, but he grew bored with the game when he saw that Jacob was no longer even perturbed by it. He was becoming an object of inspired interest more than one of ridicule.

"So tell me, how is it, taking care of that woman's estate?" Luke queried, as they sat outside in the shade of an oak tree with their dad. Loretta and Mom were in the kitchen sitting at the table drinking tea, discussing the insoluble trials of being entangled in what is called a close family. The men were drinking from bottles of Stag beer; the only brand their dad would drink, unless there happened to be a cheaper brand to be found.

"It's not really that bad, not at all." Jacob stared up into the leaves overhead.

"Keeping your feet on the ground?"

"Pretty much."

"Do you have to wear a uniform?"

"Not yet, I think I'm supposed to wear shoes. But I'm not very good at sticking by the rule book."

"I was never any good at that either." Luke started laughing. "I'm just messing with you."

"That's for sure," Dad exclaimed, looking at Luke, shaking his head and chuckling. "None of my sons—except Mark; he's the only one who would do what I told him. I mean, most of the time."

The two sons remained silent, exchanging between them a tacit appreciation of the special relationship Mark enjoyed with their father, and by extension, the entire family.

"He could always be depended on." The father added, and his two present sons were provoked to groan in open resistance. The motif of Mark's ancient filial piety was a seasoned matter, ripe for casual kidding.

"Most of the time." Jacob said, feeling called to action.

"That's right, only in those times you knew about." Luke addressed his father with playful ease; alluding to the early days, before the Marcan priority was established. Mark had been a different person until tragedy tore Johanna from the family, and the miserable father's resulting carelessness at work.

"We can't bother much about what we don't know about." Henry spoke in those sage tones he had earned after a long period of physical suffering. He puffed delicately on the stem of his pipe as if he were the resident dean of classical studies, reflecting on why it made perfect sense for Dante to choose Virgil as his traveling companion, in that very catholic and glorious romp through the underworld.

Earlier in the day, as they listened to Jacob expound upon the prodigious flower beds he was erecting on the Spencer grounds, they noticed his strong pastoral yearnings. They were compelled to mock him for being a lord in all but title, and holdings. Beer became superfluous as they lapsed into spells of reticence, swayed by the protracted dying fall that heralds each sunset in bucolic settings.

"Hey Luke, I almost forgot, do you want to do some work at the Spencer house?" Jacob asked.

"Maybe. Like what?"

"Beatrice wants someone to fix up The Joint; to make it into a guest house. She wants me to see if you are available to bring all the electrical work up to code."

"Well, I probably have the time."

"Is that something you would be interested in?"

"Sure, I can come and take a look at it for her. That's an old building, that could cost her some money."

"She knows; she's got money."

"Yeah? And you said she's paying you, right?"

"Yeah. Little stipends, now and then."

"She's paying you?" The dad came out of his reverie. He had been listening and not listening at the same time; ever at a certain remove, dreaming the dreams of old men, as was forecast by the first prophets. His hand grasping the pipe came down to rest on his knee. "That's a good thing."

"She has a lot of work she needs done around the place. Say Dad, can I borrow some of your tools? I need to learn some more carpentry."

"More carpentry?" The father asked innocently, which caused Luke to begin laughing as if he'd heard a fine, satiric joke. The father became even more excited. He exchanged a look with Luke and took pleasure in seeing the contrasting expression on Jacob's face.

"What are you saying? You're going to be a carpenter now?"

"Well, not union." Jacob smiled as if puzzled by his own situation. "I guess we can't all be union."

"You're the exception to the rule," his father said, a merry gleam in his eye.

"He's the exception to something." Luke's tone offered up his appreci-ation of something rather good, and unintelligible, now flourishing among them.

They erupted in laughter. It was not clear to any of them why this sud-denly seemed so funny. When the convulsive fit subsided Luke went inside to get a piece of paper and a pen to write down the contact information for Beatrice. The mother came out after hearing the laughter and fussed around, clearing away some of the clutter they had accumulated, picking cans off the ground, after scolding them for being so messy. It was a com-mon routine because they abided by construction site rules, cleaning up at the end of the day's labor. Her hand grazed Jacob's shoulder as she swept behind him on her way back to the house.

"That might be a good side job for you," The dad said to Luke after a while, as if he had had to deliberate on the matter. They interrogated Jacob about the exact nature of further renovation work Beatrice might need to have done. As long as Jacob had been aware of adult conversations he had heard a constant flow of information between the men regarding small construction jobs to be had, and how they might keep them in the family. Only Jacob had never worked as a craftsman in any of the building trades, and was therefore exempt from these discussions.

The men began to slump into their chairs, taking a survey of the deft gilding suddenly brushed on the fine edges of still objects; a perfect accent for enjoying the lassitude they plumbed as journeymen. The mom came out with a platter of moist, succulent brownies, and told the dad about someone who had called him about a golf outing. It used to be a highly prized annual event.

"I'm not going." He said.

"Why not?" She challenged him.

"I can't do it anymore." He said irritably.

She went back indoors in a way that suggested this matter was not over. Jacob and Luke concentrated on devouring the treats that evoked strains of their childhood.

"I better call them, let them know." The dad said and clambered out of his chair and followed after his wife. "I don't want to have to keep doing this."

The brothers began to talk about the father's inability to play golf. Since his accident he had mended quite well, with diminished capacities, to be sure, and after a long lapse he tried to take up the game again. For a good while he was able to play a more sedate game, and his friends accommodated him, concocting new ways to tease him and each other from that basis. But of late it had become too much of a struggle. He was older, and the frailty pained the sons to see at first hand. The damage of his old injuries was yet lodged in his lower back, and he found it awkward and sometimes jarring to become incapacitated when he was out on the course. He had finally decided to stop forcing the issue. Not all of his friends were aware of this abdication and he was having to decline invitations. Luke and Jacob exchanged a look of helpless commiseration. Neither of them had ever been avid golfers and could not really understand the sense of loss, but they knew it was real.

Later on Jacob marveled over the fact his strange new life was being accepted by the family. No one had even asked him if he were looking for a job. That was incredible. His mother told him the money she had been sending him was going to be deducted from whatever he might have gotten after they were gone. It was only fair. Jacob had not said anything; in total agreement that this was just; and besides, it made him extremely uncomfortable hearing his mom talk of her own mortality. It later made him feel good that it was not just charity dispensed to an irresponsible son. He was also still drawing out of his own savings, but not very much. Beatrice had begun to increase the amount she disbursed for his jobs around the estate. It was clear she enjoyed being able to come by and have him at her beck and call; as she was forever making notes regarding new chores she wanted him to complete for her.

◆

One day a brightly polished BMW 750 pulled into the driveway and drove confidently under the brick archway and proceeded to the the wide paved area in front of the garage. A man got out and started looking around as if he had come to purchase a piece of property. Jacob was using an axe to chop out old shrubs growing near the tennis court. Jacob walked over and recognized Robert Carouselly.

"Hey," Robert said, "How you doing Jacob. Working hard?"

"Yeah."

The man advanced a step and held out his hand to be shaken; something they had not done when they had met at the convenience store on Father's Day. "I heard you were up here."

Jacob nodded, suspicious he was going to be asked to play an unwitting part in some scheme. Robert's eyes played over Jacob's begrimed clothes.

"You look like you could use a break. You got a minute?"

"You look like you're getting ready to sell something."

Robert laughed. He was wearing dress slacks that had a permanent crease, a pressed shirt, and a jaunty suit coat. His thick dark hair was swept neatly into place and held there with some kind of gelatinous product. His face had been hewn by rough strokes, along handsome lines, but it was fairly gaunt, as if his hungers were impossible to appease, and constantly fed on vital tissues.

"I just thought I'd stop by. See how things are going with you."

"As you can see. I'm a busy man around here."

Robert chuckled, his head bobbing up and down in calculated movements, as he continued to assay Jacob's features. It was an odd show of deference, because in high school, in that medieval society, Robert had more social standing, being on the football team; moving among the varsity jocks and cheerleaders. Jacob had been a virtual nomad, loitering on the fringes of various Hippie clans, formed after breaking away from the hordes of Nobodies, many of whom went on to achieve success in life.

"I could see your truck from the street, so I figured you must be hanging around. I wanted to see if I could have a word with you."

"Sure thing, but I'm not in the market for a car."

Robert laughed affectedly. "No problem."

"You sell quite a few high-end cars, don't you? I walked by your lot the other day."

"That's all I sell." Robert provided a succinct explanation of his business model.

"For a long time I was doing it on the side, as a broker; selling Beamers, Mercedes, you know, and I had established this great network; people were calling me. So then I decided to buy an existing business, and set up my own shop."

"Sounds like a good deal." Jacob said, still confused as to why Robert had come onto the Spencer property to advertise his business to a poor groundskeeper who drove an elderly truck he had never paid for.

"So you're actually working here?" Robert asked, looking over at the tennis court where he had seen Jacob hacking at old shrubbery stumps.

"Yeah. I keep an eye on the place." Jacob had little interest in defending this phase of his life to someone he had not really liked that much while attending McDermott High, and whom he had hardly seen at all since that time.

"I've gotten to know Beatrice a little. I sold her a car. Have you seen it?"

"You mean her red Cadillac?"

"Yeah, burgundy. I don't usually mess with Caddies, but she was set on that Brougham model. She could have bought a new car; she's got plenty of dough. But she watches her money. So I found her a '92 that was just cherry. I didn't make anything. My best deals are with BMWs. They have the sweetest ride." He looked lustfully at his gorgeous white exemplar of automotive engineering, and Jacob leaned over to ogle the sumptuous interior.

"Have you ever driven one of these?"

"Nope."

"Do you want to?"

"No, I don't have any money to buy anything like that—"

"Come on, it's just a ride I'm talking about. Let's take her for a spin."

Jacob looked at him with a dubious expression. He looked over at the
tennis court, as if considering a ruse of pretending he could not afford to
leave his post; but that sounded ridiculous in his own mind.

"What the hell."

Robert directed Jacob to get in the driver's seat and he took for himself
the shotgun position.

"Where to?"

"Go out to Florissant and head towards 270."

"Okay." Jacob was feeling pretty good. The precise feel of the car's handling was impressive; no play whatsoever between the steering hand and
the wheels.

"Man, this car is fun to drive."

"I told you. Sweet ride, isn't it?"

Jacob nodded. As they climbed the ramp to get on 270 the car accelerated with a surge of smooth, thrilling power. On their right they passed
by McDermott High School and Robert let his eyes roam over the buildings on the campus. After a moment of reflection he turned and looked
straight ahead.

"You know about the big reunion, right?" He asked.

"No. What reunion is that?"

"Our class reunion, at McDermott. I wanted to discuss that with you."

"What do you want me to do?" Jacob felt his hackles rising, sure now
he was going to find out what all this spurious diplomacy was about. He
wants me to help set up tables or something. He's probably on some damn
jock committee addressing the labor shortage for menial tasks.

"Were you planning on going?"

"No, I didn't even know about it. I probably saw something, but I
threw it away, I don't really—"

"Well, how would you like to help me get a party going at The Joint?"

"The Joint? The place at the Spencer's?" He was suddenly very interested and rather confused.

"Yeah, like in the old days. Remember?"

"I wasn't a part of that whole scene."

"Oh man, it was wild." Robert explained that he had been a friend of one of the Spencer boys during the renaissance years. Apparently the older Spencer girls had first used the space for innocent sock hops and petting parties. The oldest son had dabbled in group howls inspired by the beat movement. Robert was involved later, when they were lounging about one evening, playing cards, and smoking cheap little cigars. The beer was tasting too good, as they were fond of boasting at such times.

Someone accused the others of cheating, in mock of a TV commercial then airing. The shtick was for a player to interrupt the game to declare in a slow, rising, minatory voice, 'These cards are marked!' Then he would tip over the table in outrage. It was done several times, and finally they all tried to upend the table in the same instant. They stood up in unison like an Olympic team hurling the flimsy card table straight upwards to smash resoundingly against the ceiling. It recoiled downward like a gigantic spider bent on revenge and they dove out of the way to avoid injury. There was a storm of helpless laughter that left them rolling on the floor. In the ensuing lull someone suggested they ought to build a bar in the corner of the large room, and the motion was carried by acclamation.

In the following weeks they scavenged building materials and manufactured a neat structure in the corner, where a crawl space let out into the enclosed area over the garage. This became a storage area for stockpiles of beer and other baronial necessities. It then became self-evident to the peers that the room's lack of décor was unsatisfactory. The covetous nature of castle dwellers came upon them. Someone suggested the bare walls might be adorned with actual street signs. The motif was apropos, since the military had so recently gone astray into Cambodia; inspiring students in Ohio to object and draw fire upon themselves. The local authorities were mystified at the disappearance of so many street signs (one was pulled up by the roots!); and could not possibly deduce these prizes were now on display as works of art. The contemplation of these abstract designs made for droll commentaries, in the ghostly glare of black lights, while passing around joints. Soon the place had its official designation.

"My uncle gave me that flag we draped across the back windows." Robert said.

"Oh yeah, I remember that, on the back wall."

"Yeah. It was his friend's death shroud. The guy's wife gave it to him. I guess she didn't want it either. He said the war in Vietnam was just wrong. He told me these crazy stories about his tour. I mean, he made it sound like it was all terror, drugs, and once in a while some pussy. These insane blood sports in the bush, utter boredom, and hallucinogenic parties. Hey! Remember Jimi Hendrix playing the national anthem? We had that on one of those records we kept in The Joint. Remember that little stereo?"

"I remember the loud music when I went there. But there weren't very many people there at the time. I didn't really know anyone."

"You must have been there on an off night. That was the thing, you never knew when it would happen. There were plenty of wild times, believe me. People would go on the roof; out along that trail in back . . . we'd even go down into the stables!"

Robert continued to reminisce as they wended their way along the winding two-lane roads leading to Sioux Passage Park, situated along the Missouri River. Once they arrived and parked the car and ambled over to stare at the river they became pensive. For a vivid moment each separately recalled the days of chasing around in cars, coming to this park to drop off rope swings into a slough of the river, or to play tackle football with braless girls wearing flimsy tops when no one was keeping score . . .

Both men were leaning against the car, staring vacantly at the harsh sunshine of the prosaic day as it flashed like a welder's torch on the river's seamless surface, sealing every crevice allowing entry into the past. Robert had exhausted his capacity to imbibe such intoxicants from the stream of consciousness. Jacob thought of Jenny in stirring silence. They drove back in abstract moods. Jacob began brooding over his lack of prospects.

"You want a smoke?" Robert asked him.

"No." Jacob answered firmly. "When was that, when I saw you last, I mean before I saw you at the quick shop." Jacob was recalling better days.

"Down in the Loop, right? Yeah, where was that?"

FLORISSANT GIRLS

"It was at Pliny's Café." Jacob confirmed.

"Oh yeah, about five years ago. That woman you were with, she was pretty nice. She had a great sense of humor. Seemed pretty wild, too. Are you two—"

"That was Jenny. We used to go there all the time. We lived right by there, just off the Loop."

We loved that place, he thought to himself, we could look out from our lofty stoop and feel at home in our own, special, resplendent sphere. Across the street reposed that strange city hall building, that looked like a magic castle built by a prince, who had used his talents to good effect. That structure's pretty dome was complemented by the larger hemispherical roof of a synagogue standing nearby. He could watch the last light glowing there before evening, feeling like he had risen above everything; for the Loop was his kingdom, it belonged to him.

"We had some great times there. We were party animals."

"Are you two still together?"

"We broke up. We weren't right for each other."

"Any kids?"

"No." Jacob stared ahead in silence for a moment. "You still married?"

"Oh yeah. Bound and gagged. No, just kidding. A son and a daughter are both spending my money in college."

Jacob remembered that Robert was married to his letter-sweater girl before graduation. Neither said anything for a while, both were contemplating unsettling matters closer to home. Jacob began to let his emotions overpower his reasoning.

"I wish I could afford to buy a car like this. Is this one for sale?"

"They're all for sale, that's the whole point. Finding the seller to match the buyer. You see, it's really about timing. Wait, are you serious? Do you really have an interest?"

"No, no. I don't even have a real job."

"That's your white truck? You own that?"

"Well . . ."

"Do you want to sell it? First, you paint it, spruce it up, then sell it to make a little cash. I could steer you towards some things, and after a few smart trades, maybe you could start to accumulate some equity."

"No, no. It's not something I want to sell, as of yet . . ."

They passed by Wabash Park on Florissant Road, swung to the left, and began their final descent into the heart of the city. Glancing above the road, beyond the buildings, Jacob could see nothing but a dense canopy of trees. He imagined he was heading into the depths of a virgin forest.

"Well, what do you think?"

"About what?"

"Throwing a party at the Joint! We'll invite a few people at the McDermott reunion to come over after they leave that boring affair. Or, we could even send out invitations! What do you think?"

"You've talked to Beatrice about it?"

"Yeah, pretty much. She's okay with the idea, I mean, she will be. She wants to hold parties out there, herself, in the future. This will be like a dry run. It won't be dry though, right?" He rapped Jacob in the shoulder with a fist.

"Not likely." Jacob felt a stiffening resistance to being drawn into someone else's delirium.

"The main thing is, we have to get the information on the McDermott attendees. So we can decide who we want coming to our party." Robert spoke with a quiet intensity.

"You want them to fill out application forms?"

They were standing beside the car on the driveway in the same spot where they had begun this adventure into the past.

"We need to get Kimberly Lahore to help us. She's gathering information to write short biographies on everyone. We need to get our hands on that data."

Jacob stared at him, not saying anything, pondering what he might offer for his personal notes; I am presently serving as choirmaster for the cicadas of Old Ferdinand.

"She's your cousin, right?" Robert insisted.

"Yeah."

"Do you think she'd share that information with you?"

"I have no idea. I haven't seen her in a while." He was wondering if he had been truant at any of her family's events since the advent of his hermitage.

"Can you ask her?"

"Look, I'm not really sure about any of this." He frowned, shaking his head. "The Joint is completely unfinished, there's nothing up there now, nothing but decayed ruins. Your project seems a little haphazard to me—"

"No, I know. I need to talk to Bitty some more. Look, I just came here on a whim. She told me you were keeping an eye on the place for her, and it seemed like a good idea to talk to you, to see what you think. It will take some work, I know, but I'm really starting to think it's a great idea. Imagine the divorcées who live in other cities, coming to town for a party! "

"You want to roll a joint?" Jacob asked him in a deadpan manner.

"What?" Robert appeared mildly shocked. "Really? Do you have any stuff?"

"No. I'm just kidding. That's what we'd be doing back in those days."

"No doubt. I never get high any more. Well, unless a customer initiates it. You'd be surprised how many respectable types—"

"No, I wouldn't. Like I said, we used to have a party joint in the Loop."

"Yeah. I don't see the point anymore of getting high just to get high."

They looked around in silence. Both were feeling the strange effects of having the tides of time washing through the nervous system faster than the normal psyche was equipped to handle, with any sort of equable mien or manner.

"You know, this party could get out of hand. What if too many people show up?" Jacob posed.

"I don't think that's going to be a problem. What can happen? We're old now!" He threw out his arms to emphasize his point, but the energetic gesture itself belied his assurance. Jacob was intrigued, and somewhat rankled at the idea of being manipulated by a salesman. Then Robert said,

"Here, take the keys. Have some fun driving this car for a couple of days. I'll pick it up on Friday, about this same time."

"Are you sure?" Jacob wanted to refuse, but he couldn't bring himself to do so.

"Take care now. Well, I have to drop by the bank, and I can use the walk. See you later."

"Do you want me to drop it off at your lot? I can walk home from there."

Robert shook his head as he loped away, his arms swinging in happy sweeps.

"Do you want to use my truck," Jacob yelled at the retreating figure, feeling foolish as soon as the words had come out of his mouth.

Robert raised a gallant hand to dismiss the offer; in his other hand he held his fancy Motorola flip phone, and was now dialing a number. In another minute it was obvious he had raised someone on the other end; as he walked down the drive one of his arms waved around to add emphasis to his voice as he addressed an unseen party. Then he clamped the phone on his chest and turned around to deliver a parting shot.

"Go see your cousin, Gates!"

"What the hell just happened," Jacob asked himself, looking at the BMW, and then at the keys in his hand.

He returned to the spot where he had been laboring to extract roots from the ground. He sat there with his arms on his knees. He had to piece together many disparate things in his mind. He moved to the shade under the maple tree behind the stables; taking up a twig to scratch crude symbols upon the ground. A gray squirrel cackled over his idleness. He thought of his first year attending McDermott High School. He was bowled over by all the Florissant girls who emerged from the surrounding community of small houses, built in droves after the great war. The place was a colony producing stunningly attractive young women just in time for the onset of his carnal exaltation. He was struck again by the choral movements from that divine symphony that shook his entire world. What explains that innate, physical artistry of people who are coming of age; freely tramping into sublime joys, and quaking sorrows, venturing out where the gods fear to tread.

He pictured Connie Garnet coming to his sophomore Biology class. He could look out the window and see her floating down the paved path, soon to join them at their lab table. Her head was held up high as she pranced with the invisible Graces who bestow rare powers upon those they favor. Her firm body was splendid to behold as she swept along, her short plaid skirt swirling around her gorgeous bare legs. Her feet were bound in flat exotic sandals, which had straps laced up onto her calves. The earth unrolled in stately splendor beneath her steps. The vision touched him with that solemn purity of notes rung from church bells on quiet mornings, announcing days of service . . .

Jacob decided to inspect The Joint again. The space was more interesting now. He stood at the compact little bar they had built in the corner; now badly scarred and tarnished by age. Time ruins everything, he thought; and then he was pleased to reflect that it was also time that had cast a spell of romance about the place. It was not half bad, after all, this haunt where swarms of unbound young people once brought their innocent cups of desire. He noticed that one of the street signs had survived; he had not noticed it before when he had ducked into the room with Beatrice. It showed a squiggly line and warned of a winding road. Instantly it made him want to learn to play a particular Beatles' song, using only the spare passion of his own pious strings.

He circled the room, touching his finger on dusty panes of glass. At his feet were fossilized roaches and dry rodent droppings. He stood for a long time at one of the back windows looking out over the trees in the direction of Elizabeth Avenue. He imagined the sycamores were holding out their arms like high priests, exhorting all those who still struggled to cherish idols poured from melting pots, to come join them in seeking after higher things not yet known.

15

I t was Friday, and Jacob could still remember how sweet it was to get off
work early on a Friday afternoon. A privilege earned after he had worked
many long hours for his uncle, and weekends too; and in the early days he
put in extra time without pay, and later on, working without overtime pay,
as a matter of course. He did not mind. He enjoyed the trust and confidence that was placed in him. It was a matter of pride, nothing ever had
to be said about this pact they had forged through mutual commitment.

Then his uncle began to thank Jacob effusively for his past efforts, and
it only served to taint what they had established through their tacit adher-
ence to shared values. It now occurred to him that when that started, it
was after his uncle Julius had sold the company, and it must have been after
he had learned the true nature of his illness.

While out walking, coming down Adams and crossing to get to the
other side of Elizabeth, he decided to go to Marlow's while he had access
to the BMW. It was Friday, some of the old crowd was sure to be there, possibly Jenny herself. While heading back he did something he had not done
since he was a child, he cut across several yards and climbed 'Spencer's Hill'
to speed the course of his journey.

An hour later he was climbing the steps inside Marlow's, heading for
the second floor. On the landing he stopped. The din of voices and laughter was like a powerful buffer holding him back. He leaned forward and
glanced around, his eyes resting at once on the face of Jenny, seen in profile.

Her excitement was shining forth from her features. He shrank back, and made his way back down the stairs.

"Jacob?"

He looked up, a woman had arrested her ascent and was staring directly at him.

"Oh, Elaine. How are you?"

"Are you leaving already?" She asked, before laughing in a pleasant manner.

"I was just . . ." *Skulking away!* He couldn't find any words. The woman's face released freshets of automatic empathy, and he considered she might have valuable information to divulge.

"Do you want to get a drink downstairs?"

"Yes, sure." Her eyes were alluring, the filigree of age on the mask of her composure was somewhat glaring.

She climbed down before him on the narrow enclosed stairwell, brushing by several couples coming up who stared at them in silence. They found a booth in the back of the long room on the ground floor and he went to the bar and paid for a beer and a glass of white wine. She began to chatter, since he was acting furtive, like a wild creature who has strayed out of his territory. She launched into a comedic account of her most recent love affair. He could not help but laugh as she spoke, in between long pulls on his beer.

"So that was the end of that." She wound up her tale. She was a fairly good-looking woman; as some of the old wags said, 'built for action.' She had never settled down, and her cheerful attitude seemed to have been plastered over an obdurate mold of bitterness.

"Sorry to hear that," he said mechanically, hearing the idiocy of his words as he formed them.

"Carpe diem, right?" She cried in her throaty voice, raising her glass, then she took a great swallow of the vine's restorative nostrum. She extracted a pack of Marlboros from her small scuffed brown bag and offered him one. He declined. She lit one and began blowing out jets of smoke as if a tremendous volume were trapped inside of her under great pressure. "I knew it wasn't going to last, right from the start. No regrets though, right? You and Jenny, you guys had a good run, though, right? How long was it? She . . ." Looking at Jacob she stopped talking. "I'm sorry. This is probably, I mean, you haven't been around for a while."

"I know. I probably shouldn't have come."

"Why did you, then?"

He looked at her closely, having chosen not to do that while she had been speaking, making instead a study of her nicotine-stained fingers to strengthen his resolve. He was determined to avoid doing something stupid. "I don't know why I came here," he said simply. "Other than the fact I am an idiot."

"Do you feel like getting out of here, getting away from these people? How about going to the Loop, maybe?"

"Let's do it."

The next thing he knew they were outside, standing by the BMW.

"This is yours?" She phrased the question in slow, breathless wonder.

"I've been sort of test driving it."

"Good for you. It's beautiful. Well, take me for a ride, man!"

As they drove away the song, "I'll Take You There," by the Staple Singers, came on the radio and he turned it up to drown out his intemperate thoughts. She began singing to the music. He exclaimed over the quality of the sound system. He felt her increasing interest in him, as she stole glances at his face while she swung her head to the music. Her keen appetites were quick to the whetting.

Passing along the edge of Forest Park he thought, "I can't go there, into that world, forever sampling spoiled goods."

"Where are you taking me?" Elaine asked excitedly.

"How bout Pliny's?" He was devising an exit strategy for himself.

"Great idea," she purred.

He felt a miserly twitch, calculating the money he would be spending for no reason he could fathom. Why had he not told her this was not his car; that he had no job and could hardly afford even this inexpensive little outing.

At Pliny's there were only a few patrons in the place. It was one of the long-established restaurants in the Loop, and offered a wide variety of beers. Jacob perused the sticky menu to find one he had never had before; finally choosing a sweet amber ale. Elaine ordered her usual vodka tonic.

She spoke to him satirically of the old gang, as if it were incredibly trite that everyone was still doing all the same things. She avoided mentioning Jenny. He found himself telling her honestly about his present circumstances. He could see the amorous glow fade on her features. He was finally able to tell a lie she would be grateful to hear.

"I've got a chance at this new job, and I need to be ready for that in the morning, so I can't really stay out."

"I understand," she said politely, not looking at him, making ready to leave immediately, anxious to be rid of him, too.

"I hate to cut the evening short." He added, and the falseness of his statement echoed off her steely resolve. They finished their drinks and walked out the back entrance into the parking lot. When he was driving her back to her car they made small talk out of very banal material that caused them to retreat further into silence for longer periods out of sheer embarrassment. He offered up the coup de grace, telling her the car was not his, and to whom it actually belonged.

"You're kidding? Robert Carouselly?" She turned a pale face towards him, and he glanced quickly at her and was surprised by the contorted look of her visage. She scrambled to light another cigarette. He wanted to ask her not to smoke in the car, but he had not the courage. She acted as if he were still trying to deceive her, even though he had come clean about everything. They drove in silence until they came again to the road along the boundary of Forest Park. Many healthy young women were running along the paths, wishing to stay in shape. Elaine glared at them fiercely. She had been working herself up, and now she struck.

"You know that abortion Jenny had, that wasn't yours; or this motorcycle frat boy's, either."

"What?" He looked over at her, feeling a strange anger building in his chest. He no longer had any clear focus on anything. He felt only the upheaval of black visceral anguish. That was none of this woman's business . . .

"She told me."

Jacob shook his head about as if trying to discourage a flock of gnats that were trying to land on his face. He could not speak.

"Unfortunately, when you drink too much, with some people, they start to tell you things." She continued, seeing that he was dazed. "Then later on of course they wish they hadn't been so careless. They don't want to be around you so much after that, and of course it's all your fault; there's something wrong with *you*, all of a sudden. It's quite a system. It really is."

"I'm sorry to hear that," he said rather ineptly. It was hard to breathe. An emotional Notre-Dame caught fire and was already collapsing; he was chased from his holy seat by the flaming timbers crashing down around him.

The drive became a purgatory for both of them. The radio was turned down very low for some reason and he had not the will to turn it up. She lowered her window and looked out breezily as if being taken on an official tour of a natural disaster. He changed the radio to a public station and they were playing a song by Suzanne Vega called "Calypso." He wanted to turn it up but refrained from doing so. It would have involved too much effort. Arriving at Marlow's he could see the expression of betrayal on her face; blended with satisfaction for having delivered a lethal blow. She was done carrying around that toxic knowledge, at any rate.

"Bye Elaine."

"Yeah. Take care of yourself, Jacob." An icy current rippled through her voice.

"You too, Elaine." He was feeling stupid about everything.

As he was turning around he looked up at the second story where the people of his past were caught behind the windows being as caricatures. The image stayed with him afterwards; a mental tableau of animated figures engaged in boisterous social conventions. He was strangely moved by that primal scene; the intricate exchange of auditory and physical signals designed by the species over untold millennia, and which individuals are prompted to act out by rote, and barely understand all the while.

16

He parked the BMW in the garage, as if trying to hide an infernal machine designed to torture an ego into confessing it's most dependable sophistry. He made his way into the basement of the Spencer house, where they had left a great jumble of old furnishings. Everything was arranged and stacked as if this were the cargo hold of a ship making ready to found a new suburban colony somewhere.

He discovered a sturdy wooden chair on wheels that would be ideal for use when he was practicing his guitar. He lugged the chair up to the first floor, then to the second floor, and sat on it, breathing heavily. He decided to carry it up to the third floor, and the only way, other than the servant's stairwell, was by going up the narrow staircase leading off from a door in his bedroom. It was a heart-pounding exercise to wrestle the chair the last way up to the third floor. He set the chair in the middle of the large room and listened to the pristine echoes washing back over him.

He retrieved his guitar and brought it onto his lap; tuning the instrument while his mind whirled about in the open space. His eyes began tracking motes seen in the sunlight as if they were rare musical ciphers he might make use of for his own compositions. He tried to play, "I'll Take You There." The song had lodged in his brain. He was teased by subtle licks. He had never tried to learn the song before, and now he had fun making up his own version. He had never really tried to be a songwriter before; but now alternate lyrics were coming to him without conscious effort when he covered other peoples' songs. He enjoyed weaving his improvised lyrics with his novel take on the original song's structure. After practicing for a while he stared out the window. The summer day was dissolving into the vibrant water colors of early evening. He decided to go for a walk.

In no time he was pausing at the bottom of Adams, peering across Elizabeth at the handsome Victorian house where the nuns of Saint Margaret's were once housed. Jacob let his eyes rest on the conical roofs and the large covered porch that swept around from the back and wrapped across the front of the house. That was back in the glory days, when the church maintained a full stable of sisters. Now the stragglers lived in a tidy brick bungalow stationed next door to a nearly identical edifice where the priests lived, close to the church. When not on duty the fathers peered out their windows to wonder at the sort of private life that might be going on inside the other building.

Jacob made his way up Elizabeth in the close breath of a warm July evening, bemused by the oddity of feeling physically invigorated and morally depleted. In the rustling foliage he heard many familiar root chords that bolstered his spirits. It was one of those purple suburban moments, composed of glowing darkness, when the earth seems one vast consciousness, too lavish in its latent riches to express anything other than brilliant airs. The human animal quickens to this presence just as surely as the cicadas and snowy tree crickets, now heard singing of generations yet to come. In fleeting pulses a mortal life touches upon the infinite patience that resonates with swarms of ticking stars.

His mind was in a ferment quite often these days. Being alone was different than it had ever been before; no, that wasn't really true. It had been like this when he was a boy, terribly so, during those cheerless months after his sister Johanna died of scarlet fever. He was thinking of this more and more; after he had finished the fifth grade, how everything changed, invariably for the worse. Now he was having to wonder how much of that unhappiness, in later years, was of his own doing.

"Oh Jenny, my lost girl," he thought to himself. "I wish things had been different. You were the one who lifted me out of myself. We changed together, for a while, and eventually, we fell apart together." He laughed bitterly. "I wish I had tried to be different with her, instead of going back into my refuge." Now something gave way and he was flooded with a scouring tide of emotions. Ahead he could imagine the wrecked ark of his dashed hopes strewn about the dead elm tree at the corner of Darst and Elizabeth. The black figure loomed up as the apotheosis of all his wasted efforts and unfulfilled yearnings . . .

He turned off into the parking lot and walked to the end where the drive made a steep curve and descended to the lower lever. To his left he could see the Grotto. Something inside of him stiffened against the inclination to pay a visit to the shrine. He walked down to the bleacher seats. There was no one else in sight. A vast emptiness pervaded the grounds. He took a seat on the top tier and looked up at the first stars as they began to glimmer faintly through veils of earth's sheer atmosphere.

Jenny had moved on with her life. Not until he had seen her face at Marlow's did he accept the incontrovertible fact she was gone. He had to laugh. He had truly felt that she would not be able to live without him. He never quite asserted that as a truth to himself, but he had held on to it like it was a flotation device, and he was a man lost at sea, his ship reduced to flotsam tossing around him. He began to think of her in that honesty that comes to a mind after it has run its course in one direction, and takes comfort in knowing all that past suffering does not need to impede his future steps.

We were so good together, in the beginning. I put all my faith in that, holding on to that truth, even after it was over, and we were, each of us, in another place altogether. Before he had met Jenny he would always become aloof by degrees after getting into a new relationship; as if there were a predetermined schedule that governed these things, and he was simply following a prudent set of precautions. It was because he never believed any of those relationships would last, and so he would not give them a chance to evolve into higher planes of complexity and meaning. The simple process of aging made him understand that he would not be allowed to remain as one of the blithe spirits taking part in the parade of youth. Looking ahead he could see that the rules were vastly different for mature people. He became afraid to be alone. When it was too late, he decided he wanted to settle down, and then absolutely refused to do so . . .

Do you want to have children? You asked me this very early on, and I vehemently declared I did not. What had I said, exactly? You acquiesced to my selfish rationale, at the time. Didn't you? What if I had not been so adamant? Or you, more insistent, deploying a full complement of the maternal force. We always returned to the party routine, convinced we were happy. Everyone thought so. They commented on it. We took pride in being social animals. But there were no children. In time all the others we cared about had borne offspring, or were trying to, and then the whispers came. What is it? Some sort physiological deficiency? Merely selfishness? I actually put forth the notion that our biological restraint derived from that noble, shopworn ideal; we were sparing the proposed unborn from the ravages of this rotten world. To deprive others a chance to prove themselves, and experience the joy of this marvelous world, out of a sense of morality? Because of one's own failures? How many of these counterfeit bills are kept in the currency from one generation to the next for such dishonest transactions?

We started coming apart even as the larger circle broke into smaller factions and it became a time of wild, destructive games. Anything was possible. Maybe we did not have to face the usual consequences. It is strange though, I never strayed; taking pride in being faithful, even taking pleasure in casting aspersions. That made no sense. To congregate with them, watching them, to laugh and party with them, while judging them, from the confines of one's secret monastic temple.

The fatal problems did not start in the bedroom, but collected there; and once the corruption reached that harbor, the bond was doomed. That debasement is repellent to any who have been happy in the carnal union. Natural sympathies grow rancid, generous emotions become stale, in every and even the legal sense, and then you cannot look upon one another. You strove to initiate a renewal, out of panic, after the illicit conception, dragging us back to a period of sexual carnival. And it was getting better, until you said those words.

"I'm pregnant." The way she said it was strange enough, but also utterly inopportune. She told him as they were dining at a restaurant, so they could not really discuss the matter; and she sat there, wiping her mouth, watching him get angry. On her face an ominous expression he would never forget. She had already condemned herself, and him, knowing what his reaction would be. She concealed one important detail: the fetus, or whatever you call the mass of cells at that stage of its evolution, had been formed from her egg and the spermatozoan of another man!

Later at home, our first and only grand opera. Shouting, pacing, and fuming. Did I want it or not? Did you fear I would say yes? I was mad because it seemed like the height of deceit for you to do it on your own and not include me in the decision. Although I am pretty sure that happens all the time. He had experienced that sense of being trapped before. What if they had taken different routes to that moment, and it had been his child she was carrying? What would have happened to us? Then disgust, fatigue, and indifference. It became absurdly normal to live together while not being together, until it was intolerable.

"Which of us is going to move out?" She finally asked.

"I'll move out." She moved on and he accepted a shambling life of drifting along. His mother must have perceived the gravity of his loss right away. She would not listen to him equivocate about extraneous issues of blame, nor let him belabor his distress. That damning perspicaciousness focused in her narrowed, pale green eyes, leveled at him precisely the way she had trained them on her fallen husband. Jacob recalled he had also received this look when he was a boy, when he was unable to comprehend anything . . .

Jacob left his perch on the bleacher seats and walked across the parking lot to take the sidewalk up the hill on Chambers. He swept his eyes over the granite walls of the school buildings erected on different elevations carved into the hill. At the corner he turned and walked by the church building. The stained glass windows were bleeding outward a faint suggestion of the trembling tongues of fire sheltered within the empty house of worship. The figures depicted on the windows seemed to have no life because the sunlight had ceased to illuminate their passion. It would come back in the morning, precisely on schedule. He moved himself as if being governed by a series of inexorable constants.

He remembered being right there on that corner the day his fifth grade ended; the nuns walked them out by this unusual route, taking them up the hill to the corner and releasing them into the glory and grandeur of another summer. He had looked around at the nuns, and the other kids, in a state of amazement. How should such happiness be explained, or put to use, or preserved? Now he followed in the footsteps of the child, with no trace of the joy that overcame that boy anticipating another epoch in the wilds of Ferdinand. It was right before tragedy struck the family. And now he could only go home to what was not a real home. He had almost had one and he had sabotaged the inner structure of his emotional makeup so that no real life could be established there. It had been his fault. There was no doubt of that anymore.

17

H e pored over one of his books. His thoughts wandered off the pages as he recalled a dream from the night before. He had been wrestling with a woman who bore a disturbing resemblance to Beatrice! They had been struggling over an enormous set of keys that Jacob could barely lift off the ground. She had thrown them at him. He had felt the gash on his head, bringing away red fingers. He tried to run off, losing his grip on the cumbersome ring, and then he scrambled to find the bunch of keys in the grass on his parents' lawn. He could not remember anything else.

He cooked himself a pan of scrambled eggs in the large kitchen and ate his food at a picnic table in the back yard. Dogs could be heard barking plaintively in the distance. A blue jay raised the alarm as a cat padded across the driveway. Jacob noticed the BMW and laughed silently. He had forgotten it was there. He showered, shaved, and made all his standard ablutions, and drove the BMW down to Ferdinand Motors.

"Gates!" Robert called to him. "So you brought it back. I was about to call the cops." He had emerged from his little office to greet Jacob at the car.

"I bet. Thanks for letting me use it. Great car, man."

"You want to keep it for a while? May as well enjoy . . ."

"No, no."

"There's no problem, all these cars are for sale. You see?"

Jacob did not see quite what that had to do with him using the car for no reason. It was just more pressure to get him to join the cause, to help him with the great party to be held at The Joint.

"This thing could get me in trouble." Jacob said looking at the handsome car. "I have my truck, that's all I need."

Before he knew it they were both walking towards the office, a sort of glass cabin where the salesman could sit and see his whole lot, like a spider couched in the hub of his web. In the office Robert took his station behind the desk. Jacob was sitting in the chair on the other side.

"What will it take to get me into that car?" Jacob said.

"What?" Robert's face lit up in astonishment.

"You want to put the sales job on me, don't you?"

"No, I know you can't afford any of these cars. Isn't that what you told me? I mean, do you think maybe you can? Because, yeah, I'll start selling . . ."

"About the reunion thing."

"Oh." Robert leaned back in his reclining chair and locked his hands behind his head, staring out now like a cobra with his hood inflamed. "Have you talked to your cousin?"

"No."

"Not at all?"

"No."

"Do you think it's a stupid idea?"

"No, not really." Jacob had been intrigued by the idea from the outset; his recalcitrance was more troublesome, pertaining to his position as a nobody. In the old days he would have leapt at the chance to be a part of this improbable festivity. When he enjoyed his life, and his job, he and Jenny had been eager impresarios, offering up the apartment for many such occasions.

"I think it could be momentous. I really do. I'm not gong to lie to you." Robert leaned forward and fell into his most confident mode; he was completely sincere, because he was selling products of his own desire. There was no fire that could disprove the pure gold of one's imagination.

"All that was a long time ago."

"I know, you can't relive the past. Who wants to? I want to create new memories. I want to watch other people doing the same thing. I want to be a part of something outside the same old, same old. You know?" He looked at Jacob who only stared back, as if in wonderment. "I want to have a night where time stands still, and nothing matters outside of the whirling moment, when everything else falls away."

"I guess I see what you mean."

"Instead of all that standard reunion business, remembering the past the way it never was, bragging about your mortgage, and how much you have to pay for college tuition. No, this would set us apart. It would be a real party."

Ah, Jacob thought, there it is. The desire to throw 'a real party.' He must have his own fresh ideas about that platonic form. Jacob knew something about this yearning to reach for what lays beyond one's grasp. He recognized that Robert wanted to be the lord host of this mystery tour. Now it all made sense. He stood up and before he could say anything more Robert also rose to this feet, extending his hand. They shook and Robert spoke as if they had concluded a nifty transaction. He kept looking at Jacob, attempting to get him to concede the wisdom of at least trying to pass through the looking glass, once in a while. Seeing that his message fell on deaf ears he ceased his tactical sales pitch to salvage the larger campaign.

"Well, think about it."

"I will."

"Go see your cousin. See what she thinks. Let me know if she has a problem with it; and if she wants to come herself, that would be no problem. Just let me know. What harm can it do?"

"I'll see." Jacob moved adroitly to evade the snares of another man's unraveled obsession.

"Hey, Gates!"

Jacob spun around and halted.

"Do you want to test drive a Mercedes for a few days?"

Jacob just looked at him, dumbfounded at the man's persistence.

"That's the ultimate car for settling down, in comfort!" Robert's sardonic smile seemed to indicate the offer was ironic.

Jacob smiled weakly, his gait made somewhat wobbly after the repercussions of that parting shot. What had it meant, exactly? To settle down comfortably with the family in the suburbs, that was one thing, to do so as the self-anointed Maharishi among a tribe of cicadas, that was something else, for which there were no songs yet in his repertoire.

———

He was glad to get back to his own thoughts. A liberating spirit was once more released on these streets where he had romped as a child. He could remember riding his bicycle along these routes with the excited patter of childish heartbeats, powered by the flow of his blameless pulse. The former child served as an elegant private escort to the adult, or deposed emperor, who reigns over the glory and ruins of the present moment. The romantic promises of one's imagined life mobbed his steps in a triumphant march, that did not last for long.

He trudged up Florissant Road, breaking a sweat; arriving at Wabash Park he sat on the grassy hill for a while to watch the people in the swimming pool. It was now a fully integrated facility. Jacob wondered about the system of American apartheid that had always seemed invisible to him, and was now apparent for what it was, and always had been, a purposeful desecration of the vainglorious American creed of liberty. More and more his reading of the newspaper made society itself seem like the prime suspect, time and again caught at the crime scene, and thus forever under investigation by itself. One glimpsed behind the curtain a perpetual conspiracy of those in authority using their power for personal aggrandizement, at the cost of democratic values.

Before heading home he decided to walk around the lake on the asphalt pathway, taking in the landscape with the eye of a groundskeeper. Midway in his walk he looked up at the Junior high perched on the plateau on the far side of the lake. He found himself climbing the hill to get to the football field, and going beyond that to the rustic plot in the far corner. He waded into the wind-blown grasses to reach the giant cottonwoods. He laid down under one of these trees, staring up through the sonorous leaves at the clouds that appeared to be airships coming from the old country. What was left to be discovered?

A work party of ants began scaling his garments like emissaries from Lilliput, wishing to disabuse him of quixotic notions. Being a good pedestrian, he rolled over and hoisted himself off the ground. He brushed off his clothing and began his trek back to Florissant Road and down to Chambers. He climbed down the steps leading to North Clay Avenue, the heart of his childhood. He turned right on Darst and looked up at the wooded property saving a portion of the wilderness where he played as a boy. In such plots children are teased by the spirit in the land, when befuddled consciousness is yet clean, and drawn to the verge of things, where beliefs are engendered and sanctified.

Once at home he suddenly decided to drive to his storage facility and pillage his locker again. He soon found what he was looking for; a box of school papers from his time at Saint Margaret's. At the house he carried his loot up to the third floor and rummaged through the sheaf of papers upon which he had copied the lyrics of his favorite songs. He had transcribed each in his studious script, adding his own form of musical notation. He now held in his hand a version of Gordon Lightfoot's, "If You Could Read My Mind."

He settled himself in his chair, the music stand in front of him, and began playing the song. He now knew it better than ever before. He played it all the way through, whispering the lyrics as he played, concentrating on the musical structure of the song. He played it several times and then took a break. He sat on the floor again, sifting through more papers, passing them before his eyes. His penmanship was rather good; he had taken great pride in that after Sister Ellen Mary had praised him so highly. She always made a fuss over him during music class. He realized she was probably the one who had informed his mother of his love of music, because after that one conference she bought him the guitar for Christmas. His first passable song was a clumsy rendition of "Silent Night," which he had played for his sister Johanna in his bedroom. She had smiled with a cocked head, as if she were bemused by his behavior. After he concluded the piece she had thrust out a hand to brush across the strings, making them thrum.

"Are you going to keep at it? Get really good, do you think?" She had challenged him; knowing all about his frequent projects, each abandoned before very long. She had been the serious one. Her report cards always perfect . . .

How had he replied to her? He must have been irritated by her skepticism. That was a common theme in their relationship, her doubting him; but also, pushing him, encouraging him, inspiring him . . .

He got up and ranged about the upper story, looking out the windows at the trees everywhere crowding the landscape like green clouds. He felt himself to be in the middle of everything that mattered in a way that caused his pulse to flutter and his head to swim. He sat down again and began playing the Gordon Lightfoot song, this time singing the words as well as he was able. He had never been comfortable singing before an audience. He was too self-conscious about the limitations of his voice. But when he was engrossed in his music, and feeling good, he often began to sing without belaboring the material, and it sounded good to his own ears. It was his voice, after all, and a part of what had come up out of his depths, to become the salient thread of the power that created the song itself. He played the song over and over until he could not concentrate on the material any longer.

Then he admired his homemade sheets of music some more. He decided he should write a song about the old days—he would write a song for Connie! The inherent irony of someone his age attempting another variation on the theme of young love, this did not even occur to him. He was now completely on board with the plan of having a party at The Joint. He wanted to see Connie again. Why not? She was undoubtedly married, with four, no, three, no, *five* beautiful children, and a nanny, and her husband would be the president of a bank, or a steel mill, or they might own their own island, and arrive in a helicopter . . .

"The divorcées!" He recalled Robert's excitement. He began laughing. The whole thing was so preposterous; he accepted his outlandish mission. Being the fool in the attic, it was irresistible to him.

18

After some more reflection he had second thoughts about the party. What role was he to play? Not master of ceremonies. Robert was sure to wear that mantle. As for cleaning up afterwards, that would fall on his shoulders. Beatrice would expect him to look out for her property—was she even in favor of this crazy idea?

When he did see her again they walked the grounds in their customary fashion. She confirmed that she had granted permission for the party. She then asked him what he thought about installing a fire pit in the yard, and Jacob was enthused by the idea. They decided it should be placed between the back porch of the carriage house and the tennis court. He said he would call his brother Matthew for guidance.

The other brothers called Matt 'the cabinetmaker.' It was a derisive form of flattery; being a commentary on the often unprofitable nature of his sedulous craftsmanship. In fact, the superb quality of his work had spread by word of mouth across many lush and heavily groomed suburban tracts; places where sumptuary laws are flouted in grand style. In spirit, these folks are worthy of Augustus, who renovated Rome in the motif of marble; in nerve, the equal of Herod, who fashioned Jerusalem to be a gross tribute to his ultimate patrons, Pride and Ambition.

"People like having elegant workmanship. They don't always want to pay for it, though." Jacob had heard Matthew's mantra quite often. "You have to find people who are used to paying for nice things, and then you have to make sure you treat them the right way. You have to believe in the value of your own work, and you have to let them see that you do." It was agreed upon to have Matthew come out and have a look at things.

One afternoon Jacob went by to see Cody and Sally. He was enjoying their company on the patio when Frances came out and commandeered his truck. She needed another load of mulch and she didn't want to pay the delivery fee.

"We're all beasts of burden, you know." This was one of her favorite aphorisms. Cody rode with him to get the load and it gave Jacob a chance to discuss the party with him.

"I never went to The Joint," Cody said. "That scene wasn't for me."

"I thought you would have been all over that, back in the day."

"No, I didn't really know anybody who went up there. I never hung around with the Spencers."

"I remember just going to their yard, when I was a kid. I'd play outside with them sometimes; but when they wouldn't come outside, I would just play on the grounds, like I had a right to be there."

"I know, like it was a park. You have to wonder how that looked to the parents."

"Yeah, when they were there."

"What did he do, anyway?"

"I have no idea. Everyone called him the ambassador, but I doubt he was an actual ambassador."

"I remember those huge parties they would have. The whole house lit up, people all over the yard, torches set up outside, the big fire pit!"

"They had a big fire pit?"

"Oh yeah, don't your remember?"

"Not really. You know, Beatrice wants me to build one for her."

"Will you be able to use it, for your own use?"

"I guess so."

"I could help you. I've built some of those in the past."

"Really? I'll give you a call. Say, I need your number, I have a phone now."

"Beatrice is paying for it?"

"Yes."

"You loser."

"She pays all my utilities." Jacob began laughing. "I'm living in style Cody. I'm Chief Groundskeeper of the Spencer Mansion."

"Well chief, you better get this load delivered or you'll have Frances all over your ass. She outranks any groundskeeper."

"Yeah, I guess she does, at that. Did you quit smoking?"

"Trying."

"Good deal. I was afraid I was going to start bumming them off you. I used to really enjoy it when I was younger, now it's like puffing on death."

"Yeah, no shit."

Frances supervised as they worked, peppering them with questions of the sort that had become so routine they hardly noticed it any more. They often warbled as children responding to a mother, who, in her doting audit of childish accounts, graces every act and trifling achievement with an aura of wonderment. She was always gathering information on the people she considered to be in her spiritual charge.

———◆———

A week later Jacob was on the screened porch of the second story observing a spectacle taking place in the distance, far out over the garage, as a cool front moved down from the north. He could imagine furious battalions. One might be reminded of those forces Tolstoy attempted to describe at the end of *War and Peace*, when he wielded the philosopher's crayon to describe blind, evolutionary forces directing and molding the shapes of history.

What was he supposed to tell people at the reunion? He was a rolling stone collecting moss on someone else's land. His trade? Landscaping artist. How explain that he roams about like a rustic hobo in the mystery rags of romance? He imagined how everyone would take the time to update each other on their social profile. You have procreated, no? Show us the proof. How many? What are they doing? Okay then, what are you doing for a living? So, let me calculate the annual salary, just a minute—a groundskeeper? On a golf course? Wait, what now? Where did you say you are living, again? Here?

"Who cares," He thought defiantly. "Being outside of things is nothing to feel bad about. That's where I have taken up residence!" Jacob returned to his chair in the third-story auditorium to practice his music some more.

He played without singing, listening very intently to what he was creating with his hands. He loved the dexterous, tactile sensation, heightened to the order of unconscious movements, as natural as the labor of his tireless lungs or melodious heart. Beyond the intellect's grasp there was an intimation of something special happening, when he was submerged in the refrains that lifted him into euphoric transports. It never lasted very long. He stopped playing to stare out the window. The rain clouds were breaking up and the sunlight was striking all the wet surfaces; the visual analogue of hearing the sudden onrush of beautifully composed notes. He rose from his chair to make a circuit of the third story, looking out every window to see as much of the glittery landscape as was possible. It was going to be a gorgeous afternoon. He decided to call his cousin. She agreed to meet him in the Loop that afternoon; fortuitously, she had taken the day off from her job.

He stopped at a self-service car wash and sprayed out the bed of his truck, afraid people might think he was hauling manure for a living. He met Kimberly at a restaurant in the Loop called Vedi Napoli. The décor suggested an ancient villa buried by Vesuvius, and later restored by successful hippies, who festooned the walls with rock 'n' roll paraphernalia. Many vistas of the real eternal city clung to the walls. Plate glass windows let the patrons observe strangers passing by outside. He had gone there as a teenager with a fake ID and coltish pride; much later he took Jenny there during their courtship to drum his wings for her.

"It's been a while, Jacob." Kim said when she came in and found him seated at the glass, staring outward.

"I know." He watched her sit down. She was an English major who had many times caused his mind to flounder when she began speaking about her love of books. He wondered if he should try and explain his own new-found fascination with a certain author's collection.

"We didn't see you at the wedding." She was referring to the marriage of another first cousin. All of their mothers were sisters.

"Yeah, I missed that one."

"People were saying you might be going underground on us."

"Why do you say it that way?"

"What way should I say it?" She seemed happily amused. Her thin, sharply-drawn face was too often an irreproachable mask of blanket disapproval. She harbored tacit reservations about the world, and everyone in it, and was not willing to relinquish these lightly, not for anyone. She had been happily married for a while, bore a child, and became a glowing mother; and it was obvious she enjoyed her life. Then she wasn't married anymore, and you could tell what a difference this made in her altered demeanor.

"Have you ever read *Notes from Underground?*" He ventured.

"I wrote a paper on that book; back in the dark ages. Why do you ask?"

"Oh, just wondering."

"Have you read it?"

"Some parts of it. One thing I couldn't figure out; why is that guy so angry about everything?"

She laughed. "He suffers from existential headaches, I guess. I didn't think you were one to read such books; or, any books, for that matter."

"I never was before, but then while I was living in this basement—"

The waitress had come to the table and Kim put up her hand like a policeman to halt his speech. They ordered drinks and discussed the possibility of ordering food. The issue was left undecided. Menus were left on the table.

"You were living in a basement, you said?"

"Yes, up in North County."

"I had heard you were living up there. The old stomping grounds, right?"

He provided a synopsis of his past year, leaping over certain parts to obviate the sense he was seeking her pity. He described the old Spencer house, which she knew nothing about, and she did not press him unduly. By her face it appeared he was not making much sense to her. He asked her about her family and listened politely; he was interested in the people she spoke of now. It seemed to Jacob that they had been close to becoming friends all their lives. As children, being the same school age made them confidants, and sometimes accomplices at family gatherings. On many occasions Johanna and Kim and he had formed a little isle entire unto itself. Pretty soon they were rambling on about their loved ones in a wry manner, putting themselves at ease. He began thinking of his sister Johanna rather intensely.

He had tried many times to quit this practice of imaging what she might have become in life, had she lived. It always left him feeling much worse after he plucked at those fatal strings. To his dismay he seemed to begin such excursions only when he was getting excited about his own future. But now, something felt different. He believed Kimberly and Johanna would have become close friends as adults.

"Like I said, now I've got the post of Chief Groundskeeper, but the position of head steward is not out of the question." This was the second time he'd used this joke, and her narrowed eyes showed her annoyance. They ordered food and chatted about their siblings at more length.

"I'm living in style." He concluded when she brought him back to his present circumstances.

"Well, one thing's for sure; you've been on something of a personal journey." Kim said this as he munched into a fat juicy burger, the specialty of the house.

"Does that mean, I'm going someplace?" He asked her ironically.

"We're all going someplace." She said with a whisper of spirituality. Her dark brown eyes were enlarged portentously behind the lenses of her round glasses. Her straight sandy hair fell like silken veils around her face as she looked down, and then flared back into position when she sat upright. He watched her stabbing at pieces of chicken in her bowl, one of the house specials, called the Crazy Salad.

"Maybe the first thing one should do is strive to end up in the right place." He spoke without fear of sounding foolish, not knowing why he had just shared this sententious thought, which must have been stolen from one of his texts.

"That sounds about right. Of course, striving and waiting can become pretty tedious."

After their plates were taken away by the waitress they decided to stay and have another drink. Outside it was deepest afternoon, far past the point of no return for those who needed full daylight to pursue their livelihood. They both stared out the window for a moment, lost in their own thoughts. Kimberly recalled a certain Capriccio by Antonio Canaletto, hanging in the Art Museum, which depicts an incongruous assemblage of stately ruins by a placid lagoon, seen in that beautiful, solemn, dissolving cast of light at the end of day. She remembered the first time she had viewed it; on a date with a man she thought might end up becoming her second husband. The statistics bear out that the second conjugal bond usually proves more durable than an earlier failed experiment. Her eyes were open, but she did not see that he was in a different place himself. He had queried her about the setting of the picture; 'So you mean, none of that is real?' He soon escaped the betrothal and fled with a younger woman, who had once been a cheerleader for a professional sports team. She looked very good on his arm, and apparently never found it necessary to challenge the validity of his infallible opinions regarding anything that was being discussed at the moment.

"So tell me, what's the deal with your friend Robert?"

"I'm not sure we're friends."

"But you want to help him put together this reunion after the reunion, at a place called The Joint, which is at an empty house, where you live, like it's a set where they're getting ready to make a film based on a forgotten novel by Balzac?"

"I'll plead the fifth," he said laughing. "Not knowing what the hell all that means, or who Balzac is, or was."

"Was!" She shook her head slowly as if his ignorance were a very sad thing; and grievous for a blood relation to observe. "Look, I almost refused to help out on this McDermott reunion because it's just not where I'm at anymore; but everyone still sees me as I once was, you know? That girl who helps on every committee. The one eager to pitch in for every stupid pep rally."

"The whole idea of celebrating that time does seem pretty strange."

"Rich and strange. Well, so tell me, do you want me to help you put together an exclusive after-party?"

"Not sure how exclusive it's supposed to be."

"I'm just saying."

"It just seems like he's trying to conjure something out of the past. Life never works that way . . . It is pretty weird."

"Something is there to celebrate possibly, though." She spoke as if in league with Robert for reasons of her own.

He laughed as he fell once more under the spell himself. "I love the location. All the haunted sidewalks, the great trees. So often I find myself walking the streets and scaring up memories like I'm flushing wild game." His visage shone with his enthusiasm. She thought suddenly of one of her friends, Hank Norden, who managed to steer every conversation around to his doctoral dissertation, on the grade school years of T. S. Eliot, and how ground-breaking it was going to be. He'd been working on this magnum opus for almost ten years now, and had recently been dropped by his second program advisor.

"It's funny how you keep going back to that neighborhood."

"I live there now."

She laughed. "In our conversation, you keep meandering back to that topic. Do you really like it there that much?"

"I guess I do."

"Why?"

"I don't know. I haven't thought about it that much. Not thinking too much, that's critical for a good groundskeeper," he quipped. Her face did not change. "No, after everything that happened, I felt like I should be ashamed of myself, for living this way. But I wasn't, really. I was sort of ashamed of not being ashamed, of not being serious enough, or something. It was like I'd quit doing something you're not supposed to ever quit doing, and I was getting used to it. You know what I mean?"

"Sort of, yes. For some reason talking to you makes me think of my own childhood. It's pretty wild to think about those days now."

"Did you play with Johanna much?"

"Your sister?"

"Yes."

"Gosh." She leaned back, looking upwards. "Yes. I have so many memories of her. We were always together at family gatherings. Don't you remember?"

"Yeah, but I just, I mean, we all have our own memories, and I can't remember her so well at those events. I remember a lot of times at our house, out in our yard, and up at school, for instance. But I don't . . ." His voice trailed off as his emotions galloped away from his words.

"That was so terrible." Kim shook her head, biting her lip. She wanted to reach out to him some way, but she was thwarted by his subdued detachment. He stared out the window. She sipped her white wine, stealing glances at him, feeling very awkward, until a thought came to her, wholly formed, demanding to be articulated.

"I remember one time Jo and me were at your house, in the basement. We were trying to play some kind of trick on your older brothers, something about lining up all those ship models they had down there?"

"Yeah?"

"I don't know what we were going to do, but you kept coming down and bothering us. You were always pestering us. You wouldn't leave us alone; anyway, this time Johanna finally told you to go hide in your secret place, and to wait for us there. Do you remember that?" Her mouth hung open in anticipation.

"No, I don't. I remember our secret place, in the attic, but not that incident you're talking about."

"You stayed there so long. We laughed so hard over that. Oh, we had a lot of fun together." She looked out the window. Jacob began to feel that he should not have invoked his dead sister, it only made people uncomfortable; and he hated the idea that they would somehow think he was playing the martyr in the affair. He waited a few moments and tried to get back on track with his putative mission.

"Look, the truth is, Robert is just trying to invite a select sampling of people to throw a great bash, but he's also got some notion of getting together with a woman named Jessica Lozoff."

"Oh, I remember her!"

"Is she divorced?"

"What? How do you know she even got married?"

"I don't. That's the kind of intelligence I'm supposed to get out of you. Oh, and Robert wants to make sure everyone you ask to show up at The Joint is aware that he was on the football team."

"He said that to you?"

"No. But I have a feeling he's afraid a lot of people might have forgotten that he made the team senior year."

"Yes, I remember. Is it more difficult to make the team in senior year?"

"According to him!" He laughed. "I suppose it is. He was a wide receiver. He was pretty good. That was his big deal."

"Yes, he started going around with a new group."

"I'm not sure he ever really broke into that crowd."

"What was your big deal?"

"I didn't have one. No wait, my guitar. In case you hadn't noticed, I was Dylan's protégé, for a while there."

"People noticed." She chuckled. "Are you still playing?"

"More than I have in a long while, actually."

"I don't think I've ever heard you play."

"No?"

"I remember once, we were at your house, and your mother wanted you to play for us; but you refused. You were so rude."

"I don't remember that." He acted hurt to be accused of such a thing; but he recalled how true it was of him, then, to be obsessively protective of his music. It was really just fear, but of what, though?

"So maybe we should send out invitations with pictures of Robert wearing his football jersey—"

"In my bio let's say I was in a band; just put down Mama's Pride, or REO Speedwagon; nobody will know."

Kim laughed, remembering her infatuation with the song 'Riding the Storm Out,' which had been a part of her sound track the year she graduated from high school.

After a curious pause, Kim offered encouragement. "The idea does have promise."

"Yeah?" He was intrigued by her unexpected interest.

"Jacob, tell me, how'd you get into all of this?"

"That's a good question." He was tempted to tell her to just forget it, he was sorry he had troubled her about such a silly thing.

"It sounds like you want me to help Robert become Gatsby? What about you?"

"I might come as a Russian monk."

She smiled appreciatively, wishing there was more time to quiz him on his curious new reading habits. "Should we send out formal invitations?"

For one instant Jacob could not tell if she was being serious, or mocking him. He laughed weakly. "It sounds ridiculous, doesn't it?"

"Not completely. Tell me more about this place, The Joint."

"It was a local phenomenon. A perfect venue for the teenage waste land years. Not for me, so much. It's above the garage, part of an old carriage house, and it's on the highest ground around there. It's this beautiful corner of the world." As he spoke Kimberly caught again a strain from her flowering youth, somewhere outdoors; scented petals were falling through the air, her hair was blown across her face, and the music was inside of her . . .

"Well, if you want to, we can get together to talk about this some more. I can show you what information I've collected so far; most of the people have responded favorably. It is intriguing. I was friends with Robert's future wife back then."

"You're sure you don't mind doing this?"

"Not at all." She almost confessed that at one time she had had a crush on Robert, until he made the football team; then he was trying so hard to belong to that crowd of athletes and cheerleaders, he became insufferable. He had even neglected his girlfriend rather badly, until they got engaged.

"Okay, well, that's great! I thought you were going to laugh at me just for bringing this up." He really had feared she was going to think he had taken leave of his senses.

"Let's all pretend we're back in high school again, what can go wrong?" Kim presented a smile as enigmatic as any he'd ever seen on a woman's face (it was an extensive catalogue).

"How about I call you then?" He said.

"Do it." She rose and held out her hand for him to shake. He did not think he had ever done that with her before.

"Probably sometime next week."

"That's good." He had remained seated.

"You'll have to come out to Ferdinand to see The Joint."

"I guess I will at that." She smiled genuinely and vanished.

Jacob looked down at the tiny bubbles in his tepid beer. He had not been able to finish it. He mourned the past enjoyment of cigarettes; the moment was perfect for that ritual of the café experience. One thing was still the same, the pleasant habit of viewing people strolling by outside. He sat there at his table for a while, watching the night come down and the people gliding by on the other side of the glass. He imagined himself in an observation car plumbing the depths, peering out at exotic specimens more strange than the tropical species found in household aquariums. Earlier, in the fading light, he had enjoyed the surreptitious game of watching these people swim up into view and then disappear into the gloaming. Now they seemed to have no world around them, but lived only in darkness. He sometimes feared he was losing touch with his humanity, but some divine breath always swept him out of this heresy. Sometimes he was left feeling like the last reluctant pagan during a religious revival.

19

Jacob was standing in a shallow hole, grasping a shovel close to his chest, as a prophet might lean on his staff while Yahweh delivered a long sermon. Cody is sitting on the grass, legs raised and arms wrapped around the knees. Matthew stands at the edge of the hole rubbing his unshaven chin, appraising the situation.

"Not sure that's deep enough," Cody said. The other two men looked at him and did not say anything.

Jacob had questioned whether he should excavate the hole a little more, and Matthew had not commented on the matter. He only looked on pensively.

"I'd say it's okay, that's plenty of depth."

Jacob stepped out of the hole and let the long-handled shovel fall to the ground. Cody got up and came over to inspect the hole.

"What I'm saying is, why not break a few stones and bury them upright, to make sections."

"That's a good idea, Matthew concurred. "Mark the four compass points."

"Let's do it," Jacob said. "Now, who has a compass? Wait, there's one in the garage. They have just about everything in there."

At that moment a Mercedes-Benz came under the arch and crept slowly down to the end of the driveway. Robert emerged from the car and sauntered over.

"This looks like a Street Department crew; one man working, and two watching. If you want to speed things up, I can help supervise."

They all stared at the talkative newcomer, studying his brash manner. Robert wore creased khaki pants, a pressed shirt with flaring unbuttoned collars, and shiny black shoes that were like miniature boots. His hair was brushed back and cemented in place. The other men all wore jeans and T-shirts and their hair was disheveled by work and wind.

"Mind if we use your Mercedes to haul some rock?" Matthew asked Robert.

"It's not mine. Belongs to Ferdinand Motors."

"You working there now?"

"He owns it." Jacob said.

"No shit."

Robert held his hand out and introduced himself to Matthew. They shook hands and appraised one another.

"My brother." Jacob said.

"How many you got?"

"Three."

"You were the baby, then, weren't you?"

"He still is the baby."

They all laughed. Jacob laughed at them laughing at him, not at all clear on the nature of the joke; other than the fact he was the closest thing to a babe in the wilderness one would be able to scare up in these parts. Robert asked Matthew what high school he had attended; he had graduated from McDermott High six years earlier than his class.

"What year did you graduate, again?" Robert questioned Cody.

"I missed that one." Cody retorted with a hard, fixed stare.

"Hey Robert," Jacob spoke up. "Did you talk to Kimberly?"

"Oh yeah, she called me. That's why I'm here. We need to talk about when we want to get together. She has everything we need."

"She wants to see The Joint."

"Yeah I know, so when do you think?"

"How about on Sunday."

"That probably works. I'll find out with her."

"Come over here a minute," Jacob motioned to Robert. "I want to show you something." They walked around the garage, over to the flat shelf of ground above the hill. As a child Jacob was drawn here when it snowed. Many would come. They would lay on their stomachs on sleds and pass down the hill, at the bottom pushing hard on the steering bar to swerve to the right, passing over several more yards in the white crystalline mist. He remembered sweeping down the last decline and out into the back yard of a house facing Elizabeth Avenue. You had to let the sled come to a complete stop, spending every foot pound of force stolen from Spencer's Hill, before trudging back to repeat the cycle.

Now they were looking down into the sunken area behind the garage, and over at the large open doorways leading into what had once been the stalls. Jacob asked Robert if he wanted to invite people to the event who had not been in their class. Robert said they would have to wait and see.

"Oh yes, I saw Elaine Spazz recently." Jacob said. "Do you remember her?"

Robert began laughing in a guttural tone.

"I used to know her."

"She seemed to indicate as much."

"What did she say?"

"Not much."

"We had sex down there, in one of the stalls. That was some party that night. Oh man, I almost forgot about that night, damn." He laughed almost soundlessly.

"I can imagine you two down there."

"We did it standing up."

In all that filth, Jacob thought; instantly amused, and somewhat perplexed at the images now assailing him. His own sex life had always been rather prosaic. He adhered to no radical dogma when attempting to be a troubadour in training during the sexual revolution. He believed monogamy mattered; although in college (that aborted stint) he learned the prudence of conducting research for the next match while engaged in the present one. He carried the belief that none were going to last; that was clear enough. No, nothing had been very clear, actually, but he was sure those relationships had no chance of leading to anything of lasting value. In time he learned that for many others it had been quite different. Many used that time in the great Hormonal Sea of higher education very productively, to select a suitable mate.

Over time he began to have a better understanding of the basic mechanics at play in carnal relations. He had come to believe that the wiring diagram of human desire was too complex to be explained by sententious fools. He thought suddenly of the fact he had just used the term 'filth' in his mind to describe possibly the cleanest form of waste there is, ancient dung reduced back into the earth and covered over by many layers of fresh dust that altogether forms the outer skin of the earth.

"You haven't said anything to Cody about the party, have you?"

"Yeah, I asked him if he wanted to come."

Robert frowned heavily. "No, we don't want to start inviting everyone. My god, you didn't invite Elaine, did you!"

"No! But look, if Cody and Sally aren't invited, then I'm not going to be involved in it either. You'll have to do it on your own."

Robert was furious. They stared at one another for a seething moment.

"I just don't want this getting out of hand. Beatrice—"

"I don't know how you can prevent that, from everything you've said about the good old days. If the word gets out, it might end up being just like the old days."

"No, we'll keep the list down. But you're probably right, to some extent it will increase by word of mouth."

"It might not, that much."

"Let's just assume it will, and try and keep the numbers down. But we have to see what Kim has for us. That's the main thing."

"Anyway, see all that brush, I'm clearing that out, but it's taking me forever. Do you think Beatrice would want to put a garden down there? Maybe a field kitchen, some fountains . . ."

"Slow down. I know she has a lot of money, but we can't scare her off talking about installing Roman gardens. Come on, man."

"Roman gardens? I'm just talking about a place where people could sit and enjoy the evening; nothing in view but what we would plant here, and on the other side there. They'd have nothing else to see but the sky overhead. I know she wants to host her own garden parties on the grounds."

"You mean later, down the road?"

"Yeah. Not for this party. The whole idea should be to get people comfortable being in a natural setting, right? "

"She does have ideas percolating in that busy head of hers. She's not sure exactly how she wants to proceed, just yet. I know she wants to see how this party goes. I take it her affairs are going to be much more elegant, mostly up in the house, once she gets that ready. Did you ever go to one of those open house parties they had every December?"

"Heck no. I never even knew about them until recently."

"Me neither. Well, if we're lucky she will put some money into The Joint. I'm working on her."

"Do you think she will?"

"Not sure. I sold the idea to her as mostly an outdoor thing. She wants to come over next week and go over our plans. I'll call you."

They made further arrangements to bring Kim out to see the grounds and compare notes. Returning to the backyard they found Cody alone at the hole.

"Where's Matt?" Jacob asked.

"He went in to have another look at The Joint," Cody answered.

They looked over to see Matt coming out onto the little roofed porch on the right side of the carriage house. There was a small suite of dilapidated rooms on the ground floor, where a kitchen and a bathroom facility were located. The rooms were cluttered with an assortment of antediluvian pots and pans, broken furniture, and other refuse. All was coated in layers of velvety dust that belonged to the ages.

"This place needs a lot of work," Matthew said as he approached the others. "Does Beatrice want to renovate all of it?"

"Not sure," Robert said.

Jacob was feeling a twinge of something he could not consciously grasp; an almost imperceptible slight at the thought Beatrice was now confiding in Robert more than himself. Before long Robert took his leave. Jacob started digging again. Four holes were dug and two stones broken in half; the jagged ends positioned in the ground, the finished ends serving to mark the four cardinal directions. Before spreading gravel and sand at the base they decided to take a break. Matthew and Jacob sat on the ground and enjoyed the comfort of being at perfect ease.

"If she wants to put the money into it, this could be something really nice." Matthew announced.

"I don't know about this party, though." Jacob said. "I get the feeling Robert is working her over pretty good."

"Yeah, he's an operator. How long you been hanging around with him?"

"We're not hanging around. He dropped by some weeks back with this idea about holding another party at The Joint, and I wasn't too hip on the idea, at first."

"Sounds like now you're all in though?"

"I think so. It will be a trip, seeing some of those people again."

"Jacob wants to see Connie Garnet," Cody said to Matthew.

"Who's that?" Matthew asked, looking attentively at his brother with a huge grin. Jacob felt sheepish. He looked at Cody as if he had betrayed him somehow.

"Tenth grade, man." Cody said.

"Is she coming to this thing?" Matthew asked.

"Who knows. We haven't even decided who to invite yet." Jacob started to laugh. It was fun trying to imagine what might happen if a lot of people showed up as besotted as Robert was, and he was becoming himself as the event took shape.

"Did you ever go to one of the open houses the Spencers held every year, during the holidays?" Jacob asked his brother.

"Oh sure, those were a big deal. It was all about being among the fashionable folks, I guess. I didn't really belong! They were really something. I was going with Mary Spencer for a while, there." He smiled and released a sigh. "You know, when clients hear I'm from Ferdinand, that topic comes up quite a lot. Those parties are still remembered by people. It helps me land jobs." He began to laugh.

"You probably bring it up for that reason."

"You bet. In their eyes it makes me more worthy, somehow."

Cody went home and the brothers repaired to the kitchen and Jacob made two bologna sandwiches with mustard for each of them and took two beers out of the refrigerator. He produced a large box of Cheez-Its from the cabinet. They devoured their meal at the picnic table in the back yard in comfortable silence. Terse comments were made about other family members. Mention was made of future events concerning the family. Jacob brought the empty plates and depleted box of crackers back to the kitchen and brought out two more beers.

"Cody seems like a good guy." Matthew said as he contemplated the carriage house, still going over the figures for a total renovation.

"Yeah, he is."

"Are you feeling pretty good, living out here, like this?"

"I . . . I don't know. I can't say what exactly I'm doing here."

"You seem to be in a pretty good place, though; all things considered."

Jacob was not sure what 'all things' referred to, but it was not difficult to infer his sabbatical was being sanctioned, contingent on the warrant his situation would change for the better at some point in the future. "I know it can't be a permanent thing."

"Probably not." Matthew looked again at his brother's face. They resumed a stately, brooding silence, as if intent on listening to the rare recital of soughing maple leaves. After a while Matthew looked over at his brother.

"Why didn't you ever marry Jenny?"

Jacob involuntarily drew in a deep breath before responding.

"I don't think we were right for each other."

"Don't you think you could have figured that out a little sooner?"

"Yes, I should have. I know that now. But I don't know how I could have, really, looking back on it now. She wasn't exactly acting like she wanted to go down that path either. I wasn't thinking right, I guess. I wasn't thinking that it would make any difference."

"Any difference? Didn't you want to have kids?"

Jacob shook his head slightly as if he was falling into a trance.

"Did she want to have kids?"

Jacob stood up and acted as though he wanted to take his beer back into the kitchen, but after one step he turned around and came back to stand at the table. He was very agitated.

"Why do you want to dog me on this right now?"

"I'm not trying to dog you, Jacob."

"I fucked up." He turned around and looked at the house, still wanting to go inside for no reason he understood himself. He turned around again.

"I'm not saying that." Matthew said, then he lightly slapped a hand on the table top. "Let's finish up the pit." He stood up, crushed the can of beer in his hand and let it fall onto the table, where it rocked, emitting a series of hollow notes, that struck Jacob as extraordinary. It was the coda dubbed over a prerecorded track; a falling cadence added to signify the end of something. He took the elegiac tone to heart, forced by life to move beyond the wasted part of a life that is no more.

"I just want you to know, if you need anything, you can come to me."

"No, I know. Everyone has been so good, it's really . . ." He looked down, shaking his head. "I hate to think about what everyone thinks of me now."

"Little brother, it doesn't matter. What you have to do is think of yourself now. Next time, you want to be sure. That's all."

After they finished the pit and put away the tools Matthew chastised him for the disorder he found in the garage, in the immemorial practice of older brothers. After Matthew departed Jacob went up to the auditorium to play his guitar. It was becoming like the old days when solitude was a fortress, a place where he played his music and collected his thoughts and distilled drops of his own goodness out of swirling clouds of messy inchoate dreams. Many times this reliance on seclusion had been interpreted by others as a form of selfishness. He knew it was not always only that, though; he had a sense of what might be possible in the future if he could only keep his mind right, while passing through this wilderness of uncertainty.

He wondered how it must have been for Matthew when he was going out with Mary Spencer. Jacob had not even known about that history, although he was not surprised. Family lore had enshrined Matthew as the handsome brother, who had been very popular in high school. Jacob wondered if he had been one of those people who comes to look back on those days as the pinnacle of personal success. No, not Matt. His maturity was more advanced than that; he had always accepted the obligation to take measures to ensure he was satisfied with the lot he has chosen. To a large extent it was simply a matter of acceptance, living honorably with the choices one has made. His marriage to Judy could not be as troubled as it often appeared from samplings taken at family events.

It was just that Judy was not happy in her role as the daughter-in-law who must serve under the aegis of Sharon, Mark's wife. Their mother doted on Sharon and delegated ceremonial functions to her. Jenny had always talked about this favoritism with a satiric bite that revealed a bitter feeling she was being treated unfairly. She had not been close with her own mother, either; but it was true she had been excluded by his family, in very subtle ways. Now they acted as though it had been mostly his fault! Possibly he should have intervened on her behalf more often. The truth was, even the in-laws never quite accepted Jenny for some reason; that's what she alleged, and now Jacob understood her accusations. He had been too complacent in espousing her cause, lacking conviction, and his people had divined this instinctively.

Kim brought over the data and they began compiling a prospective list of people they wanted to invite. Spirited debates broke out among them as Kim stood her ground on certain selections, vying against Robert's wishes. Jacob took her side, staying loyal to lineage. Robert had to relent. She finally was able to move forward to have the invitations printed and mailed out. Robert was paying for the bunting and favors. Beatrice decided to rent a large tent for the back yard where a cash bar would be installed; many tables and chairs were ranged around the yard. Her idea was to let people take a tour of The Joint, then afterwards have many places to sit and visit. Over the course of the next week Robert lobbied to have Beatrice put more money into renovations of The Joint, and she readily assented, surprising him with the ardor of her feelings, on these, and other matters.

20

One day Robert dropped by to consult with Beatrice. They were sorting through options and tying up loose ends; both assigning chores to Jacob! While they were walking the grounds, talking of the upcoming party, Matthew drove up and strolled over to join them. Jacob noticed how Beatrice changed when his brother approached them in the area above the hill. She put a hand up to her bronzed hair and patted herself. A resplendent smile emerged on her face. She extended her hand with a coy, feminine gesture, rather exceptional for her.

"You must be Matthew, the older brother." She spoke in a rhythmic cadence.

"Yes, not *the* oldest. You must be Beatrice."

"Everyone calls me Bitty."

"I was telling him about The Joint," Robert said abruptly. "There's no time to gut it and remodel. We're thinking of what can be done for the interim."

"For the interim?" Matthew's deliberative tone questioned the wisdom of taking this approach in any constructive endeavor. "Let's have a look."

"Yes, you tell us what you think." Beatrice encouraged him. Her hand came up reflexively as if to reach out to take hold of him, but then she dropped it as she spun around to walk towards the garage entrance. "Well, let's go up and see what you can get finished before August twentieth."

They filed up the narrow reverberating stairwell and surveyed the space, murmuring over the challenges that lay ahead of them. Matthew quizzed Jacob regarding his skills in the building arts. Jacob was thinking, "Great. Now I have three bosses."

"If you're going to have Luke do the electrical work, then you should put up new drywall, at the very least." Matthew said as he came to a stop after circulating around, inspecting every aspect of the structure. "I guess you can leave these old windows alone. Spruce up the trim, keep that quaint aspect."

"Could that be done by the time of the party?" Beatrice asked.

"It wouldn't take that much time. I could teach this bum how to hang drywall." He put out his hand and gently shoved Jacob on the shoulder. "I'm no painter, though. You could do that, couldn't you Jacob?"

"You want to teach me to do dry wall?"

"Why not? There's a chance you might want to earn an honest living some day." Matthew spoke further of other improvements to the estate that could be staged over time.

"Bitty doesn't want to spend money on that kind of thing right now," Robert said. Ignoring him, Matthew suggested she might want to consider expanding the living space of The Joint by extending the room into the garage area by several feet. They climbed down the stairs and walked to the back area, peeking into the cavernous space where the stalls had once been. Beatrice kept close to Matthew. They shared a style of conducting business that accelerated the proceedings. Robert kept a vigilant eye on the attention she was paying to Matthew, aware his own influence was diminishing before his eyes.

"I have enough to start with; I'll get with Jacob on the schedule." Matthew spoke with assurance.

"But we haven't discussed price," she said, an edge entering her voice.

"Oh, sorry. I didn't mean to presume anything. It's just that I know you won't be able to get better pricing anywhere else."

"I'm sure, but—"

"When we're done here, we should sit down and talk, you and me. You're ready to make a decision, right?"

"That is correct."

"I'm the one putting the party together," Robert said weakly.

They all looked at him and no one said anything.

"Where did those huge rocks come from?" Matthew asked.

Jacob explained that he found the rocks buried in the underbrush. He was working like Sisyphus (except that he had a level playing field), moving the rocks to the back of the lot. He was able to trundle them along, in slow, heaving, thunderous steps, using a great plank he'd found in the garage as a lever. Cody was helping him with that strenuous labor. These days Jacob was moving his entire world, unconsciously using the principles laid down by Archimedes; wielding cardinal virtues of long standing against the pivots of his life. He had to lift himself into the clear to see himself; the preparatory work of inspiration.

"They almost look like sections of ancient wheels," Matthew reflected out loud.

"Something the Flint Stones would have used." Robert offered.

"You could put a sunken garden there." Matthew said.

"Oh, that would be elegant." Beatrice responded fervently.

"Cleaning this up would be a piece of cake. We could give you an estimate so you could see if it fits your budget. I mean for later."

"I'm already clearing it out," Jacob said.

"You'll need to grade it and do something with the ground afterwards."

"Beatrice," Robert had moved closer to her; "I know some guys we could call, if you want to get this area finished." She nodded, biting her lip, not looking at him.

"Yes, we might get an estimate from them too."

Robert turned away, a sour look coming onto his face. Beatrice walked over to Matthew and asked him for his advice on how best to bring the carriage house back to a fully habitable condition. He spoke to her at length as they made their way over to inspect the rooms together. Jacob began to imagine his life as an indentured servant, a creature always being directed by others. There might be advantages to not having burdensome responsibilities . . .

A week later Matthew came over and he and Jacob ended up sitting at the top of the hill. He had been working up the pricing structure and talking to Beatrice on the phone, keeping Jacob appraised of their discussions.

"How did it go?" Jacob asked him.

"Good, we've got the job." He answered. He handed over a list of materials to Jacob, telling him to call his old place of employment to get pricing on some of the items. They always had an inventory of overstock materials they were willing to part with at reduced pricing. "Beat 'em down on price. You know the drill."

"No problem."

"That Bitty's a pretty sharp gal," He said.

"I think she's loaded," Jacob said, "She just isn't sure what she wants to do with the place yet. But I know she has some grandiose ideas swimming around in that head of hers."

"Grandiose? Swimming around, you say?"

"No doubt about it."

"Yeah, anyone can imagine castles once they get their hands on some real money. Look, the thing is, we have to keep track of hours and all expenses. I want this job to be extremely tight."

"Okay."

"I'm not charging her for my labor."

"Why not?"

"Luke isn't either."

"You talked to Luke about it?"

"Yeah, this Saturday we all start the job. You better be ready."

"I'll be ready." Jacob sounded defensive. "What do I need to do?"

Matthew leaned back, looking around. "Just be here brother."

Before leaving, Matthew motioned for Jacob to follow him, saying he had something for him. He reached into the cab of his truck and extracted a bundle and tossed it to his little brother.

Jacob caught the white cloth and let it unravel from his two hands. It was a pair of carpenter's overalls. The garment was freshly washed but it retained many faded stains from numerous jobs sites.

"We're about the same size. Those ought to fit you."

"Thanks." Jacob was startled by the gesture.

"Here," Matthew had reached into his cab and brought out another object which he gave to Jacob. "You'll be needing a good hammer. It was Dad's."

"Thanks."

Matthew climbed into his truck and drove off, leaving Jacob with a curious pang of compassion. His brother was getting older, the old vigor was diminished, and he rarely noticed it, but just now he had seen it clearly. He held up the overalls in front of him and studied them a moment. He experienced a childish rush of happiness. Receiving unexpected gifts that promised to open new vistas brought him back in touch with a younger mind's penchant for prizing modest treasures. There was also a heady trace of the child's exuberance at being encouraged by an older brother.

Working on The Joint with his brothers proved to be very satisfying; learning to do this work instilled a sense of pride he had not known he coveted. They instructed him so that he could work all week on the project, taking time to do so when he wasn't dashing off to cut someone's lawn or perform other yard work. Frances was getting him more landscaping jobs and it was hard to keep up. Cody began helping him with some of his paying jobs, and was enlisted on the work at The Joint as well. Even Gregory showed up and helped, mostly hoisting refuse into the huge dumpster they had rented.

One day, after they had flung the last of the debris down a chute built atop the roof, and it was all thrown into the metal container, Beatrice showed up dressed like she was prepared to give a showing of the house. She brought platters of snacks and a case of beer. It was understood once she had parked her car and popped the trunk the guys were free to take charge of removing the fresh provisions. They had an old wash basin they used for keeping the beer cold. Beatrice always brought ice with her.

Someone would give a cry at the sight of her Cadillac, knowing it's arrival meant work was about to be concluded. It was Matthew who determined when they were finished, and released them accordingly. He was impressed by Cody, who worked diligently and accurately. He talked to Beatrice about paying him.

"Well certainly, I think you ought . . . I mean, I should be paying all of you for your labor."

"No problem. We feel like this is something we want to do. You're doing right by Jacob. It all comes out even, at some point, right?" He flashed his boyish smile at her and she took in a great breath of air. He reminded her so much of a crush she had when very young; it was uncanny. "But like I said, I found out Jacob has been giving some of his money to Cody, so I suggest you actually get him a paycheck too."

"Well, why don't you act as general contractor, and I'll just pay you and then you pay everyone."

He made a face showing his dissatisfaction with that idea. "On this, I think it will be better for you to pay them. I don't want to get into that role, not yet. If we go forward, with the other plans, then we'll have to sit down and talk again. You may want to get bids—but for now, it's best to let Jacob handle that part."

"But you're already doing it for the materials."

"Yeah, but on the labor, I would prefer to only keep track of the hours, and let you take care of the rest."

"If that's what you want."

Matthew began to walk away but she halted him with her voice.

"Now, Matthew, can I ask you something about the kitchen over in the cottage area?" She had begun to call the lower level of the carriage house the cottage; which confirmed she was ready to put money into the renovation of that space. "I think I want to speed things up. And for this project you *will* give me a price that includes your labor."

"Sure, sure."

"I've talked to some people about your work, you know. I've heard very good things."

"Good to hear. I have fond memories of going to one of those open house affairs they used to have before Christmas."

"Really! You were there too?"

They spent an hour discussing the past, and ways they might truly incorporate the upstairs of The Joint with the downstairs quarters to serve as a proper guest house. Jacob saw them coming out of the cottage and taking leave of each other. It was rather strange for Jacob to see Beatrice acting so girlish, and the responsive lights twinkling in his brother's eye.

"Jakey! We'll be seeing you, man." Matthew yelled out as he left. Jacob waved back, watching the almost slouching manner in which his brother left a job site.

Beatrice was finding herself in a novel predicament, having to curb manifold states of giddiness for the sake of appearances. Her dreams were not only coming to fruition, but gathering momentum. After she made the leap, buying the Spencer house, on what felt like a whim, she immediately began to worry. How was she going to find good, honest people to do exactly the kind of work she wanted done; according to her preferences, without getting bled dry in the process. It was such a small project, to the contractors, and yet it loomed so large in her heart. Now she found herself placing supreme confidence in the counsel given to her by Matthew Gates. She found herself musing upon his fine qualities. He was just the sort of man she should have married, although she had thought that of other men in the past, who turned out not to be such men, once a longer acquaintance revealed more unsavory aspects of their personalities.

Nonetheless, it felt good to be dealing with a man she thoroughly respected, and it was becoming more clear to her that she wanted to keep the house as a sort of eternal debutante, belonging to the town, a place where special things happened. To be a venue where everything was always very pleasant, and the most elegant town folk wished to come out and be a part of her latest sensation. She wanted more than that, of course, but she was too enthralled presently to worry over the spiritual imperatives of the project she was undertaking. She now lived in that euphoric, fretful bustle of getting ready for gala events.

It made her breathless sometimes to be on the ground in the midst of the work that was really taking place just as she had decreed.

"Jakey!" His head spun around. Now Beatrice was calling him by that diminutive. He strode over to her.

"Yeah."

"About Cody."

"Yeah?"

"If he's going to be working here, then I need to pay him."

"Okay."

"I'll give you his check too, when I give you yours. Okay?"

"Sure."

They discussed the matter of keeping track of the hours and that Matthew would continue to forward that information to her along with the receipts for the building materials.

"I'm still not sure about your brothers not taking anything."

"Well, that's what they said; so, good luck changing their minds. It's a family thing; because you're letting me—"

"No, I understand. I understand." She drew in a long breath, glancing around at her estate. "Everything is going so well, don't you think?"

"Yes, it is. I think we're making great progress."

When he was alone again he felt as if he was the only one stuck in place, and after a moment of dour reflection he had to laugh inwardly. At least if one is going to get stuck, this is a pretty good place for that to happen. Then he repaired to the auditorium, to work on the song he was trying to write for Connie; the girl from Florissant, the first woman who put a mystic glory into his heart that was never to be forgotten.

21

I've heard it said that all great parties have in common the sense of strangers being gathered to celebrate certain shared values. If you accept the dire psychological premise that every person is a stranger to every other person, then that axiom makes more sense; or maybe it falls apart altogether. I am not sure. One should never discount the power of those imperishable dreams people carry to such gatherings. That is why teenagers are able to scrape together orgies that evoke ancient mystery cults, with hardly any means at their disposal. Suffice it to say, this fête at The Joint brought together people who had been breathing heady fumes for quite some time.

For the most part, the drinking that evening did not register on the heroic scale. And yet Beatrice was able to defray all costs from the proceeds of her cash bar. She was elated when people questioned her about her plans for the Spencer house. She was delighted to become the grand dame, to whom the guests paid tribute. She had only wanted to drop by to make sure the carriage house was not being set on fire by barbaric hordes.

In the days leading up to the gala Jacob began to loll in private fantasies. He imagined Connie in a succession of florid details that compelled him to bear down and finish his song. He called it, "Secret Places," as a working title. He spent an inordinate amount of time in his auditorium, working on the instrumental parts by which he hoped to impress her. Some of the embellishments were stolen from great talents, but the lyrics remained a problem. As he practiced Beatrice was sometimes listening, at the top of the servant's stairs, on the other side of the third story, indulging her own reveries.

Robert arrived at the party early. His anxiety drove him from the McDermott reunion just as it was coming to a simmer. His wife had refused to go to that reunion with him, as he had foreseen, and he was reeling under the effects of his freedom. He arrived at the Spencer house and found a dozen cars in the driveway and became excited.

"What are you doing here so early?" Jacob asked him, as they strolled about the grounds.

"I couldn't wait."

"How was the crowd at McDermott?"

"Not bad. Not many here, though."

"It's way early. Well, actually, it's too late, by twenty years!" Jacob laughed, amused by Robert's anxious state.

Robert was dressed in a way to make one imagine disco had suddenly made a bizarre comeback. Jacob cryptically teased him for flouting the spirit of The Joint by wearing such attire.

"Didn't you say this is the house that Jimi Hendrix built?"

"What? Where's everybody at? Maybe I should have talked to more people at the McDermott thing to let them know about it."

"What is that, a silk shirt?"

Robert looked down at himself, as if startled, then became perturbed. "Do you have enough chairs up in The Joint?"

"Go look."

Robert made no response; he was going through such a range of emotions now it was impossible to play host to any single one. Jacob lifted a drink to his lips and fantasized some more about Connie. They took seats at one of the tables placed outside the tent. The bartender brought them fresh drinks just as they sat down, even though they had not quite finished those they had already purchased. Beatrice had placed the man on a commission basis, and he was eager to maximize profits.

"What about the house?" Robert asked. "How does it look inside?"

"People aren't suppose to go in there. Except for using the bathrooms."

"Well, you know they will. Hey, what's that table doing up on the balcony?" Robert had in fact walked around the property before coming into the back yard, and this one small table caught his attention.

"Oh, that's nothing."

"It has a table cloth and candles."

"I may be using it later on, for a little private dinner date."

"Oh really? With who? Tell me."

"I'll let you know."

"Well, whoever gets up there first, right?"

"No, no way. It's mine, all set up . . . I don't want anyone else using it."

"Good luck there, man!"

Jacob was hoping to entice Connie up there for an intimate conversation over drinks, away from the madness, but with a view of the same, and he might even get the chance to play his guitar for her. The balcony was on the side of the house opposite the driveway, and close to the room he was sleeping in, just one door down the hallway . . .

What pretext could he use to induce Connie to come and listen to the song he had written. Somehow he had to let her know that he remembered her very fondly, while making it clear he was not deranged nor obsessed! He wondered if he was prepared to tell her he was a song writer? He practiced the arts of humility. 'I'm just a guitar player.' How did Dylan try on humility, in the first flicker of fame? He must do better: 'Oh, I dashed this off. It's nothing, really.' No, don't say it's nothing!

Jacob drank quickly. Before his cup was empty a fresh one arrived. He took another long gulp.

"This could really turn out to be something?" Robert murmured, staring into space.

Jacob looked in the same direction. There were colored bulbs on an electric string wound about the back yard and these cast a lurid contrast upon their features. In the dusk these diffuse aureoles around the lights weirdly matched the painted atmosphere of the western skyline. The capricious fates had given them just the right dose of dry temperate weather to feed an enriched mixture to the fires of romance. Robert began wishing there were furnished bedrooms in the house, that might be reserved for the night.

"Did you see Connie there, at the school reunion?" Jacob asked him.

"What does she look like, again?

"I don't know. Oh, you're shitting me."

Robert laughed.

"I don't know what she looks like *now*!"

"Let's check out The Joint." Robert felt a need to get control of his rampant faculties.

They went upstairs and pretended to inspect the furnishings and came to rest at the refinished bar, both leaning on it and musing on the myriad paths that were even then winding people towards this very spot. The space itself was a mystic apparatus that allowed hearts, plugged into mortal bodies, to distill precious drops of love from an infinite ocean of time.

The bartender left his post to bring both of them unsolicited replenishments, taking their money and making change out of his pockets. They thanked him politely and exchanged a wary look as he vanished down the stairs. They even walked over to the windows to see him resume his place at the bar under the tent. They looked at each other, both thinking the same thing, but not saying anything out loud. If he works the crowd like that all night, it was going to get pretty wild.

"She was smart to put that cash bar there." Jacob said.

"Oh, I think she knows what she's doing." Robert replied.

"I hope there aren't a lot of unintended consequences; stolen street signs, added legal costs, et cetera."

"Fuck the costs." Robert said in grand movie star style as he puffed on a cigarette.

Later they stood around outside as a young woman drove across the lawn and up to the side door of the house and exited her sports car. She posed for a moment, as if modeling the elegant dress pasted to her svelte carriage. Her head moved abruptly to put her bouffant tangle of blond hair into motion. She swept her eyes across the two figures standing beyond the archway staring at her. She turned with a choreographed maneuver to ascend the steps. They were mesmerized by the flash of her sculpted legs bounding up the stairs.

"Wow, who is that?" Jacob asked. "She's not from McDermott."

"No." Robert agreed. "Word's gotten around."

They realized that it would be a fool's errand to try and police the grounds too closely. Robert decided it was time to start enjoying the bash. Jacob mused over possible stratagems he might deploy to lure Connie up to the balcony.

"Beatrice was pretty emphatic about not letting people run wild in the house." Jacob asserted as a clutch of new arrivals swung past them in a bright stream of excited chatter.

"We're into it now, my friend. We'll just have to hope for the best."

"The house is mostly empty. There's not much damage they can do." Jacob sounded unconvinced by anything he was saying. He was thinking of his guitar, hidden under his bed, the case swaddled in a blanket. The cloth might be snatched away, his guitar ripped from its womb . . .

"Hey, don't worry about it." Robert was amused by the stricken look on Jacob's face.

"How often did things get broken at The Joint parties?"

"There wasn't anything up there to break. Records got scratched . . . Did Beatrice say it was okay for you to put that table on the balcony?"

"Don't worry about it." Jacob felt he was within his rights as general overseer of the estate.

"I don't want her getting pissed off at us. She won't ever let us do it again."

"Are you kidding me? These things never happen again."

"Not like this, exactly, but there will be other events. She wants this to be a venue that people use on a regular basis."

"Not for things like this, you dumbass. A mob of middle-age people trying to resurrect a chapter out of their teenage wasteland years."

"Well, you better keep an eye on things, when it gets late."

"Me! What about you?"

"You're the groundskeeper."

"You asshole."

"Check it out." Robert's attention was drawn off by three women coming under the archway along the driveway, all in short dresses, striding with brazen resolve, in the manner of Helen after she took up residence in Troy. They were vocalizing many loud, shrill sounds, couched in piercing laughter; the primal, insuperable ululations that act to galvanize men.

"Are *they* coming from McDermott?" Jacob asked, looking down at his North County clothing.

"I don't think so." Robert began considering all the people who might have somehow caught wind of this affair. Jacob worried the event might draw specimens of that breed who start fights and revel in the destruction of property. What if the surrounding burghers had to call in the National Guard! He was listening to "Ohio" now playing on the stereo in The Joint. He rocked his head back to laugh as if he were slightly demented. Robert tilted his cup of beer and let it drain out, his bravado fortified with malty gusto. A trace of his high school football days, cleats churning up fresh turf, wafted under his nostrils. He was sensing the spoils now, not the battle, which had already been forgotten.

"And so it begins my friend." Robert was no longer among mere men, he was being called by Charlemagne to stand up (at a memorial service) to show his medals, not his mettle.

"In the spirit of The Joint." Jacob said holding up his plastic cup. The bartender had already plopped a fresh one in front of Robert so he picked it up and clashed it with sloshing camaraderie against Jacob's, dousing both their hands in suds. Then Jacob paid the tab.

"I need to slow down," Robert said, getting up and strolling off to inspect the grounds. He was thinking he should have waited and come later. He was also having such gorgeous daydreams that nothing sensible penetrated very far into consciousness. It didn't matter to him what happened from this point onward. He just wanted to experience some fragment of that wild excitement known in his youth. He wished to stir those embers forever lain at the bottom of his heart's decrepit furnace.

After a while Cody, his wife Sally, and Frances strolled up across the green sward that is Allen Place and took a tour of the house. Coming out of the house they came over and sat at the table with Jacob and talked about the party. They were dressed and acted as if they were attending the wedding reception of distant relations. The tent man appeared before them. He now had an acolyte to keep down the fort, allowing him to circulate among the customers like a war-profiteer thrown among the general staff, leering with them down at their great war table.

Jacob watched Frances pour the contents of a beer bottle into a small plastic cup. She filled it half full and drank half of that in the next half hour. He watched Sally pull the bottle over to herself and pour more of the beer into her cup. Cody was not drinking at all; his wife had insisted he stay sober. He said they would not be staying late, they were expected later that evening at his mother-in-law's.

"Oh wow, I have to slow down." Jacob stood up. "Who wants to go see The Joint?" They all stood up at once, ready to do anything that allowed them to leave the table and move about. They trooped into the little carriage house kitchen, and Sally and Frances paused to run their hands over refurbished structures.

"You did good work here," Frances said to Jacob.

Jacob was proud of their work and nodded enthusiastically. He bounded up the stairs as if he were trying to scale the euphoric cloud that had engulfed his mind for a moment. Anything was possible. The song "Baba O'Riley" started playing on the stereo system as Jacob and his friends entered the room, where a good dozen people had collected in frothy spirits.

"This is where I heard that song for the first time." A man was explaining to a few others about his days visiting this infamous den. "Man, that's the best song ever written."

Some people began to argue about that assertion, and then over the question of which albums were originally stashed in The Joint. The first speaker claimed to know every record in the original collection, but another person vehemently rebutted several items mentioned on his list. They could not agree on *Surrealistic Pillow*. The two women attached to these men laughed at them for caring about something so inane. The debate was interrupted by the profiteer who arrived with a tray of beers for sale. He left with an empty platter and a sheaf of credit cards. The argument resumed but no one remembered where they had left off, and it continued that way henceforth. Jacob later found that trying to remember when anything in particular had happened was hopeless.

He circulated among the people in a fugue state. He talked to a lot of them and encouraged many to reveal their Joint stories and he noted how many of the tales conflicted one with another. He liked that result, though, because it meant he was getting deeper inside their memories, where certain things could never die and were always appearing in a new light. It was inevitable that if he did not make a fire in the fire pit, someone else would, so he tended to that chore and collected a party around him. He heard many stories that could not possibly all have been true.

Many people were assembling in The Joint, flouting fire codes. During one of his visits Jacob could hardly move in the crush of bodies. The din was enormous. The cloud of pot smoke was authentic to the occasion. Back outside again he strolled around with his cousin Kim, and a few of her friends. They asked him more questions than he could answer. Trying to appear nonchalant, Kim told him what he wanted to know about Connie.

"Yes, she's coming, you fool. What I want to know is, have you seen her since high school?" Maybe, no, he wasn't sure. She then directed his gaze to her figure.

"That's her?" His eyes flared open as he looked at a woman standing in the middle of the yard. It was Connie, in the flesh.

"Well, go on. Go talk to her."

Now he *was* a teenager again. He looked at Kim and she burst out laughing.

"I'm afraid to," he said. "What is she going to think of me?"

"No comment." Kim surveyed the spectacle revolving around her.

Then Jacob saw Robert striking up a conversation with one of the people clustered around Connie. So Jacob girded himself and strolled over to the little group. He stood by, smiling as the others acknowledged him with polite nods, before turning to listen as Robert regaled them with tales of his trafficking in used vehicles.

"I can always tell when I've got somebody hooked, because they don't bring the car back right away. They prolong the test drive. If they call me to ask about the price again, I know I have them hooked. All they want is to feel like they're getting a good deal, to see if I'll negotiate with them."

"Where do you get all the cars?" Connie asked him eagerly.

"I've got contacts all over the country."

"My first husband always had to have new models," she said brightly. "He said he didn't want to bother with mechanics all the time."

Several men nodded their heads, calculating how much money you had to make a year to afford this beautiful woman, and by what deficiencies of merit or intelligence, did this former swain she spoke of now, manage to squander his conjugal rights. One of her friends began teasing her for being such a 'high maintenance girl.'

"I was always like that, I can't help it." She became suddenly as a girl again. She was having enormous fun. She was free to do whatever she wanted; the world had no problem bowing before her.

Jacob quickly ascertained that Connie was now Constance, as she began to hold forth about her life in Florida, which seemed to blot out his boyish starter set of dreams. Her confident gaze took the measure of these natives from the old village with exquisite sensibility. She was too sophisticated to flaunt her obvious splendor. She was wearing an elegant gray dress that let one see how shapely her figure was, and how fine her legs still were, and that she was able to hold herself with the poise and composure of a princess.

"She's stunning," Jacob thought to himself, viewing her face with great pleasure. The string of lights in the yard shone a luster on her features as if a secret world of glamour revolved around her, and the obeisance she attracted was part and parcel of the invisible energy binding the cosmos. She conjured respect from the shadows and fires that had forged the bare elements of life in the first place.

He never did find out if she knew that Robert and he had engineered the party, and further, if she was aware that he had dearly wanted to see her again. It didn't matter. She would have been on the most desired list by the majority of the respondents. She was still this sensuous model of a woman who had matured and now exuded taste and culture as a natural perfume. Her perfect smile was dazzling. She had short hair and the wholesome look of a supermom who reigns in any number of venues as soon as she shows up; at family events, at school, at work, and here, as a celebrated personage that exalts the whole group by her presence. Jacob was enthralled when she spoke of the days she had attended parties at The Joint. Then suddenly she addressed him with a warm smile that passed over him in reverberant waves. It was the essence of courtesy, smothering any fears the recipient might be harboring.

"And you were my first crush!" She exclaimed. He was amazed, having been afraid to make anything of it lest she did not even remember those mesmerizing weeks.

"I was so stupid then."

"You were sweet."

He felt a tinge of embarrassment; his sentence was being read out loud for all to hear, after all these years. No woman wants a 'sweet' man; or at least not until after she has taken him in, to be disciplined and housebroken. At the last he becomes a household pet she must care for much more than she ever bargained for when she swore to uphold her vows. Shared time in the vale of marriage renders old papers obsolete anyway, as tender mercies flourish in what has become native soil for both parties.

"A fool." He said, still utterly charmed by her attention.

"You were a good kind of fool." Her demeanor charmed everyone.

He was staring at her face in a sort of silly rapture. He just wanted to bask in the beauty of this women, who had been physically blessed, and composed herself with such certitude and grace.

"Do you want to take a tour of the house?" He asked her.

"Oh, we already did that. It's really something. I had never been in it before. Now, is it true you are living there?"

"Yeah. I have to say it is."

"Wow, that's so neat."

"It's quite a life."

"And what do you do, for a living?"

"I'm the groundskeeper."

They all started laughing as though he had made a clever joke. Then they started looking at one another as he sank into embarrassment. Connie changed the mood by confessing to her own great awkwardness in the old days. Somehow her natural graciousness detached Jacob from his preposterous dream of courtly love, and made him glad he had met her again. He was proud to know how splendidly this McDermott girl had turned out.

"Tell me your best Joint story." He petitioned her. The little group gravitated over to one of the tables and they sat and told tales for a while. He kept hearing the same thing over and over, that people remembered how, 'You just went there.' And that you never knew what you were going to find once you got there. What kind of crowd would be there? What would be happening? The universal refrain became, 'It was just crazy.'

The party was deemed a success, at least by the criterion of having had a sufficient number of people in attendance. Swarms of people moved about the grounds, massing in The Joint, and then floating out into the glamorous night again. Many local pilgrims had come just to attend the 'Spencer Open House.' Jacob enjoyed moving about, observing people, engaging them in conversations, and then breaking away at strategic moments to feel his own wondrous, inexplicable momentum. He declined frequent offers to take shots of liquor. He had less success avoiding the peace pipes, charged with the once again quasi-religious weed. Some folks were intent on proving something, which he thought foolish; he was still looking for something else that had not been defined. He wanted to explain it to someone but then became amazed at how many people were entering and leaving the confines of The Joint. He became convinced many were crawling out the back windows and scaling down the wall. He could hear them laughing down in the stalls. He had to go investigate for himself. He forgot his mission when he saw people on the tennis court standing in a circle. He sat on the ground and stared at them . . .

The past engulfed him. The album *Paranoid* by Black Sabbath was being played and a man's booming voice could be heard singing the lyrics to "War Pigs" with remarkable fidelity. It suddenly struck Jacob as astonishing, for some reason, that they had all passed through the same historical period at precisely the same time. How could that be? Now he was sharing a joint with the party on the tennis court. Someone he knew but couldn't name handed him a bottle of Boone's Farm wine. He tilted it up to let the sweet syrup gurgle down his gullet. He thought these people were staring at him because he was thinking of Jenny and Constance, and it must be obvious to them that he was losing his motor skills and could not run out of his own dreams.

In the next instant he was in The Joint again, with a tangled swarm of bodies set aglow under the black lights, speaking an ancient allegorical dialect of English. The song, "A Day in the Life," came on the stereo and he rose and made a stately progression down the stairs and through the cottage kitchen, where a man and woman were locked in a succulent embrace. On the tiny porch he stopped to look around, breathing the rich night air, feeling in his marrow the pulse of deathless elegies. This was something, anyway; this phantom energy, still moving people who instinctively grasp for the lost grail of youth, which is never known by its possessors until it is lost.

"It's only one evening." He began to laugh. "Completely full of time." He tested more phrases on how everything revolves around the past; that resounding nothingness, where songs are born in tribute to the hollow ache that has never gone away, and around which we find it necessary to arrange our day.

He viewed the dark figures scattered about the lawn. He considered most of them to be mere tourists who had come because they had heard about something taking place, and had nothing else to do, and needed to occupy their time in a way that might be talked about afterwards. There were other pilgrims who knew their quest was futile; the most reverent of the whole bunch. The knowledge they seek is like buried treasure hidden beneath human consciousness.

"Who am I?"

"There you are, you ghost! I've been looking for you." Robert had appeared. His aspect was that of a madman, returned from a private abyss. "Man, oh man, Constance! You were right about her. Wow!"

Jacob just stared at him, incredulous he was acting as if he were Robert, and nothing more. It nonetheless seemed proper to be respectful of every persona, even those lacking an explanation.

"Have you seen the fair Jessica?" Robert demanded.

"I have no idea anymore where I am."

"She's so great, she really is." Robert was paying no attention to Jacob as he spoke of Jessica; facing only his roused daemon.

"I'm sure she is all that you imagine. Everything is here if you want it to be."

"But you know what she did? It's unbelievable. She did it again!" Robert leaned over and knocked a fist on Jacob's chest. "She just did it to me again." He looked at Jacob as if answers could be found on his countenance; then he realized there was nothing to be sought there. He stood upright once more and swung his head around to stare out at the grounds. Jacob fixated on the fire pit where a band of people were gathered; all faces resolved to flamboyant masks, coming alive with the streaming impulses of revealed thought.

"She did what? What happened?"

Robert explained how Jessica told him again he was not her type. She had done the same thing in high school, delivering her line in a calm steady voice, 'I will never feel that way about you.' He and some buddies had gone to raid the backyard camp site of some girls they knew, one of whom was Jessica. After a round of games and chasing them and letting them scream and settling down and being told no, it really was time for them to leave, and this by the mother of the house, who had come out in her bath robe. He could never remember anything else either of them had said to each other that night, except for that closing line that had crushed him so.

"Constance told me about her kids." Jacob said after waiting to see if Robert was going to say more about his debacle. But he was smoking a cigarette and gazing around like a secret service agent who has lost his politician (JFK, hookers) and no longer really gives a fuck.

"She's such a knockout. Did you talk to her?"

"Quite a bit. She's a very impressive woman."

"Jessica is so full of life. She's not settled down like everybody else. That's what I loved about her back then. She acts like she's not afraid of anything." Robert was resigned but still entranced.

"You have to keep yourself in tune . . ." Jacob had looked away as he spoke, and when he turned back to Robert he saw that he was gone. He had taken flight over the open fields of illusion once more. Jacob did not know what to do next; he thought he might take another trip up to The Joint. He was climbing the stairs when someone exclaimed,

"I was at Altamont!"

"Was that the Stones concert?" Someone asked.

There was laughter, at the question, apparently. Then as Jacob was able to see over the banister into the full room, the cloud of smoke was repellent. He turned around and went down the stairs, and outside he walked to the pathway at the end of the yard, behind the tall pine trees, where there was darkness to be had. He leaned against a section of the fence and stared at his surroundings. He was drinking from a bottle of water. He turned around and pissed into the thick tangle of brush at the top of the yard beyond the fence. As he was thus engaged, the world began to flutter in whirling colors; he was drawn inside the aurora borealis!

Turning around he saw that a patrol car had gone around the house and had come to rest in the back yard. Its lights were revolving, as if to tame the crowd, and was having the opposite effect. As this Ferdinand cop exited his vehicle he was swarmed by celebrants. He had not come to enforce ambiguous laws regarding hallucinatory substances. The officer was an alumnus of The Joint. He had his own stories to tell, of how the imagination refuses to be held in custody, but he remained silent on that score. He lingered a moment to enjoy the sensation he had caused, and then drove away while sifting through a cache of his own memories. He left his lights whirling long enough to titillate the neighbors.

Jacob wended into the yard and encountered Beatrice. She was flushed and at first Jacob thought she was angry about something.

"Is everything okay?"

"What?" It took her a moment to focus on his face. No, I mean yes. Did you see Deborah Spencer?"

"No."

"I was told she was at the party, and I figured she wanted to take a look at the house. But when I met her she acted funny. I told her that of course she could take a look any time she wanted. She didn't say much. She just put her hand up, like this." She raised her palm in front of Jacob. "And then she walked away."

"Where did she go?" He asked.

"She went inside, taking her own personal tour, I guess. I don't know if something happened. She wouldn't talk to me. Oh, I'm sure she's okay. How are you?"

"Pretty good." He raised his water bottle and looked at it. "Things were getting a little crazy. Not too wild, I don't think. But it's been a good party."

"I think so, too. We had to send out for more wine."

"Not surprised." He almost added, no need to send out for more pot. Beatrice was distracted, and suddenly she was gone.

Jacob went to the other side of the house to enter the screened porch on the ground floor. He wanted to find Deborah, surprised at this sudden resurgence of bravado. She had been the crush of the whole fifth grade class at one time. He recalled the face seen in her photograph on the wall above the stairs, probably from her high school graduation. A delicate face of even lines, long straight hair, and glowing eyes to lure heroes to crawl ashore over foaming rocks. He climbed the servants' stairwell as though ascending a secret passageway in search of his destiny. He wandered through the halls and empty bedrooms, brushing by other strangers who were appearing in private masquerades of their own.

Then he found her alone on the balcony. He approached her and introduced himself. She answered in a terrible voice, ensconced in the role of suffering heroine. Her eyes were shiny. He knew to remain quiet for a moment.

"It seems so strange being here," she said, "with all of this going on."

"Everyone is so interested to get just a glimpse of the place, and you lived here all the while." He spoke while looking out over the yard and the shimmering figures moving around and sitting before the fire.

"I didn't even know it had been sold. Or that the realtor had bought it."

"She has a lot of plans for it. I set up this table here to be able to get away from the madness," he explained to her. He poured her a glass of white wine, astonished the bottle was still there in the cooler. She sat down and accepted the glass.

"Did you go to The Joint a lot?"

"I went there." He said, mesmerized by the searching way she was looking at him.

"I wrote a song—"

"About The Joint?"

"Well, about that time, I guess. I can get my guitar." She did not reply but looked at him as though he had spoken to her in a Phoenician dialect not heard since the reign of Tiberius.

He rushed off the porch, down the hall, and into his bedroom. He got down on all fours and brushed aside the blanket and pulled the case towards him. He ambled back with his guitar and sat down, getting comfortable. He looked up at her. She smiled imperceptibly, but it vanished in the tremulous frieze of her pained expression. He was struck by how very sad she looked. He began to play a rather long instrumental piece, but looking up he saw she had moved to the railing in a corner of the balcony. She was looking out at the back yard. Jacob laid his guitar down and walked over to where she was standing.

"You seem to have a lot on your mind," he said.

"Yes, I've lost someone recently. That's why I came . . ."

"Oh, I'm sorry." He felt very awkward, not knowing if he should ask whom she had lost. He did not feel it was quite his place to console her. Her reticence seemed very significant. He stood there not saying anything for a few moments, noticing the full moon, as though facing a god too long neglected. He glanced again at her face, and was moved by her anguish.

"It's difficult when things change."

"It has changed everything," she confirmed. She began to talk about the lost person as if speaking to someone not present. She told him how she had heard the bad news from someone else. He did not interrupt her. She looked at him a few times as if she had almost forgotten he was there. Then she was silent and he could see on her face that she no longer wished to continue her monologue in front of him. He stared out at the grounds.

"I must be going. Thanks for listening—what's your name again?"

"Jacob."

"Thanks, Jacob."

"Take care of yourself."

"You too."

"Oh wait." She turned around. "You're the one who's living here?"

"Yeah, I'm sorry, I should have mentioned that; I'm sort of helping Beatrice. She has some ideas—"

She wrenched forth a smile from her misery. "I hope you enjoy taking care of the grounds."

"I do, I really do."

"Are you intending to stay on a while?"

"Yes, I am."

"Well, I really hope you're able to do something with the place." She had stepped forward to put her hand flat on his chest.

"I'll try." He replied, as if in awe, not knowing what he was saying; utterly smitten by the dignity of her solemn gesture.

Then she left him standing there, feeling empty, as if a strong gust of compassion had cleaned out his consciousness. He retreated to the corner of the balcony, staring out at cartoon characters seen through the windows of The Joint, and the glowing specters collected around the fire pit. He lifted his eyes to find a few trembling stars keeping time to a musical notation that has baffled all ages.

He carried his guitar back to his bedroom and secreted it beneath the bed once more; after wrapping the case snugly in the blanket. He paused a moment to look at himself in an old tarnished mirror, that had no doubt reflected many still, quiet feelings over the years. In a flash he saw all his brothers in his own visage. Leaning closer he was amused to be reminded of figures seen in pictures taken by Mathew Brady; ghosts bearing witness for the world they would never know and which they had helped to create.

Leaving his room he turned to walk down the hall to the front stairs and encountered an amorous couple involved in a stumbling waltz. They clung to one another as if to keep from falling down.

"This isn't a real house." The man said as Jacob swept by them.

"Maybe he's not a real person." The woman said.

"You are, my real, pie sweetie." The man cried as the woman let loose a piercing laugh. Then there was silence. Jacob imagined the two were getting ready to become as one flesh, and hoped they did not use his bedroom for this purpose. He did not turn around to see. How many overwrought pillars of salt can be spared for one blue planet?

22

Outside Jacob observed that the party was all but finished. He lumbered around as if attempting to shepherd the last weary celebrants to their cars. He noticed the extensive damage done to the lawn.

"Beatrice ain't going to like this," he said out loud, making a wry grimace. Much of the repair work would fall on his shoulders. He picked up a plastic cup off the driveway and poured the dregs at the base of a huge scarlet oak on the property line.

"Feed your head, old master," he instructed the tree. He craned his head backwards to look up at the still leaves. He experienced vertigo and flung his arms out in a crazy, unbalanced gesture.

"Jacob, what are you doing?"

He whirled around and staggered, having to catch his balance, before he recognized Beatrice. Her grim face in the poor lighting presented a wild gothic mask.

"I don't know how these things happen."

"What?"

"I am keeping an eye on the grounds."

"Jacob, tell me, have you seen Robert?"

He was confused by her consternation. Everything was over, wasn't it? She was holding the same brand of cellular phone Robert owned, and regarding the device as if it had just bitten her. Jacob's ruminative silence rankled her.

"Have you?"

"I saw him a while ago. He looked like the rag man, going in circles."

"Are you drunk?"

"Now?" He meant to ask why that would be relevant at the moment; but instead teased more lyrics. "I took both cures. I lost my debutante."

"You're not making sense."

"Not on principle." He said, repeating what he had heard some pompous character say earlier in the evening when he was challenged on a political issue by another character just like him. Having a circle of spectators, the two had battled over ideas like two knights who had gotten knocked off their horses, and then had continued their struggle down in the mud. "I'm seeing everything twice."

"Oh, please stop talking nonsense! Now this stupid thing doesn't work." Beatrice was addressing her phone. Apparently there was mechanical malfeasance afoot in the universe.

"Did you try The Joint?" Jacob suggested.

"Of course, I looked there." She shook her head, looking at Jacob more wrathfully. She began to stalk off, but stopped, turned and raised her finger to let Jacob know she was still directing him. "Do keep an eye on everything."

"I see everything." He said, staring at an oak trees on the front lawn. He did not see where Beatrice had gone in the next moment. He saw huge spiders on the roof of The Joint. This made him laugh. Other nocturnal beings were near the pine trees, entering the path, as if seeking utter darkness. There was enough moonlight to record their mythological passage.

Someone was playing Dylan's album *Blond on Blond*, which Jacob had placed in The Joint for the party, and then forgot about it afterwards. The high camp of the first song brought Jacob closer to himself. Dylan must have been stoned out of his mind when he recorded that one. The party was not quite over, not yet. He ventured towards the music. He shook his head to dissuade the barkeep from trying to sell him another drink, before looking; even the profiteer had decamped!

Who *was* playing that disk? He couldn't decide whether to enter The Joint through the garage or the porch door of the cottage, and while trying to decide he found himself heading for the sunken garden. He glimpsed two people sitting close together at the top of the hill. He watched as their heads tilted up and down, as both remained staring outward, sharing intimacies. He stood very still and some of their words became intelligible. They were discussing trivial ordeals that would be forgotten in nine months, as life gave birth to new troubles. As he was about to retrace his steps, he heard sounds emanating from below in the stables. The sensual groans and pig grunts of two bodies coupling as God intended; for he covets good ratings. Jacob had to slap a knee; hilarity began resounding inside of him. No laughter came forth from his mouth.

"Who gives a fuck?" He cried to the stars above. "Where? When? And with whom?" The two heads above the hill swiveled to stare at him.

"Who is that creeping about?"

He raised his hand high with an open hand to let them know he was only a harmless vagrant. "Have you seen all good people?" He shouted at them. He was put out of temper by their haughty attitude and spun away. The song, "Visions of Johanna," began playing in The Joint. He kicked at a plastic cup that was not empty and knocked a spray of mercury pellets up into the starry atmosphere. He then noticed a great spawn of empty cups littering the lawn and driveway.

"All the waste," he murmured. "I've seen all good waste beneath our fun." His whirling mind paused to latch on to the Dylan song. He thought of how the singer had labored over the song while his new wife was pregnant. He never ceased wrestling with the demons who came to test him in his craft. Jacob regretted that he had missed the beginning of the song, that haunting introduction was in perfect accord with his present mood.

Just then he saw Mulligan coming out of the garage, marching towards him. Jacob started to ask him what he was doing here; but the man kept walking, barely acknowledging Jacob's existence. That's the way brother, stay your course! He was the quintessential ghost of the evening. Had he been of that merry crew who created all this phantasmagoria in the first place? The Joint certainly had a storied past, but no historian will ever put the chronicle into print; it remains for an acolyte of the Grimm brothers to capture the obscure, transcendent romance of the place.

Jacob thought he might call it a night; repair to the house and maybe see about plucking out a few last chords before bedding down. He was awash in new lyrics he knew he would forget. He might close the evening by playing the song written for Constance, and almost for Deborah; now he would play it for himself. The whispery night air on his face felt like a caress; something precious being offered, a petition to be heeded. He stood like a lawn statue for a moment. Then looking around he noticed he had drawn the attention of two women by the fire pit. The taller one was using a stick to stir the ashes, causing trails of glowing embers to rise into the gloom, as if tragically attempting to return to the mother stars.

"Let's go, this place is dead," the shorter woman said as she stared at the intruder.

Jacob headed over towards the pit along with his moon shadow, as if he had been nudged to do so.

"And who are we?" He said to them with obvious bluster, to make it clear he did not mind looking ridiculous to them. They smiled derisively as they stared at him. They became amused while they waited for him to continue his performance. He reached out for the woman's stick so that he could stir the fire. She relinquished her hold, glancing at her friend, shedding sardonic mirth from her flashing eyes. "Doesn't matter. You don't need names here." He mumbled, his spirits flagging.

"Who are you?" The taller of the woman asked him. Her hair was a thick wavy mass around her face, which confronted him with keen appraisal.

"I'm a Russian monk."

"Okay." The shorter one answered, stretching out the word.

The taller one had a more subtle reaction as Jacob assembled the charred stumps in the fire pit to cause a spurt of sulky flames to rise and reflect seductive gleams onto her face. Struggling against his stupor he stared at her visage, so full of marvelous life and movement. Then she was smiling at him, without using any of the usual facial mechanics needed to produce that effect. He had the strange sense of basking in that smoldering intensity.

"Have you lost someone?" The shorter one asked him.

"No. I live here by myself."

The taller one named Molly made a wry face. It was impossible to know the exact nature of her silent criticism. Jacob could see only the swaying embers in the dark pools of her eyes.

"Was this your party?" Molly asked, cocking her head in a sweet movement of forbearance, passing over his befuddlement.

"No, not really. Some of it was."

Janey laughed in his face. He looked at her and nodded glumly.

"Did you connect with any old acquaintances?" Molly asked.

"I made a fool of myself a couple times tonight."

"Only twice?" Molly gave voice to delicious irony, drawing him hence, as towards the next measure of a newly discovered song destined to be placed for all time in the body of one's personal canon.

"Was that difficult for you?" Janey added with blunt, piercing glee.

He laughed. "Not all all. I have a gift for doing that sort of thing."

"I'm Molly, and this is Janey."

"I'm Jacob."

"So you didn't have much luck tonight, huh?" Molly asked him.

"I think I was pretty happy when it started. The anticipation, I guess. It seems like you can't ever hold on to anything you really want to keep. The feelings you remember."

"Like what?" Molly asked, after a long pause. She was younger than him, by how much he could not tell. Everyone spoke of him as one who looked young for his age. When would that suddenly change?

"I met a woman I was crazy about in high school. She said she remembered I was sweet."

"Well *that's* sweet." Molly replied. She was keeping him at arm's length, poking fun at him, and offering him a modicum of encouragement, all at once!

"Have you ever been to The Joint before?" He asked them.

"It was pretty much over by the time we were old enough to be a part of it," Janey said.

"I remember sneaking up there one time during the day." Molly said.

"I was with you!" Janey squealed. "You drank a warm beer!"

"I did not. I only wanted to taste it."

"She drank a warm beer with cigarette butts in it."

"I did not!"

He noticed they were not dressed for the party as most of the other women had been; wearing casual shorts and light flowery blouses, and sandals. It was now rather cool for this attire.

"Do either of you want a drink?" He asked them. They all looked over at the liquor tent, which was no longer staffed.

"Were you going to drive somewhere to buy us drinks?" Molly asked.

"I do have a truck," he said, glancing over at the vehicle resting in the garage.

"We have to go," Janey said. "We're already late."

They began walking towards the garage, and he wondered if they were going up into The Joint, but they kept walking around the garage towards the hill.

"Hey, where are you going?" He shouted, trailing after them.

"We're from Margaret's."

"Margaret's?"

"Our cars are parked at Saint Margaret's." Molly called back to him.

He stared at her figure as it passed down Spencer's hill and passed into the darkness beyond. So there you have it, he thought, the village children had come to explore the amusement park of our dream world, and they found it unimaginative. He climbed the reverberant wooden stairs once more and found The Joint was empty; nothing left but the shabby litter left behind. He looked out a back window and caught a glimpse of the two women going forward under the sycamores. He sat down on a couch, feeling relieved that the whole thing was really over at last. There was a sense of loss that must be pushed away; dealt with at a later date. Then he noticed there was a single bottle standing on the bar counter, and he had to get up to examine the label. It was a Château Margaux.

"Fancy stuff," he exclaimed, hefting the bottle to gauge the fluid level. He sipped a little, just enough to coat his tongue. He knew it was probably better than he was able to perceive with his rude and ravaged palate. A vestige left behind for that last toast that never comes to fruition in common hours. He grabbed the bottle by the neck and scrambled out a window to get on the roof. Once outside he stood up and surveyed the grounds. Everyone was gone.

Then he saw Robert and Beatrice exiting the side door of the house. They stood facing each other at the bottom of the steps. Their heads touched and got stuck and the necks began to tussle; then they managed to free themselves again. Robert craned his neck around and by happenstance located Jacob on the roof, his arm raised in salutation. Jacob moved his hand back and forth in broad sweeps. Robert kicked his head back slightly in acknowledgement, then it came down and fused itself to the other head once more.

Jacob scrambled up the tiles to reach the pinnacle of the roof and sat there facing out over the land below. A pearly darkness clothed the suburban vista as nicely as the primeval woods had been exposed to the full candor of the moon in ancient times. He watched as several house lights were extinguished. On Elizabeth Avenue tiny somnolent moons in pairs wended slowly along as late automobiles proceeded over the old trace. He looked out over the colony of slumbering houses, considering that every person shared that need to feel 'at home' someplace. He noticed one solitary yellow light in full blossom in the gloom; one reluctant household was keeping a lamp burning.

He knew the house; the elderly occupants had been there for a lifetime. He watched as that light disappeared and darkness enclosed all the yards. There was no getting out of the woods. There had always been a pact made with the night, so ancestors could reside in another homeland; much as those early colonists who once moved across the sea, when ocean travel was a venture of great peril. They could only turn their thoughts fondly to their mother country, which they might never see again. We have a primal need of seeing in both directions at once, and consciousness only thrives among great troubling unknowns by telling stories that make sense out of nonsense.

"Well, Jacob my boy, a toast to our habitat." Jacob was then under the care of Eben Flood, and he congratulated himself for enjoying this moment. "But it is time for sleep," he confessed to himself. He listened to sounds that punctuated the silence; intonations so faint they might be insects, but you could not be sure they weren't noises occurring in one's mind. The heavens spoke with that insubstantial stream of mystifying particles that has crossed a vast nothingness, merely to suggest to ordinary mortals there is an unknown provenance of things. How do such signals manage to confirm the value of one's own music?

"Anyone out there?" He shouted to alert anyone below in the area outside the stables. "You awake? All good serpents?" He hurled the empty wine bottle in a high arc to fall into the last bastion of riotous vegetation. He climbed off his perch and made his way back inside and down the stairs and effected a quick rambling circuit of the grounds. There were no cars in sight, just the tire tracks left in the ground; a Sumerian script left by modern machines to register the fact humans tend to move in circles.

Arriving in his bedroom he saw at once that his bedsheets were rumpled and looked as though they had been removed and gathered up again and thrown back on the mattress with rude complacency. He looked closer and fell back aghast. Some people had used his bed for a tryst. He stripped the sheets off and bunched them distastefully in his arms and hurled them into the corner of his room. He would have to remember to wash them the next day. He thought of his guitar and getting down on the floor he reached under the bed and brought the case forth along with its blanket. As a teenager he had named his guitar Melanie, after the lovely singer who played at Woodstock. He considered her to be the perfect hippie chick, whom he actually wedded in his dreams. Before very long he had decided it was idiotic to name a guitar . . .

"What do you think now, Melanie?" he asked to mock his own confusion. "We've come a long way from those candles in the rain, but you can't outgrow everything."

He decided to play something from another era and dragged himself up to the third floor, taking the almost secret passage from his bedroom. The blanket was clutched in one hand and trailed behind him on the stairs as if he were some plodding ghost who's been caught in the act of losing his shroud. He held his guitar close to his chest with the other hand. In the auditorium he rolled his chair close to a window and sat down facing outwards, looking at one of the great white oak trees on the front lawn. The silvery limbs were in perfect repose. It was pleasant to see this lovely familiar shape standing there, composed for his eyes, as though this instant was always supposed to be one he would arrive at, feeling this eerie sense of gratitude.

At first he tried to play the song he had composed for the party. He couldn't do it. He didn't care about that song anymore. His fingers fumbled at the strings as if he had lost his motor control. Using brute concentration he played one chord progression with precision, and then another one, and then he shook his head and carefully laid the instrument down on the floor. Then he folded and spread the blanket on the floor and laid down on top, curling up and falling fast asleep, as a shipwrecked voyager, who has washed ashore and feels the lyrical waves as a lullaby arranged perfectly for one heart.

Part Three

Beyond Déjà Vu

23

My travels have proven to me that you are never too old to learn more about the human heart. It is when other people inspire you that things begin to happen. Those mysteries that bind the living to the dead are manifested as genuine ties sustaining a single, attuned purpose. Promises are made afresh. The dry river beds of history stretch out before you as the leafy mirage attracts the wanderer in a desert. I shall not tax your patience any further in that direction; however, there is one fragment I wish to hold up for all eyes. It has to do with the origins of Ferdinand, and has an appeal like truth. It deserves a passing glance from the shores of our main story.

It concerns a remarkable Spanish soldier, or say, a galley slave. He decided to jump ship to seek better parts, in regions largely unknown, in this historical anomaly, once called Spanish Illinois. He felt the ache of freedom in his bones; the call of destiny prompted him to exercise his will against the constraints of his time. I know this concept is fraught with intellectual perversities. I have friends who tell me we have no free will; others tell me that of course, we do. Recalling these events, I am resolved to take the latter position, what choice do I have?

As far as our Spaniard is concerned, he took the magisterial leap, and swam like a man possessed. Before undertaking his amphibious flight he had listened to his officers, while feigning the stupefied indifference of the debased minion. He heard them discuss the illicit French traders ranging up and down the interior rivers, and how there was no way they would ever be controlled without a larger Spanish presence. That would never happen, because the king was in thrall to silver and gold, and cared hardly at all about his remote colony in a vast continent that had nothing but fertile lands and fresh streams. Our deserter at the oars had been raised by a French woman; he could speak the tongue like a captain. He knew he would be able to befriend those French traders and volunteer to row for them on their excursions up the Missouri River.

His confidence soared as he entered the unknown. He thrived at building relations with the tribes and the traders. He ended up establishing a mill on Moline Creek, and a sort of trading camp on the very site of the Spencer estate. The Chouteau brothers once chuckled affably over the audacity of the man while quaffing imported ale at his camp table. He was glad to pay tribute to these fur barons and participate in their lucrative and often outlawed trade. As an old man he disappeared down the Sante Fe trail with a slave woman. In time his land was divided into lots for the elegant bourgeois homes worthy of a rising nation. The extant house was built by an agent who worked for a railroad titan. He came west with hardly anything except an enormous amount of credit, after the Anglo-Saxon frontier had crashed through the region and gone tearing westward. The field was left open for law officers and lawyers to establish order for men like Herb Spencer, who came along much later. By then the edifice needed extensive repairs; but his indefatigable wife sang a wet, luscious aria into his ear one night, and he soon took up the task of refurbishing the old mansion.

Introducing the Spaniard into our story is not to suggest Jacob was such a heroic figure himself. He had never leaped from a ship to get to this place where he was now living; but his mind had taken leave of much that he once thought of as settled values. It often felt as if he were abandoning too much, before he was even aware he was seeking a purchase for his next move forward. He was out there thrashing in that obscure medium where change occurs. It was a different man who attended the funeral of his uncle Julius, than the one who had worked for him not that long in the past.

He had been dreaming of his First Communion; there were two girls in white dresses, both of them laughing. One was his sister, and the other one he did not recognize. They were looking at him and laughing. He was staring at them and listening when the phone rang; the news of his uncle's death was conveyed to him by his mother. She gave him the particulars and he had to retrieve his only suit from storage and take it to the cleaners. He wended through the prescribed funereal motions in a sort of haze; whenever he thought of his likely inheritance he was wracked by guilt. At the wake he roused himself and began asking many questions about his uncle, wanting to hear other people sharing their memories. The time elapsed in great emotional stops and starts and he was left at the end utterly spent. After the funeral mass, and the burial at the grave yard, the family repaired to his mom and dad's house.

In the last hours all the brothers were together in the basement, where their dad had created a den for himself, and a playroom for the grandchildren. At one time his father had assembled a little shrine for Johanna in that space, placed on an ornate shelving unit he had built himself. Over time his wife had slowly dispersed the clutter of relics about the house, to lessen the jarring impact of such a display. It did not strike her as a proper way to treat with one's grief, which must become settled in the bottom layers of memory. To her it was too morbid, or macabre, or just too suggestively pagan, perhaps. Jacob was peering at the effects, and noticed that now the rosary was missing. Several framed photos of Johanna remained; he was searching for one in particular, taken after their First Communion, out in the back yard. It was not there.

"Here's one more to Julius," Their father said, rising a little snifter half full of Irish Mist, which had become a favorite toddy of the brothers at such times. Henry was always one to give toasts, if the occasion arose, or was hauled up by main force. He now poured out a glass for each son. They all sipped like clumsy bears having to feed out of tiny goblets.

"He used to get nostalgic after hours," Jacob said, and they all looked at him. He had not meant to speak of this but the moment overcame him as he remembered the uncanny honesty of Julius that cropped up at random times. He would tipple and cavort with spirits of the past in a mood of pedagogic reflection "He used to talk about you a lot, Dad."

"When we were young, we thought we were going to take over the world." Henry said, a mist collecting in his eyes.

"He always talked about that Dodge truck you had."

"Oh, he always laughed at that truck. I had to hang a pan underneath the engine to catch the leaking oil, then I'd get out and tip it so I could pour the oil into a can and then back into the engine."

They all laughed. It was an old story. Now was one of those rare times when it was hilarious again. Jacob took great comfort being there with his family; an almost ethereal sense of belonging lifted his spirits. He felt confident, and such values are impossible to gauge; but its effects are plain to see in every aspect of social intercourse. He weighed things with a revised set of standards. He thought of how tolerant the people in his previous circle of friends had been regarding racist humor. It was a malignant acquiescence to vile rhetoric, and it trickled through their lives like an iridescent stream coming off a broken sewer line. He had not learned any of that prejudice here, in this home, he thought, nor certainly not in their first one in Ferdinand. He felt pride in that fact, and also that he had not been true enough to them, and himself, in many things.

They were playing pool, the two youngest brothers pitted against the two eldest, each party insulting those of the other with gusto. It seemed like another inevitable ritual that was taking place at the proper time when his mother came down the steps and served tiny scrumptious sandwiches. She stayed to watch them a moment, her hand on her husband's shoulder. He sat there, smoking his pipe, peering out from his vantage of august equanimity. After a short while she removed herself again and could be heard upstairs moving about in the murmur of other womanly voices. The men continued talking in a desultory fashion of the past and there were long lapses of silence when they stared into their cups as if performing secret rites of divination.

"He said you were no salesman." Jacob said to his dad.

Henry roared out in reply. "He was right, there. Yes, yes." He slumped back into the couch. "Julius was, though, that's for sure. He would go out drinking with the customers, before they were even customers. He could get anyone to laugh. No, I have to say, he built that business himself, there's no doubt of that, none."

"He said you were more steady and reliable, where it mattered most, than he ever was."

"Oh, I don't know about that." He coughed, clearly touched; his love for his older brother freshened quickly upon him.

"He said when you married Mom he knew he would never have to worry about you again."

"That's when I started to worry." He spoke as if he were being totally serious, and all his sons laughed heartily; so much so, that the primal first cause of this laughter ventured down the steps in person, to see what was happening. She stared at them with that imponderable, expansive, puzzled, inexorable compassion that forms the bone marrow of a woman's love for her brood. She had found the picture Jacob had been looking for earlier, and she now handed it to him. His moist eyes thanked her profusely. He was feeling in that moment very fortunate; not trusting any words to express to her why this was so. Her eyes were shining at him in such perfect concordance that it felt like he was hearing music in his mind, as if in fact he were actually rehearsing.

24

H is days became incomparable to anything he'd ever known before. He found himself to be rather happy, even while spending time cutting grass for people. Frances brought him new customers and instructed him how to approach each account. Some of the old ladies, who were supposed to get his services for free, came out and pressed dollars on him. He took whatever was offered, informing Frances of his experiences as a salesman might report back to his manager.

One afternoon, after he was done cutting grass for a woman who lived on Elizabeth, they sat on the terrace in her back yard, looking down the long rustic hill. Her husband was a reticent man; all her children were living in distant cities. She spoke of these people to Jacob as he sat and listened. He talked to her of his family. They spoke much of the natural beauty of Ferdinand and how it was a great place for any couple to raise a family, and that anyone should have the right to do so. Upon taking his leave of her hospitality, he motored to the drug store. He was dressed in what had become his standard work uniform, his white carpenter's overalls. He parked in the lot as though his mower were an equal to the standard peerage of American automobiles. He was standing in line behind a middle-aged woman who was talking to the young woman behind the counter.

"It's men! Men did it." The old female customer exclaimed.

The younger woman agreed emphatically. Jacob had missed the first part of their conversation; the indictment was unclear to him. He looked down at his 22 oz. can of beer. Looking up he saw both woman staring at him.

"That's why we drink," he responded. "So we can bear our sins."

The young woman smiled dubiously; the older woman eagerly returned fire.

"That's why we drink our wine, so we can bear you men!"

Jacob began chuckling. That was good. Yes, they do all the bearing. They even have to bear the enemy! In that oldest of all contests for power, it is all about holding two opposing ideas in one's head at the same time. He left the store and straddled his mechanical charger, proceeding homeward at a rate of progress once common to the buggies, broughams, and phaetons that once prowled these streets. In the days when the good people sported about town holding whips, attired in fashionable garments, collecting tithes of envy from the slow pedestrians they scattered out of their way.

A few days after the party he encountered Beatrice with misgivings. He had told Cody how he saw her and Robert kissing at the end of the party.

"That's hilarious. I'm not surprised."

"Really? I didn't expect that at all."

"That turned out to be some party, eh? But not for you so much."

"I had a good time."

"Serenading the stars?"

Jacob had divulged the particulars of his comedy regarding his official song; a composition for an occasion that never comes about.

"What was it about, again?" Cody sought to stir the farce afresh.

"I have no idea. Something about not ever leaving high school in the past, trying to remain an adolescent forever . . ."

Cody interrupted to propose new material for Jacob's Magical Crisis Tour; in the melody of a famous Stones' song.

"You can't always piss where you want, but if you try, you might just find, you get into some pretty good weed!"

"I could do a score for the movie; A Hoosier Piddling on the Roof."
They spent an inordinate amount of time composing lines that would never be played during a tour that would never happen. They had a good laugh.

"That was a classic." Cody said, referring to the tryst of Robert and
Beatrice.

"You weren't even there at the time. How can it be a classic for you?"

"It just is." Something to wield against Robert should it be called for.

"I gave them my blessing from the roof of The Joint." Jacob raised
his right arm to show his version of the papal sleight of hand. Cody made
motions like he was aspersing holy water on a docile congregation, and
quickly altered the mime to exhibit another more solitary procedure a man
does exclusively for himself.

Now Jacob was remembering these antics as he was talking to Beatrice
and he had to dispel those images from his mind to keep a straight face.

"Did anything happen?" She asked him.

He appeared dumbfounded.

"Did anything happen that I should know about?" She amended her
question rather irritably.

"No, not really. I think we came out of it pretty good."

Once they commenced strolling about the grounds everything became
more natural. He had learned to exercise discretion; laughing inwardly;
keeping his own counsel as a good minion. On the front lawn they appraised the extensive damage. Some of it was deliberate, the work of suppressed spirits released from the crypt of maturity.

"There's no excuse for that." Beatrice said.

"The lawn is torn up pretty bad all over."

"The parking was a huge problem." She mused over possible remedies.
"You can repair most of that, right?"

"Yes, I think so, some of it."

We can bring in a company to do sod work."

"That would be a good idea."

"I'll give you the name, you can call them. Look, Jacob. I wanted to tell you; I've talked to Matthew about it, and I think we're going to start on the cottage. When we get that done, you can live there, okay?"

"Yeah, that would be great." By cottage she meant the downstairs kitchen and bathroom area, plus the larger upstairs quarters of The Joint, which was going to be expanded, pushing over into the garage space.

"Okay then, let's see how this goes, shall we?" She was also going to finish one of the upstairs bedrooms for her own private use.

Henceforth she dropped by often to see how the work on the cottage was coming along. Matthew had a way of teasing her that put her in mind of her younger days when her fulsome feminine figure did not meet the specifications laid down by the Cheerleader Committee. It was ruled by one indomitable woman, otherwise a complaisant housewife; an alumnus of the squad, who explained, "It's just that I have high standards for the girls. I'm not going to apologize for that—never!"

Becoming a cheerleader had been a burning ambition for the young Beatrice, and she never forgot being thwarted by that one woman. She was vexed whenever such resentments bubbled to the surface—and she could not explain this to anyone. It was too embarrassing. It no longer mattered! So why the recurrent tides of regret washing up from dismal memories? Meanwhile, her oldest daughter was chiding her for being afraid to try new things! She never knew what to tell her when she was pressed about her past. The daughter was becoming more curious as she settled into the most burdensome, and rewarding, years of her own motherhood. Quiet moments over wine often turned into inquisitions. Beatrice wished she had a friend with whom to share these outpourings, without resorting to clinical expurgations, or whatever dime store psychology was in vogue.

She had always been at odds with certain kinds of imperious women who reigned in the circles where she had vied for position. Lately she had been tempted to unburden herself to Frances, feeling such implicit trust in the woman. There was something amiss, however; for instance, she acted funny about that Gregory character. The brute scared Beatrice. More than once he had looked at her funny. When she mentioned this to Frances, the tactless woman had lashed out at her in a peculiar way. The wretched feeling of being at odds with another woman, whom she respected, came to the fore and she plunged back into her work, where she was able to obtain tangible results. Matthew seemed to have an intuitive feel for how important these changes to the house were for her. He shared his notions on his craftsmanship in the most touching manner, and that fostered more intimacy with her own designs.

One afternoon, after Jacob, Luke, and Matthew had finished working at The Joint, Mark swung by just as everyone was getting ready to leave. They were puzzled by his sudden appearance. Late in life he had become rather stout. His long, jowly face was endowed with enormous dignity nonetheless; and his short peppery hair put Jacob in mind of an English cleric for some reason.

"I just wanted to tell you in person," Mark said gravely to Jacob, who leaned forward in suspense. "I've heard about the will." Everyone trained their attention on his face. Mark reminded them that their uncle's housekeeper was actually his consort. Jacob was irritated; he had learned this fact at the wake, and felt stupid for not knowing it all along.

"So, you're saying . . ." Jacob began.

"Everything went to her." Mark confirmed.

"I never said I was entitled to anything," Jacob looked away. "I only . . ." He had to stop himself from speaking his mind out loud. Julius told him more than once he hoped Jacob would be able to use the money to improve his lot in life.

"It's tough, I know." Mark said.

"Well, I thought so." Jacob was hurt. "After what we heard at the wake, and everything." His shoulders slumped. He had not known till then just how much he had expected to get his hands on some of that money.

"I can't believe Uncle Julius would do that to you." Matthew said.

"What did Dad say?" Jacob asked.

"Ah." Mark made and held a pained expression on his face. "Not much. You know how that was, between them."

"Yes." As young men they had argued over money and the business, and then forged a truce; and finally a genuine peace after they were only brothers once more.

"The will they used was drawn up a month ago." Mark spoke as if reading from a transcript.

"You might be able to contest it." Luke said in a strange tone. He had not really gotten along with uncle Julius; they had argued violently about the Vietnam war several times, and the rift was a cause of embarrassment for everyone.

"Do you think she had undue influence over him?" Matthew asked.

"No." Jacob said emphatically in a low, angry voice. "But why didn't he ever marry her? Why didn't he acknowledge to us that she actually was his wife, for all practical purposes?" His anger increased as he spoke, and his words reflected back poorly upon himself, and so he lapsed into silence.

"Yes, imagine how she feels." Mark's voice could tremble like organ tones, as it did now, much to Jacob's dismay.

"Was he of sound mind?" Luke asked.

"Yeah, yeah." Jacob and Mark spoke nearly in unison. They had both seen him several times right before the end, and could attest to this unequivocally.

Mark continued in measured tones. "He was as lucid as he was weak. No, trying to fight this, that would not be something to consider." He put his hand out and placed it on Jacob's shoulder, and that made him feel worse. It was clear he had no right to feel bitter about this, that it was wrong for him to feel this way. He was wanting to be alone. He wanted to play his guitar. His music was becoming a true refuge for him now as it had once been so long ago. He could play the instrument and transform bad emotions into beautiful sounds that had been brought forth from the purity of unfathomable sources.

"I wanted to come and tell you as soon as I knew." Mark said.

"I'm glad you did. Oh well, thanks Mark." Jacob said. "Do you want to see our work in the cottage?

Mark said he certainly did and they promptly gave him a tour of the place. He was very appreciative of their work, and his brothers sought to tell him how certain aspects of the work had been accomplished. They still accepted without reservation the terms of his approval, just as he deemed it proper to dispense such to them. When he was leaving he paused to look at each of them, and as always, you had to infer what he might have said if he put into words even a tenth of what other people did when thoughts ran through their heads during such moments. He had become taciturn as a surrogate father, having to control his unreasonable rage at being placed in such an unfair position. Much later he had learned, after being tempered by marriage, the power of letting go of things. He had learned from his wife how to let another person help you carry burdens.

"Well, be good, be safe." He paused before adding, "Have fun."

The other brothers watched the eldest of them get back into his car; from behind the wheel he lifted a hand to wave a familiar salute. His face remained somber as he drove away.

Luke shoved Jacob on the shoulder with one hand. "You got the 'have fun!' You Saxon dog!"

"He had to think about it, though." Matthew added. "You almost didn't get that part."

"Yeah, I guess there's no hope for you now." Luke spat out as if in contempt.

They erupted in laughter. It was the same salutation Mark always gave at solemn occasions, but it did not always go the same way. Some people only heard him say, be good, others, be safe; the full equation was reserved normally for people outside the family, upon whom Mark was conferring the full sanction of family approval. Jenny swore she had never heard the last portion of the salutation regarding the importance of having fun. Jacob assured her his brother must have said it to her, in the early days. But really, he wasn't so sure.

It doesn't matter, Jacob thought, once he was alone; at least that's finished. No need to worry. I'm chief groundskeeper. Master over all of this. He flung an arm out to encompass his metaphysical station in life. Suffused in a rich strain of irony, containing many germinal parts of the active truth, he enlarged his vision of all things. He resumed his work in the lot behind the defunct stables, hacking away at the last of the luxurious vegetation. The snake clans had been thrown back on their Bedouin roots. Jacob knew this part of his life could not last indefinitely; but some force he could not possibly grasp was moving him through the span of his days and holding him snugly in place. He felt compelled to persevere, to see if the provenance of this power might become more clear to him in time.

In the midst of his manual labor he remembered a passage from one of his texts. The idea of being the Napoleon of one's life. What temples must be destroyed along the way in such reckless campaigns? In order to establish a new Code, must one first scatter wreckage and debris all about his passage? Napoleon? Who was he kidding? A man who only emulates Monsieur Onan in his amours, who has become a leper of Capitalism; in the social hierarchy reduced to the ranks of untouchable ones. His only faith was that of the pagan child who worships the outdoors . . .

Pausing, the sweat dripping down his face, he listened to a dying generation of cicadas. The harsh collective songs of these little red-eyed demons shook the air around him. The rolling measures had such an incredible, insistent, latent power. He listened to the monotonous dissonance pouring out of the trees where unseen choirs seemed to be challenging other life forms with the significance of their epic sagas. It seemed strangely urgent, and too impertinent, for the human mind to countenance; being convinced of its own divine right to hold dominion over this earth. Already, it was felt, the depths of another summer had somehow filtered through one's care.

In the noise of life's smallest creatures there was dread reproof, perhaps tinged with encouragement, in the celebratory march of life. One suspects we have only gotten to know time as the galley slave does the sea. Fruits of the ultimate voyage cannot be known by those chained to the oars. Songs are sung to encourage the mass to go forward in concert;

but the complexity of the human personality, that miracle of evolution, this beautiful enigma, in thriving, beggars its own sovereign imagination. Nonetheless, one must strive to know his own true voice, should he wish to properly belong, as do these brash winged things. He got lost in reveries as he listened to natural songs. For one instant his whole being was raised in sonorous response, and he was truly of this vibratory earth whence he came and must in time return to again.

25

Jacob's manner of living was conducive to his health. He treated occasional bouts of despondency as if taking shelter from inclement weather. You retreated indoors for a while, to meditate over a glass of ale, or to play a melancholy song with religious devotion. You shed despair while scaling large steps to reach higher registers. At times he sought out the bad weather; wading through downpours to replenish hidden cisterns. He had a sort of mud room, between the garage entrance and the cottage door, where he could stow his foul weather gear.

The Joint was now finished. On the first floor there was a shower and other bathroom facilities, along with a large kitchen. He gladly accepted help from several women to furnish the place. Cody's wife spent several tense moments discussing window treatments with Beatrice, while Cody and Jacob stood by, awaiting their orders.

"Maybe you should steal some more street signs and put 'em up." Cody jested. It did seem that the only specimen remaining of the once notorious motif deserved a place of honor.

"The Book of Life is scrawled over with many glyphs, never understood by anyone." Jacob said before he could stop himself.

"Whatever Gandalf; wearing overalls."

"Getting those signs must have been an adventure." Jacob mused.

"I remember one time, a cop questioned me about them," Cody mused. "He probably thought I was a likely enough suspect. The jackass! I didn't even know what he was talking about."

The favors of time were freely granted throughout the course of every day. Being outside was like taking a cure. At present one season was making haste to flee as its successor began tromping on its heels. Seasons often turned upon each other and squabbled like cubs testing strengths and weaknesses. Frances put Jacob to work almost as often as Beatrice did, and he had come to depend upon it.

"I want you to help us up at church," Frances said to him one day, as he was on her patio having tea. He wasn't much for tea, but she put great store by the ritual; and he thought it best to accommodate himself to her ways, even though it seemed to aggravate her propensity to put him to work.

"Sure. But right now, I have a lot to do up at the house, for Beatrice." He added the last to try and keep her aware that a healthy balance of power in the struggle over his surplus labor was only to be expected from the separate heads of state enclosing his little Switzerland. He feared that 'doing work' for the church might expand ridiculously if he were not careful. He was not too keen on assisting that barbarous hierarchy.

"We're getting ready for the Fish Fry."

He could only stare, seeing how solemn Frances was acting. Her age was difficult to assess. Her complexion was lightly mottled, but her features were still firm, and handsomely molded.

"Doesn't that start right before Lent?"

"We start . . . well, we start whenever we want." She concluded the comment as if to the officious assembly of her private doubts.

"And when is that?"

"The first Friday after Labor Day."

"What do you want me to do?"

"You see, we have very tasty fish; but those damn Lutherans seem to get all the trade. Even our Catholics go trooping up that hill to their fish fry. Do you see the problem?"

"I do." Jacob had been around her long enough to know once she was comfortable with someone she would speak her mind as one might to a passive audience. Here Jacob had no idea where he stood on the recondite issue of rival churches vying for the local, blessed fish trade. She appraised him sharply, aware he might be considering her in a satiric light.

"You do, what?"

"See how perfidious the Lutherans are."

"Okay now, no one said that. But they are vexing!" Her right hand clenched into a fist and rose up over the table as if she had a council there before her ready to put her words into action on fields of battle. "I just want, I just think . . ." She steadied herself and bore in. "Jacob, we need to make our Fish Fry the one people want to come to, so we can raise more money for our causes. So, can you be up there, with your truck, on Thursday? That's the last day the professional workers will be there, finishing up what they have to do."

"What time?"

"Come around two or so, we're mostly going to map out our plans, for moving forward."

"Where should I meet you?"

"Do you know where the Grotto is?"

"Yes." He felt his head swim a little as though the air were suddenly a fluid medium and his senses needed a moment to adjust to the change of elements. Frances became a little blurry.

"What's the matter?"

"Nothing. Thursday. Bring the truck. I got it."

"At the Grotto."

"Yes. Yes."

"Okay." He started walking off.

"Wait!"

He stopped in his tracks and turned to look back.

"Thanks, Jacob."

"No problem." He spun around, waving an arm high over his head. He decided he wanted to improve his version of one of the old cherished songs; doing so had an almost narcotic effect on his temperament these days. It felt like the highest grade of sinful pleasure a wandering child could possibly know. As a boy he used to skip mass and use his knowledge of the labyrinth beneath the church to try and play one of the guitars kept in storage there. He just now understood that his getting caught one morning, by one of the nuns, must have resulted in his mother buying him one for Christmas! It seemed as if ever since he had never been able to put away this penchant for retreating to his musical sanctuary, almost as if he were making an act of contrition.

———◆———

Saint Margaret's is located at the corner of Chambers and Elizabeth. The latter artery rises gently from the south with the grace of a country lane, sweeps by all the parish structures, and issues northward to lose its name in the Missouri bottomlands. The original church was much smaller than the edifice standing there now. It faced onto Elizabeth. A large addition was added in the flush postbellum years, and this wing ran parallel to Elizabeth, and presently it serves as the main body of the church. The original interior was greatly altered, and afterwards there remained passageways secreted behind the altar leading into the school building. Several alcoves once used as confessionals in the earlier structure were left idle.

Jacob parked his truck in the upper lot and walked past the old gnarled buckeye trees he remembered from his childhood. He turned into the paved area that swept around the back of the church and spotted Frances and the workers over by the Grotto. They had just finished laying down a pad of bricks in a decorative oval design, spread out in front of the Madonna. Four venerable sassafras trees were ranged around the perimeter of the little courtyard. He saw Frances put her hand on one man's shoulder, saying something that caused his head to jolt upwards. He started laughing from his belly. As he walked off towards his brethren she spun around to accost Jacob.

"Good." She said simply.

"That looks great," he said, looking at the new flagging.

"It was a splendid idea. And they've done a superb job." She was beaming. The aspect of the Grotto was transformed; it now begged for a human presence to gather there. Two nuns assigned to the parish came out of their abode and turned in unison to look at the construction site as they strode by, heading for the school building.

"Those aren't really proper habits." Frances said as her eyes flicked over the modern vestments of these two younger women. Jacob knew he was not expected to act as though he had heard this pronouncement. He reverted to the previous moment when they had been admiring improvements to the grounds.

"The sassafras trees are perfect." He said.

"Yes, I told them no way are they cutting those down. I could see how that would complement the design." Frances put a long finger up tapping at her chin. "I told our volunteers we need a rock wall around the flanks of the grotto structure." She said, turning to look at him for assurance. "I wanted you to help them with that part."

"A wall?"

"Just a low wall." Her tone rose slightly. "To keep it separate from that section at the crest of the hill with the birch trees. I want to keep that area separate, as natural as possible."

He thought suddenly of his satisfaction when he had worked for his uncle, making sure material landed at the job site when it was needed. He made sure the superintendents were kept happy, and their crews productive, so the owners would come back for more trade. Something else was on his mind, though; he had been trying to avoid thoughts of the last time he had stood here. One time he had been there at the Grotto with his sister Johanna, it could not haven been very long before her death. Afterwards, he had come back, to stand here, before the Madonna, to pray to her. He was not clear why he had done so. He had been too young to seek redemption. He looked away as the memories assailed him, provoking a surge of unsettling emotions.

"I can't pay you for this work," Frances said to him, sensing he was disturbed.

"Oh, that's no problem."

"I am asking Cody to give us a hand, and I think he should be paid."

"Absolutely. I used to attend this school, you know."

"Yes, I know."

He nodded, afraid to look at her; he was thinking of his sister again and he didn't really know what Frances knew about Johanna. His mother had initially suggested he contact Frances about getting an apartment in Ferdinand, but he forgot what she told him regarding her own relationship to this quite remarkable woman. He had almost the little boy's innocent faith that all older women were confederated in a league that watched over little boys to make sure they did not become hopelessly besotted by the seductive joys children hold in trust for higher powers, that are not altogether of this world.

"Let me introduce you to some of the men."

He offered up his truck so that others could use it to round up materials, tools, and people. He became one of the day laborers working for the masons who were building the little wall, and adding other touches about the Grotto with a variety of stonework. He was put to work with a shovel and a large, nasty wheelbarrow, which sought to embarrass its handler at the most inopportune moments. Jacob managed to turn his clumsiness into comic relief. They appreciated his wit and strenuous efforts. The day they finished the job and were being cut loose Cody and Jacob took a moment to talk with Frances outside the cafeteria under the church, where they held the fish fry.

"Well, thanks for the help, you two. And the use of your truck earlier, Jacob." Frances spoke with quiet sincerity.

"Do you know that woman talking to those guys at the picnic table?" Jacob asked her.

"Why yes. Why do you ask?"

"I met her before."

"Where?"

"At our party, at The Joint."

"She was there? That's not really her kind of thing, I can tell you that."

Somewhat startled by her dismissive attitude Jacob studied her face and saw that Frances was staring at the woman with a protective look that increased his curiosity.

"Does she go to this church?"

"Oh yes, since she was a child."

Jacob noticed Cody was also staring at Frances, waiting to see what other information she was going to share with Jacob. He was mindful that Cody belonged to this parish, and he did not, as he watched her countenance undergoing the effects of strong emotion. She kept her silence. They took their leave of her and began walking home. Jacob had walked to the church that day because they no longer needed his truck, and now walking on these sidewalks evoked countless subtle feelings that were but the barest rudiments of memories, and all the more precious for that reason.

"Did she pay you for this work?" Cody asked.

"No."

"Then why is she paying me?"

Jacob looked around at the neighborhood as he walked, acting as if he hadn't heard his friend.

"Huh?" Cody insisted.

"Fuck, I don't know. You know Frances. She still calculates everything with her nun's rosary, not an abacus."

"What does that mean?"

"What's the problem? My family gave me a truck. Do you want to explain to me why they did that? Why do you give a truck to a derelict? Can you tell me that? Oh, never mind. I never know what you're talking about Cody; ever since you told me you prefer the Stones to the Beatles, I can't trust anything you say."

"I said I listen to them more, just because there's more there. You can't deny it. The catalogue is amazing."

"More there . . . I don't want to hear it."

"Just look at the length of their career. I mean they're still going! The sheer output of the group is incredible."

"You don't know what you're talking about."

"All those albums with Mick Taylor, you can't tell me those aren't as good as what the Beatles were doing; and they were starting something new, around that same time the Beatles were ending their run. The dumb shits. And what about *Exile on Main Street*?" As he warmed to his argument Cody resorted to tactics analogous to those banned by the Geneva Convention. "Besides, everyone knows the Beatles are overrated."

"You're an infidel. You'll burn, Cody, you'll burn for that."

"It's like trench warfare and mustard gas."

Jacob had lectured Cody on music several times, with extreme unction, perhaps, and now had to pay the piper, perhaps. He could be a pompous fellow in matters of musical appreciation, and it didn't take much for him to feel suddenly ridiculous, when passions ran too high. He had learned much since his dogmatism had begun to wane. The enjoyment of music was in the care of each listener, and the arcane knowledge that lay underneath one's subjective love for a particular song was beyond the reasoning power of human intellects. In some respects, we are all tone deaf to the original chromatic scales pulsed earthward by the spheres. We have no knowledge of how they were first spun together, nor why they move us as they do, from such distances.

They were passing underneath the huge dead elm tree. This corner house had been a definite mile marker to the boy, who numerous times turned there to go down Darst towards home. There were two stately sycamores down that way leaning over the sidewalk, which is constantly being fractured and molded over their ancient roots.

"Cody, do you know that woman?" Jacob was reflecting upon the way she had folded her arms across her chest, dropping her head, reserving judgment as the men at the picnic table strove for her approval. Her composure seemed to cast them under a spell. The image resonated in his own breast as he recalled seeing her at the fire pit at the end of the party.

"Who are you talking about now?" Cody exclaimed.

"That one sitting at the picnic table. I asked Frances about her, but she wouldn't really tell me anything. You know the one I mean. Is her name Holly?"

"It's Molly!" Now he was acting irritated by Jacob's curiosity.

"That's right! I talked to her at the party."

"Yeah? I was surprised she went to that."

"They came late, to check it out, probably on a whim—"

"Her and Janey?" Cody had become rather solemn.

"Yeah. They came up through the yards, and then left the same way, just like we used to do in the old days."

"She lost her husband and her son in a car accident. A drunk driver hit them. Only the drunk survived."

"Wow," Jacob whispered, thinking, so that's why Frances had been looking at her that way. He was about to ask when this had happened when Cody supplied the answer.

"It was three years ago, on her birthday; they were rushing out to get something, last minute . . ."

"Oh man. Oh, now I see . . ."

They kept walking down Elizabeth towards Church Street. Everything was familiar and strange to Jacob. All the trees were as friends and they were of a forgiving nature; never holding anything against humankind.

"Are you going to the Fish Fry?" Jacob asked him, then thought again; "Oh, you probably have to work, don't you?"

"Yeah, I'll have to miss the opening this year. You going?"

"I don't know; I guess so. Do they get a pretty good crowd?"

"Well, we're starting to do better, since Frances got involved last year. They gave her the franchise to run as she wants, and it's done a lot of good. All these improvements on the grounds, that's her idea; she wants to serve more people outside this year."

"That should help a lot."

"She's the one who convinced them to start it early, take advantage of the good autumn weather. Her idea is, why lock yourself into the religious calendar. She's a pretty sharp old gal, you know."

"No doubt."

Cody explained how Frances originally became the manager of the Fish Fry by force of her personality. One day the head priest perceived some irregularity in her methods and she dismissed him from *her* scullery. He became incensed and rebuked her; whereupon she departed in wrathful protest. The next Fish Fry the entire staff, which she had recruited, failed to show up, and many parishioners refused to attend as well. Subsequently, there was a great stir among the flock; emotions grew heated, feelings hardened, and factions began to coalesce.

In her distress Frances decided to call a very unorthodox bishop she had befriended in Baltimore, alleging she had noticed sinful proclivities. The worldly prelate, whose idol was Cardinal Richelieu, engaged her in a round of licentious badinage. Her retorts made him cackle. He inquired further into the matter and discovered a dossier on her irascible foe, taking it upon himself to call a prominent personage in the St. Louis diocese. In due time the priest was told to stand down; and shortly thereafter was transferred to another parish. Frances was invited to enter into contractual obligations concerning St. Margaret's Fish Fry.

Jacob was thoroughly delighted by the tale. He could imagine the behavior of Frances throughout the ordeal; seeing in his mind exactly how she would have conducted herself in each moment. He experienced a curious feeling of having been there with her, as one standing on the sidelines, cheering lustily at the final gun.

"You don't mess around with Frances," Cody said and they both laughed.

As the story unfolded they had stopped walking to stand by the concrete post at the top of Church Street. Now they commenced walking again, but only for a short while before parting ways. Jacob tramped over the fringes of several yards to get to Spencer's hill, and from thence climbed up to his abode. Cody continued up the slight grade and then down the steeper hill on Church Street to his home at the bottom.

Jacob began pondering various things he had heard about Frances. He tried to imagine her in a nun's habit, like those he had seen the nuns wear when he was a student at St. Margaret's. Those sisters belonged to the *ancien régime* and wore the long heavy black dresses that were truly befitting an ancient cult, girded about by decorative chains attached to fearsome crosses. A sort of personal chapel structure was clamped onto the head, setting the face in a position of being bound to face demurely and directly whatever tribulation was forthcoming. The upper body was adorned with an inflexible white breastplate, fashioned to keep the tender entreaties of school boys from touching directly upon their hearts.

He recalled seeing them glide in their long gowns up the sidewalk on Elizabeth, their feet invisible, their hands also buried in folds of black drapery, and by miraculous means seeming to move forward like figures spun out of fairy tales. There was a gentle motion of the costume heaving back and forth as they made ponderous headway. He imagined the stern, unbending characters striving against a relentless gravity, ascending the long suburban grade, making gentle progress towards some abysmal destination sequestered in their hearts. He laughed at the picture, eager to get back to his guitar, keen on having a productive session before returning to his chores. Keeping time was about heeding the correct measures; and he often moved these days in accordance with a melody that was never heard, but only sensed, as one might feel an unseen energy source. Something as pure (and dangerous) as the sunlight that has refined from dull matter a symphony of desires for sentient blood to resolve into final, lasting products.

26

Jacob was leery of going to the Fish Fry. He rarely attended church services as an adult; his religious practice had definitely lapsed. And yet he knew so many good Catholics, and preserved so many good memories gathered in while attending St. Margaret's. The church and school had comprised inseparable parts of one whole that embodied a better part of his happy childhood. He still felt ecstatic responses to the music in his heart; recalling the glorious moral weight of those soaring carols. He used to stare up into the heavy finished rafters, wishing to perch there like an owl, wanting to sing in a manner that would fill certain girls with rapturous wonder.

He finally decided to go in case Frances needed his help. As he walked through the yards to get up to Elizabeth he was nagged by a nervous uncertainty, as if he'd left something behind. The parking lot that wraps around the back of the church was blocked off to traffic to leave space for the attendees to congregate. Jacob gravitated towards the area between the school entrance and the doors to the cafeteria under the church. Frances soon put him to work setting up tables and chairs on the patio at the Grotto. After he and a few other men had finished the task he took a moment to inspect the familiar Madonna. The blue robe was fading into dingy white; the cosmetic plaster was badly riven by the defacements of time. Jacob was sure there must be a plan afoot to supplant this replica with a newer model to achieve harmony with all the other improvements.

Standing there in something of a trance he thought of Johanna; how good it would be if only she had lived to give of herself, from that good heart she possessed. She would very likely be active at some parish just like this one. She would be a mom. He wondered, would they still be best friends? He was approached from behind by Molly, who eased up beside him.

"Have you brought the lady a special petition?"

He swung around, startled to see her. He had been stealing glances at her all the while he was busy setting up the tables. She had been sitting at a picnic table over by the tall chain-link fence along the crest of the upper level, conversing with two men; one of them an elderly fellow, the other was about his own age, somewhat foppish in his attire.

"I was just taking a moment." The words just came out of him. At once he was fascinated by an almost imperceptible shimmer clearly active in her eyes. He felt delicate notes of receptive warmth passing through a veil of infinite reserve. A pained expression came onto his features. She watched as a shadow passed over his face, as though he had seen a ghost. She knew immediately that he must be aware of her tragic losses. He looked away, adjusting his demeanor, and then turning towards her again he spoke with enthusiasm.

"I really like how they've used the sassafras trees." He could feel her eyes on him.

"They really accentuate the space. I have to say, you've done good work here."

He looked at her, becoming unconscious of himself, enraptured by the color of her eyes.

"He's certainly admiring me!" She thought to herself with delicious whimsy. And he most certainly was; transfixed as by a sort of luminous presence. To him the rich gray color was suggestive of those thrilling clouds that stir up suddenly over houses in the spring and augur storms that leave one mesmerized while sitting on a front porch.

"I was just a laborer." He said, somewhat flustered. He had been thinking of her since he had arrived, and was caught up in superstitious sensations now that she was standing before him. He looked upon her visage; imagining a rare sort of sanctity. He recalled how she had acted at the fire pit, and for reasons he could not comprehend, a curious reticence beset him.

"I thought you were a Russian monk?"

His head tilted up after a quick glance at her face and he began to chortle.

"Yes, I suppose I am. But I've got another job now, I'm chief groundskeeper."

"Yes, I've seen you outside a time or two on my walks."

"Did you go to St. Margaret's as a kid?"

"Oh yeah, graduated at the head of my class."

"Really?"

"No, but I might have been at the head of the mob rushing out at the end."

He was intrigued by the expressive show of subtle variations in her mood. She seemed always to have several themes going at once in her mind as she spoke of common things. Now she displayed a natural, delightful curiosity to know more of the stranger she was addressing. The honesty of this benevolent trait was evident in her voice, and shone forth perfectly from her eyes. He thought if only he knew her a lot better, he would accuse her of being a sorceress. That smile! She seemed to know things about him that he himself could hardly guess. He was surprised by an inexplicable wave of playfulness that lifted him up out of himself and pushed him forward against his will. Her personality spoke to him like a beloved musical passage he was struggling to master.

"Did you go to Margaret's?" She asked him.

"Yes, through the fifth grade; then I went to public school."

"Why?"

"We moved out of the parish."

"How come?"

He wasn't sure what to tell her. "My father couldn't work for a while, he had an accident at work."

"Oh."

It felt so natural talking to her. He was on the verge of broaching the subject of his sister's death, but he caught himself before tumbling into that pit of remorse.

"Say, who are those two guys at the picnic table?" He asked her.

"Oh, that's Cook and Hereford. I've known Isaac Cook for about a year now. He came home to care for his dying mother, and then he had to settle her estate. He's from Margaret's. Paul Hereford is a friend of his. I've just met him recently. Not really sure what his story is. They make quite a pair—if you like senseless arguments—I can tell you that much."

"They like camping out at that picnic table."

"Yes they do. That's become their post. The workers from the Grotto dragged the table up there from the lower level, and now they've taken it over for their deliberations."

"Deliberations?"

"Come on, I'll introduce you." Her hand grazed his elbow as she turned around.

"What?" His eyes followed unchastely after her retreating figure. She was petite in her upper body, the breasts under a white lacy blouse appeared to be models of voluptuous understatement. Her hips swelled out in her worn jeans like fulsome paeans to motherhood. She had long slender legs. She moved with sure gracefulness, despite a medley of peculiar motions, which belonged to her alone. She wore plain white tennis shoes, and was no athlete, and did not need to be one to exhibit the more valuable charms that were the cardinal features of her feminine power. As they approached the picnic table the men there began to speak louder, as if to put forth an example of local customs for this unexpected emissary.

"What's the difference between the English Empire and the Third Reich?"

"Masterpiece Theatre?"

"Cleverly done, babu. No."

"More humane treatment of the coolies? No ovens."

"That's closer, yes. The tolerance of squalor and misery for an under-class, by the governing power, versus the attempt to devise a pure Valhalla here on earth."

"Treating the potato famine as a piece of bad luck for English land-lords; having to work that much harder to export the grain out of Ireland."

"Not to mention the nasty business of having to evict tenants while they are also starving."

"Bloody awful, and beggars everywhere! A blight on the lovely scenery."

Jacob was struck by the relish they took in making shocking state-ments. It reminded him of his nieces and nephews when they were little children, always desperate for attention, wanting adults to watch them in some act they believed they had just mastered. The mantra was, "Look at me, look at me." Why *did* humans crave attention from others in that way?

"It's a savage, wasteful game, this thing we call human progress." Isaac Cook said in his best rendition of magisterial calm.

Molly put her closed hand up to her chin. Jacob saw that she was frown-ing, as if going over unpalatable alternatives in her mind. Then she inter-rupted the two men at the table to introduce Jacob. He had noticed how the countenance of the more elderly man became resplendent as soon as he saw Molly approaching; then it reverted to a philosophical cast to make his speech. Now it was again almost boyishly solicitous of her approval.

"Isaac says you're attracted to our Grotto because Russians like their icons so much." Molly spoke to Jacob.

"You were talking about my order, were you?" Jacob said, taking up her facetious tone; flattered that she had been talking about him to these men.

"We talk about everyone around here, that's what we do." Isaac confid-ed, peering at Jacob out of guarded brown eyes full of seasoned merriment.

"Molly?" The younger of the two, Paul Hereford, caught her attention. "Isaac tells me all of this would make a good movie."

"Or maybe a good novel." Molly retorted, narrowing her eyes as she looked at Hereford, who was a novelist.

"All of what?" Jacob asked, feeling excluded from something essential to the ritual unfolding before him.

"Too long," Paul said, meaning an explanation wasn't worth the effort.

"Too tedious, as well." Isaac affirmed.

"And too boring, definitely." Molly put the final touch on the little joke. "Jacob, you have to know, these two never stop talking, and if they run out of topics, they just chatter like parrots." Molly glanced over at the tables by the Grotto, where several people were sitting, casually observing her movements in a furtive way. Some smiled knowingly, while others took pains to register sour disgruntlement at seeing others behaving in a way they did not understand, and were sure no one should countenance.

"Do you want something to drink?" She addressed Jacob brusquely. He heard the word 'drink' as a fish feels the barb, and froze for an instant.

"That's right, we have a liquor license now." Isaac said. "We're up against the degenerate Lutherans. Come on, Mr. Gates, you need to do your part. You can't just be hanging around for purposes of private edification. Offer up your liver."

"Will you get drinks for us?" Paul pleaded with Molly in what he must have thought was an appealing manner for a gallant beau.

"Okay, okay. You two are helpless, and hopeless. More red wine?"

"Yes, give strong drink to one who is perishing," Isaac said with glee.

"Let all who are simple come in here." Molly fired back, a wicked twist on her lips.

"He gave to men the vine to cure their sorrows." Isaac savored this reference to Dionysus with his eyes locked on Molly.

"For curing maybe, not drowning," Molly quipped.

"Whatever is needful for men, who claim more than mortals may."

"Which *you* always do." Molly leaned closer to needle him.

"You are the enemy!" He declaimed. "You rise above us without pity."

Molly shook her head, very pleased, and they both started laughing with unaffected delight.

When Isaac's mother had been alive Frances convinced him to teach an adult class, providing a secular context for the Bible stories, on Saturdays in the cafeteria. Molly had assisted in this endeavor, and they fell into a routine of repairing to Isaac's house afterwards, where they greatly amused his mother with the most ungodly banter. They treated her to comic versions of the historical curricula they were teaching the inquisitive students, who had previously only tasted the church pabulum fed to them as children. A vital gleam returned to the frail woman's eyes as she was included in their purgative fun.

At a much younger age she had been notorious, in some circles, for her wholly irreverent and caustic wit. These commentaries regarding the historical basis of scripture were conducted in a very relaxed tenor, over glasses of wine selected from the richly furnished cellar. The atmosphere was conducive to sharing personal feelings on even the most delicate subjects. Jacob had no knowledge of these things, but he could see the warmth passing between these two people, and it subconsciously predisposed him to a favorable opinion of Isaac. He was startled when Molly turned to him with fierce determination.

"Now tell me, what do you want?"

"Me?"

"Do you want beer or wine?"

"What kind of beer do they have?" Jacob acted very serious.

"I don't know." Molly's voice was instantly that of a maternal scold. "It's cold, probably. We charge 'exorbitant prices,' according to Hereford, here; but it's served in a plastic cup—and you will be served by me! Maybe. So, yes or no, buddy?"

"Yeah, put up or shut up—what's his name?"

"Jacob."

"He's a young patriarch."

"In training, are you?"

"Well?" Molly leaned closer to him. He wanted to tease her in a monstrous fashion just to see what she would do, but her imploring eyes made him relent.

"Yes, something fermented, in a plastic cup. That would be splendid." Jacob caught the glint of a mischievous smile as she turned to go.

So then he was left with these two voluble characters. He stood there, looking about, trying to think of a good excuse before taking his leave.

But no, now he had a beer coming! He was unaware of how closely he was still watching Molly as she walked to the area between the church and the school where there was a low decorative iron fence around a group of tables. Several groups of elderly people were dining there. Molly stopped outside the cafeteria entrance and began talking to a young girl; when she finished that discussion the girl traipsed off in a skipping dance. Then several more people closed around her at once. When she broke free from that group the only two black women present drew her aside for a conversation. It grew very animated. Jacob watched as the three women began laughing, several times bending over and reaching out to touch one another lightly in their merriment.

"That little girl was her daughter Sophie," Isaac said to him. He looked around and saw that both of the men had been watching him intently as he had continued to observe Molly.

"How long have you known Molly?" Isaac asked him.

"Not long. I met her, very briefly at a party, and then now, here, again."

"You met her at that thing held up at The Joint?"

"That's right." He wondered how they seemed to know so much about everything.

"You look somewhat smitten, Jacob."

"No I don't," he said, flushing. "How old do you suppose she is?"

"I don't have to suppose, she's thirty-five." Isaac said. "I'm sixty, and Hereford here is forty, and he thinks he has perfected an ageless prose style."

Hereford shook his head, smiling. "I never said anything about having perfected anything. In fact, I said everything ages! You should probably know that Cook here has spent his life scripting very lucrative but trashy TV programs. He thinks nothing lasts, or is meant to last, and that all is in flux; and therefore TV is the perfect medium."

"That's not even close to being accurate. And you meant to say pap."

"Even better."

"Don't they show reruns all the time on cable TV?" Jacob asked.

They both looked at him.

"What sort of books do you read?" Hereford asked him.

"I have a complete set of Dostoevsky in my quarters. I've been reading that in my spare time."

"Ah, very good. Have you read any of that other blasted Christian, Tolstoy?" Hereford asked. "You don't want to end up like him, of course—"

"No, nothing else, much." They began interrogating him about literature and discovered the only thing he had ever read was these texts he had recently found, and his study of these was cursory. They prized out of him a succinct, expurgated story of how he ended up in the basement with tiny, furry footmen, and then became a groundskeeper at the manse. Cook sort of leaned back, as much as one can while sitting at a picnic table, to appraise Jacob in silent meditation.

"Well, I think that's damn fine, really." He looked at Hereford. "That's the stuff, right there. That's what I mean, Hereford. There's your fodder."

Paul Hereford appeared somewhat suspicious. First of all, there was the fact Molly had brought Jacob over to them, and that was sufficient cause to accept Jacob graciously, simply to stay in her good graces. Then again, one should have to pay his dues, before being seated at the table.

"Why quibble over what someone has read?" Isaac pronounced; and then they launched into another diatribe fashioned as a duet.

What had Henry David Thoreau read? None of the gospels put down by our Lost Generation crowd, nothing by the modern disciples, Hemingway, Fitzgerald, Steinbeck, Wolfe and Faulkner. What had Isaiah read? Or Jeremiah? And Homer? Moses? What salacious pulp inspired Adam, or his patron, Yahweh? What essential scrolls are there, really? Who's to say that anything needs to be read? Wasn't the moral law said to be written upon the heart? Jacob tried to read their faces as the two erudite Gregorians released a flood of plainsong over the old weathered table.

Then a woman sadly not Molly brought them their drinks, and appeared to be none too happy about it herself. Molly had explained to the other woman, 'I don't have time to start jabbering with them right now. Please. Pretty please.' Jacob had seated himself at the table upon invitation. He was intrigued by the way they moved from topic to topic at a frenetic pace. Their dispassionate curiosity about the human species seemed endless. They spoke of white flight, the new crime bill wending through Congress, yet more church scandals, Max Weber, and suddenly they were engaged in an excursus on the human penchant for creating hierarchies.

"Maybe the only way to have a consistent vision of society, is by viewing it from the very top, or the very bottom," Hereford said.

"That doesn't help you very much, does it?" Cook said sardonically.

"In one case, you have to look up through the distorting lens of resentment; and from the other end, you are forced to look down through the foul atmosphere of contempt, bred by the callous growth of entitlement."

They interrupted the rhetorical flow on occasion to ask Jacob questions and he gladly answered them. He took pleasure in feeling no obligation to try and keep up with their incredible verbosity. They filled his ears with words he did not know and he considered he might get a dictionary, mainly for use with his own texts. He sensed the source of their steady scrutiny; they wanted to know why Molly had brought him over to them. He did too.

After a while Molly returned to the table, which instantly inflated the lungs of these men. To amuse her they spoke about those people of the parish she knew well, ever careful to monitor her reactions. Isaac and Molly exchanged information on matters of which the other two men had no knowledge. At one point Isaac grew reflective.

"I think I'll go to Santa Fe before too long."

"What's out there?" Hereford demanded.

"A desert girds it round. If I pack correctly, I could become a Bedouin."

"Make sure to search the fringes for broken faiths." Paul suggested.

"And then there's that magic staircase in the chapel. I might try and walk up that rickety thing, if they don't stop me. Cry out like Job from the top."

"Bring a bottle of good vintage wine, so you'll be able to give a toast when they find you in the wreckage."

"No, I'll brandish the Book of Changes at them."

"If they throw you in jail, you can write a letter to the world from Santa Fe. The pitfalls to avoid on the stairway to heaven."

Jacob noticed that Molly kept a fond eye on Isaac. She knew more about his thoughts than were revealed by his speech alone. The man appeared frail in his physical bearing, but he roused himself when espousing a cause. When he spoke of himself, however, he became as the aged Roman patrician, who suddenly finds himself having to live the simple Stoic life he had extolled and avoided his entire life. He was one of those rare expatriates, the conquistador who carries his flag at last to unspoiled lands of wisdom.

Before leaving for the evening Jacob stepped over in front of the statue again. He was possessed by a memory of looking over from another section of the school grounds and seeing his sister Johanna standing in the Grotto area, facing this same statue. Her arms were pressed at her sides, or possibly clasped down in front of her. She had been perfectly still, as though lost in thought. He could not remember when that was, or anything else about the episode, even the time of day, but he knew it must have been shortly before her death. He now remembered there were leaves in the air being blown about his sister's steady, unmoving figure. She stood there as if she were praying. He tried and failed to do the same now. Molly was watching him from inside the cafeteria, remembering what Frances had told her about his sister Johanna dying of scarlet fever. She watched Jacob turn and walk away down the hill towards the field below. She understood at once that he was trying to get away from something and closer to it at the same time, and he needed to let his emotions run away for a while.

27

On Saturday Jacob rose at dawn, put on his overalls and loped from window to window making his customary surveillance of the grounds. He could not have explained why he did this every morning; it was now ingrained habit. He gulped down several cups of coffee while poring over one of his texts, almost insensibly, not able to concentrate on the printed page.

He devoured an apple while walking the grounds. He threw the core onto the path by the pine trees. He was cutting the grass when one of the neighbors beckoned him to come over, requesting that he cut her lawn for a fair exchange of legal currency. Afterwards they sipped Coca-Cola from large glasses filled with actual ice cubes. It brought him back to an effervescent state, having sweat running dry on the face in the shelter of a mature tree's generous shade, while sharing old sovereign pieces of his mind with a congenial woman. Then it began, the sensation of being in a role, and the necessity of staying true to the spirit of this ordinary life he did not understand.

Once back at the Spencer estate he armed himself with garden tools and tackled the Stalingrad of shrubbery behind the stalls. On previous forays he had made good headway, but the offensive had stalled; today Cody came over and they renewed the attack against the stronghold in great fervor, determined to remove it root and branch. They moved massive boulders by main force towards the trees at the back of the lot. A mess of rusting cans and other human litter had to be disposed of, and they cut and stacked pieces of dead wood along the back of the lot. There, a stand of trees and shrubbery separated the property from the hill that descended down to the back yard of a house facing onto Elizabeth. They were sitting on two of the boulders when Beatrice came by to check on things. She exclaimed over their progress.

"You've gotten most of it cleared away!" She had her hair clamped on the back of her head in a casual knot that was very becoming, and she was wearing loose comfortable clothing that made her appear more youthful, at ease, and comfortable.

"It's a clean slate," Jacob said.

"The sunken garden," she replied. "We'll have to think about this some more. We'll need trees. When we have the design ready we should plant some ornamental trees immediately. I guess we should get a rendering done." She was now friendly with a landscape artist who was a consultant for one of the larger nursery chains, and she kept him busy sketching out her visions. Many of these plans would never be brought to fruition; but she enjoyed collecting the various scenes, reveling in the act of designing positive change.

"Your brother Matthew says he has something for you."

"What's that?"

"He didn't say. Some tools, I think. He said he tried to call."

"I guess I missed it." Lately Jacob had heard from some of his old friends, and others were responding directly to those first strange letters they had received when he was going through his bewildering phase of withdrawal from the world. He felt obligated to restore proper relations with certain people, who seemed to understand, somehow, that he had gone on hiatus for reasons of his own keeping. Some people were able to overlook his retreat; others wanted to maintain a safe distance, lest he become a burden, or an embarrassment, to them. He could only smile at such exemplary caution used by ordinary folks so naturally.

Earlier in the day Cody had complained to him that he did not think his wife was getting enough exercise. Jacob responded by saying she had to exercise caution every day, being with him. You ass, was how Cody answered him.

"Who in this world is not a beast of burden?" He had asked Cody, apropos of nothing, in emulation of the terse sermons of Frances.

"That was another good Stones' song," was his reply, between gasps, sweat dripping off his face as he tugged on a stubborn sapling.

"Jacob, you can always use the phone in the house." Beatrice said to him now.

"No, I know. I'm just never up there to hear it ring."

"Do you want one installed in the cottage?"

He hesitated, only now realizing he was imposing on her generosity again.

"I'll get that done, no problem," she said, not waiting for a reply.

Cody looked at him and smiled. "You derelict," he whispered harshly.

"That's Chief Groundskeeper to you, dog."

"You just can't get no satisfaction."

Beatrice watched them having their fun, not even sure what they were jesting about most of the time.

"You have anything going on here this evening?" Jacob asked her.

"No." She shook her head, then began looking around, very pleased with the prospect of having a sunken garden, and possibly a field kitchen where the stalls had once been.

"I was going to make a fire at the pit. Burn some brush; relax a little."

"That's fine. Would you have time today to look at that kitchen cabinet?"

"It's done."

"Oh, great. I haven't gone inside yet."

"Matthew said we should probably strip off the wallpaper in there. Do you want me to start doing that?"

"Sure, sure. Is he coming by this evening?"

"I don't think so, I could call him."

"No, that's alright. Okay, then."

She took her leave after some more small talk. Jacob wondered why he was becoming exuberant about trivial things, and remained at a loss when facing important issues, such as his future. He attempted to address the nature of this malaise, using Cody as a sounding board.

"You just need to get laid, Gates." Cody had little practice listening to a groundskeeper struggle to build from scratch his own apologia.

"That's true enough. I don't see any prospects, though."

"They're all over the place. You could take a run at Bitty."

Jacob began laughing. "That would be so wrong. That would become a gargantuan mess. Besides . . ." But there was no need to say anything more; the evocation of Robert's precedence decided the matter. Cody's face showed that he was no longer interested in the topic anyway.

The truth was, Jacob now deemed that sort of casual sex to be untidy. There was nothing wrong with it, per se, and if a young person wasn't really sure yet how to effect a more lasting union, then it was necessary to find out how cohabitation can be revelatory of a person's convoluted intricacy. Carnal knowledge leads one directly into the inner sanctum of personality. Selfish egos collide, heat is generated, defenses go up, come crashing down, peace is waged; ultimately the home front becomes the lair of that domestic monster boredom. One could go on, but for Jacob, now, it would be like working hard, and assiduously, to earn one's daily bread, and then not caring that it was always stale.

After a while Cody began talking about his wife, and how she was doing better and enjoyed being at work again, but he had a grievance to lodge against his mother-in-law. These complaints were not for public consumption and he knew he could count on Jacob's discretion, so he dumped on his friend as freely as one does when moved to tap an irritable spleen, siphoning off bottom grades of vitriol. Jacob enjoyed the show of trust involved. He took the mother-in-law's side on every point, and Cody, knowing he was just doing that to annoy him, acted oblivious to his barbed wit. He needed to pour out his resentment to the last drop, and then he slapped his hands together, and was done with it, for a while.

"I've got to get going," he said, starting off, then halting and turning. "Hey, who are you having over for the fire?"

"Just me and my ghosts."

"Oh."

"You want to come up, with Sally and the kids? I can get some hot dogs and marshmallows"

"You'd have to get everything to make s'mores, to keep the barbarians happy." Jacob routinely referred to all children as barbarians and Cody had adopted the term.

"Okay, will do."

"No, better yet, we'll get all that stuff. You get the beer, and white wine for Sally."

"Okay. She likes Chardonnay, right?"

"Too damn much, just like her mother."

Jacob snorted his commiseration.

After Cody left Jacob mused upon the old wives' tale that women gossip and men do not. He had known members of both sexes who were terrific gossips and others who were as reticent as the guards at Buckingham Palace, and almost as flashy about it. Maybe an old husband's tale should address how the male is the weaker sex in the arts of mending a broken heart. These days the world often became as his own toy sphere, something to turn over in his mind. He took a sumptuous break with his guitar; playing "Longer Boats" by Cat Stevens, only partially whispering the words, and with painstaking care trying to perfect his own version.

He gathered dry sticks and branches down in the path along the back of the property, piling them in little stacks. He knew Cody's children would enjoy using the sturdy wagon kept in the garage to haul this ready fuel to the fire pit. In the dusk they were all assigned duties and a fire was built that used elementary magic to hold them encircled about the flames in a trance. They sat on the ground talking of their own little kingdom; drinking soda, beer and wine, and talking listlessly of topics that touched on grave matters of the world, and coming back ultimately to the dire necessity of getting drowsy children to their safe, comfortable beds.

Jacob watched them leaving in a troop and felt a pang of fugitive loss, being left there alone. He stirred the embers of the dying fire for a long time. He was full of deep, nebulous emotions that collected around him like the night's glimmering atmosphere. He could hear the coals ticking. Even the insects could not sleep and took turns singing mournful songs. He was feeling tremendous anticipation, but he could not have told you what he was expecting to see change in his life. Something was there; something worth waiting for. It was exciting to have even this intimation of a blessing lying in wait, somewhere out there in the suspended gloom.

Sunday morning he woke up feeling the course of wholesome energy that circulates after a day of enervating labor, and eight hours of sound, wild-eyed sleep. He had dreamed furiously, and remembered nothing. He was taking delivery of the Sunday *Post-Dispatch*, and now he walked to the end of the front yard wearing only a pair of old shorts. Stamping about in his bare feet he suddenly wanted to bellow. He understood why apes pound on their chests and roar when it is suspected neighbors are peeping out in search of damning intelligence regarding peculiar eccentricities. As he retraced his steps he rubbed his impoverished paunch. His bare feet felt good on the grass and the asphalt and the wooden steps and floor of his abode and then up in the air tingling as he ruffled the paper in front of his eyes. The natural integument on the bottom of his feet was getting tougher; he recalled going about barefoot one summer in his childhood, as an experiment . . .

He took up his guitar and ran through scales like a mad student, pushing accelerando flights out past his control. He improvised wild variations of songs already known. He lost himself in his passion for music. Then he was drinking more coffee and reading another story of political scandals; but he couldn't finish the article because he was thinking of the Fish Fry he'd just been to, and the one coming up in only one more week! He found himself pacing again, looking absently out his windows, for a second time that morning, as if he had been left too long in a remote sector on the great wall of his empire.

To calm himself he played an album, *Songs for Beginners* by Graham Nash, and listened to every phrase and nuance of the music. He had his large stereo system with him again, taken out of storage, and it made a difference. The space resonated with the quickening of his most joyful essence as he experienced that sweet renewal of being moved by one's favorite songs. In a short while the spell was broken. He needed to do something. He set out to clear his mind on the sidewalks and wound up at Wabash Park. At the far end of the lake he noticed a triad of black cherry trees. One was was quite remarkable; not much more than a sapling, already possessing unusual grace in the sinuous structure of its limbs.

The pond was a placid mirror reflecting the trees and the premature autumn colors seen on several of the branches, flung over their own dying shades. The trees stood there, as if contemplating the water in that silent majesty of unquestionable beauty. Jacob experienced a feeling he had not felt in a long time, and he was unable in that moment to place it in a rational context. Life just seemed to have such an infinite range of possibilities; conscious life was a shocking book of innumerable pages. Understanding required more than just leafing through the same pages in the same order time after time. The first and the last were bound by the same threads. There was something to be said for letting the whole be whole, for getting out of the way, and not thinking, when the mind was drawing upon miraculous powers of vision.

He began walking again; it was not advisable to spend too much time standing like a vagrant searching for scraps of something precious reflected off the water, or gathered out of the fleecy clouds hanging overhead. It was no good grasping after something unknown lying between the world and the mirror of the world. His steps were bolstered by the sound of the cicadas going mad again. They acted as though they had a reliable source confirming that the Book of Revelation was coming true, and only the chosen were aware of this momentous news. They were no longer singing to promote social movements, but to encourage themselves individually as they entered into the actual prophecy of their apocalyptic faith.

Jacob climbed the hill towards the quarter mile track of the junior high and walked around the grassy skirt of that plateau to get to the far corner where the cottonwood trees stood like forlorn sentinels. They had the bearing of knights and lords who have fought and borne wounds, and now are retired in the country, and care for nothing but the courtly songs of troubadours that excite old memories. The leaves of the cottonwood trees regaled him with soft noble chatter. He took his fill of these songs in which trees attempt to give voice to the wisdom regarding the necessity of experiencing the splendor of summer days.

Jacob listened attentively while looking up through the tree branches at the beaming sky. He appraised the bronze hue coming over the leaves and heard the changed timbre of the sound when the earth's breath made them flutter. He began wondering what was the earliest time people went to the Fish Fry; the first ones who were part of the crew, who had volunteered to help out. He wanted to get there in the first wave, to see if there was anything more he could do to help out. He would have to wait all week, though, and that plunged him into this curious state of confusion that was trailing him at every turn. Why did he have to wait to stumble upon something ready made before mounting his own spirit of wonder? No winged messengers appeared to guide him. He questioned himself, under the spell of leafy incantations; staring up at lazy, puffed-out clouds, clearly under full sail and yet seeming to stand still from his vantage. His longing to embark upon his life's true course allowed a deeper breath to enter into his spirit.

28

On Friday Jacob performed a variety of chores in the Spencer house and then cleaned up certain areas around the yard. Taking a break, he walked down to see what Cody was doing, and found, to his dismay, that Frances was in the process of forming a press-gang, comprised of Cody and Gregory, and he was too slow-witted to avoid taking a shift himself. The day's task was hauling rocks to her patio area in order to replace the concrete retaining wall with one made of natural stones. She had selected large flat rocks with rich, colorful tones, and the vendor had promised free delivery. However, they ignored her instructions and dropped the load along the curb at the wrong end of the property, right at the street sign for Allen Place.

So they deployed a huge dolly Cody had borrowed from a dubious Mr. Haney, with old rusty wheels, that did not want to follow a straight course. Using much foul language they moved all the stones to the drive-way. Gregory had been wielding a sledge hammer for days to bring down the old wall. They had cleared away most of the rubble, making piles in the driveway for later removal. One of the masons who had worked on the Grotto at St. Margaret's offered to build the new wall for Frances. Jacob inspected the blisters on his hands and sailed off with an airy salutation.

"You going to the Fish Fry?" Cody yelled after him.

"Yeah," Jacob shouted back. He climbed a grassy incline at the end of the driveway and plunged into a thicket of shrubbery and came out on the other side with cobwebs threaded across his face. He looked back smiling, striding down the side yard, then veering to the left and passing out of sight.

"He's psyched up about something." Cody said to no one.

Jacob broke into a jog as he crossed Clay and forced himself to walk again as he went towards home. The weather was ideal for outdoor events. He shaved, showered, and dressed himself in jeans, a button down shirt, and old walking shoes. He tromped down the steps and emerged from the large garage opening, and suddenly spun around and returned, climbing the stairs two at a time, to change into a pair of penny loafers; a signature piece of his attire since high school. He did not reflect on the decision, it just happened. Now he felt it was necessary to take the shortest route so he stepped out like a giant, taking huge, loping strides down Spencer's hill; several times, his loafers losing their traction, his arms flailing, he almost went crashing to the ground. Upon regaining his balance he began laughing in lusty drafts. Once at St. Margaret's he wasn't sure what he should be doing, at first, but then he saw that Cook and Hereford had already taken their places at the picnic table.

"Jacob! Hey boy, how are you!" Isaac yelled. "You're coming pretty early."

"Yeah, who are you looking for?" Paul queried.

"She's not here." Isaac added.

"Yet." Hereford replied.

"Who?" Jacob asked foolishly. "I thought I would come early, to help set up." He remained standing, ready for a bout of playful bantering.

"Sure," Paul said, looking down at his loafers. "They always need good help. They told us they aren't serving drinks yet; so can you go and see if you can use your influence to get our table some wine?"

"My influence?"

"As a Russian monk." Isaac explained with a glint in his eye. "Don't you have some sort of reciprocal arrangement with the fathers of the Mother Church?"

"Well, I may have fallen out of favor with my own order these days. The word is, I've gone rogue."

"You mean, you've gone native," Isaac said.

"God only knows what's happened to me. So, you two heretics want more wine?"

"I don't think it's fair to say we're heretics," Paul acted as though he took umbrage, and wanted to go on record, speaking in a serious tone. "I certainly don't believe in God more religiously than he doesn't believe in Him." He turned towards his friend. "You still *want* to believe, and therefore you're susceptible to believing whatever refurbished concept is dredged up."

"Now I'm thinking of something James B. Eads may have hauled up from the bowels of our great brown god. A primeval skeleton maybe."

"The bones of the Santa Maria."

"A giant gar fish." Jacob contributed.

Isaac and Paul both chortled, happy to be touching their rhetorical foils briskly together in a demonstration for the initiate, and having him partake with some dexterity.

"Now you're going to start loitering around here, flapping your jaws?" Molly was among them, making them all stop to appraise her visage. She was there beside him. Her voice brought forth a virtuoso woodwind section from the far glades of his aching heart. The breathless power of that desire to be in someone's good graces! He had that feeling of hearing a favorite song, which has been heard a thousand times, and which loses its power in the usage; but then the magic regenerates while you wait to hear it again, and when you finally do, it sounds richer than ever. He was lost in a state of exalted confusion.

"They're serving drinks," she said to them invitingly.

"That's good, these characters need some wine to keep their words flowing without too much stagnation." Jacob answered.

"I'll see what I can do for them."

"Wait! Molly?" Isaac did not want to let her go, even on such a vital mission. "We've decided to incorporate the C & H Treacle Company, forming a partnership to work on our ideas."

"We think we have our first project," Paul said with satisfaction.

"What are you going to be selling, footnotes?" Molly's voice had a crisp, dry finish like an expensive vintage.

It was evident Cook and Hereford had been poised to receive her rejoinder. Now they both pitched forward, roaring out their approval. They knocked hands together awkwardly, not adept at such tactics of male camaraderie, being almost exclusively rhetorical gymnasts. Jacob seized the opportunity to observe Molly, as she bit her lower lip in her own delicious savor of this sudden frenzy. She was highly amused by these two incorrigible men who spoke to her so freely of nonsense and weighty matters; as if it were all one prolonged dialogue that constantly needed her imprimatur. Everything was offered for her perspective. She turned to look at Jacob and her eyes gleamed slightly at the sight of him staring at her with that open boyish wonderment. His manner was in stark contrast to the histrionics of these others seeking her approval.

Jacob was too puzzled to respond adequately so he looked away.

"We're thinking of doing a script together." Isaac explained.

"Like experimental theater? Two men and a picnic table? I can't wait." Molly peered down at Isaac with a precious smile.

"Actually," Isaac addressed her in a thoughtful manner, "We want to exploit some of the material we both know; delving into our roots—"

"Grafting what we know of the world to other wild things found in our lost suburban woods." Paul's voice retained the ironic ring of their usual bombast.

"We're really hoping to turn over something fresh." Isaac said, still looking at Molly, who was now listening with her arms folded across her chest.

They laid out the grand scheme. The idea was to use historical personages, along with many people they've actually known, to weave together a narrative.

"It sounds too ambitious," Molly interrupted the presentation. "Why not pick a particular time period, focus on that, and do it justice."

"Justice?" Isaac queried satirically under his breath.

"We won't spend a lot of time on the distant past." Paul protested.

"She's right, you know. Your idea requires too many flashbacks." Isaac stated, looking reproachfully at Paul, who had been raised near the Mississippi River. He wanted to drag the narrative back to a time when the fur trade was thriving.

"The main thing is to capture the arc of the sensibilities, resulting in those that obtain when the main characters enter the stage, in the modern era." Isaac explained.

"Where does the name Florissant come from, anyway?" Jacob interrupted their discussion.

"The word in French was said to mean, blooming, flourishing." Molly recited exactly what Isaac had once told her. She was bemused by the looks she was getting from everyone, simply for knowing this one simple fact. She was preparing to leave them when one of her friends came up to the table and began to physically pull her away to establish more intimacy. Once separated from the table Janey challenged Molly with fierce whispers. Janey was a mother of three, with a wild tangle of curly dark red hair that enclosed a sunny, freckled face. She had very nearly mastered the art of balancing the needs of her willful, gregarious nature, that did not lightly brook being thwarted by social conventions, with the exigencies of being a superb friend. To her family she was a lioness. Since the first grade she and Molly had been as rivalrous sisters.

The men at the picnic table caught themselves pausing to listen to these unintelligible whispers; and then, when the sibilance ceased, they began looking around nonchalantly, falling into that awkward pose of guilty parties.

"You want wine, then?" Jacob said. "I can buy a round."

"No, I'll get it," Molly said, coming back to the table. "Isaac has already paid me." She turned to watch Janey going off in her wonted hauteur. She exclaimed in mock weariness, "I guess I have to take care of our precious winos, for the good of the cause."

"You might add that we are winos with superb taste," Paul demanded.

"Do you want me to bring you a bottle of our cheap stuff?"

Cook and Hereford looked at each other, smiling gleefully in affirmation. They had not thought of ordering a bottle, it was suddenly very novel to be able to do so as if this were like any other fine culinary establishment.

"Are you sure you can do that?" Cook asked, acutely aware of the irrational propensities of local powers and principalities.

"You doubt me!" Molly cried.

Isaac was overcome by his present happiness, and seeing it reflected in her eyes made him giddy. "That would be splendid Molly!"

"Isaac, you know we do what we want around here. Big Sistah said we could." Molly here referred to the honorific bestowed on Frances by one cabal at the parish.

"She is the final authority on things of this world." Hereford said facetiously.

"All hail Lady Frances!"

"Okay, okay. Settle down." Molly admonished quietly. Janey had come back, pulling at her elbow and they moved off together. They could hear Molly's sharp rebuke; "I'm not going to start a temperance league, Janey! Her friend stalked away again. Molly returned to the table, a bright, shiny look on her face.

"How about you?" She addressed Jacob. "Did you come to help? Or to sit out here drinking with our resident philosophers?" She turned to go towards the cafeteria. He scrambled to his feet and lunged forward to catch up with her. She was wearing jeans with an expensive label, and tasseled loafers that looked pristine and smart on her elegant feet. Her sleeveless blouse was a mauve color, decorated with all sorts of lacework. Jacob felt oddly proud of her, aware how strange it was to feel that way about a woman he regarded as a superior personage. It was more of his unfolding confusion, that already seemed normal when he was around her. This being swept away, as if in the most happy dream, was too exceptional to jeopardize with clumsy acts of intelligence.

She put him to work helping the people behind the counter; providing them with the boxes of food and other supplies. Then she had him help carry a few extra tables and chairs out to the Grotto; they were not sure whether or not they would be able to draw many people to that location. Jacob did the chores assigned to him and stopped off frequently at the C & H Company to swap jokes and endure their ridicule for being a church lackey.

"Keep a pious attitude, brother."

"And if thou dost see wrong, hold thy tongue."

"And other parts, as you must. Prey not on our sisters, brother."

"Know thy place is meant to be lowly."

"Seek not wisdom, but fear of the mothers."

It occurred to him that they were jealous of his relations with Molly. She was constantly coming up to him to keep him abreast of official business and to share fresh gossip. He didn't completely understand it, and that only made it more satisfying. She regaled him with elaborate stories. She fleshed out the lives of parish folk with her provocative sense of humor, which held everyone, including herself, accountable to an exquisite set of values. He was her confidante, moving in familiar rounds, devising private jokes that could be shared with a single word, or sometimes just a glance, flung piercingly through a crowd. Much unexplained laughter ensued between them, and people took notice.

"What do you expect to get out of this work, brother?" Isaac asked him.

"It doesn't pay, and there are no benefits; but they tell me there's a lot of room for advancement."

"I have no doubt," Isaac exclaimed in a hearty voice. Then he chuckled in his most winsome manner. Paul smiled in a wry fashion.

"No benefits?" He muttered. "Seems like he's making good headway."

"It's more than that, though; he's a hard one to figure."

By the time the vibrant colors of dusk had faded out and blended quietly and without notice into the ether of night, where the stars burned as votive candles, the scant outdoor crowd had dispersed. The only people left were those inside the cafeteria, sitting in the bright, harsh glare of the fluorescent tubes. Many of the older folks lingered over their empty plates to partake of nutritious lore that spanned three and four generations. Hereford made a comment about another place he was expected, and promptly decamped. Cook was alone at the picnic table, an empty bottle of wine standing before him.

"About time to call it a night, huh?" Jacob had developed a protective feeling about the man, influenced by Molly's devotion.

"One hates to leave such a lovely evening."

"It was a good time. Not enough people came."

"Now you've started on it? The mercenary instinct, infecting the faith, and all her minions."

"Sistah says we need more people!"

Isaac laughed in a shallow manner that often, and did now, precipitate a series of coughs soon after.

"I was watching the chimney swifts before it got dark." He said after regaining his composure. They both turned to look at the empty space above the middle level of the school grounds, where the birds had earlier been swooping by and around in extended loops, closing out their day with joyful aerial feats. It was common to see two mated birds flying in tandem, going into curving glides, and leveling out wingtip to wingtip, as if overcome by connubial bliss.

"I used to be able to watch them from the windows when I lived upstairs on Allen Place. They swarmed around Vogt School." Jacob recollected.

"They seem to be such happy creatures," Isaac pondered aloud.

"Makes a man envious. They have permanent homelands, which they keep sacred."

"Which they leave every year."

"But then they come back every year."

"I think you will find advancement here, Jacob, I really do."

Jacob looked at Cook, wondering about his storied life, that had brought him worldly success; and then back here, to curate his gift for sorrow, that he did not seem to share with anyone, except maybe Molly. He made sacrifices at the modern altars of intellectual detachment; cynicism, irony, and added his own flourish of honest, worldly despair. Around Molly he received the liberal sacraments. He enjoyed burning sticks of pagan incense with Hereford. There was another, very personal aspect to his personality, permeated by humane aspirations so fine they seemed to disperse into the atmosphere at the first breath.

"Do you need anything else, Isaac?"

"No. Composing myself to go home."

"Do you want a ride home?" Jacob wasn't sure who would be driving him, he had left his truck in the garage, but someone must be present with a car willing to help out.

Isaac looked at him, waiting for Jacob to acknowledge the absurdity of his suggestion. Isaac lived a short distance away. "I don't drink as much as it looks like I drink. Hereford drank most of this," he said putting his hand out towards the last bottle.

"He's a terrible lush." Jacob confirmed.

"No, don't say that." Isaac looked around culpably. "He's a pretty good writer," he added pensively.

Jacob nodded agreeably, seeing that Cook was no doubt having thoughts that cannot be expressed. He was once more lost in the pathos of bygone sorrows and joys, beyond all regret, striving to appreciate that innate love of life that burns like a filament in the cavernous depths, and which no amount of healthy despair can extinguish. He had been thinking of something Molly told him about her faith, and he wondered if he might be able to achieve something like that for himself.

Jacob started bringing chairs back to the storage room under the church. During one of these trips he stopped at the Grotto and faced the statue. He was feeling so many strong emotions he could not seem to catch his breath, as though he were fatigued. Working actually helped him to regulate his breathing, whereas being in repose brought on a riot of emotions that besieged him like a rebel army. What was all this public worship about?

"You Russian monks really have a thing for this chick, don't you?"

Again she had appeared, as though he had conjured her; like a witch was given unto him instead of a guardian angel, and his only hope was to learn the language of the coven. Where does one find such instruction?

"I was just paying my respects."

They both turned to watch as Isaac departed in his rambling motions. Jacob ventured to break the silence of the strange mood he had fallen into.

"I guess you didn't get the crowd you wanted, did you?"

"We'll just have to wait. I think it will happen." She spoke with serene confidence. They both lifted their eyes to take in a portion of the sparkling bits shed upon the earth by unimaginable galaxies.

"It was a perfect evening to be sitting outside, with all of this to enjoy." He extended out his hand to encompass what he meant.

"That's why it will work out. It just takes time. How did Isaac seem?"

"What do you mean?"

"Was he getting maudlin?"

"Yes." Jacob nodded. "He definitely was."

"Did he start talking about his lost woman?"

"No, just the—what do they call it? The dialectics."

"The endless dialectics." She exclaimed and laughed in a low musical key that gathered a sonorous pitch from deep in her person.

"He seemed pretty sad, I feel for the guy."

"That's how he gets. He's always wallowing in memories. He's told me so many things. He knows everything about the history of Ferdinand. He's the kind of man that turns his heart over to a woman like a piñata. Here you go, smash me, let me dump out my best stuff for you. Now rake through my guts!" She laughed in a wild, high-pitched squeal he had never heard come out of her before. "You just can't do that to a woman!"

Jacob looked at her, amazed by her trenchant appraisal; it felt almost indecent to haul this out for his casual examination. They were silent a moment and then Molly said, "Isaac." They both began to laugh, thinking of their gentle-mannered friend.

"I remember seeing my sister standing here one time." Jacob spoke without forethought. He wanted to disburden himself to this perceptive woman.

"Yes? When was that?"

"I don't know. I just remember her standing here, very still, right here. Looking at the statue there, so still. I guess she was praying? I don't know."

"How old was she?"

"I don't know how old she was then."

"I mean, when she died."

"Oh, it was right after fifth grade, that summer. I must have seen her standing here that previous autumn. I'm not sure."

She had watched him speak as if struggling to enunciate something in a language he did not fully understand. "And then your family moved away?"

"Yeah, my father had an accident at work right after she died, and then everything changed for the family."

"It must have been horrible for you."

He looked at her. She was a person who knew more about suffering than him. Somehow his distant pains did not seem to equate to anything she had gone through so recently, as a mother, and a wife. He could find no words. He feared his own malignant sorrow. He stared ahead.

"Did you like going to school here?" she asked.

"Oh yeah. I mean, it was before I had to think about growing up. You know? It was that early period of childhood, when . . . it was like every year the world kept getting better." In his mind he remembered how everything got very bad, and continued to get worse, even the idea of a future seemed to be ruined . . .

He could see she was about to leave him.

"So, I'll see you next week?"

"See you next week," he replied, turning to watch her walk away. She had left so abruptly, and he was glad she had done so, for he was about to become visibly distraught. Her presence was bringing up feelings he had suppressed for so long there was no way to control how they broke to the surface, and flowed along from there, sweeping away his defenses. Time was different now. It was being modulated by the presence of another being. He felt an extraordinary calmness. Everything was different; he had been released into an unspoiled country, ripe for discovery.

29

Jacob became religious about mundane occurrences. At any moment liable to feel a faint, anticipatory shiver, followed by a premonition of something momentous, surely imminent, certain to come. There was that feeling of lingering twilight, of mysterious truths glimmering on the verge of consciousness.

Frances put him to work on her retaining wall and he began whistling as he labored. He and Cody exchanged frequent gibes about their respective deficiencies as novice craftsmen. The handling of the brute rocks was assigned to Gregory, who felt pride as they were aligned and secured with mortar by his confreres.

The artisan taught them how to get started, advising them a 'rough look' would not be that bad; then he bowed out. The apprentices continued to learn while on the job as Frances moved about, fussing over her project. Once in a while she jumped in to do the work herself, as Cody and Jacob stood by and watched, highly amused that she could not quite leave anything completely alone. She relinquished the trowel after a short period and stood back to resume her role as superintendent. For lunch she fed them poor boy sandwiches; when it got late in the afternoon she took off in her bug and brought back cold beer.

They were standing in the driveway admiring their work when Robert drove up in a Corvette, He asked Jacob if he would mind delivering the car to its new owner in Kansas City.

"When does it need to get there?"

"You would have to drive it there on Friday. It's easy money."

"You want me to drive there this Friday?"

"I'll pay you to stay over there, bus trip back. Kansas City is a great town. I'll make it worth your while."

"No, I can't"

"Why not?" Robert insisted, only increasing Jacob's sudden fit of anger.

"Look, I don't want to, okay?" He did not know why he was so mad at Robert, but he wanted to have a good reason. "I'm getting sick of doing everyone else's chores." He was fuming now, embarrassed and angry.

"Well, fuck it, then. I thought you could use the money. I forgot you're a regular handy man now, in great demand."

"What about you, Cody?"

"No. I can't do it. I have the family—"

"Why don't you and Beatrice make the trip?" Jacob fired his words like live rounds.

They stared at each other. Robert began to smile in a glaring, offended manner. "Let's not get bent out of shape. I'll find somebody else."

"You do that."

Robert made the tires chirp as he sped off.

That night Jacob spent four hours practicing one song, driving himself to continue practicing, long past the point of diminishing returns. The mechanical efforts to produce harmony also restored equanimity to his perturbed reason. The next morning, after a breakfast of eggs, bacon, and heavily buttered toast, he began playing the song with far greater control of the measures. He finished a rendition and was assailed by a loud sound.

Cody was yelling at him from the driveway outside the garage. He went down to see him.

"What was that?"

"What?"

"What you were just playing."

"Oh, that's called 'Classical Gas.'"

"That was awesome, man."

"It needs sore work."

"I told Frances you can play really well. She might ask you to play at church."

"No, I don't want to play at mass."

"I think she means for the Fish Fry. It was Molly's idea."

"Really?" He was wondering how did Molly even know he played guitar; he had been fantasizing about playing a set of songs for her. So they were talking to her, about him? What else did they tell her about me?

"Could be a cool gig."

"I don't know. I'm not sure that's a crowd that wants to watch some dude playing old rock songs on his acoustic guitar."

"You never play rock—"

"Hey, whatever. Just because Dylan went electric—I never did. So that means I'm better than him. You think he'd stoop to playing a church gig?"

"He might have in his Christian phase."

"I forgot about that, but he came back to the temple."

"Hey, how many people are they getting up there?"

"Not as many as they'd like."

"I'm anxious to check it out tonight."

"You're going?"

"Yeah, me and Sally will be there."

"Cool."

They had been walking the grounds. They wandered off through the back row of tall pine trees just beyond the open area around the fire pit. A long stretch of ground lay along the back perimeter of the heights; a broad leafy trail redolent of all seasons at once, as the earth underfoot was a sodden quilt of moldering layers.

"I hope she leaves this area alone for a while," Jacob said.

"Places like this are like museums of my childhood." Cody answered.

"I feel that way, too." Jacob remembered how this ground had been one of those tracts children claim by right of childhood; they deem such property to be exempt from certain legal strictures. They hold to a primitive concept stated in the Bible, somewhere, when the prophets first divined where the march of civilization would eventually leave the people of the land. On their parchments they renounced ownership of the earth, by all humans, to protect themselves, and to protect her.

They tramped along the length of the trail in luxurious silence, passing along the fencing on the left, having similar thoughts that neither would have been able to put into articulate speech. It was a vague feeling of regret that this trail was not more extensive, as it had seemed to be when they were children. They wished the path was enclosed by an expanse of real woods, so one could break away and get lost for the day, and hear the sirens that send one crashing through the underbrush to discover that other side of nature as yet undefiled by human designs. Most of the path was covered by a high canopy of foliage, and this made it immensely attractive to pedestrians for mysterious reasons.

"I haven't been out here in a long time." Cody said.

"It hasn't changed much, has it?" Jacob asked.

"No, but we have. I feel like I'm trespassing now." They were in fact behind the last house on Clay, and this rustic, sun-dappled remnant of land belonged to those in possession of that title.

"Let's go back." Jacob said.

Back to the source of all beginnings . . . his mind often resounded with his own interior phrases. He found it soothing to jot down his thoughts and lyrics in a college notebook he had purchased. There were also many curious doodles that resembled his high school sketchings. On the first page enormous letters had burgeoned forth, enfolded in sprays of decorative foliage, spelling out, Molly T. Fuller.

———◆———

The principal officers of the C & H conglomerate were holding their weekly board meeting. The two men sat side by side at the pine table, facing out at the church parking lot, where those who toiled were making the rounds in a bustle of productive activity. Several workers trained reproachful looks on these indolent ones, which they in turn appreciated tremendously. Out before them, slightly to their left, was the patio in front of the Grotto. There were many unoccupied tables and chairs. Jacob was on a ladder helping to string lights between the sassafras trees. People driving by on Elizabeth would be able to see these lights, and it was hoped they might be encouraged to investigate what was happening there.

Cook and Hereford were in good spirits; they had a bottle of red wine placed between them and each fondled his plastic cup like an ancient toddler. The talk was desultory; at certain times it became briefly intense, before subsiding again into a cursory rhythm. Many affirmations gave off that morbid note of the angry, unhappy liberal swearing over his battered missal, à la Robespierre.

"I heard people are seeing beavers down in Moline creek," Cook said.

"The suburbs are becoming wildlife preserves," Hereford added, "Foxes, coyotes, turkeys. "Instinct is driving them, and they accommodate themselves to the friendly environment."

"Friendly environment? That's a good piece of dramatic propaganda."

"Is that a Chinese dragon?" Hereford asked, looking over at the Grotto. The men stringing the lights were also hoisting up and tethering, between a corner fence post and a light pole, a gold and scarlet dragon.

"I don't think Frances is going to like that."

"It was her idea," Jacob said as he came over to audit the proceedings while remaining aloof from the official poppycock cherished by the company elders.

"No kidding?" Isaac exclaimed. "She's not one you can predict, is she?

"No sir." They began to compare the present Chinese government to the time when an emperor was head of state, and putatively, everything else.

"Why do we need heads of state?" Jacob asked.

"The Romans had two consuls," Hereford said.

"But there's only one pope." Cook offered.

"That hasn't always been the case," Hereford said and laughed dryly.

"We should have nine popes, like the Supreme Court; let them vote on issues like birth control."

"That way, at least some of them are sure to have children of their own to worry about."

"And mistresses to take into consideration; that would temper their bulls dealing with women."

"They would rule on behalf of Jephthah's daughter."

The conversation stalled as they observed the final erection of the dragon and then enjoyed how the breezes animated the creature with innate desires such that his fierce demeanor seemed warranted. Cook and Hereford began to argue over the institution of marriage, for no apparent reason.

"With you it's always about the eternal husband, even when he's a social Ronin." Paul spat his words.

"Isn't the story of these past ten thousand years, for our species, the trapping and domestication of the violent male?" Isaac offered. "We're nearing the end of the age of violence."

"So, there are no more wars? No plague of domestic abuse?"

"Life is long."

"And you would say that ultimately we will see the unleashing of the infernal female?"

"Instinct is not to be denied."

"That is just habit carried along for untold centuries."

"Don't spit up your Nietzsche at me!"

"Who's spitting on whom over here?" Molly asked. They all spun around to look at her. "Everyone behaving himself over here?" She inquired. She was wearing a swirling blue sundress. Her bare arms were the quintessence of seductive nakedness in Jacob's eyes. To be twined in those! He ranged his eyes down her figure, marveling over her skimpy white footwear that adorned her precious feet.

"Hereford is getting ready to castigate his former wives," Isaac said with a triumphant note. "In chronological order, I hope, I can never remember how it goes."

"I've heard those tragic songs." Molly said with a mordant bite.

Initially she had been drawn to Hereford, as a fairly handsome, intelligent, and suave individual, with evidence of a redeeming air of self-reproach about him. However, his cultivation was marred by savage tattoos inked on the bare patches of his ego. These tribal stains made her feel revulsion; like smelling a carton of bad milk. He was damaged in some fashion which she couldn't identify. She had seen this enigmatic suffering before. If the afflicted one happened to be a great talker, it was likely to grow tedious as the tale was constantly devised and revised. She smiled pleasantly at him to alleviate the injured look she had just put on his face. He had been married twice, divorced twice, had chased beauty for its own sake; and now his misogyny was blended so thoroughly with his chivalrous veneration of 'the fair sex' that he invariably spoiled the desires of any woman taking a central role in one of his dramas.

Cook, on the other hand, married late in life. As a romantic student his heart was broken incurably; which condition sent him reeling into the world like a prophet of the Sexual Revolution. He became a sort of faith healer. Much later his potency was conscripted by impregnable matrons, whose unfailing grasp of things had clamped their hearts to the iron ribs of opulent trust funds. These women prized the idea of having a discreet affair at just the right time, when the chatter afterwards over cocktails was possibly as delicious, and lasted longer, than the physical play itself. He scripted a climactic chapter by courting a younger woman for several years, instructing her in all the worldly things she hardly cared about, and, when she finally consented to marry him, her friends all laughed. They said it was the only way she could get rid of him. The marriage lasted one year; she broke it off on the anniversary; saying she could not possibly live up to his 'theatrical vision' of what her life ought to be about. The collapse of this delusion crushed him, again; he found solace in playing that quixotic role for the feminine sympathy always on sale somewhere in genteel quarters.

The consonance of these two histories of reproductive failure helped to explain why Cook and Hereford bared their teeth at one another when the issue of marriage was raised. They preferred to enact savage banquets where hearts were served up in a figurative sense, like steak tartare, with much bitter relish, as pride took revenge on itself for the sake of appearances. It was much better and safer to hold forth on society at large, than to examine too closely the ugly wounds of those present at roll call.

"Oh yeah! Go Dragons!" Molly shouted, directing their attention to the paper creature struggling in the wind. She prompted Isaac to explain to the others that at one time the teams at St. Margaret's were called the Dragons, because of the legends of Saint Margaret of Antioch.

"But weren't the dragons, the enemy?" Jacob asked, somewhat tentatively; having already heard Isaac speak effusively of this particular saint; daughter of a pagan priest, who converted, and was beheaded during the reign of Diocletian.

"You're so literal," Hereford replied.

"That's why the church finally made them change it. I still have a soccer jersey with Dragons written across the back. I was number ten. Just like Pelé." Isaac was suddenly very animated.

"Here we go, the great soccer player." Hereford said. "He could have been a star."

"I bet he was very good." Molly said with obvious bias.

"I was pretty good." Isaac said, "Playing at that level, anyway."

"You played in high school?"

"Yes, and college, for a while. I didn't really feel as much enthusiasm for it then. I don't know why." He had a far away look on his face. "During high school the best part was everything that was happening outside of the games. And I was becoming enthralled with movies and everything was becoming like a great movie for me. Even if we didn't win a game, I rewrote the script in my mind, using the experience to produce something else altogether. Making up and weaving together the most vivid scenes I wanted to film."

"Like this story about you being a star?" Paul asked.

"Oh, I would always manage to score the winning goal in my script." Isaac rejoined at once. He began to laugh. Jacob saw how Molly's face reflected the delight pouring from Isaac's visage. He had watched her absorbing his happiness as a part of her own. Now she allowed Isaac to bask a moment in her affection; it shone down as from a mysterious font.

"The good old days," Paul said.

"There were times, when just stepping onto the field," Isaac continued his rhapsody, "or at the end of practice, I could *feel* the experience I wanted to somehow capture on the screen. The feel of that late afternoon light, the cool air, the surge of youthful vigor, wearing cleats that tear at the ground as you make plays. Everything was part of my destiny. I knew beforehand how it was going to make me feel, being out there on the field, and then afterwards, being among friends in bars and restaurants."

"You miss having something to center life?" Jacob queried, in a rhetorical sense, distracted by the chimney swifts swirling around in ceremonial flights.

"Yes, that sense of knowing the part you have, even though you don't really know anything. But just being healthy and happy; being in touch with life, that precious thing." Isaac concluded his reverie.

"Being in touch." Paul agreed, under his breath.

They all raised glasses to sip the syrup of nostalgia, and each fled into private reveries. The moment was interrupted as Janey came up and wanted to take Molly with her to do something inside the cafeteria.

Molly resisted her officious tactics.

"So where's Sophie?" Janey asked her spitefully.

"With her grandmother."

"Lainey was looking for her. I told her Sophie was going to be here."

"I'll get with you in a little bit." Molly said irritably. Janey frowned and swept her eyes over the men gathered at the picnic table, and then, with focused hostility, latching onto Jacob's form. He sensed she was ready to invoke the sort of Furies who had mauled and torn apart men, according to Euripides. Molly moved suddenly closer to her and they exchanged harsh, angry words. Janey shook her head in negation and turned to effect another righteous withdrawal. It was still worthy of being observed and they all watched her; until Molly grabbed Jacob by the hand, tugging him forward. She released her grip once he was propelled into motion.

"Come on boy, let's go."

"Where to?" He began laughing as he followed her determined steps.

She strode rapidly through the parking lot, up the broad drive and back around to climb the steps to the walled terrace at the front entrance of the church. She stopped outside the doors, turning to him. Jacob felt a pang of regret, thinking she was interested in getting him to play his guitar at mass, or even worse, he feared she wanted to get him on the parish rolls. Why else would she haul him into the church?

"When's the last time you were in here?" She asked. He glanced at several red bud trees near the bottom of the steps on the lawn that ran along that side of the church. The leaves looked like comically swollen hearts. How old were those trees?

"I don't know. A wedding, or a funeral maybe; pretty long ago."

She led him into the building, walking around the wooden pews on the right and up along the row of stained-glass windows. Down below them was the parking lot, not far from the entrance to the cafeteria. He slowed down to look at the scenes depicted on the windows; as a boy the stations of the cross had always intrigued him, when he was not having grandiose daydreams during the mass.

"All these images." *Have become a part of me now, despite everything . . .* "This one always used to get to me."

"Really?" They stood together to inspect the scene described in the liturgy as the first fall of Jesus.

"The great pains taken to document every step of his physical ordeal—"

"Assigning each fall a number." She whispered.

"Exactly."

They walked slowly along the wall looking at the other windows, the rich afternoon light suffusing the vibrant panes. Jacob looked up at the marble Jesus hanging high on the wall. He was wearing only a marble loin cloth; in his last breath, bearing his immortal wounds. His tortured limbs and hands and feet had been fashioned with gruesome verisimilitude by an unknown sculptor. Jacob's mind was unable to move past the grotesque symbolism, or detach itself from the verities of human cruelty. He heard the sounds of children directly beneath them; a young girl's innocent, playful cry fluttered through the interior of the building.

"What is it, Jacob?" Molly noticed that he was looking at nothing, a mist gathering in his eyes.

"Those children playing, that was us, once." He was adrift in a state of introspection which she did not want to disturb. "I used to wonder what kind of person my sister would have become, having her own children . . ."

Molly only stared at his face in silence as he caught himself.

"We were twins. We did everything together. And then one day she told me we would have to walk to school separately. She didn't want to walk to school with me anymore."

"That's perfectly normal," Molly assumed her maternal voice. She put a hand on his shoulder and withdrew it again. She waited for him to speak further from the vantage of those grievous recollections. His face responded warmly after a subtle wrench of the mouth.

"I know. It's just that we were on the threshold of the next phase of growing up, and it's like I'm still stuck there . . ." He tried to laugh but choked up instead.

"Come on. I want to show you something."

He felt her hand grasping at his wrist, using almost no force at all she moved him forward, following in her steps. She led him to a nook behind the altar area where two wooden doors were almost hidden in the molding of two adjacent wall panels.

"Go in there," she instructed, giving him a gentle shove. She disappeared in one door and he passed through the other. She took up the clerical seat. It was an old, superannuated confessional they had used in the early days of the original church, before the expansion and remodeling. He was feeling rather silly, taking a position on the kneeler. He peered at her face through the wooden lattice, having to smile at how she was behaving.

"Tell me more about your sister." She commanded softly. He began very simply and directly to provide a narrative of the last terrible days, when he did not know what was happening. He had never gone to the hospital. He was aware his parents were going to see her, and they discussed over his head the idea of taking him, and then they came home devastated. They told him she was gone. It had felt like he kept waking up, not from, but into a recurring nightmare. Then it just seemed everything of his old life was gone. Those outside the family had no need to continue wallowing in sorrow, while he was inconsolable. It set him apart. His father was visibly wrecked. He fell at work and the family structure was terribly altered; and soon the onset of remorse, and waves of guilt, accruing from a host of other incomprehensible sources, left him shaken to his core . . .

"It was such a terrible loss for all of you."

"The strange thing, though, was how I responded, on my own. The first thing, afterwards, when I was alone, I came up to the Grotto, and I made a vow to the Madonna that I would live for her, for Johanna. I would be a better person, for her."

"That was a fine thing for you to do."

"But I never did any of it."

"I'm sure you did your best."

"No, I don't think so. And then, much later, it became a part of my music, but that was really about my own vanity."

"You're being too hard on yourself. A devastating loss will do that to you."

He looked at her face again. He had not been aware of it as he spoke. She was just there, a powerful benevolent presence breathing in front of him.

"One time, after my dad fell at work, and Mom was taking care of him, I was wanting to see her for some reason. I went to her bedroom, and she was sitting on the bed crying. I started to go in and she got up and rushed up to me, but only to say, 'Not now, Jacob!' And then she closed the door on me."

"She was probably—"

"Only now do I see how difficult that must have been for her. She had to be our rock. Mark was doing a lot, but she was the parent, she was there for him, too. Looking back, I see the selfishness that comes out in grief. That was really hard to bear for me."

"For anyone. For anyone. It's part of life."

She felt him staring at her face; his own looked strangely serene.

"Do you want me to say some Hail Marys, now?"

"Come on," she said, "Let's get out of here."

They traipsed down the other side of the church than the one they came up earlier, passing quickly, and without noticing the orderly bank of scenes portrayed in the windows.

"I think I could use a glass of wine." Molly said, turning to see that he had stopped again, and was now inspecting one of the windows. "Let's go." She spoke in a subdued voice.

"Hold on." Jacob replied, staring at the colored glass; then he was walking behind her, glad to be able to observe her bodily movements. These affected him as beautiful melodies every time he was close to her. In another time he thought of how music enters the ear as sound waves, the fleshy drum working delicate bone structures, and these transduce the mechanical motion into electrical signals that become in the mind a form of incredible beauty. In a kindred strain of magic the visual apparatus, once directed at the woman you are beginning to love, composes sonorous beatitudes that shiver throughout one's entire being. His cup was wildly sloshing over as he strove to catch up to her.

30

One day he found himself driving up Florissant Road just because he wanted to stare out at the world while speeding along, while listening to music on the radio. The old songs never sounded more relevant to him. One of his favorite medicine songs from the past, "Magic Carpet Ride," evoked again the first blooms of manhood. He was drawn ineluctably to those tortuous, two-lane roads winding over verdant, fissured hills, and the stubby, harvested fields, passing through a labyrinth of time, returning to Sioux Passage Park.

Back in those primitive days the land was barely touched by the earthmovers of progress; their frolics took place in messy, rustic splendor. Adam's first descendants seemed to be in charge of things, and the fig leaf was optional. You had to trek a long ways to get to the river, traversing rough terrain, clad in bell-bottom jeans, collecting pollen and burrs, slogging along like refugees driven out of Pharaoh's city. Now one could drive a vehicle right to the river's edge, and use the concrete ramp to launch a boat, to chase after the ghosts of lawless fur traders, if such desires pulsed in your bloodstream. He stared at the river for a long time letting his excitement bleed off so that he could merely drive his prosaic vehicle back home.

Once back in Ferdinand he pulled into the drive of Cody's duplex.

"What's up?" Cody had come outside upon hearing Jacob pull up, shut down his engine, get out of the cab, and slam the door with a reverberant clang.

"Frances said she wanted to borrow the truck."

"When?"

"Wednesday, I think she said. Here." He handed Cody a spare key he had gotten made just moments earlier.

"Are you going to leave the truck here till then?"

"Yeah. I don't think I'll need it. Use it if you want to."

"No, I don't think . . . " Cody quit speaking, seeing that Jacob was already striding along the side of the house towards Allen Place. He was definitely doing this more often; not really paying attention to anything anyone else was doing or saying, but rather bouncing along to the tune of some strange sound track he was playing in his head.

"Oh good. You asked him to borrow the truck?" Sally asked, after coming outside and coming up next to her husband. She had wanted him to get the truck to help her mother with some items purchased at an 'antique store' which she needed to get delivered to her house. She had mentioned this in front of Jacob the last time she had seen him.

"No."

"No?"

"He just left it here, he said in case we need it. Apparently Frances needs it on Wednesday."

"Well, can I use it now, then?"

He looked at her. "What do you need it for?"

She did not answer immediately, but pried the key ring from his hand. "Just some things." She paused before mentioning the name of a troubled friend of hers who Cody was not fond of, but whom Sally had known since her memory began recording her life.

The last time Cody had gone with his wife to help this particular woman there was an angry ex-boyfriend involved; he had to be chased from the house, and then off the front lawn. Cody had armed himself with a poker he had taken from the fireplace. He hadn't been sure his bluff would work, or that the other man would stand down, or not have a firearm in his vehicle. He wasn't sure himself that it was a bluff; he had momentarily lost control of himself. He still had visions of himself bashing in the stupid man's head. His wife's shrieking had initiated the episode when the boy-friend had grabbed her friend by the neck with both hands. The police had been called and they questioned Cody, but seemed to conclude a certain form of justice had won that day, after they jostled the last spasm of anger out of the ex-boyfriend who had completely lost track of what his rights were, and were not, when he was an uninvited guest inside an ex-girlfriend's house.

"Let me know if there's anything I can do." Cody said, looking at his wife, waiting for her to look back at him. When she finally did, her only response was to smile as if he had said something very subtle and satirical about an arrangement known only to the two of them.

———————

Jacob's week had been a blur of activity; he sought out chores as a way to ensure the clock performed its duty in an honorable fashion. On Friday morning he sprang out of bed like he was twelve. He was in a state of excitement not seen since he had waited for the opening of his last school carnival at St. Margaret's. This was held on the two lower levels, a few days after the school year had expired, when summer officially began. It was a time of orchestral winds and dancing trees, narcotic growth and thrilling, fragrant airs, cotton candy, diesel fumes, and those great, half-monstrous contraptions designed to wring from children screeches of untamed joy. At such times an enlightened boy finds himself believing in human perfection, as those apostles who shaped in their empirical workshops a new fable that had no need of original sin.

He took the quickest route to the church, skidding down the hill and striding across the lawns like a Vandal, using routes approved by Euclid, before getting back to the linear rectitude of his trusty sidewalks. He saw quite a few cars in the upper parking lot by the rectory and this added to his excitement. Molly would be happy. Once at the Fish Fry he noticed several of the tables at the Grotto were occupied and the people were having drinks. Cook and Hereford were at their table, a bottle of wine between them on the rough, warped boards. They were in a fine fettle, Jacob could see at a glance, with so much human activity out there before them to provoke their dry commentaries.

"What are you fine gentlemen doing here?" He asked, as if surprised to see them. "Oh, that's right, you live here as kings and counselors. We are here but to serve you, out of the parish plenty." He had found an old family Bible in the Spencer basement, and he was dipping into it occasionally.

"Ah, the eternal footman," Paul replied smartly. "He's come to shame the idle dreamers."

"There's no need to give you, or anyone else, a moral lecture."

"Well, you're feeling pretty good about things, aren't you?" Isaac said to him.

Jacob peered around, surprised at how many people there were; searching for Molly, wishing to congratulate her on this prodigious increase in attendance. Over at the original outdoor section the usual grandees were planted in their chairs, staring out at the children playing in front of the school entrance. Some of these old ones were in a ritual trance, observing the mechanics of youth's irrepressible nature. Jacob's heart began roaring like a forge, stoking the most combustible materials imaginable. He was ready to recast his whole world into new shapes. His thoughts of Molly were akin to those that drove the archangels mad; as was told to us by a very clever Latin Secretary, who allowed them to peek inside Eve's boudoir.

"Where are the chimney swifts?" Jacob asked, glancing out over the second level where it seemed he had just seen a pair gliding by in tandem.

"They've decamped," Paul said. "Damn gypsies, like this one here."

"You're no different. Have you seen our waitress?" Isaac exclaimed to Jacob.

"Waitress?"

"Look!"

Jacob turned to see a woman serving one of the tables at the Grotto. She was attired in a lacy, ruffled, white shirt, black shorts, and white sneakers. The ensemble comprised a recognizable utility uniform. A pouch was attached in front and held in place by tethers knotted on her lower back. The young woman had her blond hair pulled back and woven into an intricate braid that fell to the middle of her back. She had big icy blue eyes that held one in suspension if you looked directly at her when she smiled your way. Her white shirt was just tight enough to let her buxom charms wreak havoc on the casual observer who a moment before might have believed he was beyond the reach of mysticism.

"Wow," Jacob whispered. "That's one way to get more customers."

"She's smoking hot, isn't she?" Molly said as she arrived on the scene.

Jacob looked over at Molly's face, seen in profile, as she and everyone else kept a keen eye on the waitress, whose name was Lilly. Jacob continued to stare at Molly, at the precious mold of her features; the neat snub nose, prominent chin, the wide thin mouth, which could say so much without words. His eyes stroked her sun-rinsed hair until he became fascinated by the gold pendants in her ear lobes, befitting an Egyptian princess. He was falling before a new form of worship as she turned to face him. Her clear gray eyes had a stupefying effect, becoming suffused with a lavender hue. Something fluttered outward from that perplexing light to touch hidden keys planted much deeper than all the loose images flitting through his consciousness.

"What are you so giddy about?" She queried, her eyes now flashing behind her drawn lashes.

He shook his head in dumb negation, unable to accept the terms of his present happiness. He smiled at her with enigmatic fervor, and she crinkled up her nose; her eyes lingering on his face for an instant, before turning away.

"What fresh mischief is afoot?" She spoke now to Isaac.

"Your boy there looks like he's intoxicated."

"I'm not." Jacob responded at once, as if surprised at his ability to speak. He had not had a drop of alcohol all day, and hadn't thought of having any. Now he was puzzled by her blue eye shadow; he couldn't tell if this was a look he had seen before. So much was not about normal chronological time anymore. His dreams were coming true, but remaining as dreams;

he was but the confused visitor to this surreal netherworld. The behavior of all these people and his own actions were incomprehensible to his sedated faculties.

"God help us if you do start drinking like these two." She said, somewhat hurriedly, to close out the eerie moment that could not last. Then she was off to perform some chores inside the cafeteria. She returned requesting his help and he was put to work hauling and unloading boxes for the cooks who were busy in the steam and fume of an overtaxed kitchen. He was swept up into the pageantry just before sunset when luminous colors streaked the horizon and deep pools of shade stretched out over the grounds, which had become a bedlam. All the tables were full; everywhere he looked numerous groups of people stood close together in convivial knots. More people kept arriving.

Lilly was rushing back and forth, her face shone as brightly as a new penny. She was laughing just trying to keep up with the insatiable demand. Molly and Janey had begun to help her at the height of the rush. Jacob was also pressed into service as a bartender, after suggesting they should bring coolers out and sell beer out of them, over on the hill near the Grotto. He had meant to suggest they devise something for next week, but Molly directed him to commandeer two large coolers kept in the school storage locker and then dispatched him to buy ice and in what seemed like hardly any time he was hawking beers like a carnival worker. He kept stuffing damp currency into his pockets while exchanging mock insults with the patrons, whom he trained to stop expecting change.

"Contribute to the cause or I'll tell Sistah you're turning Methodist on us."

"Don't go telling Sistah!" This became a sort of spirited battle cry for the men who were climbing joyfully into their cups.

"Now go on, you Catholic bastards; seek and ye shall find—more thirst!"

Molly came up, her eyes dilated by his excited antics. She took his receipts, smiling at him in a way that made him feel he was part of a grand conspiracy, known only to the great ones of this world.

"I've never seen tips like this," Lilly cried to Molly as she passed by.

"Where did she come from, anyway?" Jacob asked breathlessly. In the general uproar they could hardly hear one another; Molly led Jacob to some privacy on the edge of the hill beyond the Grotto. They stood looking around, sharing their happiness without saying anything.

"Frances found her somewhere. She said we needed professional help."

"I probably do."

"You could use a lot of things."

He began to talk to her of Johanna, as she was in the good times. Molly told him several cherished memories of her son John. As they spoke to one another they stared at the crowd enlivening the Grotto. They were perfectly at ease, as though it were a pause, near the end of a ceremony, before the real festivities would begin. They watched Frances moving among the people, bossing them as she made her way through their ranks.

"Frances," she said, shaking her head, emitting light breaths of mirth. They both began laughing.

Janey came up to them and attempted to take Molly away by pulling on her arm, but Molly resisted and both women frowned at each other. Janey was not one to lightly cede ground. Her three children were running around somewhere, her husband was ambling about conversing with other peers of the realm, her own inner circle was in crisis.

"Molly!" She cried as Molly slipped back to talk with Jacob. Her hands on her hips, Janey looked on, knowing how stubborn her friend could be, but it was rare that she was the person being resisted. Molly was not confiding in her, as she always had in the past. These distressing confrontations kept happening. She called again, loudly and plaintively, so that Molly came over to her, shaking her head in exasperation.

"Honey, what is the matter with you?"

"Why is he calling you Margaret?"

"That's my name."

"Did you ask him to call you that?"

"Janey, what is the matter?"

"Well, people want to know; are you and him together now?"

"No." Molly shook her head, acting surprised, and somewhat hurt by the question. "Who's saying that?"

"No one, but . . ."

Just then one of Janey's sons came up and began pestering her with an urgent request; he wanted to go upstairs into the gym and he wanted her to escort him. Janey whirled off with an angry glance at Jacob, which he accepted in that gallant manner happy souls reserve for the less fortunate.

"Why is she so mad?" Jacob asked Molly.

"She's not, really, she's just frustrated. Everything is changing so much." Her face lost its solemn mien and broke into glee as she spoke to him. "Oh, this place is hopping, isn't it?"

He marveled at her resilience, a quality he had already come to depend on without being quite aware of it. He wanted to thank her, but he had no idea how to do that for something so nebulous. In the tension of strong feelings he blurted out something that had occurred to him repeatedly in the past weeks.

"You're like *the* St. Margaret of this place."

"No." Her face contracted into a grimace. "Don't say that, please, don't do that."

He had watched a sudden, uncontrollable anguish contort her features for just an instant and then vanish. The impression was lasting. He was afraid to tread further on whatever issue it was that had upset her.

Just then the principal priest of the parish emerged from his lair intent on having a word with Frances. It was indeed hellish dealing with this awful woman, but now he was resolved to make her stop, or at least curtail, all this horrible license. One must maintain acceptable levels of control. This gross handling of the flock resulted in more money, to be sure, and the bishop was eminently fond of increase, as any good shepherd would be, but the brand itself had to be protected from tarnishment!

He steeled himself as much as he was able for the ordeal of confronting this *woman*! She must be made to understand. She must concede his authority to advise her on these matters. His stealthy approach put him just outside the circle clustered around the Treacle Company, where they could observe but not hear the interview. She had spun around like Joan of Arc, expecting to do battle. At their table Cook and Hereford provided commentary on what they imagined might be going on, as if the Inquisition had been reinstated to enforce the canon law concerning the serving of fish on church grounds. They vied with one another in their histrionics, playing to their small audience.

Frances was more animated than the prelate; her hands rose about his face. Once or twice she pointed a deadly finger emphatically at the smaller cleric. A bet was made; would she poke him or not? It certainly would have deflated him terribly. He was naturally a servile creature, but his collar made him think he should assert himself in situations like this one, even when he was matched against a superior opponent. He had thin wisps of hair on his upper lip, that served little else than diverting one's attention from the misshapen mouth. He had a curious habit of smiling unexpectedly, and then, before it was even noticed, furtively resuming his worried, injured look.

Frances turned away abruptly before he was finished speaking, and left him standing there beside himself. He began emitting weird suspirations as he imagined murderous phrases and was instantly wracked by guilt. His hand was still raised to make a final point. But no one was there to receive it. He made the fatal mistake of turning towards the Treacle gang; all were facing him like they had paid to see an Elizabethan farce, and he had just come on stage in his motley. He remained in a ridiculous pose for several more awful seconds before he managed to break away to the rectory, where he might prescribe a shot of bourbon to the long-suffering mental patient which he was in fact. Once fortified in spirits he would reimagine his trial and vanquish the wicked hag like a veritable Jove!

"I don't think she helped herself there." Molly said. "Oh, that was not good." She looked down at the little sign she had improvised for their picnic table at Isaac's behest. In cool, ornate, handwritten watercolors it declared, The Mermaid Pub. Her fist rested against her chin as she wondered if that had been such a good idea; and not just that, but all of this riotous fun they were having.

"She clearly bested him." Cook said.

"At what cost?" Hereford chimed in.

"She hates having to do that." Jacob said, knowing how Frances acted when she was very angry at herself.

Frances had gone into the cafeteria and all around the entrance area people were coming and going in swarms. The Grotto was overflowing. People were at every table refusing to relinquish their seating, while others stood on the periphery silently beseeching them to do so. The lighting strung in the trees gave the faces of the petitioners an eerie, unearthly aspect, as if they were specters standing in for their breathing doppelgangers.

"Oh, wait!" Molly remembered she had wanted to show them something. She loped off to arrest Lilly and spoke to her and came back with a cup of wine.

"Taste this?" Molly offered Isaac the plastic cup containing a dollop of wine.

"What is it?"

"It's a more expensive vintage we're going to be stocking."

"Oh, splendid."

"Frances said we ought to have at least one expensive bottle, so we can fleece people like you two."

"Good stewardship." He tasted the nectar delicately. "Not bad at all." Isaac spoke in reverent tones. Hereford took the cup away from him and tasted it as well.

"Have them bring us a bottle, at once." Isaac said. "Maybe we should buy one or two, for other tables, to advertise—"

"Too late. Lilly said we've already sold out. This is all that's left." Molly said, waiting for his reaction.

"So, you're just teasing us with this drop?" Isaac cried out. "Ay, you know how to break a man's heart. But I am the foolish drudge, I toil for your delight."

"This is good stuff." Hereford was smacking his lips for effect. He held out the cup for whomever wished to sample it next. Jacob took it and sipped. He made a face as he imagined a gourmet might, before rendering his final opinion.

"I can't tell. My favorite used to be Boone's Farm, Green Apple. Is that something you can stock?"

"Maybe just for you, my lost boy." She leaned towards him extravagantly, feigning a coquettish swoon. Her face loomed before him, blotting everything else from his vision. Her faint perfume was now a powerful aphrodisiac. His senses had no use for anything besides her. He was lifted onto a magic carpet, floating inside a private globe, where nothing of the outside world mattered to him. She whirled away and the world's insane routine fell upon him once more.

"Make sure they stock a lot of this stuff." Cook demanded. "You can't tantalize us like this. It's not civilized!"

"This is much better than that other swill you were forcing on us." Hereford said.

"Forcing on you!" Molly challenged him in a loud voice; causing everyone to laugh.

"Let us transubstantiate our mortal woes." Cook spoke as if acting in stead of Ecclesiastes, raising his plastic cup with both hands, to mimic the sacerdotal procedure. "There is a time to break down, and a time to build up."

"Yes, a better vintage must come, as has been foretold by our great Sistah, the prophetess of the masses." Hereford continued to craft midrashim for the table's exotic scripture. He was far into his cups and not entirely lucid.

"The goodness imbibed removes impurities from the blood." Cook added with enigmatic fervor. Jacob assumed they were both showing off for Molly now. He decided to join the fray.

"Man does not live by loaves and fishes, nor even wine, alone; but must have his music as well." Jacob spoke as one of the brethren. Cook nodded towards him in a cordial fashion.

At this point the unusual entourage at the picnic table dispersed, leaving only Cook, Hereford, and Jacob, who was suddenly under interrogation.

He could not take any of it seriously. He was unable to care what they thought of his educational attainments. He could not measure up to all that erudition they hauled around like a wagon full of mulch, to what end?

"Just so you know," He announced to them emphatically, "I never haul manure in my truck." He paused. "It's only done out of necessity, and then I only carry the highest grade. Unlike the Treacle teamsters." He tried to mimic their speech patterns to amuse them.

They redoubled their efforts to press Jacob regarding his relations with Molly, and he became uncomfortable. He parried their questions with incongruous humor to let it be known that this was not a topic he would delve into with them. He began asking them about the genesis of their respective intellectual portfolios. Each one took his turn, expressing a wry view of his own history, waiting for the other to offer a withering critique of same. It had the flavor of a practiced routine. They had become friends long ago; both being from the St. Louis region, both having achieved some success in the arts, or as Hereford said of Cook's career, in the gross entertainment field.

Jacob watched them in a profound state of disinterest. He broke away at an opportune moment when they were heatedly discussing the future of the novel and whether or not a digital platform for television would finally drive a stake through the heart of the moribund demand for fine prose. He drifted along. He sat with Cody and Sally for a while and listened to Sally talk about her challenges at work. She was happy to be of use once more. One could feel the weight of her pride buttressing Cody's own. Her strength was integral to his fortitude. She had crafted his nicely-fitted suit of armor from the homespun effects of her emotional dowry.

"You should convince them to play music out here." Cody said during a pause in the conversation.

"Yeah, we could inaugurate the Crisis Tour here."

"You ever hear Molly sing?"

"No. Have you?"

"In church. Oh man, she's pretty good."

Jacob swung his head around as if looking for something. "She said something about getting a deejay."

"Really?" Cody was excited. "What kind of music?"

"I don't know." Jacob began wondering what this diverse crowd would want to hear. He noticed there were more black people on the premises than in the past; it was a promising start. "I would do soft rock, classic anthems, Motown, all the good pop tunes."

"You know, I've done some deejay work in the past. I could do that in a way they'd really like." Cody said with conviction.

"It's true. He was really good." Sally concurred.

"What kind of music?" Jacob asked.

"Disco."

"Oh no. We're not going to play disco here!"

"I know that, but it's all the same process. I'd be playing the music you like—that's my music too, you know."

"Well, have you talked to Frances about it?"

"No."

"Why not?"

"I didn't even know they were considering it. You could have told me."

"Well, look around, this place is hopping. They've got a waitress for crying out loud. I think they're going to set up a bar and more tables over there at the crest of the hill."

Jacob saw Molly coming out of the cafeteria by herself and he got up to go and intercept her before any of the multitude had a chance to nab her first. His excuse was that he wanted to see what she thought of the deejay idea, but really he just wanted to be near her. All the hubbub swirled around them as a storm around its eye and he felt enormous calm being with her, separate from the commotion, standing only in her glow. It was exciting and somehow exceedingly safe in a way he could not comprehend. He didn't want to understand, for fear of destroying the enchantment.

They spoke of using Cody as the deejay while standing in the penumbra at the base of the church terrace.

"Come on, let's go." She clasped his arm to get him moving.

"Where? Oh no, not again."

"My turn."

They were treading softly down the main isle between the pews. It was so odd, he felt as though he were holding her hand and clearly they were not touching one another. He looked up at the heavy, smoothly-finished, ornamental beams that formed the framework holding up the roof. He imagined the carpenters must have enjoyed manufacturing those pieces a great deal more than building out the bones of another shopping center or factory.

They began walking around the altar area when Jacob stopped to dip his fingers into a marble font. He raised his fingers above the bowl, listening to the droplets fall onto the tympanum, making perfect circles. Molly approached him, tilting her head and narrowing her eyes in reproof.

"What are you doing?"

"This idea of holy water. I'm not sure I've ever thought about it before. It's so bizarre. It makes me feel like I'm stoned."

"Stop acting weird."

Molly directed them into the confessional again, this time swapping places. He sat and listened; she knelt and spoke to him in a way she had never spoken to anyone before.

"I don't know what to say," she began.

"In that case, say twenty Hail Marys—"

"No, stop."

"Sorry. I'm listening." He waited. "You brought us here." He was amused, and afraid—of what? Something besides getting caught at playing a sacrilegious game. Something seemed wrong, and exciting; he sensed a danger impossible to decipher . . .

"That thing you said, about me being a saint?"

"Yes."

"That has been a real problem for me. After my loss, I let them put a halo on me. It was like I knew I had to stop mourning, but they wouldn't quite let me. I felt like I was losing myself." She had several times alluded to this before but never in such a direct manner. He had divined it, not being sure of his intuition. It had served to maintain a distance, Jacob suddenly understood, and he wondered how much effort she had to put forth to do that, and if she had always done it with everyone else.

"I was numb," she continued, "for so long. Everyone took care of me, and Sophie too—but it's different with a child. They have such powerful, natural defenses. And it was terrible to see that, too! It was frightening for me to think of her having no father, *and* a mother too distraught to be a good mother! But we came out of it, together, each of us following a different path. I'm not so sure of mine anymore, but we've always stood together, you know?"

"Yes, of course, you must live your lives."

"I know that, but how? That is always the question. Sometimes I think the best thing is to be her mom, and not to worry about being anything else. Still doing all the usual things, of course, but to really make her the focus of my attention, and myself, to be a healthy woman; one who takes care of herself. To be a role model for her, nothing else. But that can become a problem as well." She became silent. Jacob leaned closer and looked at her averted face. He had never seen her so grave, nor intense, when talking about herself.

"I don't see anything wrong in what you are saying." He felt odd speaking to her this way, but his formulation of inane support flowed naturally.

"Maybe I don't want to get married again."

He was startled by this assertion; only murmuring in response.

"Maybe I want something completely different."

"I'm sure you don't have to do anything you don't want—"

"I'm not sure I even believe in marriage anymore. I've never admitted this to anyone, but I'm not sure our marriage was going to last. Can you believe that?"

Jacob did not know what to say; an old dread whelmed up to hold him fast. He feared fumbling away something by not handling his responses properly. She had struck upon something at the heart of his insecurities.

"I'm not sure I even believe in monogamy anymore." After hearing her speak thus, Jacob was keenly aware of her face, and how her eyes were sparkling at him through a mist that passed through the wooden mesh to engulf him. His confusion increased, becoming like a blinding fog that obliterates the view of the road in front of you. You're still going forward, having no idea what is out there, and knowing one should not just keep driving forward into a vast unknown; but if you stop, other motorists might pile into you from the rear.

"I'm sure you don't mean that, do you?" Jacob spoke before he could weigh his words. He wondered if she were trying to shock him; but why would she be doing that now, in this way? And to what purpose? That was ridiculous . . .

"Everyone wants me to get married. Janey is mad at me. Heather is furious. But why? It's like you have to be married to be a part of all this. Why does everyone have to live the same life?"

"I know about that." Jacob said feebly.

"You never did get married?"

"No. I probably should have."

"Probably? Should have? How would you have any idea of what I'm talking about?" Her words stung him.

"Jenny wanted to get married, at the end anyway. I'm the one who always argued against it."

"Do you ever feel like you're just playing a role?"

"Other than when I'm being a Russian monk?"

"Jacob?"

"I think that was my whole problem. I never thought about anything other than being part of a crowd, and one that did things that were considered fun. That was all that mattered. Having a child would have changed all that, so we—"

"Is that why you and Jenny didn't have children?"

He didn't know what to tell her; in his silence he balked. The truth he had always relied on in these matters seemed no longer a viable construct, but only an illusion pasted together from shopworn clichés.

"I don't know."

"Did you try?"

"I always said I didn't want to have children."

"Why not?"

He laughed a nervous laugh, composed of rotten, dredged up things, mostly self-disgust. "It would have interfered with my assigned role, I guess."

"Assigned?"

"Molly, can we get out of here now? This doesn't feel right to me."

"I know. Listen, don't pay any attention to me. I guess I just don't know what I want."

He had begun to reply, but found she was gone. He exited his cubicle and walked after her, going out the original front entrance. They made their way down the sidewalk in a depthless silence, passing the main steps and turning down the wide drive, returning to the Fish Fry. Certain people rushed up to Molly and she was spirited away and Jacob felt the flock ranging their eyes over him. He repaired to the familiar picnic table.

"Where have you been? Offering sacrifices to Yahweh?" Hereford asked. "He no longer requires that sort of thing."

"You should read the old prophets." Cook advised.

"He's not like the Aztec gods. You don't need to offer up your beating heart." Cook spoke as a wise man.

"We went to confession." Jacob said quietly.

"That's the spirit," Cook replied, assuming an unclear note of irony.

"They're holding that right now?" Hereford asked incredulously. "Are you even a practicing Catholic?"

"You didn't really go to confession?" Isaac challenged him.

"Just going into that building is a sort of confession, isn't it?" Jacob said.

"You seek in vain if you do not wish to find, or be found," Isaac recited from his metaphysical book of gloom. Paul smiled in appreciation.

"Hey, who's Heather? Do either of you know her?"

"She's a friend of Molly's. Well, she used to be." Isaac explained. "Molly was dating her brother, for a while there. He's divorced . . ."

"Really? How long ago was that?"

"She never told you about any of this?" Isaac sounded uncharacteristically at a loss.

"I've just learned there's a cabal trying to overthrow Frances." Hereford said.

"That's old news." Isaac replied.

"What do you mean, overthrow her?" Jacob asked.

"What potentate is not being plotted against?" Isaac seemed annoyed. "They want to get the Fish Fry under the control of a regular church committee. The parish council voted to give it to Frances, but now everything's changed. Heather and Janey are on the council. And Heather's brother is the treasurer."

"And he's the one who was dating Molly?" Jacob asked, leaving his mouth open after speaking.

"They might still be, as far as I know." Isaac spoke softly.

"You mean, our wandering Jacob, you have never seen Herr Hindermarch, marching?" Hereford jested. Cook seized the narrative to offer Jacob some facts.

"His name is Kenneth Hindermarch. He's a lawyer. My mother knew his mother really well. One of the Founding Madams of the town's latter days." Isaac was ashamed of his mother's peculiar opinions regarding the slave owners who participated in that horrific custom around these parts at one time. Among those in local historical societies there was a propensity to pass over or even condone the horror when it pertained to their own ancestors.

"I've heard his people have been in Ferdinand for a long time." Paul added, and Isaac frowned at him over his cup of wine.

"Molly is dating this guy?" Jacob was becoming only more bewildered.

"I'm not sure she is any more." Isaac insisted weakly. "Not since you showed up."

"Since I showed up?" He sat there in a strange vortex of thoughts that had no meaning for anyone but himself, and the other two began a separate discussion as he stared dumbly into the night. They had been discussing a recent children's movie that had come out and was proving to be very popular with the suburban distaff population. It presented a brief against the French Revolution and the nasty, matriarchal hyenas; making the case for royalty and the mandate of heaven, and all that supports an absolute monarchy. Cook and Hereford were joking about a movie they ought to make in rebuttal, to be called *Revolt of the Hyena Queens*.

"It would be a story about the overthrow of Hollywood. Civilized men get nervous when those things slip lightly along the edge of their lives."

"A portrayal of the last days in the battle of matriarchy versus patriarchy." Hereford said with fresh vigor.

"If violence were ever removed from the equation, then women would rule again."

"Again?"

"Asherah will come back to reign on earth."

"We will have one of her temples right here."

"That one serves for the time being, doesn't it?" Jacob was prompted to contribute, peering over at the Grotto, where the eternal personification of Woman was consecrated in her demure pose. A persona molded by chivalrous warriors to be the perfect queen of mercy, further exalted in status by a priestly caste to appease the half-pagan populace, who might worship her as the singular, maternal goddess. She loves all and must not exert undue influence regarding temporal matters of power, which are only deemed safe in the hands of the holy and elected brethren. She survives because she was invested by the whole people. She stands her ground above them all, in all times, dressed in robes of moral purity; holding her tongue, and so god help us if she does not!

Jacob began to listen more closely as the others paraded their knowledge; describing the fusion of pagan mythology and the rites of the Mother Church; which had needed to wean the primitive people from a rich, protean diversity of temples. After a moment he felt as though he were listening to complete strangers. How could they talk incessantly this way, and seem to have nothing else in their lives to distract or trouble them?

The waitress came up, and seeing that he was out of sorts, directed her charms at him for a mesmerizing instant. She's come from another world too, he thought.

"Do any of you want a nightcap?" She spoke as freshly as ever to the entire group.

All the men looked at her. Jacob stared into her eyes; it had the effect of lifting him out of his gloom; but her social mask left him feeling dizzy, and even more uncertain about everything that was happening.

"I'm good," Jacob said. "I have to get going."

"It's too bad you don't serve brandy here." Hereford said.

"One snifter of cognac would be nice." Cook agreed, putting his hand reflexively over his wine cup. "No more for me."

"What time do you get off work?" Hereford asked her.

"Right after you leave for the evening, sir." She thus jabbed him in a sore spot, his advanced, relative age. There was a fine antiphonal chortle for response, and then silence, for everyone was a little frayed after a long sodden evening. They put forth weary smiles, having to face the risen monsters of somber self-reproach that breed in the lees of wasted hours. The young woman had once more tactfully braved the usual fire, the jocular bolts from men attempting to lure back an old imagined glory. In that awakening of the past, and the breath of that once vast yearning, comes the haunting atmosphere that swirls about noble ruins at dusk. It was deepest night. They sat there unmoved in the silence, as if awaiting the last chanted prayers conferring leave on the congregants, when the liturgical voice intones for all to go in peace.

31

There had been a spate of curious activity on the street in front of the Spencer house. Jacob watched the cars driving by slowly. Some pulled over to the curb. A few of the pilgrims exited from their cars, pointing in his direction. He had no idea what to think, until a blithe, middle-aged couple drove their dusty sedan right up to the mouth of the garage and solved the mystery.

"How are you?" The rotund man called out with hearty bravado. He stood there looking up at Jacob, who was at a window, staring down at them. He rushed down the steps to greet them. They were decked out in crisp, casual attire.

"We just had to come." The woman explained.

"Hope we're not disturbing you."

"He wouldn't let me pass through this town without coming here." She had a coiffure built like a luxury cupola atop her head, her earthy face was composed of a complete autumn palette of colors.

"I used to attend parties up there, back in the day." The man thrust out his arm to indicate for Jacob where some of his idyllic memories had been formulated. Jacob explained that he had some knowledge of those times; the man said they had just met someone who had been at the recent party."

"Small world."

"That's exactly right!"

"Can we see it? Do you mind?"

He told them that in fact he lived up there; hoping to dissuade them from touring his living quarters. He thought he would humor them, by suggesting they take a stroll about the grounds. He would let them reminisce while he acted as tour guide.

"We won't be but a minute." The man's demeanor changed, becoming that of a senior manager presiding at the company picnic, still directing his subjects in their leisure hours.

"Is this the way?" The portly woman was on the move, apparently having learned from her husband how to ascend to the upper chambers of his shuttered dreamy factory. He heard them clumping up the stairs. He surmised they wished he were not there, nor all his incongruous belongings.

"See, we've just come from Montenegro." She turned from a quick survey of the room to address Jacob, holding out a pin on her blouse for Jacob to inspect, as though he would know what it symbolized.

"That's nice," he said, rather befuddled.

"It's been such a whirl. Carl would never forgive me if we just passed this by. I've heard so much about this place."

It turned out there had been a proto-Joint before the one Jacob had known, and had heard so much about recently. The man admired his seasoned guitar sitting upright in its stand.

"I used to play guitar, in those days," he said pensively.

"It's still in the attic sweetie."

He didn't seem to hear his wife, reaching out to touch the neck as one might feel a totem. We have evolved our perspectives over the course of untold millennia; in every human breast are buried thousands of other lives that might have been ours instead. At times we become aware of occult misgivings that are but the trace echoes of those lost destinies.

"Feel free, go on." Jacob encouraged the man to pick up the instrument. He slung the strap around his shoulder.

"Oh, look at you now!" His wife purred.

He played a few chords, then began finger-picking with crabbed awkward hands that once had known how to perform the task much better. Jacob concluded that he must have been pretty good at one time, but he was obviously very rusty, and besides it was not his guitar.

"Not bad," Jacob said as one journeyman to another of the same guild.

"So much time," the man said, "not being able to play. Ah, there, that's in the past." He placed the guitar back in the stand very carefully. After perfunctory salutations they got back on the road, having another item checked off the list. They were going across the country to see a daughter in California, and they had a fear of being stranded in the mountains because of snow.

Jacob took a stroll about the grounds. The man had said, apropos of nothing, that this was where he had first heard "Bye Bye Love." He did not expound on this sentiment, and Jacob thought it very fine to leave it at that, with just a slight mention of the ineffable holiness. He also could remember exactly where he was when he had first heard many songs, those that would comprise a lasting legacy of the best part of his life. Returning to his room he sat down with his guitar and began to practice; then he decided to bring his guitar down to Cody's, or actually, to the patio belonging to Frances, and started playing there. By the time he played "Country Girl" Cody and Sally were sitting at the table listening to his performance. Even that bastard Mulligan stood on the sidewalk for a moment, nodding in time, before taking his leave, once more the nomad living apart.

"Oh, nice one." Cody said. "From an album as good as anything the Beatles did."

Jacob had to laugh, as way of consenting. "No doubt."

"What album?" Sally demanded. They both responded: "*Déjà Vu.*"

"You know," Jacob said while playing. "If you had to try and give a young person an idea of that time, with just one album, this might be the best choice you could make."

He continued to play and sing other songs as if he had been performing there for this crowd for a long while. Before long a little group of people had collected on the patio to hear him playing his heart out. Most of the time he was hardly aware of their presence.

———◆———

Later in the week Jacob convinced his dad to play golf with him. He had been reluctant because he said he wouldn't be able to keep up, and it just wasn't worth it anymore.

"I'll be your caddy."

"No, I can't walk the course, Jacob!"

"I mean I'll drive the cart, and handle your bag for you. I'll be your chauffeur."

"You mean, you wouldn't play yourself?"

"Maybe I'll take a few shots, do some putting on the greens; but for the most part, I'll just help you play the course."

"It seems sort of silly."

"I'm sure we can do better than 'sort of'; we can be damned silly if we want to. We have that right!"

A snort of amusement escaped the father, sealing the pact, and soon he was breathing life into his pipe bowl. Jacob enjoyed seeing the elfin cast on his father's features. Once they were out on the links they made good progress. It had always been one of his dad's favorite courses; a long, winding, undulating test for a golfer's skill and endurance. His dad always maintained an accurate stroke. He knew it made no sense to shoot for distance, now that age had aggravated the disability he had largely overcome, until of late. In his fall he had bent his frame so badly out of its optimal shape there was a dramatic loss of power in his swing even after he partially recovered. But he always had a facility for striking the ball straight.

Jacob would ferry him from point to point, sometimes in disregard of course regulations concerning the proper use of the electric carts. He told his father about Cook, Hereford, and the Treacle Company. Throughout the day he was gratified to hear his father's genuine laughter breaking out for no apparent reason. Jacob had learned as an adult that he shared this trait with his dad, that of giving vent to delayed humorous reactions. It were as though some situations had to gestate inside of him before giving birth to a full appreciation of the hilarity involved. He knew they both liked to carry certain occurrences around with them as personal amulets.

"There's nobody back there." The father advised, "Go on Jacob, you take a shot." He felt obliged to encourage his son to participate.

He did so. They slowed down for the last few holes since there was no pressure to do otherwise. Jacob had hardly any interest in golf; he had tried to acquire at least a modicum of the cult-like love so many men he knew had for the game. It was very useful in the business world. He wasn't in that world anymore and now he was enjoying himself and he was not keeping score. Observing how his father reacted to this semblance of his lost game proved to be rather pleasant. The mystery of caring about anything so ridiculous as golf was not that much different than any other deep human mystery, especially if you had smuggled a bottle of Irish Mist onto the cart.

"Where'd you get this?" His dad wanted to know.

"I stole it from your cupboard at home."

His father began laughing. "Your mother will notice, you know?"

"She always does. I'll blame you. This is your favorite poison, not mine."

Jacob had also purloined two plastic cups out of which they now sipped the shockingly sweet, delicious whiskey. They sat in the shade of a huge cottonwood tree that stood like a retired emperor down in a low spot near a tiny trickling stream that burbled by, offering mature commentaries upon the goodness of fresh, running water.

"When I was younger, I was known for playing a fast game." His father said. They were both watching a foursome of duffers on a distant green dawdling over the results of some truly wretched putting. "I would have made them skip."

Jacob laughed at the vision of his father, in another era, scattering the slower golfers in front of him by plopping balls among them. "That's considered very bad etiquette, isn't it?" He gasped out.

"I've been on both sides of that nonsense." He sounded very sober all of a sudden.

"Seeing things from a different vantage now?"

"I suppose so. I'm too old to pretend I've done everything well."

Jacob nodded respectfully to honor his father's reflective mood.

"It's true, everything changes. Love changes, friendships fall away, over stupid things, but you must keep close to the family. Those bonds you have, with your brothers . . ." His tremulous voice became halting.

"We're all good, Dad. We're good."

"I know. Ah, I'm not myself. This has been a lot of fun for me, but it brings a rush of memories back, just the same."

"I understand, believe me, I do." An image arose of his father in the bad times. He perceived how his valiant heart must have been punctured; having lost his flesh, his blood, his daughter, at such a tender age. He thought he could see that pain transfigured even now on his age-mottled face.

"I'm sorry about you and Jenny." Henry broached this dreary subject for the first time. Jacob was suddenly at a loss for words. He wondered if his father, or anyone else in his family, knew all the sordid particulars of their rupture. "That can't have been easy."

"No." Jacob gulped down the last syrupy contents in his cup. "I'm not sure I did right by her, at the end. It feels wrong how everything ended between us."

"When I was in a bad way, your mother was my rock. Granted, she wouldn't take all my shit, but she never let go."

Jacob looked at his father's face; he wasn't quite there with him. He was searching through the annals of his life with his helpmate, and feeling uncertain about having shared even this small portion of their trust. His normal protocol called for reticence on such matters; and yet strong emotions had come upon him, and he wished to bolster the spirits of his son. He wasn't sure how to do so. It were as though his wife was there, her hand on his shoulder. There was an echo of the dark days; a voice telling him, 'You know what you have to do.' He wanted to impart something of this powerful energy of love that has passed through purifying fires, delivering one safely to a new realm, where you are established among your loved ones, as firmly attached to immutable truths as humans can ever be.

"I let go." Jacob plunged, as if in sympathetic motion, back into his shame.

"That's not what I mean," his father was back, looking at him. "Jacob, we all have to live with the past, but you have to figure out what you want to have for yourself going forward."

"I know."

"I just hope you can find someone who can be that rock for you."

"Me too."

"Pour me some more of that stuff. We may as well dispose of all the evidence. I don't think we can afford to take it home with us." Henry's highly affected manner made Jacob laugh instantly.

"We don't want to get caught red-handed."

"That's right!" His dad laughed as one does after an emotionally charged moment has cleared away nicely.

When he dropped his dad off at home, his mother seemed irritated with him for some reason he could not ascertain. They had walked in the door laughing about some quip one or the other had made relating to something that had happened earlier in the day. She met them at the door with a concerned look on her face. Her son knew this could turn into peevish complaints regarding matters unknown, pertaining somehow to the incontrovertible guilt of all males.

"How did it go?" She asked, clearly avoiding something else she wanted to know.

"It went really well."

"He's a good caddy," Henry said. "Not a great caddy, though, my game suffered because of that, but it wasn't too bad. I will say, he knows how to provide the right refreshments."

"I saw you took the last of your Mist."

"That was the doing of the caddy. He was breaking rules all over the place."

"We had to improvise, based on the local conditions."

After finishing their round they had downed a few more beers in the clubhouse, where they met some of Henry's friends. Things had gotten boisterous. The old men agreed Henry was surely on to something; they vowed to make their sons act as drivers for them too, soon enough. Now

Madeleine could see they were oblivious to the fact she was upset. She had only been informed of this outing at the last minute; and her youngest son had quit writing those strange letters to her which she had so wished he would stop writing. He was not calling her as often as he used to do, or as frequently as she thought he ought to be doing, considering he was dependent upon her to such a large extent.

It was she who had called upon her friend, also from Iron County, to help her son find a place to stay after he quit his job. It was she who had talked to him several times when he seemed desperate, and had reached out to her in a wretched state, and was soothed, and found there was no need to delineate all his malfeasance since his mother had gentle ways of assuring him things were never as bad as they seemed when one was most at risk of believing the worst. She was greatly vexed to know he was going to the Fish Fry at St. Margaret's every week, and had met a woman there, who had turned his head, and he had not once mentioned any of this to her! Meanwhile he's out on a golf course, blabbing to his father, about God only knows what nonsense . . .

The local conditions? She studied Jacob's face as he loitered, preparatory to taking flight again. He seemed extraordinarily happy. She was glad to see that, but she was also very desirous that he confide in her. "Say, have you been going to the Fish Fry up at St. Margaret's?"

"Oh yeah. It's great what they're doing up there." He started laughing. "We've got this whole outdoor thing going—it's like a carnival."

"Are you meeting people?" She asked as they moved into the kitchen. She suggested he stay for dinner but he said he couldn't possibly.

"Yes, indeed. There are a lot of characters up there. Do you remember a man named Isaac Cook?"

"Yes, I think so. His mother, didn't she pass away not too long ago? We weren't close."

"He's an interesting guy. He's always up at the Fish Fry. They renovated that area by the Grotto. They have tables out there. I helped them string lights in the trees. Remember all those sassafras trees?"

His mother was looking intently at him. On a recent phone conversation she had had with Frances, a certain woman named Molly had been mentioned, and apparently her son was showing a lot of interest in this woman. She would like to hear more about this topic from her son's own mouth, if he didn't mind! He detected his mother's simmering frustration.

"Mom, is something the matter?"

Her mouth tightened into a mute refutation of that line of questioning; it was not a proper means to enter into her thoughts. He knew the problem might not be anything he would be able to solve in this moment, and he wanted to get back to Ferdinand.

"Mom, listen, don't send me any more checks. I'm pretty much breaking even now, even better actually, things are looking up, so—"

"Well sure, sure." She watched him turning to go. "Do you go up to that Fish Fry every week?"

"Oh yeah." He was nodding slowly, as if he had fallen into a sort of trance. "It was a good day, Dad!" He called out and heard a muffled reply from the bedroom.

"Are you losing weight? What kind of diet are you keeping?" She poked him in the midriff.

"Mom! I'm not hungry. We had those beers and—"

"You should get something in your stomach."

"Not now, I need to clear my head."

"Jacob, are you okay to drive?"

"Oh yeah. I'm fine. Your husband was the one . . . No, I promise to be good, and safe."

A subtle smile creased her lips. "Try not to have too much fun." They smiled at one another in that way two kindred natures use to honor the sacred edifice of shared values that is the bedrock of the faith they have placed in themselves.

Jacob exited the 270 outer belt onto Elizabeth Avenue and drove towards Ferdinand. The lazy speed limit was notoriously enforced by local cops who had not much else to do, if you were to listen to those who had recently been cited for speeding violations along that route. At the moment, Jacob was annoyed that he could not slow down even more to better observe how the late afternoon light changed all earthly forms. A golden, very fine, active spray transformed the world. It made tree branches pulse in the air like metal castings laid aside to cool. The leaves shone like illuminated manuscripts put together by unseen hands; one could only imagine the brilliant, cogent lines copied from original sources. The open mind could only gape at such material splendor.

Once he climbed the steps to his space in The Joint he felt oddly at home, possibly for the first time since he had evicted himself from the apartment in the Loop. It was not just a refuge anymore. He drank a glass of water that quenched his parched insides. He started playing his guitar, but he couldn't concentrate and had to set the instrument aside.

He climbed onto the roof to look out over the mystic suburban woods, but even the first stars brought no relief to his melancholy. He decided to take a walk and soon found himself gliding past the elegant sycamores on Elizabeth. They stretched out before him like a race of giant wizards, walking in single file towards some ancient shrine. They had gotten lost somehow, and were now arrested in the act of moving forward, becoming as creatures stranded in tragic legends. The yellow lights wafted softly from windows, pressing outward into the gloom, and dissipating in the yards.

He doesn't want to think of Molly, but finds it is impossible to do anything else. He struggles with the idea he is not good enough for her. Why else would she say those things? What did she mean with all that blasphemous talk about marriage, and monogamy? Was she trying to scare him away? Why had he failed to pursue her in an honorable fashion? He was only hovering about her, like a sickly moth drawn to a porch lamp . . .

He walked into the upper parking lot, going to the end and around and down the hill to the lower level. He passed by the little structure of bleacher seats, and soon found himself climbing up the grassy embankment towards the Grotto. It looked strange now, with no tables and chairs and devoid of human life. Only the string of dead lights wound about in the trees reminded him of the happiness this venue had brought to him. Now it was again part of the somber past, that never was really past, given the nature of human consciousness.

"I wish I could talk to you." He said out loud, having become oblivious to his surroundings.

"Jacob? Is that you?" Janey had come up to stand beside him. Her face twisted around to appraise him with keen, instinctual curiosity. "*Who* were you talking to just now?" She asked in a tone laced with that suspicion reserved for those straying dangerously beyond social convention.

"Janey." He had not been able to come out of his reverie at first, and imagined it was Molly; his soul had wanted so badly for it to be Molly, and for her to peer into his heart once more.

"How long have you been out here?"

"I just got here. I was walking."

"Two of my boys are up in the gymnasium playing sports." She stared at him as she spoke to him and it was unnerving; he understood she disapproved of his friendship with Molly. He shared her confusion as to what it was all about; never more so than at this very moment. He wished he could ask Janey certain questions about Molly, but it would not go well; how could it? He could not begin, as he ought, by stating he had in fact been addressing his dead sister just now, before she had surprised him.

He stared up at the large windows of the gymnasium, barred on the inside with a heavy mesh to protect the glass from the errant throws of exuberant youth.

"Is Molly here?" He asked her, after deciding not to do so.

"No."

"Oh." He could feel that she wanted to ask him questions; but she refrained, not wanting to actually discuss anything with him.

"Well then, I'll let you get back to your walk." She swung away and strode across the parking lot.

He proceeded down Elizabeth looking up at the crescent moon caught in the black branches of the elm tree near the corner. The little globe's full luster was being blocked by the one world close enough to share in its glowing rapture. He was moved by his certainty regarding the recurrent phases of virtue; his steps began to bounce off the sidewalk as he floated in the wonderful autumnal atmosphere. Back at his abode he climbed out the window and perched on the roof and looked out at the suburban darkness.

"What did she mean?" This refrain plagued him. She had gone through so much sorrow. Those grievous deaths had given her an aura. He thought of a saintly woman mentioned in one of his texts, who ultimately offers the comfort of her lasting companionship to the author's dearly fallen man. It was always that way in dramatic versions of life, hardly ever in real life. His mind roved beyond his own sense of guilt to contemplate that value in the abstract. For it beleaguers the mind; where does so much guilt come from?

Surely a species, once obtaining consciousness of the fact it can influence its own behavior, must then explore all the dismal outcomes in a new light. This belief soon smashes into something else, however, the knowledge each individual has nothing but the most primitive understanding of himself. Is there a moral constant extant in subatomic particles, in all those strange, defiant electrons? Or is one largely a victim of temporal desires, a product of his instinctive social handling? At any rate, too often, he feels that he is, by nature, both responsible and largely helpless. Jacob found that his foreign author was ingenious when exploring human intricacy and frailty; but then he always asserts his faith in a chauvinistic version of the same old fairy tale. How does that keep happening?

After turning out the lights inside he peered from one of the back windows. The original, imperfect glass panes distorted his vision, and as he moved the stars seemed to ride up and down on galactic waves. What if the disturbance was caused by an enormous, unseen energy source, passing through alternate dimensions, now entering this time frame, transporting nomadic gods in search of new worlds. Spectral creatures sent to find those who were yet searching for moral sustenance, still drawing mortal breaths to fortify the intractable blood, as if doing penance. Those who have come too far, and cannot go back, such as the brave siblings, Hansel and Gretel. They might be out there among those other spirits, struggling to find their way, as best they can, firm in the belief that no matter what has been lost, out there in the scary world, much else, of even more value, is there to be discovered, if only they are prepared to invade the darkness and find out for themselves.

Part Four

—◆—

In the Old School Yard

32

Janey was pestering Molly to answer her, and receiving only silence in return. Janey had a devious thought; "I'd like to slap her."

She covered her wicked smile with an open hand. She had actually done that once, when they were young girls. On occasion, after glasses of wine, they sought to reconstruct the circumstances leading up to that episode. But there was always a bad taste after conjuring the original animus, even in the spirit of fun. There had been a time when Janey was the dominant personality; her eminence had been eclipsed as Molly became one of the most popular parishioners at St. Margaret's. She had achieved this status by other means than those utilized by girls competing for rank in middle schools.

"I remember you were pulling my hair." Janey spoke as one protesting too much.

"What are you talking about?" Now Molly looked at her friend, whom she had been trying to ignore, but this statement utterly confused and irritated her.

"That time you say I slapped you."

"*Say* you did. Come on, Janey!" Seeing the strange, wounded look on her friend's face she pressed her further. "Why are you talking about that?"

"I just remembered it, that you were pulling my hair before it happened."

"That's not true."

"Because Bobby Jones was talking to me."

"Oh please. I don't believe you. Like that would have made any difference to me. How old were we then? No, *you* were the one!"

"Well, it must have been something like that."

"I can't believe you." There was a reverberant quiver in her voice.

"I'm just telling you what I remember."

"I'm not doing this. Okay?"

Molly began walking over to the picnic table where Cook and Hereford were dining with gourmet relish. Frances had added new items to the menu, and one of them was yellow fin tuna, oven-baked, and served with crisp asparagus spears and a dollop of piquant coleslaw. She had met an ex-Catholic, progressive chef, who agreed under duress to help improve her kitchen's fare.

"It's official." Isaac spoke with a slack, glistening mouth. "This is now the mother of all fish fries. I may have to revise my opinion of the Mother Church altogether."

"Our mother is a fishwife," Hereford exclaimed.

"Beauty then, must be the child of another madam." Cook responded in kind, monitoring Molly's face to avoid being thought too scandalous.

"By the laws of natural selection, we hereby decree this Fish Fry ought to get the biggest crowds." Hereford quipped.

"Thanks be to St. Charles, and his beagle." Cook delivered his offertory response.

"Yes, from here we can read to the lower-level creatures the sermon from the parking lot—"

"You boys having fun? Molly asked them, her arms folded across her chest, her eyes peering sharply from narrowed lids.

"We are all children of light," Isaac affirmed in his sardonic voice, thinking suddenly of his mother's social position, and the white sepulcher of her religious practice. He glanced over at Molly and saw that she was distracted. He wished he could lose a score of years and it were just she and he and they could talk honestly of all things to one another.

Hereford was saying something to him but he did not hear it. He waited to catch Molly's eye, holding up his cup. "Have you tasted the new Merlot?"

"No." She smiled graciously. "Not yet. They have way too many." She was thinking, people are right; I am encouraging their drinking, *me* . . .

"We must prepare the way," Paul said.

"Frances is going wild on us." Molly looked troubled. Her face still wore a residue of the irritation she felt from the incessant harassment of Janey (she could be so unreasonable!); but something else, not expressly clear, worried her even more terribly.

"A voluptuous Merlot, from the Cather Vineyards. Do you want a taste?" Paul addressed her, not aware Isaac had just asked her.

"No." She sat down at the table to let their chatter calm her nerves. They were very proud of themselves about something; stressing the importance of doing their 'field work.'

"I'm sorry, what are you going on about?"

Isaac confided, in a rush of emotion, "You will be proud of us, Molly. I swear."

They were at it again; beseeching her in ways that left her cold. This was just the sort of thing she did not know how to appreciate. It was maddening.

"What's the matter, Molly?" Paul asked. Isaac looked at her closely and then away. He did not want to pry into whatever anguish was now clearly occupying her mind, at least not while anyone else was around. Most of the time, when he was with someone, whom he cared for a great deal, he showed the tact of a courtier; at least towards that favored one. Here, however, he was often unable to uphold his own standards.

Janey appeared again, standing a little off from the table, her hands on her hips. She was reluctant to stay put, relegated to a subordinate position. The grievous aspect on Molly's face made her relent. She took a seat at the table next to Molly; all the others stared at her. She had never been at the table with the heathens before. She had concluded it was expedient, if not entirely rational; in part, it was because she could not stand being excluded from all these stupid conversations they conducted around this old picnic table. She had obviously failed to dissuade Molly from wasting so much of her time with these buffoonish old sots. It was almost scandalous, except for the fact Cook's mother had been one of the matriarch's of the parish, and Cook himself had inveigled himself into many dowager hearts by trading on his name, using gracious manners. They doted on him despite the fact he had been away making money writing for disgusting TV programs most of his life, and now of course he expects everyone to just let him come back, and we're supposed to genuflect before him . . .

"Has anyone seen Jacob?" Isaac asked, looking around.

"Yes, where is Jacob?" Janey said archly, making it clear to whom she was addressing this question.

"I haven't seen him yet," said Paul.

"He always comes early." Isaac put forth.

"Maybe he's not coming then." said Paul. "Maybe he's got something better to do. Who wants to make a bet on whether or not he makes it? Molly?"

"What?"

"Do you think he'll make it?"

"I don't know." She refused to look at anyone.

"I bet he'll come." Isaac said, nodding to further validate his conviction.

Cook and Hereford made a wager of five dollars, regarding the future whereabouts of Jacob, who was in that moment at home playing his guitar. He was slashing furious chordal riffs, much as Richie Havens, who had improvised a song after running out of material when he opened at the Woodstock Music Festival.

"Wait, it's not fair if anyone has inside information," Paul stated in a voice of great concern. "Molly, tell us the truth, do you know if he's coming?"

"No, I have no idea."

"Moll, you can tell us; has he been calling you?" Janey sometimes used this modified version of her friend's name, rhyming it with the word doll, usually when she was needling her terribly.

"What are you talking about? We're just acquaintances. My God, will you leave me out of this ridiculous game." She disentangled herself from the table and stalked off. Janey waited only long enough to register her own surprise, and then she fled from the table as well.

"What's that about?" Paul asked.

"No idea. Molly is upset about something."

"Oh, you think? I couldn't quite make that out." Hereford began laughing. "Do you usually explain these things for the director using footnotes?"

"You want to make it ten dollars?"

"You're on. But tell me the truth, if you do know; you can't be running a rigged game."

"Why not? That's how the world operates."

Hereford laughed.

"I have no idea. How should I know the whereabouts of our young wayfarer, spurned by his goddess?" He exclaimed, putting up his hands for effect. "But he's come to every other Fish Fry. Why wouldn't he come to this one?"

"Well, I think we know the reason he's been coming, and we just saw her act like Peter in the courtyard before the cock crowed."

"Oh, I see what you mean." Isaac looked up at the lights festooned between the sassafras trees. "No, that hardly colors the affair in all of its complexity. I still wager he comes."

"Colors the affair. Complexity. Nicely phrased for a TV guy. You know, I really would like to do the project with you. Do you think we would have a good chance of getting it produced?"

"For television?"

"Yes. Or a movie."

"You'd like that, wouldn't you?"

"Yes, I can't deny it. Seeing your own characters up there, bathed in all that irresistible glamour. One's story writ large, in the living scenes that you've wrought; oh yeah, I can see the allure in that."

"It wouldn't necessarily be your characters, and certainly not your scenes. We would have to get a good screenwriter if we're serious about this. I'm played out."

"Well, I don't know about that, but you know what's best."

"We're out of wine, confrere. Unless you have more water jars from Cana to tap?"

"Where's the waitress?"

"She's on the lower level."

"That crowd's getting out of hand. We should try to get Frances to forbid her from serving those people down there."

"They've forced all the smokers to go down there. Our Valley of Gehenna, the bones of priests and prophets shall be brought forth . . ."

"A whole bunch of them have come over from the Subterranean Blues Bar. She likes being down there with them."

"And they like her being with them." Hereford emphasized his disapproval with a vigorous shake of his head.

"Well, I guess so!"

Paul rose abruptly and stomped off to get another bottle of wine.

Jacob was now pacing in The Joint. He was feeling aggrieved, not knowing why. He felt foolish for staying away like a sulking brat. And then when he finally decided to go, he felt even more foolish, for going at such a late hour. The dusk had come with its rich glow and then had faded and now that time was gone forever. It was October fourteenth; the superb autumnal airs had prepared a witch's cauldron for mixing one's present emotions with haunting memories. The chill in the air brought one closer to the blood's glorious warmth; the density of each breath whetted all sorts of hungers. Jacob argued with himself: it was already too late to go; but then again, why wouldn't he go, even so? And ultimately, he knew he couldn't help himself, he had to go.

The smell of leaves moldering on the ground was intoxicating. The warmth underneath his jacket, and the cool air on his face, were equally delightful. When he came onto the church grounds he saw there was a pretty good crowd milling about. Isaac was at his table alone.

"So you did make it after all?" Isaac said, leaning back and looking up. He had been slumping forward into that tragic pose of the problem drinker.

"Yeah, I had some things I had to do first."

"Like what?"

"Nothing. Where's the other consul?" He now referred to them as the Fish Consuls.

"He had to leave. A certain lady required his attendance for certain needs. I think the writer had to prove his existence to her friends."

"Has he really written all those books you guys talk about?"

"Sure. He sells just enough books to provide him a comfortable living. There's no putrid excess to wallow in [he was here quoting Hereford himself]; certainly nothing like what TV celebrities enjoy. Now, you want to talk about decadence . . ."

"And you lived in that world yourself, for a while."

"I was mostly behind the scenes. I have played many parts. I won't ever bother to ask if I played them well." He smiled in a wry fashion as if about to continue a speech once learned for the stage. "No, I worked for the greater glory of the actors, to them belong the spoils."

"But you've done well, too, I imagine."

"No doubt."

"Why act so humble about it?"

"Why indeed? It's not something I think about as much since coming home; well, being back here, and meeting Molly . . . After wrapping things up for my mother, I have a new perspective. I've achieved wisdom."

Jacob lifted a clean cup off a stack sitting on the table and held it out so that Isaac could share a small portion of his wine with him. He smelled, tasted, and murmured appreciatively.

"I could probably learn to act like a wine snob, with some help from my friends."

"It's getting pretty high class around here," Isaac said.

Molly came up and looked at both of them. "You made it."

"Yep."

"This guy won some money betting on your habits."

"Yeah?"

"Hey, I almost forgot, Frances was looking for you earlier. She said you told her you would do something—"

"Oh shit! Is she up there now?"

"Yeah."

"I totally forgot." He got up and wended his way through dense clusters of people in the parking lot. They watched him loping away. Isaac swung his eyes back to observe Molly's face. She pulled away her gaze after a moment and seeing Isaac staring at her, she frowned and looked away.

"Everyone is getting real interested in this thing between you two."

"Oh, I know, believe me, I know." She straightened up. "Tell me Isaac, what do you think of him?"

"Me?" He reacted as if he were the last person on earth to pass judgment on another human being, despite the fact everyone knew how much fun he derived from doing precisely that, as often as possible. He even liked to turn his scathing attention on himself, after Bacchus has torn a few sheets out of his rigging, and he is becalmed among intimate friends. He trusted no one more than Molly, and he was treading lightly for her benefit.

"Come on, I mean it." She leaned forward over the table and grasped his cup and took a sip. "Tell me."

"Well, now. You ask a lot. I don't really know him that well, Molly. I don't know what to tell you."

She noticed that he was more inebriated than usual at this time of the evening. He usually tempered his drinking before this late hour, conducting himself with more prudence than was commonly thought; in large degree, because of his sense of humor. He often aided and abetted those casting aspersions at his expense, even when the slights were highly inaccurate. He no longer cared what most of the world thought of him; and the proportion was increasing with time. He didn't necessarily feel good about that fact, but it felt necessary to him now, for some obscure reason, and he knew he would not be going back to his old ways. He had been plunged into the past by his mother's death and he found it impossible to share any of the psychic repercussions with anyone else.

Molly watched him pour more wine into his glass; he looked up at her sheepishly as if reading her thoughts, begging her indulgence on this matter. One good friend to another, who is badly in need of such a favor.

"I don't really know that much either. We've gotten really close, but I don't understand what we are to one another. It's just weird." She looked truly befuddled.

"You've spent enough time with him; you have to trust your instincts."

"Don't talk to me like that."

"He's breaking himself down." Isaac spoke in a tone of deep sincerity.

"No, I don't think so." Molly felt an immediate aversion to this portrayal. Her face blanched. "I think he's actually very grounded—whatever that means." She shook her head as if dismayed by something not readily apparent to either of them. "It's just hard for me to make sense of it, somehow."

"I'm not saying he's tearing himself down. He's taking stock. He's delving into his own personality. He's testing what's really there, and what's gotten put there, by the world, by his own conceits. He's trying to understand what it is he always thought he wanted. He's gone to war with his own vanity. He's standing against all of this." He flung out an arm for dramatic effect, but the effort unbalanced his position on the bench and he had to slap that hand hard onto the board to right himself.

"All of this?"

"You know."

Molly saw that Isaac was not really in a very good way and that she might be enabling him in his weakness at the moment. He could talk about other people endlessly. He was a hopeless gossip; and for the most part it wasn't mean, or salacious, or petty, or perverse; he just took a tremendous interest in the human story.

"One time he started telling me about how he had been living in a basement." Isaac was looking up into the night sky.

"That was not so long ago. I don't think he even has a real job."

"Right, and he was telling me about the dust. He made it sound like he'd been making a study of dust motes in sunlight; and how eventually every iota falls to accrete in layers that cover everything." Isaac looked at the colors painted by the lights on the leaves of the trees around the Grotto. "He was really talking about free will, I think. And destiny. My mother's papers are like that, chronicles of slave-holders. What am I supposed to do with them? Preserve the lot as local history? Nobody cares about that material, not really; not the actual history. Not the moral deeds of the petty bourgeois Pharisees—"

"Isaac! You said yourself you should let other people in the society take care of all that; you need to stop worrying about it." Molly just then saw Hereford breaking free of a group of people and heading for the table. He had a bottle cradled near his stomach and swung it for her sake like a baby. She stared harshly at him and waited for him to see her and then she vigorously shook her head in tight oscillations. He understood what she meant and swerved off and landed at a table on the Grotto, where he proffered his fresh bottle and was enjoined to take a seat.

"What's Hereford doing?" Isaac stared after him, like a child, or a man who is hopelessly intoxicated. "I thought he'd gone."

"Isaac, why are you still fussing over your mother's papers?"

"I'm going to give them to the society. But it's not all society business, you know. I just wanted to go through it first. I've forgotten so much. All the layers, of my own past, and hers, and everything. You know? I mean, remember teaching them about the democratic nature of the ancient synagogues? We should be doing that here. Molly, let's give a toast to our better days—"

He reached for his glass but knocked it over and spilled the dregs over the pine slats and down through the spaces onto the withering grass.

"Okay, Isaac, come on. Maybe you ought to be getting home. Why don't I walk with you?" She stood up.

"I wouldn't have said that about Jacob if Hereford were still around. We wouldn't want to get him going on the topic, would we? You know how he can be. Nothing is serious. Nothing!"

"I know, come on, let me help you up."

"Oh Molly, be careful of my honor. I am not that bad, really." He struggled to get up. He reached out and put his hand on her shoulder as she leaned over, straining to raise him up.

"Everything alright over here," Paul had come up to offer assistance.

"We don't need your help," Isaac said. "Molly's walking me home. Go back to your other table."

Paul looked at Molly. "Would you like me to come with you?"

"No, we'll be fine. Are you okay to drive? Maybe you should get a cab."

Paul looked at Isaac; a stricken look came over his face.

"Do you want me to call a cab for you?" Molly asked.

"No, that's alright. I'll do it."

"Well, then, I'll see you later, Mr. Hereford." Isaac spoke with forced diction.

"I'll see you, Cook."

Molly felt herself once more in charge of a faltering situation she had not sought for herself. Listening to Isaac and Cook could be very strange. They sounded so alike, in all their verbal displays she could hardly tell them apart; but there was one stark difference. She had gotten to know Isaac, and she cared about him very much. For reasons hard to explain, Hereford left her cold. She rationalized to herself that she could not humor someone so neglectful of common decencies, who allowed the repercussions of past crackups to rattle obscenely through his persona.

She asked Isaac to wait a moment, while she walked up to the cafeteria to talk to some people. When she came back they began to walk up the drive. Jacob had been on the lower level, running errands for Frances. He was detained by some people on the bleachers who were conducting rituals of remembrance to conjure that enduring ache of great longing that marks a child for life. Now he was climbing the hill by the Grotto and as he came into the lighted area he saw Molly and Isaac, and rushed over to be with them.

"Where are you two going?" He asked them.

"She's taking me home." Cook spoke with the dignity of a man who has squandered so much of that commodity he has come upon a rare appreciation of what's been lost, and weighs with infinite care what remains.

"Mind if I come with you?"

"She has a lot of suitors. You know that, don't you? The joy of the holy heart, that's not for everyone."

"You've had too much to drink, Isaac." Molly spoke sternly.

Isaac mumbled to himself, and stated clearly, "It's not." Then he lapsed into wounded silence.

Molly looked past Isaac at Jacob on the other side of him and her expression told him to forbear the usual repartee. Isaac lived just down Elizabeth, in the second house from the corner, adjacent to the upper parking lot. They walked slowly as Isaac began to explain to them that he had no refreshments for them; nothing at home, he said several times.

"We don't need anything." Molly assured him. "Everyone's going home now. It's time for everyone to get some sleep."

"I don't need anything." Jacob echoed thoughtlessly.

"I told Jacob about my mother." Isaac spoke as if divulging a closely held secret.

"You did?" Molly looked over at Jacob.

"Do you want to see a scrapbook I put together?" Isaac asked eagerly.

"Okay." Jacob looked to Molly for cues after assenting out of habit.

"Maybe some coffee." She said.

"Don't know, might be coffee. Can you make some?"

"It's pretty late for coffee, isn't it?"

"Take your sandals off your feet, this is sacred ground." Isaac quipped as he opened his front door with a key.

"Isaac, stop it now." Molly responded gently.

They sat uncomfortably in the living room flipping through several albums replete with photos, letters and newspaper clippings, and other impedimenta of a solidly bourgeois life. Isaac murmured to himself as they turned the pages. They could not understand what he was saying. There was no more mention of coffee. Finally he announced to them it was time for him to get some rest and he ushered them to the door and they found themselves greatly relieved to be on the front sidewalk, breathing the delicious cool air. They paused to stare upwards, drawing in deep breaths, intimately aware of their own bodies and the burning stars.

"Oh, my tree won't be there much longer." Molly looked across the street.

"Your tree? That elm?"

"Yeah, I used to live right there."

"Really? When was that?"

They began to compare notes. Her family had moved there a few years before Jacob's family had moved out of Ferdinand, to an interim house further north on Hudson Road.

"I walked by here almost every day going to school. I could go a shorter way, but it didn't have the large trees. I love mature trees. I don't think I understood that about myself till I moved back." He became a little flustered, having just told her he loved trees, while thinking in a sort of delirium of how it would be to have her with him in bed, every night, and again, every morning, in that naked intimacy, and sheer honesty. Watching her care so tenderly for Isaac earlier had caused the sloppy burden in his heart to overflow. The door of his furnace had sprung open, exposing the hot seething mass, as it was undergoing transformation; to his perception it was blinding. He was suddenly very afraid to make a move and find out she wouldn't have him.

She must think I'm a complete fool, he mused.

I feel so close to you, and that I don't know you at all, she was thinking.

"Why did you come up here so late, this evening?" She interjected into a silence that occurred as they walked very slowly on the sidewalk past the nuns' barracks.

Molly was clutching hold of herself with her arms because of the cold air. Jacob thought of offering her his jacket but it seemed too presumptuous. As they walked towards the church grounds he noticed the light bulbs strung over the tables at the Grotto were lightly dancing. The same breeze made his cheeks glow like fireplace coals. Molly said she could almost smell snow in the air. He was instantly overcome by a deep anticipatory hunger for the outpouring of cultural ornaments that are used to mark the arrival of another winter solstice. He imagined Christmas carols resounding up into the church rafters, and hissing radiators at his childhood home, the smell of evergreen boughs draped across his mother's mantle. He could almost see blankets of snow at dusk swaddling every lawn with a purple majesty.

He strode beside himself, as he once was, beset by intense feelings, and a longing to embrace all that goodness the human spirit embodies; wallowing in the ecclesiastical tenet espousing the love of one's neighbor. Molly walked silently with her arms folded close to her body, and it were as though she was entwining his rampant emotions snugly into place and keeping them secure. He wished they had to walk many blocks before getting back to the point at which they would have to separate.

"I don't know, I just started playing some music. Then I thought I would learn *Songs for Beginners*—"

"I love that album." She exclaimed. "By Graham Nash?"

"Yeah. Me too." After a moment he laughed. "I really thought I would learn all the songs in one evening. That was stupid."

"There was a time when my older sister, Helen, she used to play that album before she went to school, when she was in college. Those lyrics are etched in my memory."

"I know what you mean."

"I don't know what I would have done without her. She dropped everything, took all her vacation, and came to stay with me. She took care of me and Sophie for a while there, in a way I needed very much."

"Well, then . . ." He spoke after a moment. The thought of taking care of her was overwhelming for some reason. They were standing near the Grotto; no one else was in sight; both of them were thinking rapidly, and confusedly. Molly tilted her head back and looked up into the vast glitter of the heavens.

"It's like I can hear them."

"I know," Jacob agreed; her voice was a chime struck by the stars.

The garish light bulbs above their heads drenched the empty Grotto in tones of picturesque desolation. They sat down at one of the empty tables under the gaze of a large, waning, misshapen moon.

"Well, it's too cold to sit here," Molly said, looking over at him.

"I was sort of afraid of seeing you again," Jacob said abruptly.

"What? Oh, why you came late. I thought, maybe. I knew I was involved."

He looked at her face, the mysterious liquid beauty of her darkened eyes pouring out from her unfathomable soul. His thoughts began to race. He had no idea what he could say that would have any meaning when put on the enormous scales used to put such a life as hers in the balance with his own. She felt him looking at her this way for a moment and then she leaned closer and looked directly into his eyes.

"Did I shock you that much, with all those things I said in the church?"

"Yes," he laughed nervously; brought back to where they really were. "I have to say, you did startle me, quite a bit. I don't know what I believe in either."

She studied his face, disconcerted by this answer. She made a slight murmur of dissent.

"That was some speech," he said. "Quite unexpected."

"It's just that I don't know what *I* want, for myself, right now. Can you understand that?"

"Yes. I think I'm living something like that myself."

"No, I think you're involved in something else."

"What do you mean, like what?"

"You tell me."

"You mean someone else?" He was almost put into a stupor by a strange effect of lighting that cast her face into a perfect cameo. Her mouth showed that she was in distress. Her wan smile spoke of the constraints of human compassion. She looked away and he studied the intricately woven plait of hair she had adopted of late. He stared at the nape of her neck. It made him desperate to say something. It was time to act. Kiss her! But he dared not do that; she wasn't even looking at him. He must hold back.

He couldn't ruin something that wasn't even begun yet; or had he already squandered it?

"Jacob, why aren't you working?"

"I'm going through a mid-life crisis?" He attempted to smile agreeably as he spoke to disguise his discomfiture. His tone had sounded false in his own ears. But at least the deflective humor was familiar ground where he might get his footing again.

She rebutted this with a silent scrutiny of his face. What was she finding there? Could one's shame be tangible on the brow like the script cut in bold letters across Roman arches?

"I really liked my job, when I was with Jenny—"

"Why'd you quit that job?"

He shook his head, appearing to be in a sort of trance of bewilderment over what he had once done. "Well, Jenny left me."

"You told me that."

"We broke up. We left each other . . ."

"You said she wanted to get back together, later?"

"No. I didn't mean that anyone left, in the physical sense, well, that's what was suddenly dead. But then she practiced the arts of seduction on me. To spice up the marriage, she told me. We seemed to be having a good time, but it didn't feel right. I could tell something was wrong."

"Did she want to have a child?"

"Yes."

"And you didn't?"

"No, I guess not." He was shaking his head again. She was observing him with a pained expression, which he noticed, and inwardly winced.

"All those years we agreed we didn't want to have kids, I don't know why."

"Then she changed her mind?"

"Not really, she didn't really say that, but I probably should have known." He was afraid to speak to her of these matters.

"We don't have to talk about this."

"It's just the way I was, at the time, and it wasn't who I really wanted to be. Does that make sense? I guess every depraved asshole comes to that conclusion. Wants complete absolution, because; 'That wasn't me. I'm not like that; you gotta believe me, you gotta forgive me. Yes, come away with me now. I'll buy a condo in Siberia.' Ah, I'm sorry." He shook his head and looked at her face, which he had avoided while he delivered his bitter jest. She looked even more somber, moved by this effusion that had brought her closer to understanding some things and further away from others.

"How old are you, anyway?"

"I'll be forty in November."

"Farty?" Her visage became animated.

He smiled, happy to be back on safe ground; the simple fact he wasn't to the genteel manor born. They got up and moved over to a picnic table placed beyond the Grotto at the top of the hill, and began to talk of the next Fish Fry and other casual matters. They talked to each other and about each other in a simple, cursory fashion, which revealed stronger currents running deeper within them. In this proximity the emotional windings in each engendered a strong flux of mutual sympathy. They felt that which is beyond the reach of words.

"I was supposed to be in Ithaca today; visiting with Helen, and to see my niece, Megan. She's one year old today. I'm her godmother."

"Why didn't you go?"

Molly didn't say anything for a while. "I was going to take my time, and drive, but then things came up . . . the time got away from me."

"This autumn weather makes me think of my old school days."

"I know what you mean."

"It seems all I do anymore is drift in these timeless currents."

"Where is everybody?" She said suddenly, appearing to be ill at ease.

He looked around, for the first time seeing the area by the cafeteria in what seemed like ages. He could see a few stragglers moving about like ghosts. He was prefiguring the manner in which Molly would say something about having to go even as she mentioned her mother and daughter, and then she was walking away. He followed her with his eyes until she disappeared and then he moved to a different table in the Grotto area. Now he was alone, in a familiar chapel of solitude. The lights above him swayed as a chill passed across his sad countenance. His mind composed a moving nocturne derived from a trove of heartfelt memories that shone as faintly as these many suns barely visible to the naked eye, sprinkling photons on our steadfast earth. He imagined the last time they were all together in the original living room with the lighted tree, the last time, before Johanna passed away; she glimmered in the mind's inner recesses.

He rose to walk home, feeling as though he had never been on Elizabeth Avenue before. It was an exquisite experience. He felt lost, as one having to find his way on an unfamiliar path in the woods, that might abruptly come to an end at any moment. He would have to venture forth using only his wits; being ready while not expecting anything to happen. He continued homewards in a sort of hypnosis. Strolling up the driveway he marveled at the galaxy, tolling sublime measures in utter silence.

33

The next morning, after some early chores, he tramped around Ferdinand for a few hours. He stopped to visit with Cody on the patio. Sally joined them and left again in short order; listening to them talk incessantly of the same topics was impossible. Who cared which Neil Young album was considered the best one! They were able to argue endlessly over the music that was popular when they were in high school. They tried to ascertain where the best hamburger could be had in the region. The proliferation of new brands of beer had subverted their loyalties to a single label, and they were now self-styled connoisseurs!

"Do you need the truck today?" Cody asked him.

"I don't think so." Jacob responded. "I'll see you later."

Jacob walked down Maple to cut through the school yard and lope over the tracks to get out to Florissant Road. He was lord mayor of the cheerful day, having no destination. He dropped by to see Robert at his car lot and found him in an expansive mood.

"Come on, I want to show you something." He took him back to the garage to show him some new used cars which had to be gone over by his mechanic before rolling them out under the plastic flags to make their debut. They talked in the garage and Jacob listened to him brag about his operation, and then they exited from the rear entrance and stood on a small bluff looking out over Moline Creek.

Robert began telling him about his relations with Beatrice. He explained that his wife had developed an aversion to performing conjugal acts with him. Jacob was intensely embarrassed to be put in the position of lay confessor. He tried to dissuade these confidences with a series of reproachful grimaces, but Robert was not even looking at him. He glanced down at the creek, and up into the trees, and God only knows where his visions were taking him as he whirled his arms about.

"Robert, none of this is any of my business." Jacob broke in.

"I'm just telling you, I wouldn't be doing this, with Beatrice, otherwise. It's the first time! Just about . . ." He was smoking and blowing smoke out through his nostrils. "It's the third time."

"I'm sure you will get it all figured out." Jacob felt like he was reading trite aphorisms from cue cards.

"It's a mess. Bitty understands me. I know, that sounds like a cliché. But she does! She's gone through a lot of things. You don't know her."

"No, I really don't." Jacob felt constrained to answer, seeing how Robert was gazing at him with a strange, maniacal stare. "I wish the best for you both." He wanted to effect his escape.

"Say, you go to the Fish Fry at Margaret's every Friday, don't you?"

"Yeah."

"That's why you wouldn't deliver that car for me, isn't it?"

"Pretty much."

"You're sweet on Molly Fuller, aren't you?"

"Look Robert, that's not something I want to get into. She's not interested in anything like that, right now. She's been through some really bad shit, herself, as you should know."

"No, I know, I know. I just wanted to say, we may see you up at the Fish Fry this week."

"Okay. What do you mean we?"

"Beatrice and me."

"Well, they are always looking for new customers."

"I've heard people talking about it."

"The place has been really busy lately."

"That's what I've heard." He assumed again his dominant position and put a hand on Jacob's shoulder to steer him around and they meandered back towards his little glass office. Outside the door they began to take their leave of one another; then Robert addressed him with enthusiasm.

"If you ever want to borrow one of the cars for a day or two, to have a nice getaway or something, just let me know. It would be no problem."

Jacob ranged his eyes over the vehicles on the lot, considering the fact that some forms of corruption take an actual shape you can run your innate greed over as the straying hands roam over the body of an amorous woman.

"I'll keep that in mind. Thanks."

"Hey, we'll look for you on Friday!"

"You bet. Go sell some cars."

Robert lifted his head and smiled with self-assurance. His confidence settled firmly in place, he returned to his listings.

———◆———

On Thursday Jacob found himself helping Frances tear out some old cedar bushes she wanted to replace with a bed of roses in the spring. He was working with a shovel, removing dirt and trying to wrench the stubborn roots from the earth. He paused, his heart beating in muffled throbs; beads of sweat were cold on his forehead. He looked around, taking in the October day. It was clear and sunny, erratic shadows of swirling leaves teased his sense of vision.

"I'm thinking of installing a fountain over there." Frances said.

"My back aches already."

She laughed. "Not for a while yet. Do you want some lunch?" She had taken off her great bonnet to let the sun splash on her strongly-chiseled features. Her hair was roped in back and the loose, fiery strands splayed about her face.

"You want me to go get something for us?"

"No. Let's go inside. I'll make sandwiches."

He had never been in her house as a guest to partake of her hospitality. They went in the front door off Allen Place and he noticed at once how neat and tidy and austere everything was in her spacious living room.

"Make yourself at home," she told him as she walked ahead through the dining room into the large kitchen. Jacob took the opportunity to appraise the furnishings of her home. She owned many pictures depicting pivotal moments taken from scripture; reproductions of works done by the great gloomy masters. He noticed she collected tiny gargoyle figurines which she perched on the mantel and bookshelves and other surfaces where they might peer down into the room.

"I like all these gargoyles," he said, hoping to get her talking about her place. She brought him a glass of chilled water.

They sat at a wooden table in the kitchen placed before a window that looked out on the side yard. She made tuna fish sandwiches using bread she had just baked. Sitting down she explained how she began collecting the gargoyles; after receiving one as a gift.

"You'll laugh, but I think of each one as a creature who has had a past life. They are condemned to brood over what they have done in those long-lost days when they were trapped in human form." Her face adopted a weird aspect as she spoke. Jacob considered her verb usage, and that she was touching upon that part of herself which led her into the nunnery, and then brought her back out again.

"They sure get your attention."

"You may know that the word gargoyle derives from throat, or gullet. They were used as spouts, of course, but the grotesque image, that was about something else altogether. It is always that way with the great fixtures of human architecture; about giving voice to something much deeper." She had often wondered what her life might have been like if she had pursued a secular profession, possibly as an architect—but she had to laugh, because all she ever thought of building, even now, was churches!

He ate slowly, listening to her speak of great churches she had visited.

"You said the figures became controversial?" He asked during a pause.

"Long ago, the demonic features scared people, I guess. St. Bernard wanted to have them purged from the buildings. He condemned them as monsters, unclean monkeys."

"Like those scary bastards in the Wizard of Oz."

Frances erupted in peals of laughter. "Now those were scary. As a girl I used to really shiver when I watched those flying monkeys." She passed a hand in front of her face as if to blot out each and every evil incarnation.

"I was really afraid of those things. We used to watch that show every year, in the spring."

"Yes. Around Easter time."

Frances got up to clear the table and Jacob assumed it was time to go back to work, but she quickly took a seat at the table again.

"Do you think we should keep the Fish Fry going through November?" She asked him.

"Sure, why not. So long as the weather holds out. But it could turn at any time. We've been lucky so far."

"This is the first year we've done this. People are complaining."

"Aren't people always complaining?"

"Well, that's true. Nonetheless, that hardly relieves us of the need to examine our own actions, seeking to know what lays beneath them."

He was surprised at this turn of events. "It's hard to please everyone, in each moment." He remembered at his last job how important it was to meet schedules. He could not always avoid ruffling feathers to make things happen. Once a job was done, everything could be put back in order. However, you had to be careful not to strain the good will of your best people too much; honest communication was very important. "Respect is always—"

"It always comes down to money," she said in a forlorn manner, staring at her hands, clasped together and resting on the table. She began to talk of how they decided to let her run the Fish Fry operation and how it was more difficult than she had imagined. Her revelations took the form of a soliloquy and Jacob sipped his water and listened. To his amazement she recounted to him the story of how she had come to leave Baltimore.

There was abuse going on and she had stumbled upon it; she confronted the priest involved. The brethren closed ranks and admonished her as if she were the one who was way out of line; coercing her to keep silent.

So she went outside the church, speaking to a woman who shared her passion for Gothic cathedrals, and whose husband was a partner at one of the largest law firms in the city. After much pleading by Frances, the woman took up the cause as her own. When her husband demurred she put her foot down and demanded that he do the right thing. He made some calls and grew even more leery of tilting into such an onerous battle. He tried to dissuade his wife from pursuing this thorny path, but she was now defending the ideal of her own social position. The aggrieved husband mustered his troops; falling into the grip of a younger version of himself. The fathers had powerful friends who had no trouble turning a blind eye on wrongs done to unknown persons. A tornadic cloud of damning papers arose as powerful lawyers skirmished to determine who really had the stomach for taking this fight into the public glare.

"I took the settlement," Frances said to Jacob, looking straight ahead. "They made a considerable payout to the victim, and I agreed to the provision that I would never divulge my knowledge of the case at a later date. I took money too. They made the case that I had been wronged!" She looked at Jacob. "I gave the money to the family of the boy. They gave it back, they insisted, because I lost the plea to be allowed to remain as a nun, in another parish. They weren't going to have that!" She stood up after disburdening herself, walking to her counter to retrieve a plate of cookies. Jacob stared greedily at the offering, knowing her baked goods were final proofs of Man's weakness against the lures of gluttony.

"There goes my strict diet." He said facetiously, munching into one of the soft starchy morsels.

"I probably shouldn't have put all that on you," she said as they parted.

"I'm glad you did." He answered, not really knowing why, but it was true; it was a way to understand the intricacies of her heart more thoroughly. It resonated with his strongly developed sense of her innate goodness.

That evening he played his guitar with enormous pleasure. Once in a while he could feel a surge of unusual power when he was expecting to struggle with a particular song. Instead, it would come to him with fluent ease. It has to do with the holistic memory of a musician; his mental and his physical manipulation fuse in that grace earned of diligence and passion. One is able to employ one's proficiency to partake of the exquisite savor of the piece, as composed, and sometimes, even better, in extemporizing, using one's mastery to enable flights beyond where you might otherwise have gone. He felt a sudden pang of regret that he had no way to share this ecstatic feeling. Then he began playing the songs he would have liked to play for Molly.

As he abandoned himself to the music he conjured an imaginary audience. He thought of Johanna; picturing her as she was in those months before she became sick. That beautiful spirit she shared with him so completely as his confidante. In those glorious days, when going to school at the beginning of each year was the commencement of brash new promises, made by the world directly to him. And each school year ended at the dawn of summer, and his return to his natural fief, where he strode about this realm as a childish lord. He now played for those orphan selves of lost ages, pondering the specters of innocent youth; which is not long, and always remains there in some form to be sweetly tasted again. He did not know if he was ever going to get to a better place, or not, but he had a notion that one's relation to life should not be determined by the worst outcomes of fate. One cannot simply float above things, cavorting with marvelous notions, content to live that sort of separate existence; not if he wishes to stay in tune with worthy aspirations borne by his true self.

34

The next week he toyed again with the idea of not going to Margaret's on Friday. It begged the question; did he have any say in the matter? That was another topic he might lob at the pine table professors, just to incite their 'jabbering.' Oh, how they huddle in all that erudition, kept forever in motion about them, like a brilliant mobile, made of the most allusive material. How like babes they are, transfixed by reflective shapes dangling over them as they loll flailing in their cribs.

He was enjoying the autumn weather tremendously. The seasonal must rose from the ground and lingered about him in the rich, heavy air. A trace of smoke brought forth a sense of rendered sacrifice, and recalled the imperfect past; manifold joys and sorrows were seeping from the sediments of what has gone before. Ecstatic leaves brushed by him and fell scudding at his feet, and whirled up into tiny cyclones that drew power from the emotional storms unleashed in his heart. He merged into their joyous flight. The deciduous trees offered fresh currency to the winds as he drank prophecies thereof, curing his warm, enraptured blood.

He had fears he might not know how to approach Molly, but these vanished when he saw her standing on the forecourt of the church entrance. She had seen him before he had seen her. She was leaning on the parapet, looking his way, raising her arm to catch his attention. His eyes were riveted on her tiny flaring bob of sun-struck hair. She did not descend from the terrace so he climbed the steps in a loping glide.

"Hey." He said.

"Hey." She answered, looking at him closely and then glancing around, as if musing upon deep matters.

"This weather!" He exclaimed; merging into her enthusiasm.

"Oh, it's beautiful." She replied, sweeping her head around, allowing him to feast on her radiant features.

"What are you doing up here?" He looked over at the doors, hoping she did not want to go inside again.

"I was wanting to catch you before you got snared by those people down there."

He laughed. In the past someone had referred to Cook and Hereford as 'those people' in a disparaging tone, and so now they used that phrase as a talisman of their own. She studied his face. He was keenly aware of her blooming cheeks and rich, lustrous eyes. She had been waiting for him! He saw her nose crinkle up in a lovely manner; she did this when she was collecting her thoughts and pondering what she wanted to put into speech.

"I wanted to give you this."

"Oh." He looked down. She was presenting him with an old, decorative volume of some sort. It had a dark purple cloth cover with the title scripted in faded gold lettering. "Thanks." She kept looking at him. He read out loud, *The Life of Jesus.*"

"By Ernest Renan."

"Who is that?"

"Just read it, if you want; I don't want to push it on you." She seemed slightly flustered, fearful of his reaction, possibly. Brandishing a religious text in his face was not the best way to excite his interest.

"Sure. Thanks."

"It's my only copy. So I want it back."

"Certainly."

"Let's go this way."

"Where?"

"Let's go around."

"Around the block?" He wondered if she was in the mood for a brisk walk on the sidewalks of Ferdinand! They could conjure the pagan spirits now gathering in schools, practicing their spooky arts for the children of Halloween.

"Just around the school, to the lower lot."

"Okay."

At the corner they could see the undulations of Chambers Road, crawling eastward towards the Father of Waters, strewn with processional lights the whole way. They passed along the sections of the darkened school. His mind announced to itself; 'I have to get my act together.' Something portentous seemed to be in the offing. He was afraid this gift of a religious book might indicate she was seeking to help him get his mind right. He almost said, I'm Cool Hand Luke. She probably didn't know that movie, nor how it ends . . .

"Do you have something on your mind?"

"I'm afraid everyone thinks I'm on the make, trying to swindle the rich widow."

"I am a pretty rich widow."

"Oh, well, that's great." He felt foolish. He had tried to lessen the tension and only made it worse. It struck him that possibly she was giving him a chance to declare himself. Hadn't he already botched his chances, a time, or two? She had plainly stated the fact she doesn't know what she wants. Is she still dating that other son of a bitch—Heather's brother? And now she was giving him a religious book! Was she trying to bring him into the fold of her tithe-paying herd, for the good of the parish? No, that couldn't be it. Was it pity, because she thought he was lost? Next, she would be trying to fix him up with one of Heather's older sisters!

"You're awfully quiet," she said.

"I feel like I'm on a first date, and it's my first year in high school; and it's not even a date, really, and you have no idea what's going on. You feel like you're supposed to know, but you really don't." He just said what had come to him, and immediately thought how ridiculous it must have sounded. But she responded with a genuine burst of laughter.

"I know what you mean."

Molly admired the vista of dark trees, explaining to him she had taken up water colors as a hobby; mostly painting landscapes and trees. She said she hoped he enjoyed the book she had loaned him. Then they were climbing the stairs and going across the middle level where he was accosted by the eyes of specters from his earliest school days, all looking down from the dark empty windows of the classrooms. Soundless accolades fell upon him. *He* was with *the* girl! They climbed the steps to the upper level and parted ways with the spare salutations of old friends and he had no idea what any of it meant.

As he seated himself Paul grabbed his book as soon as he laid it on the table. "What is this?" He demanded as he flipped through the pages.

"Molly gave it to me. No, she loaned it to me. She was very adamant on that point."

"Better be careful, buddy boy, she's trying to convert you. We can't allow apostates to sit with us, can we Isaac?"

"I was born and raised in the Church. I was baptized, certified, packaged and shipped out into the world with ashes on my face." Jacob announced with false aplomb.

He could see Isaac's prefatory smile emerging as he spoke. "She may want to break the hold that Russian has on you. You've admitted you don't read anything else."

"Well, I shall have to make an exception in this case."

"Apparently she doesn't want you to burn in hell." Paul said.

"She doesn't believe in hell." Isaac assured them knowingly. Paul and Jacob studied his superior air.

"Have you ever heard of this book?" Paul asked Isaac directly.

"I'm the one who gave her that copy."

"Really?" Paul began peering at the pages more intently, reading passages. "I always suspected you were a believer." He spoke without raising his eyes from the book.

"Isn't everyone a believer? You have to believe in something. How else do you manage to get up in the morning, walk around, go about your business. You must live a purposeful life in some fashion or other. The homeless man puts his faith in any kind of shelter, and the sun's unfailing goodness. He cultivates a superior knowledge of how to find edible garbage."

"Spare us the social gospel of the venerable Cook!" Hereford expostulated.

"I suppose that's the question; what do you choose to hold on to." Jacob said, ignoring Hereford's comment.

"Yes, I believe so." Isaac's attitude became formal. "You know, after Renan's book was published, in 1863, he was roundly condemned. He lost his teaching post at the Collège de France."

"Quite an honor." Paul exclaimed. "It's no longer possible to write a book that would have that salutary effect, is it?" They looked at him and he handed the book over to Jacob. "Here, I don't have any time for this right now. It seems to be more in line with your curriculum. Besides, I want to watch all this that's happening there." He swept his arm out to indicate the crowd of people enjoying the Fish Fry. "I don't want to start believing in things based on what has happened in the past. Doesn't that corrupt your vision? How do you see things clearly if you are so intent on pondering the tortured reasons given to explain unknown things, by people who are no longer here, and knew so much less than us?"

"So much less? Are you sure of that? Now who's the pop philosopher?" Isaac glanced conspiratorially at Jacob. "For progress to take place, one must know the history of how things have happened before, taking account of those faculties given to us. You must know who we are, to understand how we got here, and where we might go henceforth."

"You're going far off, my friend. Just be careful that nobody has to walk you home again."

Jacob thought that to be a cruel jab. Then he noticed how Isaac smiled, as if contemplating the delicacy of all human virtues; using his own doctrines to face the terrible odds doled out to everyone.

"I really enjoyed seeing your scrapbooks, Isaac." Jacob said with fond regard.

"You both must have had a good laugh over my behavior."

"I couldn't risk that in front of Molly. You know how much she cares for you."

"Yes, I do. And that's why I don't care what this character thinks on that matter." He brought his plastic cup to his mouth and took an epicurean gulp, working and savoring the complex fluid upon his palate.

"When were you looking at scrap books?" Paul asked, somewhat out of humor.

"There are more things in this school yard than you can dream of Hereford."

"Sure, truths more than mortal? All that classical legerdemain—"

"Who are those guys?" Jacob asked, nodding his head towards a brace of men in khaki pants, polo shirts, and leather jackets, all forming a half-circle around Molly and her daughter, Sophie. Janey and two of her children were among them.

"The Leading Men." Isaac's voice portended further elucidation.

"Heirs of the veldt, assembled in peace time." Hereford declaimed. "They all have thick hair, thick skulls, and thick skin; like pachyderms, they move in herds." Hereford grew fervid, his hackles had gone up at the idea of such men. The conjugal, knighted fellows, displaying peacock signs of hierarchy. The insignia on the shirts resembled galloping dust mites at a tournament, except such creatures only graze, usually on human detritus, and have no need to take up swords or mallets of any kind.

"They are merely flesh and blood," Cook declaimed enigmatically.

"Who's that one talking to Heather?" Jacob asked.

"I believe that's her brother." Cook answered.

Just then all the men in question erupted in laughter; heads reared back, peals of hollow laughter echoed around them. These Leading Men, like heads of state in old decayed monarchies, must be concerned with many ceremonial functions, and conduct themselves accordingly. Wolves howl, lions roar (while hyenas laugh), jackals screech in a guttural dialect, and the Leading Men guffaw. Jacob understood such laugher was meant to exhibit confidence while standing at the ramparts of this Ferdinand township.

"Do you know him?" Jacob asked Isaac.

"I've met him. He's a good guy, as they say."

"They all say that, about themselves." Paul added. "As you've said, that's been true for a hundred years."

"It's always the good men who do the most harm in the world." Isaac quoted verbatim from the syllabus of Henry Adams.

"Those are the sort who used to pass around the collection basket." Jacob said. He remembered the long aluminum poles and the wire basket which they would pass before you as you sat in the pew, waiting to hear the homily; or was the service paid for afterwards? He could not remember.

"They don't do that anymore. They have more modern ways of collecting on their usurious moral benefactions." Isaac said archly.

There was silence as they waited to see if Jacob would ask something more about this man whom Molly had gone out with, and possibly had been with; and since not much else was known about the situation, no one ventured to say anything more.

"I think it's time for me to get going," Jacob said.

"The evening is just getting started," Isaac said, looking around at the people moving about in little groups, and sitting at tables. Jacob wished he could sit by himself at one of the tables at the Grotto and sip a drink and watch everything happening. He wanted to stay and wait for Molly, but he knew it was not a good time to try and get her attention and talk with her, and therefore he wanted to leave. Sitting and listening to the dialectics at the Treacle Company would only further depress his spirits. They also seemed dejected for some reason he sensed but could not put his finger on. He couldn't imagine what was so troubling to everyone. He almost forgot the book she had loaned to him.

"Jacob!" Hereford called out to him.

"You going to leave this behind?"

"You want us to tell her that you cast it aside?"

"Oh, no." He walked back and took it from Hereford.

"You going to read that?" Isaac asked. "The human psychology is not quite as gripping as that found in one of your sacred texts, but there are many holy grains of wheat there, yet to be sown."

"I have to take a look; she assigned it to me."

"She's no advocate of all the stale dogma," Isaac said in a peculiar voice, inflected with his fondness for Molly. "But that book might better have been called Ecce Hominis Somnium. You know what that means, no?"

Jacob shook his head; echoes from Latin masses clouding his mind.

"Behold the man." Hereford translated the words used by Pontius Pilate when he was shown the Jewish convict who had started a riot at the money tables.

"No, that's Ecce homo," Isaac corrected him. "This phrase means, 'Behold the man's dream.' It's more apropos of our actual situation. Well, anyway, I know Molly enjoyed that book quite a lot. And she's—" Isaac was entering a reverie.

"She's an original." Jacob found himself interrupting his friend.

"That she is." Isaac agreed, nodding happily.

"She has no need of lectures from any of us, or them." Jacob nodded at the church as he turned and hurried away. The two men exchanged a glance, eyebrows raised, sharing their admiration. They watched him go careering down Elizabeth in his own exalted state.

"Isaac, I hope I retain half your dignity when I'm your age."

"More dubious words of praise?"

"No, I mean it."

"Don't get maudlin on me. We can't both play that role. Wait your turn."

"I defer to your expertise. Our creative manager."

"So you've come around?"

"It's your native ground."

"Yes, it is."

Something Jacob had heard in Isaac's voice when he had spoken of Molly trailed after him as he walked home. He was in no hurry to get there, so he passed Church Street and continued down Elizabeth. The three ancient sassafras trees just south of Church along Elizabeth caught his eyes. The trees were very old, broad in girth, and the ponderous limbs had been truncated many times by the Street Department, thus securing the lines of communication and power for the jabbering race. The squat figures put Jacob in mind of mighty dwarves, who once wielded fearsome axes in great wars; now reduced to being live relics of a breed that advances while battling its own kind, bearing the corporate scars with crabbed dignity.

Jacob was aware of a gigantic breathing in the air that kept the painted leaves gently astir, as if spirits truly moved among the living, as palpable as the pungent odors of this moldering season. He was inextricably bound up in this world's active mystery. He climbed the hill on Adams as a cohort of leaves tore down the street going the other way. He watched them tumbling like frenzied acrobats. He saw leaves coursing by on invisible currents, as if they had transcended earth's gravity. In such moments one is tempted to believe any faith that says he can stay aloft in dreams forever . . .

35

Heads swung around to scrutinize the pair seated by themselves at the picnic table near the river birches. They were beyond the Grotto on the crest of the hill leading down to the lower level. Even from a distance it was clear they were close. Jacob and Molly were leaning towards one another across the table; one could surmise incorrectly they were holding hands. Molly was talking about her mother-in-law.

"I'm never quite sure what she thinks about me, or anything else for that matter."

"You spend a lot of time with her?"

"Oh yes. She's a fairy godmother to Sophie. They're very good together. My mom gets jealous." Her voice had risen delightfully.

Jacob was feeling immensely fortunate. As soon as he had finished helping to set up at the Fish Fry she had taken him over to this exclusive setting. She was always surprising him in her ministrations. He had steeled himself to be prepared in case she felt a need to withdraw from their blithe game of dawdling on the verge of things. He was sure she needed to devote more of her time to others, and to bring a halt to the rumors.

"She just knows me, I guess. I've never met anyone who's better at not saying what shouldn't be said; she knows how to be discreet at the right time. Some things are just there, and you have to deal with them on your own, and nothing's going to be accomplished by constantly dredging up the particulars in front of others. You know what I mean there, Jakey?"

"I'll just say yes, hoping you respect me for not putting my foot in my mouth right now."

"See, there you could have just nodded and done even better."

He laughed out of sheer happiness. It caught the attention of people sitting at the Grotto under the luminous bulbs suspended among the sassafras trees.

"So? Come on, tell me. What did you think?

"About the book?"

"Yes!"

"Well . . ."

"Did you even read it!"

"Yes, I did. Well, most of it. It was very interesting."

"Did you read the dedication to his sister?"

"I'm not sure . . ."

"Well, what did you think of of what you did read?" She was clearly exasperated with her pupil.

He wanted to state plainly, "Whatever you want me to think!" Her passion was aglow on her dusky face; a countenance made to outshine any gloom! She really cares about this, he thought, instantly regretting that he had not spent more time trying to assimilate the meaning of the material for himself.

"I'm not sure I'm a religious person." He said, fearful she was going to be disappointed in his spiritual lassitude, and wanting to get past that point as soon as possible. But her enthusiasm was fully kindled and nothing was going to extinguish that until she had gotten a chance to explain herself.

"For me, it was a way to strengthen religion. The author plucked him out of the church, and let me see him back in Galilee. He made him a real human being. I found that to be inspirational."

"I did like how that one chapter begins, saying that he went back to Galilee, after completely losing his old faith."

"Yes, that's after the scene with the woman at the well. Where it speaks of true religion being about spirit, and truth. Renan depicts him as a sort of moral genius." Molly had been constantly turning to look out at the crowd as they spoke. The signs were clear; she would have to leave him soon.

"It gives you something to think about."

"Somehow it inspires me, knowing one person, who never wrote anything down, lived a life that started all of this."

"Do you think he would find himself at home here?"

She bowed her head and exhaled audibly; her response when a pejorative quip didn't strike the right chord for her sensibilities. He was embarrassed by his tactlessness. This was her parish, and her people; he had no right in this moment to roll the dice on such cheap aspersions. They exchanged a lingering glance, each showing a pathetic, separate strain of regretfulness, impossible to express without losing sympathy with the other.

"Tell me about your first time?" She said with a sudden glint of mischief in her eyes.

"My first time? Oh gosh." He laughed. "Didn't take long. Not much to talk about. It was out at Sioux Passage Park. We were in somebody's van. I owe it all to Bob Dylan. We were skipping school. I had just played a pretty good version of 'I Want You,' and apparently she really liked it."

Molly started laughing in a way he had not heard before, in a high, sonorous wave coursing up from deep, reedy chambers. She stopped rather abruptly. "Sorry, but I have no time right now. Let's just say, to be continued. I really have to go. I can see Janey's over there with Sophie, pulling her hair out." Her voice conveyed genuine regret and it soothed him.

He took a seat at the C & H table, enduring a round of jibes. They responded to his aloof manner by pretending to believe he had just been dumped by Molly. He was tickled by the fact they had been paying such close attention to them. He was full of some extraordinary fervor, convinced he shared something valuable with Molly that he couldn't explain. It was still reverberating in his chest, this strange, exclusive form of happiness, that was heightened by the flagellant's harsh devotion.

"Where'd you get that picnic table?" Isaac asked.

"Yeah, are you two trying to set up your own shop?" Paul demanded. "Do you think you can compete with the Treacle Company?"

"What did you two find so engrossing over there?" Isaac wanted to know.

"We were discussing that Jewish craftsman that Renan spoke of so fondly."

"Ah, she's giving you oral exams. Yes, that's good." Isaac spoke in fine didactic form. "Well, his real life, as best as we can tell, that's a good place to start."

Jacob was aware they enjoyed laughing at him, quite often, in fact; but they enjoyed doing so with fraternal innocence; there was no disdain or contempt. They singled him out in their comical rhetorical games, partly to act as witness, and also to enlist him as an ally in the great unknown creed they espoused as pious frauds. It was hardly any different than any other warm gesture of fellowship.

"We're betting on you, in your cause." Paul was ever adept at fermented oratory; his head swayed in his effort to deliver a proper affirmation.

"What cause is that?" Jacob was eager to foment more blather.

"What cause? Cook, you tell him."

"Not something to shout out like that, I guess. You're not seeking after an actual grail, something to drink out of, are you? Do you think it is like a beer mug?"

"How should I know?"

"He has you there, Cook."

"You're not weak in the head." Paul stated grandly.

"That's good to know."

"You're not trapped, or lingering on an island."

"St. Louis is surrounded by rivers."

"The thing is, we don't think you've actually found out what it is yet."

"Right!" Paul raised his cup.

"But you are confident of my success?"

"Yes!" Both conspirators said in unison.

"I'll drink to that," Jacob said, and then laughed as he had no cup and they quickly fumbled to get him one and poured out a splash of fine spirits from one of the bottles on the table.

"How do you like that?" Hereford asked.

"It ain't Boone's Farm, but it will have to do."

"That's the spirit." Cook said.

Hereford made a sour face, being more enamored of his grape snobbery and leery of allowing too much heretical playfulness to taint the bouquet of his cultured tastes, acquired at such costs.

"Look," he exclaimed, pointing at Frances, who was stalking through the crowds, the dwarfish priest trailing after her like a clumsy acolyte, imploring her to please slow down and listen to him. He made feeble motions with his hands and continued speaking to her, or rather at her imposing figure striding before him.

"She's making way like a Bactrian camel," Hereford said assuredly.

"What's that?" Cook's puzzlement was Hereford's prize. He had assumed most television writers would miss this allusion to an incident in chapter thirteen of the novel *Kim*. Had a reference been made to some esoteric passage in classical mythology, then Cook was sure to outshine him, due to his more solid educational grounding in the older styles of liberal arts.

"She's like the holy lama, when he gets back to his mountains, and regains all his strength; striking off for the high snows." Hereford swells as he parades his knowledge.

"Where are the mountains in our circumstances?" Cook teased his friend.

"You leave the world behind, trek to where the grass is singing. You follow painted leopards, scaling the heights of a vast solitude. You obtain perspective, clearing one's consciousness, facing the eternal snow."

"The innate morality of the people." Jacob added sententiously, meaning to provoke them, but they only nodded in appreciation. His knack of touching upon the crux of things moved them once more.

"That's exactly right. There is no caste system where men go forth to look, to see how things really are." Hereford seemed intent on continuing his treatise, but an even more powerful force of nature rose up before them.

The waitress Lilly stood there, her eyes dancing among them. She offered them the opportunity to serve up a distinctive brand of gentle courtesies. Hereford complimented her for being such a splendid complement to this unfolding soiree, which had assumed legendry proportions. She spoke of the importance of the Treacle Table with gracious formality. Cook smiled in a superior way to suggest he was in need of a more personal blandishment; and so she beguiled him by referring to his old world manners. She had just heard this mentioned at another table. Isaac's face came alive under the trembling lights, wildly attuned to grave matters laying beneath his alcoholic fires.

He is a sweet old man, she thought; poor thing. The other was an aging Lothario, who was unpredictable because he was not sure of himself, nor clear in his own mind what it was he had still to prove, and to whom, and why it had to be done yet again in this moment. If she cared a lot less about such things, and allowed him, he would squire her around town on expensive adventures; and then, at some point he would want her to weep with him at the shrines of his past agonies. She did not want to go down that road with someone his age.

While they were jabbering (as Molly would have described it) Jacob was observing Janey and Molly out in the parking lot. Janey was fussing over a lacy head covering she had just secured on Molly's head. It was identical to one she was wearing. They were trying them out at the Fish Fry, as a sort of ironic statement. Heather had recently adopted this fashion for when she was attending mass, and other women began to follow her example.

Jacob was astonished to see Frances confronting Molly, raising one arm to brandish a censorious finger in her face.

"What is this?" Frances asked them, looking at the ornate hair pieces.

They giggled like girls and huddled closer together in their confederacy.

"Take those off." Frances chastised them more severely than she was even aware of, and quickly spun around and walked off, not waiting to see if they obeyed her or not. She was embarrassed. The two women tromped away, landing on the church terrace. Jacob watched them appear above the wall, looking down on the crowd. He could not tell if she looked at him or not. They disappeared into the church. He felt a strange urge to follow them into those hushed confines where so much good spiritual dust is preserved in holy urns.

He became lost in his reveries until his name came up several times. Hereford told him to look, and Isaac alerted him to the fact some of the Leading Men had deployed on maneuvers. They watched as the cohort initiated a march, and then executed a smart oblique to advance upon their picnic table.

"How goes it, gentlemen?" One of them said as they formed a line to face the three men seated at the table. Jacob was on one side and Cook and Hereford sat on the other. The Treacle brothers appeared rather pleased with these developments. Jacob was merely curious to see how it would play out. One of the men seemed to know Cook and tried to exchange insincere pleasantries with him. This démarche failed and they exchanged awkward, hostile banter instead. Cook expressed disdain for this kind of probing; he did not deign to receive the man's overtures. This caused the man to smirk and whisper to another of his kind, causing low reports of derision. It was proving surprisingly difficult to bring the great battery of general guffaws into position.

"Jacob? Is it?" One man addressed the object of their mission.

"That's me."

"They tell me you live at the old Spencer house. Is that right?"

"Are you a lawyer?" Hereford asked.

"No. He is," the man said as affably as he could manage, feeling his dignity as a leading man had been affronted. "Why do you ask?"

"You possess a certain air of Whiggery, that stiff, bombastic attitude." Cook said with a careful flourish in his diction.

"And reek of forensic manners," Hereford chimed in eagerly.

The men exchanged uncertain looks. They were all proud to be professionals, but none were distinguished in their respective fields. They were the capable drones who keep the honey under production, working for the status quo so that the hive remains healthy and productive. These exotic strangers who had come into their ken really confused their ideals regarding hierarchy. They had used mystic means (Books and TV) to obtain success in the world, and it was difficult to assay social status with that misbegotten breed. And the other one, who was hovering around Molly, he was a complete unknown, and the intended target. The strategy had been to separate him from his allies; make him stand his ground as a single opponent, against all of them. It became pretty clear this was not going to happen.

"What line of work are you in?" Another asked Jacob directly.

"I work the land."

"He climbs mountains in his spare time," Hereford declaimed, his voice tainted with overmuch spume of bottled spirits. The men looked at him briefly, and then ignored him.

"You say you tend the garden up there, at the Spencer house?" One of them asked, his regimental smirk on full display.

"I oversee the grounds."

"He's learning the arts of husbandry," Isaac spoke in his grand manner.

"It's all organic," Paul added.

"You trying to start a commune up there?" A weak satiric tone quavered in the man's uncertain delivery.

"No. It's a very restricted covenant, closed to the public." Jacob was at ease, too familiar with this guild to take any serious offense; having belonged to similar fraternal associations himself. "Sometimes, I do stand in for the local — Isaac, what is it called hereabouts?"

"Kapellmeister."

"That's it. I help them with their scores. But they're very good, very natural."

"They work on very old, primitive arrangements," Isaac was sitting up, very animated. "Surely you boys understand. But also, it's rather experimental, at times, and that would no doubt leave you in the dust."

They were puzzled by Jacob's unflappable demeanor. They wondered if he might be touched; another of Molly's projects. A great show of satiric mirth went round the ranks. They surveyed the field. Perhaps there was no prize to be taken just now. Several gratuitous slights were passed among them; directed at various types of déclassé individuals in order to flourish the superior credentials of their merry band.

"He's also acting as chargé d'affaires, to the honorable Mr. Spencer." Cook announced as if he had just returned to a stage to address the whole audience.

There was silence. This strategy of deploying subterfuges, and here with a sickening dash of French élan, it was only to be expected from these people. And yet the flash from an antique chivalrous device did rattle one's nerves. There was a tremble of remembrance of how swiftly blood hardens to reckless war. One quaked to imagine the burp of Krupp guns heard across the border, or Katyusha rockets screaming back from the hinterland of another undefeated motherland. Mr. Cook's mother had been a local doyenne; not someone, even in memoriam, to be taken lightly. Daughters of her old circle still held sway, and you did not want to run afoul of that gaggle of dreadnaughts. A sporadic, irrepressible burst of small arms broke out in their frustration.

"Spencer still lives there?"

"We heard Spencer sold the house."

"It's no longer being used as a residence, is it?"

"Is that even legal? Having squatters live there?"

"What is all this about, having people going there to party?"

"I live in The Joint." Jacob stated loudly, feeling it was incumbent upon him to answer them in a fitting manner.

"What's that?" One of them asked.

"The house of the dead," he answered firmly.

"Did any of you ever congregate at The Joint, back in the glory days?" Cook challenged them en masse, as if this were a qualification that took precedence over all other social distinctions.

None of them had ever experienced that privilege; a few had heard about it. One could almost hear the furious cogitations. They knew it had been rather far back in the past, hardly germane, and if this vagrant personage was up there now, under suspicious circumstances, and coming around to cozy up to Molly, well then, they might well make that their business. Someone might strike off an official letter on the firm's letterhead, and pose questions about the bona fides of the man. And yet, who would have standing in such an affair? Well, Molly! Did they want to offend her by interfering in her life in such a crude fashion? That would not be wise. She did not suffer fools. Pickett's shabby ghost wafted among them. Whose idea was this, anyway? Such interior chatter ricocheted between the Leading Men, and the dissonance at the front had a terrible effect on the morale of the entire corps.

Several made attempts at conciliatory banter with Isaac, but he looked upon them with richly veiled contempt. They found themselves unaccountably in retreat, moving off like the Republican Guard, a smoldering Moscow at their backs. One made a final joke to set off the regimental guffaw, but it didn't catch hold as they tramped away.

It was then that Molly swung by, enticed by the spectacle she had witnessed from afar. She stared into Jacob's face and he shook his head and laughed lightly. She took him off a few paces.

"What was all that about?"

"They seem to think I'm a dangerous interloper."

"Well, you are hanging around with this heathen crowd, aren't you?"

He laughed. "That is true. You have to wonder, who is Jacob? I may as well put in an application with the C & H Treacle Company. Make it official."

"I don't think that's necessary. Isaac seems to be very tolerant of Russian monks. For reasons I cannot understand—"

"Molly!" He touched her on the shoulder; she turned to look at him. "They were defending me!"

"Why wouldn't they?"

"It was crazy watching all that stuff as if I was in a dream." Jacob was shaking his head, emitting whispery gusts of air. "It was like seeing a place where I used to be—"

"It may become a problem though; adding one more person to the table might qualify the group for cult status."

"I thought it was a cult. That's why I wanted to join."

"No, in that case we would probably have to drive you off the premises."

"Drive us out of Nazareth, would you?"

"Jacob, let's sit down." She led him over to the picnic table at the crest of the hill by the river birches. Upon sitting down, side by side, they took a moment to enjoy the scenery, looking out over the ball field, and the houses and trees beyond, ranging up the hill in the distance. They sat quietly for a moment, absorbing the haunted atmosphere of the evening as if listening to a lullaby.

"I wanted to be one of those women, who's been married forever. You know what I mean?" She looked at him, on her face a pained expression which affected him immediately. "I wanted to really be there for all of it, to have all the history, so when . . ." She couldn't continue, she began biting at her lower lip. He put his hand out to pat her on the shoulder, wanting to embrace her; not knowing what to do, feeling an odd sensation of helplessness. Her averted face was like a portrait of something utterly precious which he could never really touch. Molly looked around at the grounds and suddenly froze in place.

"Oh damn."

"What?"

"Heather. She's just standing over there, watching us . . . I'm so tired of this. She and I used to be really good friends," she spoke in a weary, tremulous voice.

"What happened?" Jacob asked.

She looked at him as though surprised he had heard her words. She seemed to study his face a moment, as though searching for something he had hidden there, resorting to the black arts of male obtuseness. Her own face was troubled and inscrutable. He felt her anguish as a leaden pall draped over his own heart.

"Let's go back over there." She said, so they went back to the other picnic table.

After they arrived Heather approached the table, her eyes glinting fiercely. Isaac and Paul were flustered by the mere fact of her presence. She wore a blouse with a huge collar that laid flat on her breast like a large bow. It struck Jacob as some kind of outmoded uniform; that of a nurse who fed morphine to broken doughboys, in a time when the heightened enormity of war led people to assume one last great carnival of death might end up being the cure for war.

"Have you seen Kenneth?" Heather spoke to Molly in a way that was more of a challenge than a query. She put her hands on her hips. "Well?"

"No, I haven't. I haven't seen him out here," she spoke her words with a fierce control that was akin to a tea kettle just starting to whisper.

"Well maybe if you'd quit flouncing around, over here, all the time." She flung one hand out at the people at the table, without looking at them, to indicate the pure depths of her antipathy.

"Flouncing?" Molly was livid. "Heather, you don't know anything . . ." Now she was at a loss for words.

"I know you prefer being out here drinking with them!" She now deigned to glance at the miserable reprobates. "That's what it looks like to us!"

"Oh, I don't want to hear it! I'm so done with this." Molly stared at her as if in disbelief. Heather put up her hand as she spun around, preparing to leave.

The men were momentarily cowed. The silent dignity of Molly's trembling outrage kept them quiet. Jacob was standing next to her, at a great remove from where she was in that moment. She shook her head a few times as if negating something only she could hear, and then plunged forward, following in the steps of Heather, going towards the cafeteria. Jacob exchanged a pregnant look with Isaac. They all sat there in silence; some exalted assurance they had relied upon was now lost to them.

After a while Frances came by searching for Molly. Seeing that none of them could account for her whereabouts, her facial expression tacitly berated them for being so useless. She began turning away as Cook stood up and faced her. He bowed like he was a prince in St. Petersburg, greeting a duchess. After a struggle to rise to his feet Hereford followed suit, even more ridiculously. Jacob watched them, frowning at the impertinence. Once again, it was the wrong kind of fun.

"Fools." He heard Frances say over her shoulder. He rose to his feet and strode behind her.

"Where are you going?" Cook yelled after him.

"Home."

He caught up with Frances and asked her if there was anything she needed him to do before he left. She smiled at him and said no, and wished him well. He hardly knew where he stood in all of this upheaval of emotions. His mind was in turmoil. He was beset by a feeling of helplessness, which he dreaded; once more he was watching as things came undone, and he was unable to do anything about it.

36

Jacob spent the next week reading Molly's book. He decided to read it very slowly, taking notes, scribbling in his spiral notebook. He found himself in the library on Church Street gathering other, more modern, reference works to bring back to his cloister. As he read about the Galilean rabbi who stepped off the planet like Socrates, a martyr flung into history like a great comet, he began his own quest to know more than was sought by the secular historians. His stealthy heart was bent on tracking the course of Molly's passion. He sought to find in these pages a path into her psyche. He wanted to know what she had found so appealing in this work, and why she had pressed it so earnestly upon him. What did she wish him to glean from these exhaustively plundered fields?

His study fell into a rhythm; reading for a spell, and then playing music, when his thoughts whirled around him in a little tempest. His mind was more clear after playing pieces of music that he knew very well; and afterwards he made use of that revived clarity to let his mind engage ideas, much as his fingers touched the strings afresh on his carefully tuned instrument. Many intriguing associations rose into his imagination, fostering a sense of impending discovery. Something valuable might come into view while riding these currents of bewilderment. He was facing squarely into that part of himself that is only seen as in a glass darkly.

He strove to picture this incomparable man whom the world had deified. The hero of the cross, in the beginning, sets out on a pilgrimage, which he himself does not understand. He is increasingly at odds with the sacred traditions of his own people. He breaks away, fearless, relentless; forever advancing towards a nebulous objective pulling him forward as he forsakes the world. He could not shake the terrible idea of his Holy Father, a personage looking down on him; an awesome king in the seat of honor at a great tournament. He must be the heir. The lost, spirited prince must step forward and prove himself. All around him the world is caught up in acts of violence and blood sacrifice. Thus, he too, ultimately, chooses the grisly task of martyrdom; scaling the heights of doubt to ascend into eternal fame. What had it all meant?

The hand of daylight savings was drawn back and the sudden darkness at the end of the days augured the solemn rites used to celebrate the depths of winter's meaning. The chilly breezes foretold the season set aside for honoring love; the melancholy of trumpets, the laughter of bells, and the cheer of having loved ones near. He labored outdoors in front of a nearly fallen sun, feeling as though mystic glyphs marked the surface of every vista open to the naked eye.

The inspired French author had depicted Jesus plodding forward on his revolutionary mission to find new life; afraid to face his own discovery, that the new life could be had right here. He struggled to free himself from orthodoxy. Today, people still argue over scripture with enormous sectarian vitriol. Jacob thought of television pastors making pleas for funds in return for health-related miracles; becoming rich themselves for assisting in the Lord's highly capricious general practice. What could any of this mean for someone as uninspired as himself?

How did one worship the original supreme allied commander? The one endowed with omniscience by the first scribes, who later produced a caste of jealous charlatan priests, who collected sliver coins like publicans at the great temple. They demanded 'pure' shekels that were stamped with the imperial eagle! Nor could he find divinity in the son, who was depicted as a gentle, radical soul, ultimately made to serve one of the largest cults ever created by men. Now they have a grotesque ruling cabal based in Rome, of all places, where phantoms of the bloody Roman eagles perch on their fantastic architecture. They've set it up so that people from around the globe, as a matter of course, collect money from the scattered tribes, and send it to them to manage—to a caste of utterly frivolous, antiquated, ridiculous, satin-clad bachelors, who collect fine epicene ball gowns, and gold trinkets! Ah, tempora, mores, the spiritual proletariat . . .

One morning he could not face any of the books, so he dropped by to see Cody early in the morning and knocked on his back door. He peered through the glass and saw Sally looking back at him, startled by his intrusion. She was wearing a robe; her hair was awry. After calling something over her shoulder she motioned for him to come in.

"Join us for breakfast," she said in a throaty voice Jacob did not want to parse too closely. The children were not there. He sat at the kitchen table drinking coffee while Sally continued preparing a meal of scrambled eggs, bacon and toast, served with freshly-squeezed orange juice.

"I loaned the truck to my brother," Cody said as he came into the room, his face unshaven and dressed in a ragamuffin's outfit of old clothing.

"Isn't it outside?" Jacob asked.

"No."

"I didn't even notice."

"Do you need it?"

"No, I don't think so, not right now."

"What's on your mind?"

"Nothing. Just thought I'd drop by."

Cody looked up at the clock on the wall, then at his wife, scratching his scalp with one hand while he reached out with the other as she handed him a cup of coffee.

"Oh yeah, Frances wants to see you." Cody said. "When did you see her last?"

"Not sure. I'll swing by and see her."

"Thanks babe," Cody said to his wife as she put down a plate of toast for him to butter. "What's on your mind?" He asked Jacob again.

"Nothing."

"You've got something on your mind."

"Do you ever think about how the church got started?"

"No." Cody answered in a tone that said it was a stupid topic to raise at this hour, or any other. He began crunching into a piece of toast he had just slathered with butter.

"Don't eat any until we all sit down," Sally chastised him.

"I mean, as far as the historical Jesus; what the scholars say about him?"

"What are you getting into now? I knew you were starting to lose it."

"Do they actually know anything about him?" Sally asked. "They don't teach that kind of thing at church?"

"Not really."

Cody's face said, "Well, there you are then; it doesn't matter."

"They have all these theories, based on studious conjectures."

"Wait. Does this have something to do with Molly?" Sally asked him, turning to look at him and then Cody; holding a spatula up in the air, as if she suspected she was going to have to swat at some male idiocy pretty soon. Both men had begun devouring pieces of toast, expressly against her wishes.

"Yeah, she gave me a book to read."

"Oh yeah? That one on Jesus? I heard them talking about it."

"Who was talking about it?"

Cody began laughing. "You're screwed man."

"What are you talking about?"

"My guess is she's trying to get you to join the parish."

"How do you know that?" Sally asked Cody, showing annoyance at his blithe, ignorant foray into the motivations of a woman. She scraped a portion of the eggs onto each of their lifted plates.

"That's what I can't figure out, I'm not sure why she'd care about that."

"Oh brother." Sally muttered disgustedly as she stirred more eggs in the skillet for herself.

"Well, don't go trying to convert me or anything," Cody said, acting wary of being set upon by his friend in the role of evangelist. "I go to church."

"Sometimes you do." Sally corrected him.

"We tithe. That's the main thing, isn't it?" Cody stated with a note of finality.

Sally sat down and they ate in silence for a while. Then Sally and Cody spoke of family logistics; schedules for picking up the children from their grandparents' house, and other such matters, acting as though Jacob were not there. He was thinking of other things, glad to indulge his own mental propensities.

"Hey, did you hear? Mulligan's gone." Cody said after wiping his plate clean with a piece of toast.

"What happened?"

"Don't know. Frances said he wanted to move back to New Mexico."

"Why New Mexico?"

"Who knows."

"He left his mountain bike."

"Really? Is it still chained to the post?"

"Yep."

"No you don't. He may be coming back for it." Sally said.

"We can buy a new chain if we have to." Jacob said, smiling at Cody who was enlivened by the thought of booty to be had.

"Talk to Frances." Sally admonished her husband, reading his face.

"Can you get a chain-cutter?" Jacob asked him.

"Hardware store rents them."

"I'll check it out." He rose to leave and gave Cody the standard salutation.

"Later."

Then he felt as if he owed a more gracious word to Sally, whose kitchen he had never been in before, and where he had just been fed. She was at the sink.

"Thanks Sally," he said to her as he passed behind her in the tight space and opened the door to leave.

"Good luck to you Jacob." She said looking at him with a peculiar intensity. He looked at Cody for clarification, but he was preoccupied with his newspaper and did not bother to look up. It didn't matter; he had gotten used to people treating him as a sort of special case; in need of pity, or contempt, or a judicious admixture of both.

"Thanks."

"Oh, hon, would you mind taking that out?" She indicated the trash bag she had just put by the door.

"No problem." He wasn't sure about much of anything anymore and the odd thing was that he was feeling completely at ease in this unsanctioned role he had carved out among them.

The issue of social rank no longer mattered to him as these other inalienable constructs towered over his uplifted gaze. He was grappling with that exotic creature known as the Christ; apparently even in his day there was no consensus on what the messiah was supposed to be. Just like today, advocates of the God Industry squabbled incessantly among themselves in righteous storms. The bourgeois (viz. moral climbers) Pharisees contended for influence against the vastly more powerful aristocracy of Sadducees, who owned nearly all the real estate, and ran the gaming tables at the temple. To a modern view the ancient arguments make for a dreary bedlam, and yet preachers still dispense preposterous strains of the same ornate, overwrought ignorance, at fabulous rates of exchange. Jacob wrestled with the fact he simply wanted a good life. Was that true? How did one define a good life?

Another day that week he picked up some garden fixtures for Frances. He was put to work raking leaves, and picking up and bagging sticks and helping to spruce up the appearance of her yard. They worked outside for several hours and she invited him in for lunch.

She made a green salad and added a dollop of savory tuna salad along with black olives. She also served oven-fresh bread with a slab of soft butter to make the mouth water beforehand. Sharing these repasts had become commonplace. He also had free reign to use her Volkswagen. They discussed various households where he performed chores at her behest. There were no more jobs cutting grass. Frances was sending him to homes where he changed out screen windows for storm windows. He raked and bagged a lot of leaves. He collected dead branches and bundled and tethered them so they could be put at the curb. Sometimes he was paid, and sometimes he was not; some of his customers thought it was Frances who was the one to be thanked for lending them his services. As if he were entailed as her serf!

"You know, some of these old ladies only give me busy work; they just want to feed me and talk with me."

"Is there something wrong with that?"

"No, but they're also paying me."

"So?"

"I can't take that money."

"If they have it—"

"It doesn't feel right."

"It doesn't feel right." She reiterated as she stood up from the table and went to her counter and opened the cupboards and removed a box of her favorite whole grain crackers. She sat down and began to nibble one of the wafers in a meditative trance.

"Did you talk to Beatrice about her plans for the house?" Frances looked at him with deep concentration. He was struck by her dark green eyes, imbued with golden streaks such as those that grace the world at the onset of dusk.

He confessed that he had not spoken to Beatrice of late.

"She wants to let certain charities use the Spencer House for fundraising events. She believes we need to bring good people to Ferdinand, so they can see what we're doing here."

He assented with a murmur after engorging a forkful of leafy greens and creamy fish coated in tangy dressing. "This is really good." He added, as if to excuse his wolfish table manners as he worked on his second helping. He munched into one of her gourmet crackers and found it quite tasty and devoured it in rapid bites. "So I heard Mulligan has vacated the premises?"

"Yes, that's true. Why do you ask?"

"Nothing. Did he say why?"

"He mentioned a woman named Maria."

"Do you think he's coming back?"

"Here? I doubt it."

"Did he leave his bike in the basement?"

"I think so. Nothing was said about that."

"Do you mind if I use it?"

"Well, I don't know. I don't think he ever used it, did he?"

"He did, once in a while. I don't know why he was locking it up like that, though. Made me feel like a thief. I wanted to take it just because of that affront to my honor."

They both smiled at the irony intended. It had been a sore spot for Jacob when he lived in the basement, taking it personally; now he realized it was mostly his own embarrassment for having come to such a pass; that had been the true cause of his resentment.

"He never said anything, so, do what you want. Take care of it, just in case he comes back."

"I will."

She rose and went into her living room and upon returning placed one of her gargoyles on the table. "For you."

He held the figure up close for inspection. "He's a fine little monster." He declared, stroking the handsome thing, crouching with half-folded wings on strong legs, his scaly feet armed with deadly claws. "I like it."

"For your place up there. Unless it's going to be too scary for you."

He laughed. "No, I don't think so. There are many ghosts up there already. He might put the fear of god into them!"

"Oh, don't say it like that, Jacob. I don't know about you, sometimes." She adopted a lofty air of tolerance; her face evocative of that ageless crone of myth who is able to throw kings, prophets, and magicians to the ground.

"Thanks Frances." They looked at one another for a moment, acknowledging in their silence that most honest emotions are impossible to articulate as they are being experienced.

Jacob would later pay a rental fee to obtain a chain-cutter to cut the bike free from its post and take it on a spin around the neighborhood. He became as the boy who first comes to know that freedom bestowed by his first real bicycle. The world sped by his eyes much quicker than when he was on foot, but much slower than that reeling canvas created by the hurtling automobile. In his rejuvenescence he thoroughly enjoyed observing so much more of this small world from his privileged vantage.

Later in the week his mother called him and asked him to come by to see her. He borrowed the Volkswagen to go west.

"Where'd Dad?" He asked her as they settled down in the kitchen. Through a window he could see at the end of the yard two huge red oaks clutching their brown, curled-up leaves. The sight had a pleasant, familiar cast for his eyes.

"He went fishing with Luke."

"Oh yeah? Where at?"

"The lake, the only place you can do real fishing," she answered, using the words of Luke, heard by both of them numerous times.

"I need to get down there with him again."

"He'd like that. Are you sure you don't want some cake?"

"Mom, I'm trying to eat healthy. I feel better." Sound in body, anyway, he thought to himself.

"Well, wait here a minute." She disappeared into other rooms of her house, and when she came back she was carrying a large envelope.

"These are some papers for you. You know your uncle's lady friend?"

"His common law wife?"

"Yes, she wanted me to give this to you. These are some papers and photos from the business that your uncle wanted you to have. She is also going to send you a check."

"A check? for what?"

"She said she knows Julius promised you he would remember you in his will."

"Well, he just wanted to let me know that I had been a good worker. That's all it was. I mean, it was a great job he gave me. I always liked working for him. She doesn't owe me anything."

"She wants you to have it."

"She doesn't have to." He said abstractly. She could tell that he wanted to know something more, probably the sum bequeathed to him. He surprised her with his question.

"Mom? Is it true you turned Dad down two times, when he proposed?"

"I suppose it is."

"How come?"

"You're really going into the past."

"I was just curious."

"I thought he was too wild for me. You know, he never set foot inside a church before he met me." Her face adopted a pensive look for a moment; her own ideas about attending church had in fact gone through a revolution over the course of her life, and she knew her youngest son quit attending mass long ago. But she knew this world was always changing, on the surface of things, and recurrence was the cardinal theme of human behavior. She was also considering that someone from their old neighborhood had recently informed her she had seen her son going into St. Margaret's several times with a certain woman.

"So then he started going to church with you?"

"Not at first. But he liked going out and doing many other things I wanted him to do with me. He would go wherever I wanted him to go. I tested him." She smiled like a naughty girl. "I could see he liked the idea of me being with him; and I liked being with him. He was proud of me. And pretty soon I could tell he cared what I thought about how he acted. Then I went to work on him." She noticed her son did not catch the intended humor of her last statement.

Jacob nodded as if lost in thought.

"We had a lot of fun together in those days. None of you children were there to drag us down."

He smiled wanly, caught up in private thoughts. He appeared to be making a study of his mother's face, as an artist might do with items found in a museum; the blood paying homage to ideals of its very own substance and value.

"I remember Johanna used to tease me for being so eager to go to school."

His mother started to look at him the same way he had been looking at her the minute before. "She was very proud of you."

345

"She's become like an older sister in my memories. It's strange."

"Everyone loved her so. Your poor father . . ." She got up and washed out a cup in the sink and stayed facing the wall after she was done.

"I didn't mean to bring that up, Mom."

"No, it's fine." She sat back down. A gust of wrenching mirth shook her shoulders gently. "I remember, I had to make her promise that she would not tell you there was no Santa Claus."

"What? I don't remember that."

"How could you?"

"How old were we?"

"Oh, I don't remember."

"You never told me that." He began laughing.

"I just now thought of it. I had forgotten about it, to tell you the truth."

"Who told her?"

"I'm not sure, but I suspect it was Luke. He doted on her, and she pestered him with questions all the time. I've never seen such a thing."

"It was so hard on everyone in the family."

"Yes. She was such a doll. Both of you . . . Oh, why are we going on like this?

In a few more minutes Jacob was restless to move on.

"I've got to get going."

"Do you want some biscuits to take with you?"

"Made from scratch?"

"Do I make any other kind?" She took exception to this semblance of a doubt; she was known for her biscuits.

"I think I'm going to take some classes at the university campus near me."

"You should!"

At the door he turned around to thank her in a general sense, but instead found himself saying, "I guess I'm not much of a believer, the way most people are."

"Nonsense. You have always loved life, just like your father. Just to be good to your people, you need to have faith. You need to know in your

heart what you have faith in, though, I will tell you that. For us, sometimes, its about showing up, and trying, about doing; and not all that other
business of being in the first pew, or on the right committee, or rubbing
shoulders with certain people, or whatever."

He could see he had activated some deep maternal instinct that made
her crouch over him in a protective stance. They both had pale green eyes.
He had light, sandy hair and plain, boyish features, which carried the heavy
stamp of her lineage in full tones.

"Well, I come from good family. I know that much."

"Yes you do, and don't you forget it."

He felt foolish, and happy. "Bye Mom."

"Behave yourself, now." She flung after him in a teasing tone.

While driving home he listens to the car radio playing classic rock
tunes. He sings along in a soulful manner. Some of these songs were those
he had spent countless hours learning to play as an adolescent; and he was
still practicing some of the same musical themes. He was lost to the world
around him for a while, inhabiting memories of days that are no more.
Then he was overcome with regrets, which made the landscape devolve
into a shabby field of mundane particulars not worthy of his observation.

He dropped off the peoples' bug at Frances' house and walked up
Allen Place and across Clay, heading up the driveway, anxious to get home.
Beatrice called out to him from the side door of the house, telling him to
come see the renovated kitchen. Together they admired the fine craftsmanship of his brother Matthew.

"Frances just told me you want to host events for charities."

"Yes, that's one of the things I wanted to discuss with you."

"It's a great idea."

"You can help me so much, if you are going to stay on. I guess I've
never really discussed your plans with you."

"Well, that's a good thing, because I don't know myself what they are."

"Well, I hope you stay on for a while. There will be more money for you
once we get things up and running."

347

"It sounds great," he said, feeling a little feeble about his response, and his own part in the forward movement of these things being proposed. He headed for the back door.

"Oh Jacob, you used to play your guitar up on the third floor, didn't you?"

"Yeah, I did . . . the acoustics up there are phenomenal."

"I've been thinking of setting it up for rehearsals. Little intimate affairs, for small crowds. A place to hear chamber music."

"That's a really great idea."

"Your brother is coming over to look at the space, to see what we might do. We wanted you to weigh in also."

"I'd like to. Tell me when."

"I'll let you know."

Once back in The Joint he looked out his windows at the waning sunlight caught in the last translucent leaves. He thought of Molly, of her goodness. It was plainly evident in how she treated other people. She herself was almost like a tangible prayer, constantly being acted out instead of chanted in empty structures. He was not at all sure he was good enough for her. She had gone through so much, and now she was suffering doubts, because life was so dear, and she had been wounded so badly. She deserved to not have anyone interfering with her spiritual convalescence. She was in the prime of her sexual life. She had a great need to remove her halo and fully enter the world again. She had her daughter to think of, and she didn't need the added burden of supporting some clown who used to crow about his proficiency at hosting a riotous barbecue . . .

He was playing his favorite songs on his guitar, but if you had walked in and asked him what he had just been playing he would not have known what to say.

"I'm afraid I don't have very much to offer her," he confided to himself.

Late one night he picked up the book she had given him and began scanning the pages. He was not able to concentrate on the words. He looked out his windows to stare at glowing bits of the firmament scattered above his trees. Then a brilliant aperçu came to him as he considered how the Galilean conceived his notion that the kingdom is within us. Henceforth he strives to wield the idea; the flesh itself is sacred. The temple where all the real work is actually done by humankind. It must have terrified him; he was never quite able to extirpate himself from old sorceries. He constructed an enormous idea; that the divine machinery of the universe (the Logos of St. John), was the very substance that had formed his own mind. This knowledge swept him away from his people, and he had to sojourn in the desert. He comes back to nothingness. He has only the songs emanating from his own loving nature. He is seen going half mad attempting to explain himself to his disciples. Paradise might be all around us, and in us, and needs only our final touch for it to flourish. It makes no sense to the people, who worship heroes, and since blood is the ointment used by mobs and nations, the man lays hold of the crucifix. He places himself there to wrench himself against the wheel of civilization, and is thereby crushed . . .

The war-besotted Greeks and Romans were ever grappling with the same mystic questions, but in their quest to understand the source they only engendered hysterical caricatures of themselves. They also focused on personal honor and love, drawing closer to nature. What really constitutes moral beauty? There is no doubt, from the struggle for survival, our essence has evolved moral imperatives that make no sense to us in our daily affairs. We house the meaning in vacuous structures, and weakly fumble away the ennobling mechanism. It is certainly not something that necessitates learned doctors of the law for explanation. No, it's a lasting part of us, and passes our understanding . . .

"That is the soul." Jacob reasons out loud. That sense of a higher purpose that we honor collectively, because it exists in each of us; and therefore we know that it is true. He was not completely sure of himself; but he knew that he had discovered something for himself. The soul is not immortal. The important thing is that every human being has one, which is uniquely his own. It is a deposit of very pure, refined psychic energy; the flame above the candle. It exists beyond the easy convenience of today's concept of right and wrong, as bleated in the public square. It defies the tortured exegesis of altruism as merely a sophisticated stratagem to benefit the species; no, we have evolved something more grandiose.

We strive to achieve sublimity, knowing it may never be achieved. We are bound to our mortal wick, burning through what has been bequeathed to us by evolutionary forces. Our spiritual breathing feeds off the ambient atmosphere. The flame evolved along with the fierce wiring that governs animal prowess. For what higher dominion is to be had on this earth, than control of oneself? What greater battle, than that posed by love? Jacob reflected on the potency of love, the allure of abstract justice, the beauty found in the Christmas carols; all of this comes from one singular font? His devotion to music has always drawn him closer to that source. He could go no further than this in his quest.

It was after that evening when he cut the chain off the mountain bike and began riding it around the neighborhood. He took to the streets, eager to peddle up hills, wanting to feel his muscles straining. He coasted down hills to feel the rush of air buffeting his body. He rode hard to feel his heart beating at an accelerated rate. At times he seemed to float; his balance came of moving across the earth. His faith in the strength of his limbs was stupendous. In his progress he was sheltered under the invisible cloak of his own romance. He was growing and the energy released during the process was exhilarating. He expended himself working the pedals, sweeping past familiar places and nodding to the great noble trees he loved in a way he could not understand, nor communicate to another person. It were as though all things had become refreshed in his eyes.

37

There was a time when the three tiers of land tucked away behind the church and the school were forever cast in a sort of golden shade for the boy. At recess the youngest children played on the upper level, where the nuns had quick, easy access to watch over them. The next few grades used the middle level, which was bifurcated by fencing to separate the genders. Only the oldest boys descended to the lower level where rugged sports were played on both the asphalt and the ball field. The nuns took their time descending to those barbarous steppes.

Therefore most of the early games had no rules nor officiating, and devolved quickly into a sport the boys found latent in their blood, called simply, Kill The Man with the Ball. No official rule book existed. The only methodology that held sway in these tournaments was of the individual striving against impossible odds. Jacob had never progressed down to those lower fields, his memories ceased on the middle level, and were cast in the atmosphere of storybook wonders.

The end of recess, in good weather, could seem like the close of a great epoch. One fell into mourning, remembering the heroes they had almost been. Sometimes a sentimental wisp of maturity caused them to pause their innocent games right before the end of recess, in calm reflection, with Roman stoicism, awaiting the death knell. The imperious bell, in its hideous clatter, would soon be calling them back to the regimen of the classroom. Yet for a few more moments they were under the spell of their freedom, perched on a Jungle Jim, resting like a troop of mon-keys, looking out over their territory. Each a young sachem, they spoke as peers, making sport of the nuns, and each other, sharing opinions on the injustice of long school hours, and the capricious edicts published at home. They considered improvements to be made in future games, forg-ing a separate fellowship.

One scene was imprinted on Jacob's long venerable scroll of experience. He was sitting on the Jungle Jim, grasping the cold iron bars, balancing himself with facile ease, looking over in the other sector of the second lev-el where his sister was huddled with her friends, and where other budding girls were beginning to catch him staring at them, causing riotous squeals and smiles full of some secret mirth that made his heart patter to the beat of an ecstatic melody he was anxious to learn. Now it seemed to come back to him and it was impossible for him to grasp the meaning of the elapsed time. He was strangely happy, that was all he was able to fathom. Happy, but utterly confused about what anything really meant anymore; especially when he tried to place himself in a particular social context. He was getting nowhere, observing everything from a chimerical vantage.

He arrived at St. Margaret's on Friday and adopted his role of being the sojourner in his own childish festival. He had no other recourse when she was nearby. He knew he had to stop torturing himself over what might never come to pass, but such methods were reserved for those who have graduated from the courts of childish games. He took his seat at the table with Cook and Hereford and barely touched his beer; afraid to dilute these halcyon hours. He wanted to see everything that was happening with per-fect clarity. Nothing lasted, neither would this . . .

"They make very good Catholics," Hereford stated spiritedly, referring to the house sparrows belonging to a local colony, established in the nooks and crannies of the church and the school. They lived out in the open, like the rambunctious peasants of Luther's day. The husbands and wives could be seen hunting and gathering on the parking lot; sometimes squabbling in public with a vociferous disregard for avian dignity. They performed other conjugal acts in plain sight, which the church fathers could hardly condone. But these twittering members of the flock put their faith into practice; and sometimes they observed the mass, all ruffled up in their warm niches, never protesting, too much. However, they scoffed at the propaganda concerning doves.

"The husbands and wives work together." Hereford said, looking at several of the birds hopping about at his feet.

"The little beggars are as blithe as can be." Cook said as he tossed out tiny flakes of fish to the shameless birds.

"This is their homeland." Hereford said, "They've come here to make use of all the hollow structures we've built for them."

"They live on the scaffolding, that's true; but we're all bastards in America. We never talk about the Motherland, or the Fatherland; flaunting only our pedigree, the founding papers, and whatever legal currency we've amassed."

"Maybe we're all orphans . . ."

"Under one flag."

"The rich, gaudy underdrawers of our first holy momma—"

"Maya."

"That works."

As this patter was going on Jacob was drawn away by a glance from Molly, who stood among the tables at the Grotto. He walked over to greet her and without a word she led him to the other picnic table at the crest of the hill that was now their spot. He surveyed the familiar scene in his usual trance.

"I was afraid you were avoiding me." She said to him as they sat down. She was dressed in a heavy sweater with a high collar, and the look put him in mind of the bust of a goddess he'd seen in a book. The cool air brushed color into her features and freshened his adoration.

"No, not at all. I didn't want to pester you."

"Right."

"You're quite popular around here, you know?"

"Are you still freaked out by what I told you in the confessional?"

He looked at her, somewhat unnerved, rather unprepared for this sudden leap into intense conversation. "I think you were trying to scare me off a little bit."

"I think I was trying to show you how messed up I am."

"You're not messed up. If anybody is messed up, it's me."

"I try to hide it, but, yes, I am. They say time heals, well, I need a lot of time, brother."

He sighed heavily, not knowing what to say. She was a beloved figure at the church, surrounded by devoted friends. How strange to hear her speak this way of herself. She studied his face. As often happens, the emotional forces working behind the words not being spoken were clearly in evidence, smothering the features of restraint in a sort of powerful spray, like ocean waves splashing onto the blank faces of rocky shores. His countenance was a mask nearly hidden under sprays of sorrowful frustration. He wanted to tell her that she seemed like a perfect woman to him; but he knew she would not stand for that kind of treatment right now. She was confiding in him, and expected more. Why was this happening to him, again? Oh, the intractable doubts!

"You have so many options available to you," he said, regretting his words as they were spoken. He was just fumbling, grasping for some way to get past this imbroglio of his own making.

"I don't want to go through another wedding."

He thought she meant to convey that her first marriage was still sacrosanct to her, and therefore she could not bring herself to defile it by moving on; which recalcitrance was thought by her circle to be a grave mistake. Surely everyone was telling her it was time, she had to commence her life once more. And he had never known anymore more conversant with what is most precious in life! But she wished him to comprehend that she was imprisoned in her own bastion of doubts as well. He felt the weight of a furious inertia keeping them apart. He managed to nod slightly, to avoid saying something incredibly stupid.

"What's the point?" She prodded him. "If I don't believe in it. Can you tell me that?"

"At some point you have to trust your own heart, I suppose."

"Oh, don't talk to me like that. It wouldn't be fair to him, anyway. To marry the holy widow, to take on that burden. How long would it last, after that fairy tale crumbles away?"

So, she was thinking about Heather's brother. He was engulfed in a miasma of jealousy, rising from the sickening stew of his spoiled feelings. Then he was thinking of how it must be for her, to have her friends pressing her to get married, when she did not want to confine herself that way, in the uncertain state of wedlock. To face that relentless pressure, from those closest to you, wanting you to be someone they want you to be . . .

"Under those circumstances, would you want to marry me?"

"No, I understand. It would seem incestuous."

"Incestuous? Why did you say that? That's very weird."

She had startled him and he didn't have any idea why he had chosen that word. He looked around, amazed; he felt like shrinking away to some dark refuge.

"That's not what I mean."

"What do you mean?"

He shook his head dumbly, feeling abashed. He'd put the jester's crown on his own head, just as the Corsican had done.

"I'm just a Russian monk, after all."

She frowned at him. "Why did you stay with Jenny so long?"

"I don't know. We were good together, for most of that time. Then suddenly, we weren't." He was thinking of how she had turned the question around; most wanted to know why one would break up that way after such an extended length of time.

"It's those sudden moments that are the most telling."

"I wasn't being truthful, before, when I told you about Jenny. She did want to have a child. She got pregnant."

"Did you want her to have it?"

He proceeded to recount the tale of how the relationship ended. It was the first time he had ever had any objectivity in the telling. He spoke to her of how Jenny had gotten pregnant by another man when they were in a very bad place, and then kept him in the dark about the situation. Not knowing, but clouded by suspicions, he had encouraged her to have an abortion. Then the relationship imploded and they broke apart and then he found out she had had the abortion, anyway. He attempted to explain why he had been unable to confess all of this to her in the past, but the aversion on her face told him that was unnecessary.

"Why wouldn't I want to have kids?" He asked in a pitiable voice and she did not respond. Looking at her he noticed she was animated, her eyes sliding back and forth in studious puzzlement. "I left her when she was pregnant."

"But you said she was acting weird, and she was trying to deceive you into thinking it was yours. Maybe you did know, without knowing. And maybe you just didn't want to have children with her." She spoke as if testing him.

"I hate to think of the time involved, the lives degraded . . ."

"You have to get to a place where memories don't haunt you, and those sorts of things aren't nagging at you. You have to tame the demons. It sounds awful to say—"

"No, I know what you mean."

"To be honest, that's my problem too; something's hardened in me. It's hard to describe, but I just can't indulge certain kinds of weakness, anymore. I don't always make that clear to people."

He reached out, touching her on the shoulder.

She turned and smiled at him with a face he did not recognize; one devoid of any trace of her usual mercy.

He felt as if he were coming out of a deep reverie. There was relief, emptiness, and many familiar notes from his songbook of sorrow. The inexorable nature of a life's trajectory was putting cherished dreams to flight; he perceived that much of great significance was tearing past him. They were silent a long moment, looking out over the twinkling landscape.

"Do you want to go to confession?" She asked, looking over her shoulder towards the hulking shadow of the church.

"No." He felt an arousal of intense obstinacy. He was drifting away from her at the very moment he was most attracted to her; it was almost painful, to be drawn towards her as a sensual woman and a superb moral being, completely out of his reach.

"What's the matter?"

"I don't believe in anything they do inside that building."

"You don't?"

"No. I believe in what the people do out here." He swept his eyes over the crowded grounds.

"And what is that? Making merry, getting drunk, speaking the dialectics, maybe dancing?"

"Living their lives the best they can. Families sticking together, despite all the crap the world throws at you."

"So now you're telling me you think they're all doing their best?"

"I don't know."

"But you're trying to say it's about a greater good?"

"Yes, I believe that. Does that sound trite?"

"Not at all."

"Not trite; but I mean, too easy, something too often said and not done."

He could not find the words to tell her of his belief in a personal soul, a sort of essence that makes each life so precious. He was not a cargo vessel, on a voyage to deliver one soul to eternity. No, living here, being here, and dying here; that is the glory. Taking custody of these deposits of infinite moral complexity, bequeathed to us by the legions of hard-working stars hung in the heavens, by unknown forces, it was too much, he could not tell her.

Jacob's mind was reeling. Somehow he couldn't bring himself to articulate all that was in his heart and he was sure he was making a great muddle of things. Her mention of weakness had been jarring. He shuddered in his unworthiness. She was more advanced in these things of the spirit. He faltered, losing faith in the integrity of his words. He had exhausted himself in the effort to merely approach a personage such as Molly T. Fuller on an equal plane.

"Hey?" She broke in on his thoughts.

He looked over at her, she was right there, so completely herself, her eyes full of the perfect light for soothing his agony.

"Do you want to help me steal something?"

"You want to steal something?" He grew excited. "Street signs?"

"What? No. There's a tree I want to plant right here. I love this piece of ground, looking out over the field. I want to put my own touch on it for some reason. Is that silly?"

"Not at all. I want to help."

"It's up at Wabash Lake—"

"I know which one you mean."

"No you don't!" She shoved him on the shoulder with one hand.

"It's at the end of the lake, there are several there, it's the little black cherry."

She laughed. "That's the one. It has such a perfect shape."

"Sure, I can be your thief."

Her eyes suddenly opened wide as she looked up slightly, as if seeing something very clearly, all of a sudden, in the diffuse, colored gloom hovering over the lighted Grotto. She began searching the grounds, her neck stretched out, her eyes scanning rapidly looking for one familiar form.

"I need to check on Sophie."

"Yeah. I need to pour out libations at the C & H shrine."

She turned to press her lovable sweetness upon him in one of her quick, flashing, signature expressions, and then she was gone, beyond his reckoning. He was glad to see her walking off, even though it tore at his heart. He needed to regain his balance in this vertigo he had induced by practicing the wicked arts of standing aloof, while aching in every fiber to be a part of something so eminently corruptible, transformative, and beautiful.

38

The next Friday Jacob was at the Grotto discussing the outside dining situation with Frances. She was intent on staying the course, despite a turn in the weather; he assured her they had nothing to lose.

"Now that the receipts are coming in like they are . . ." She was doing this more often, pausing mid-sentence, to flee back into her own moral confines, and then failing to find her place again. Jacob was amused by her anguished commercial sensibility. He excused himself and went to help Cody stage his sound equipment.

"Do you really think people will want to dance out there?" Jacob indicated the middle level with a glance.

"Who's the fool who won't want to dance?" Cody hurled back at him from the throne of his elation.

"If they even come," Jacob replied, feeling a chill in the air.

The weather certainly dampened the turnout for outdoor dining; but the people arrived in droves nonetheless. There was now a sense of wanting to be present at the festival for its duration. One felt a communal feeling as music was broadcast over the grounds; everyone understood this might be the year's last Fish Fry held outdoors. The hoary breath of winter put them in a holiday mood as they moved about swaddled in warm apparel, playing up to the seasonal spirits.

Jacob sat with Isaac, who wore a leather flight jacket, and ball cap, looking strangely youthful in appearance. He said he wasn't sure if Hereford was coming or not, he had previously mentioned another event he wanted to attend. But then he did show up and it was like old times. Jacob did not want to talk that much really, and he knew all he had to do was raise a topic with a bald statement and they would rush to deploy pointless arguments.

At one point Isaac began lecturing Paul after he made a comment about the inevitable failure of movies that try too hard to capture the soul of good novels. Jacob was sure he had heard this discussion before and he barely listened as they covered old material.

"Each work of art must have its own soul." Hereford stated this with absolute certitude. Jacob reflected upon his newfound belief in a personal soul; but he kept his thoughts to himself.

"Yes, that is why TV will dominate how people consume fictional dramas in the future." Cook spoke in his most insufferable tone of infallibility; which only came out, as far as Jacob knew, when he was disputing with Hereford, who matched his pitch precisely in his contending pronouncements. "Each person in the comfort of his own home, choosing from a vast portfolio, matching viewer to program."

"Each one formatted to fit the typical viewer's shrunken mind."

"Not at all." And then he was expounding upon his views.

Jacob listened to the verbal gymnastics, but he was watching the people all around him as if spellbound. He was feeling himself to be at a safe remove from the activity and yet right in the center of things. The cool air and the colored lights, flaring in melodic movements on the wind, drawing attention to the dark naked limbs of the sassafras trees, and the solemn downcast gaze of the chaste Madonna, all of it conjured a certain reverence, as one feels at times during the Christmas season. His mind registered how everything sweeps by so fast, becoming as leaves that haunt our steps along the streets.

"Jacob!"

"What?"

"Did you hear what Isaac said?"

"No."

"He just said all human progress is theoretical."

"No, I said we like to believe progress offers the chance of achieving a better way of life for all people; or rather, we pretend to believe that, but only to assuage our collective sense of our own goodness. In fact, it is like boiling down a plentiful raw material to derive a precious extract. The process is in fact very wasteful of that precious material, in achieving the desired results, for a selected portion."

"We're mostly just serfs," Jacob said, hardly knowing where the statement came from. "We're not masters of ourselves. We act like witchdoctors, dressing up a personality, and then dancing the puppet."

Hereford and Cook exchanged a look, sobered by this untaught fellow who had a penchant for delivering observations that stopped them in their tracks.

"It's a rickety thing, at best." Hereford began to expound. "My last novel, *The Scarecrow's Homecoming*—"

"Jacob, tell us about Molly." Isaac broke in, leaning forward, wishing to address himself to other matters than one of Hereford's novels.

"There's nothing to tell."

"How do you feel about her?"

"I have to mingle." Jacob stood up and stared at them like a fugitive.

"You're refusing to answer questions at the Treacle table?"

"I have no answers for this Committee of Public Safety." He threw their own satiric material back at them.

"You're out of order, sir."

"Wait."

"Hey, what's the matter?"

"You don't mingle out there, that's not your style." Cook attempted to upbraid the fellow for his lack of table spirit.

"You haunt the grounds. You drift around like a ghost." Hereford intoned.

"Maybe that's the problem." He whispered, as to himself.

"Don't let those false apostles debauch you! Ours is the way." Hereford cried out in mock horror. "Stay here, where we preserve the true gnosis. We pour out our libations to all the gods." He began laughing, raising his arm and pointing at something. They were confused for a moment, until they noticed the diminutive lawn statue of Cupid, placed at the base of the platform holding up the Madonna.

"Oh no." Isaac reacted adversely, turning on Paul. "Did you do that?"

"I'm not that clever. But what do you think? Installing that little knave in this setting?" Paul was very pleased. "It is pretty good casting, no?"

"It won't fly, not around here."

"He doesn't have to fly. He's the oldest, most cunning child. He crawls freely wherever he wishes to go."

"And he is armed for action."

Jacob stared at the plump archer with unease; Molly would be distressed by its appearance. She might consider him to be an accessory. The fun and games can be pushed too far . . .

"I need to see about something." Jacob said, turning away from the table.

"At least find a torch you can carry around with you!" Hereford flung this bon mot with glee, holding up his plastic cup in mock of some character unknown to all but himself.

"If you must go, at least bring us some more wine." Isaac beseeched him, feeling a twinge of uneasiness over these untoward developments.

"You better find Lilly, you derelicts." He yelled at them with bravado; never having used that epithet on them before. It felt good. They laughed as though it were very droll, indeed.

"Where is she, I wonder?" Jacob mused aloud, thinking of Molly.

"She's spending all her time on the lower levels, with Igor." Hereford here was referring to Lilly, and mocking her helper Gregory, the troubled protégé of Frances. Gregory was in fact now on the payroll, pushing a little cart around, chasing after the very popular Lilly, who was selling spirited beverages at a rate that kept Gregory on his toes. She could be likened to a magic Fräulein, in whose presence one confused real life and fantasy, in a manner that seemed very familiar to that part of the mind that churns out incomprehensible dreams.

Jacob passed among the skirl of leaves that swept across the lot in wild marches, only stopping briefly, while slightly trembling, to await more winds. He descended to the lower level and found people thrown together as though at a party where no one is quite sure who has put the whole thing together. They were inclined to greet people they did not know; like strangers meeting overseas and discovering they are from the same city back in the states, and thus obliged to act as boon companions.

A voluble group of people had collected on the ball field just where there used to be an actual home base. Jacob began speaking with them. Several women were eager to interrogate him regarding his relations with Molly. There was much laughter at his evasions, and for a moment it seemed he was under consideration to be inducted into the tribe. Then a round of outlandish jokes regarding marriage crackled in his ears. He was soon put into motion when he heard Dylan's portentous love song, "I Want You." He wended up the hill to the table where Cody was in control of the music.

"It's like a regular carnival." He said to him.

"Yeah," Cody replied, keeping an eye on the task at hand. The next song he played was by the Bee Gees, "To Love Somebody."

"Oh man, are you trying to take us back to disco?" Jacob feigned outrage.

"This ain't disco."

"I know."

"Besides it was requested by someone special."

"Sure it was."

"It was Molly."

Jacob looked at him. "Really?"

"She gave me very specific instructions. Had to do with her first time."

"What are you talking about? What does that mean?"

Cody ignored him with vast immovable complacency.

"You're on a power trip, Night Watchman. I'm going to tell Sistah you're out of control. You could be replaced. I bet I could do this better than you."

"No way. Besides, it's too late, everything has to run its course."

"You're losing it."

"I'm already gone." He replied. "So are you. Get ready for the next one."

Jacob had been watching as people kept coming up to Cody's table to make requests. He was happy, holding court with all his riches of CDs ranged around him. The music drew them hence, closer to the bare essence of their heartfelt wishes, drowning the noise of the world. Jacob became intrigued by the dancers on the middle level, struck by the almost formal devotion shown by each person to his or her panoply of distinctive personal movements.

"Okay, get ready," Cody said to him.

"What? You going to play 'Night Fever?'"

"A lot of people are asking for this one. I've been holding off, waiting for the right moment."

The haunting strings of the intro piece to "Maggie May" by Rod Stewart wafted over the air, stirring the crowd. Cody increased the volume while nodding in anticipation of the opening verse. The first two words of the iconic anthem were barely heard over the sound system as the assembled multitude roared them out at the top of its lungs. All over on three levels the voices reverberated against the starry sky. The awful chorus continued in delirious waves that disturbed the air around Jacob so that he could not hear himself. Cody was laughing soundlessly in the din. A shiver coursed through his body as Molly appeared; one of her mysterious smiles creeping upon those features that moved him so fearfully. Their eyes met and glimmered in harmonious thrall to this extraordinary sensation that lay beyond explanation.

"That was crazy," she said in a breathless delight after it was over. She looked at the arm of her jacket. "I have goosebumps." Her euphoria created the illusion in his mind that he had only to reach out and touch her to rise above everything. One could hear yells of acclamation coming from numerous places. Cody quickly put on a song from the *Let It Bleed* album, by the Rolling Stones, which begins with an opening by the London Bach Choir. Many people sang this solemn hymn quietly to themselves.

"How are you?" She implored him.

"I have no idea. I may be taking leave of my senses."

"Really? You still had them a minute ago?"

"No! I've just now figured it out; I have lost my mind. Do you think one could get closer to everything that way?"

"You're starting to scare me," she said, laughing with her face. Her nose began crinkling up.

"I've thrown away all responsibilities. Can that be a good thing?"

"I thought you said you had a ton of chores every week."

"I guess I do. But everything is done like I'm in a dream."

"You're logging too many hours at the C & H Company. You do know, don't you, that an awful lot of make-believe goes on over there."

"Maybe so. All I know is, I don't want to wake up." He wanted to ask her to dance with him and the moment fled past on the wind as he stared at her face in euphoric stasis.

"I know what you mean there. I looked for you over there earlier. Isaac says he fears you are becoming an apostate of apostasy."

"The professors are not pleased to have their pupil striking off to go in circles of his own?"

She laughed. Her face seemed to darken as her excitement flashed from her eyes in concert with the commotion whirling everywhere around them.

"Come on," she said suddenly, reaching out and plucking at his jacket sleeve. He followed and caught up to her. They walked over and sat down at their picnic table with the perfect vantage.

"Shouldn't you be flouncing around?" He asked her from the depths of his giddiness.

"You mean fooling around?" She reacted as if she were offended, in a display of precious irony.

He mirrored her exaggeration, taking it far in the opposite direction. She laughed in a peculiar way.

"Who says I'm not right now?" She spoke impulsively.

"Good point. You are a good witch."

"You think so, do you?" She was not looking at him. "Say, did you talk to Frances?"

"About what?"

"She's freaking out about everything."

"Why?"

"The priests want to shut this down." She looked out over the crowd on the lower level; it had all the makings of a mob, but there were only the better angels directing their motions.

"The weather will shut it down soon enough."

"That's true. But they want to strip her of her authority. They never thought she would turn it into this. Now they are working to annul the agreement."

"Can they do that?"

"I imagine they can do whatever they want. It all belongs to them, after all."

"That'll be rough, for her, to have to go through something like that again."

"I don't know; I have a feeling she doesn't like having all this financial responsibility."

"I know she doesn't."

"It's gotten to be too much for her. It has gotten out of hand."

"Say, tell me, do you still go to confession?"

"Why do you ask me that?"

"I don't know, I was just wondering. I mean, you go to mass every week, don't you?"

"Yes, I have been lately. But no, I don't go to confession. I'm not going to bare my soul to some creepy priest, chosen at random by the Curia."

Jacob shook in merriment. He was once again charmed by her unexpected responses when they were enjoying these intimacies.

"As a boy, I learned to confess the same sins over and over, to make it easier. I was mean to my parents, mostly my mom. I was mean to my one brother, and my other brothers, and everybody. I was acting selfish, like everybody else. Oh, please give me a receipt, and let me get out of here."

"Incorrigible."

"I would take a seat in the pew to say my penance, racing through them so I could clear out. I even began to just imagine I had said all the prayers."

"Anything to get back outside to your freedom."

"Strange behavior for a future monk, I guess; but really, that isn't taking hold either." He could see she was becoming distracted. "It does seem unconscionable, now; having adolescents go into those cells to confess their sins to priests! My God, what a recipe made for the devil."

"But you don't believe in the devil, do you?"

"No. Do you?"

"No."

He could not bring himself to ask her if she believed in God. He did not want to grapple with his own agnostic position in front of her. None of that mattered to him when she was near.

"Even with God," she said, I'm not sure what I believe anymore. Half the time I feel like I'm praying to myself."

He marveled at her intuitive ability to peer directly into his mind; by some enchantment of evolution, that allows one person to become so intimate with the thoughts of another that he is influenced by that other person's emotions as they happen. She almost confessed that she mainly prayed to the Virgin Mary, but decided against doing so at the present time.

Lilly and Gregory came by and stayed to chat even though neither Jacob or Molly wanted anything to drink. She poured a cup of water for each of them. She offered them portions of her resplendent youth, laying bare for them, in delicious quips, some choice eccentricities of her clientele. It caused bewitching laughter to burble out of Molly, making Jacob even more happy. Then he noticed Gregory was taking gulps out of a can of beer and it appeared as though he were drooling as he was drinking. A truly Gothic image. Just then a troop of people sailed by, coursing merrily down the hill. Pilgrims on their way to Canterbury? The Wife of Bath herself, holding a fresh bouquet of sorts, fleeing from all that 'wo that is in marriage'; she called for Lilly to follow them. She left a trail of blue hydrangeas petals as she made her way forward. Lilly and her incongruous squire trundled after them.

Jacob concluded he had to reveal his feelings regarding the church, and his soul, and life, and everything, even though it wasn't the time, nor place; and besides, he had no idea how to tear apart such a mass of insoluble strands. It seemed urgent that he make the attempt, and right now, as if he were being pressured by the relentless motion of some monstrous apparatus, bearing upon his fate . . .

"You can't live for someone else." Molly spoke without looking at him. "You can be there for others, but you have to live your life. No matter what happens, you need to restore that vital reverence you must have for your own life."

Jacob looked at her and did not say anything.

"'The man that hath not music in himself, is fit for treasons.'"

"What's that?" He was intrigued.

"Isaac." She said simply; meaning he had been her source for this quotation from *The Merchant of Venice*. For the first time he felt jealous of Isaac, and all his knowledge, and all his time spent with Molly.

At that moment Janey came up and stood at one end of the table looking at Molly. "I think Sophie is looking for you."

"She's not here." Molly spoke after looking away from Janey's face, clearly fuming.

"Yes she is. I picked her up, so she could play with—"

"*You* picked her up." Molly stood up, glancing hastily down at Jacob, and then moving over to face Janey. They exchanged angry words. Janey said something about Heather, and as Jacob strained to hear they began walking off together, heads in motion, arms flailing, still debating irreconcilable differences of opinion on these matters.

Molly looked back over her shoulder, making a rueful face for his benefit. That made him feel even more in the dark; he had no idea whatsoever what was going on between them. He sat at the table by himself another moment, very intent on listening to the music, as if he were playing his own simple instrument in accompaniment. Some early Beatles material caused a host of people to get up and dance; their good spirits depressed his even further. He repaired to the Treacle table and found them aloft in the high winds of empty rhetoric.

"Our mother is a fish." Said Hereford.

Jacob listened as their banter was raised to baroque levels. His mind began to wander and he finally slipped away without a parting word. He found himself going down to the lower level, joining a group engaged in discussing politics. One fellow seemed to have discovered the world of partisan politics, much as others embrace a new religious sect. There was pious fervor, a ready catechism, many established rituals, and fierce war songs for releasing long-bred angers against godless pagans. The novice seemed intent on pronouncing anathema upon as many of the reprobates as possible; he had a long list to choose from.

Jacob imagined the Augean stables of corruption that must exist if so many people are content to argue over high phrases, while remaining ignorant of the rotten process that dictates how the vast preponderance of legislation actually gets signed into law. Not to mention how laws are implemented once the lobbyist and the regulatory bodies become as one flesh devoted to increase and cash dividends. The exalted free press is now a place for amassing riches and fame, where the elite players are indistinguishable from the courtiers serving the Brahman caste of politicians. Promoting public policy is a game that leads one to higher status and preferment. He had learned recently that the Pharisees were frequently called hypocrites by the Galilean, because that word at the time referred to actors. There was certainly a great burlesque show scripted by Mammon going on at the nation's capitol, and there was no sign the production would be cancelled any time soon.

"Whereas, wishing to appear to be concerned about appearances, I hereby appear before you now." Jacob was walking up the sidewalk on Chambers, in the shadow of the school rising in steps alongside the hill. "I will utter oaths. I will raise my arm in salute, if you like, or become a zealot, a sort of dervish. What is a dervish?" He was addressing the white lights of cars coming down Chambers and rushing past with a litany of harsh, dismissive moans; and also holding forth for the somber retreating red lights of cars climbing the hill and going the other way. All this heedless, headlong motion being directed by manifold traffic laws ingrained as steady habit. How would it go for the one who cuts across these busy energy fields? Was there anything on the other side?

At the corner he noticed how the distant street lights on Elizabeth cast down picturesque conical spheres of filmy light on empty segments of the sidewalk. He resisted the urge to walk towards one of those spaces, and instead entered the old front entrance of the church. He stood at the railing around the altar space. It appeared to him as one of those historical sites, restored for tourists; where people traipse around in period clothing, taking pride in keeping the site authentic to an olden time that has passed away. They wish to take you back, just for a moment! He thought of one of Isaac's diatribes about a plantation he had visited: *Yes, we had slaves; but it was a merry time too, a time of plenty and gorgeous manners. Stately houses, servants, and such lovely costumes . . .*

Jacob tried to imagine himself being in this place with Molly. He feared he would never be comfortable sprawled in the embroidered lap of the great mother church of Rome. As he stood there, in direct supplication of himself, a man could be heard muttering to himself. Jacob moved closer towards the passage leading to the sacristy, and listened very attentively.

"The damned witches!" The voice declaimed.

Jacob leaned over chortling, he almost burst out laughing. He retreated down the side aisle to get to the front entrance. Turning at the door he saw the priest cross in front of the altar space, foregoing the usual procedure of kneeling on one knee while facing the altar before moving on. He turned and caught Jacob staring at him and paused involuntarily, and then spun about and beat a quick retreat back into his chambers.

Jacob exited the building, feeling better in the cool, invigorating atmosphere outside. He plopped down at the Treacle table without a word. Hereford had an unfamiliar woman sitting at his side, and was engaged in a heated conversation with Cook. The woman, dressed in fashionable attire, was very pretty, and the lambent lighting raised a nice glow on her features. Marjorie Key smiled faintly as if to acknowledge all these battles conducted by men in her presence were waged for her benefit; but she was not one to fret over the natural course of things. She smiled at Jacob as if granting him the privilege of standing in line to await his chance to vie for her approval.

"So Jacob is back!" Hereford seemed desirous of ending his argument with Cook. He introduced the woman to Jacob; sharing information regarding her social standing that left Jacob duly impressed. He was afraid to make a fool of himself by asking the woman tactless questions; so he just smiled and admired her shimmering beauty. Hereford spoke of events they had attended recently. The woman made arch observations about 'old money,' from an insider's perspective; these fell flat at this particular pine table.

Isaac began to talk in a very peculiar fashion of one of his ancestors, who had owned a steamboat that exploded on the Missouri River. Apparently there were several protracted lawsuits and no one understood why Isaac was interjecting such settled arguments into this gathering, and it didn't matter, because suddenly he was talking about Reconstruction, and the Compromise of 1877, and then he stood up to give a satiric toast to the legion of ghoulish Confederate statues that rose out of the ground all across the land (to feed on democracy) as the country became a world power. It wasn't long before Paul and his date made their excuses and departed. The woman pulled her expensive wrap tightly around herself and gave a last sweeping smile to all present. She was unaware of why she had been brought to this quaint little affair, but it had been rather 'interesting' for her to witness, and would be shared later with others of her own kind for their common amusement.

"You were in rare form." Jacob said to Isaac.

"Don't know what got into me." He made a face, feigning innocence.

"So, if you can't take the treacle, don't sit down at the table—"

"Where have you been, anyway?" Isaac asked him.

"I went in the church."

"Was it empty, as usual?"

"Not quite."

He told Isaac of his overhearing the prelate's curse while lurking near the man's inner sanctum. They both looked over at the narrow stairway, supported by bare concrete pillars, leading up to a back entrance of the church, used by priests and altar boys.

"The witches," Isaac repeated with ruminative savor. He began laughing in a gentle manner. Soon enough both men were engulfed in gales of laughter.

"Ah, that was good." Isaac said after the fit was over. He told Jacob a short while before he had seen one of the fathers removing the Cupid statuette from the Grotto area. "I hope he did not get pricked while carrying the chubby boy."

"No, stop," Jacob said, "My side still aches. We can't tell Molly about this."

"No, I know." He took a drink of wine.

"Things are going too fast."

"I hear the fathers are not too happy with Frances."

"It's been a hell of a ride. It's become a regular circus."

Isaac chuckled. "I'm just a tourist, and, when in Rome."

Jacob felt the man was too clever by half, more than half the time, and that this was only a strategic ploy to stay in one's cynical lane, and thus avoid the necessity of facing the prospect of true development. Which, he had no doubt, Isaac had done a great deal of, over the course of his life; but having to read all the true sign posts, as you go, and nothing else, all the time, that was something no one was ever able or certainly willing to do as a daily practice.

"We all chase our phantom tails," Jacob quipped.

Molly came and sat down with them. She seemed distracted, as if she were avoiding something, and while in their presence she was shielded from other malign forces.

"Who was that woman with Paul?" She asked.

"A new one in his life, said to be from good family." Isaac explained dryly.

"She looked out of place." Molly said with a curious intonation in her voice that made them all laugh.

"Oh. Molly? I saw they were cutting down that elm tree in your old yard." Jacob said to her.

"I knew it wouldn't last much longer." She said pensively.

"I sat on a hill across the street and watched them. I just sat there, my bike on the ground; I felt like a kid again—"

"Did you bring my book back?" She asked him brusquely.

"No, I didn't. I will have to get that back to you. I read it again and it gave me a much better idea of certain—"

Molly looked away abruptly as she heard her named called.

"I have to go."

"See you," Jacob said, visibly crestfallen.

"She's always running around now." Isaac said. "At loose ends."

"What do you mean?"

"Oh, nothing. Say, do you have any interest in old Ferdinand artifacts?"

"Like what?"

"Oh, just some utterly worthless, priceless relics: maps, books, some other items. I have to get rid of several boxes of an old collection. If you want any of it, I can make you a great deal on the whole lot."

"Maybe someone else in the parish—"

"I'd like to give it away to someone I know."

Jacob said he would stop by and take a look, intrigued by the idea of learning more about Ferdinand's history. He was on the point of taking his leave when a disturbance on the lower level rose to their ears. Lilly had been listening to several men boasting of the athletic prowess of their sons when Frances passed by, and one of the men said something disgusting about her person. Gregory stepped in front of the man to tell him that was no way to talk about Miss Frances, and he stuttered, as he often did when overcome by strong emotions. The man laughed at the reproof; feeling the eyes of his friends upon him. He thrust Gregory away by stamping him hard on the chest with both hands. Gregory stumbled backwards, and recoiled in a fury, landing several blows on the man's face. His foe crumpled, and sat down on the pavement, blood trickling out of his mouth.

Gregory was assailed verbally by many antagonists, who all kept a safe distance. He shrank away, and began climbing the hill to the Grotto. A trail of men followed, hectoring him, and calling out to warn people in his path. It was these cries that alerted Jacob and Isaac to the ruckus. Upon seeing Gregory's frightful struggle to maintain a grip on himself, Jacob knew the man was having what Frances referred to as one of his episodes. Gregory stooped to pick a bottle off the ground, that being a part of his duties, as he understood them, while at the Fish Fry. Jacob saw that Sophie and several other children were directly in his path. He rushed over and spoke to Gregory in a gentle manner. He could see the man's distemper subsiding into mere confusion. Then the men who had followed Gregory up the hill began circling around them; they seemed to be snarling and barking at Gregory. He peered around at them, falling into a sort of evil trance. Jacob moved closer in front of him and motioned for the others to keep at bay.

"Gregory, give me the bottle." He reached out. Gregory clutched at the bottle with his other hand.

"I didn't start it." He pleaded. "Will you tell Frances?"

"It's okay," Jacob said. "It's okay. Here, give me the bottle. I'll throw it away for you."

Gregory looked down at the bottle and changed his grasp so that he was holding it in one hand by the neck, his arm flexing instinctively, as though armed with a club. A chorus of cries began demanding that the bottle be taken away.

"Come on, give it to me." Jacob reached out to touch him on the shoulder but the man flinched; a primitive aspect blazed on his face. "Okay, let's go see Frances. Okay?"

"Tell her I didn't start it." Gregory was feeling an old dread that it wouldn't matter, because of those who were at his back, moving against him. Several of the men began cursing him. Gregory understood the feral meaning of these sounds. Someone reached out to haul at his shoulder, to get his attention, and as he started to turn around another man gave him a shove, knocking him into Jacob.

"No! Don't!" Jacob tried to quell the men, but it was too late. After being grabbed from behind, yet again, Gregory spun around, his one arm swung out in a wide arc, the bottle in his hand smashed against Jacob's forehead. He instantly saw a flock of perturbed stars swirling around, having no gravitation field to hold them in place. Gregory lunged at his antagonists and they lurched back in horror. He stood in front of them, his mouth open, his eyes wild, until Frances appeared before him. She grasped his wrist. He released his grip on the broken bottle.

"It's okay Gregory, it's okay." She repeated, speaking to him as you would to an infant you had failed to put down for an evening. He was panting and fuming, still fearing an attack from behind, but her voice and her face were the only trustworthy fixtures in his world, and he clung to these, blabbing to her of his innocence. Several off-duty policemen intervened without a word and brought Gregory to the ground. Frances began pleading with them to go easy on her friend.

While this was going on Molly was mopping at Jacob's head with a heavy scarf she had snatched off another person. She had wadded it up and was pressing it onto his wound and holding it there.

"Are you okay?" She asked him anxiously, seeing that his eyes were glassy. He kept trying to put his hand up to his head, and each time she gently pushed it away.

"Do you want to sit down?"

"I'm a little woozy."

"You need to sit down." She started to lead him to the picnic table by the river birches.

"What are you doing? Somebody has to take him to the emergency room." Frances spoke to Jacob over her shoulder as she negotiated with the men restraining Gregory. Isaac offered to take him and ambled off to get his car, an Iowa-class Cadillac left to his care after his mother's passing. Jacob was seated, perfectly calm, looking out at the strange spectacle of so many people crowded around him with somber faces. He stared at the

Madonna, who could not look up. A woman said to be a nurse was tending to him.

"Can I have a dose of morphine?" He entreated her.

"He's joking," Molly explained to the nurse.

Janey and Heather rushed up to Molly, touching her gently, speaking to her in comforting tones. Meanwhile a field dressing was applied to Jacob's wound.

"Are you sure you're okay, honey?" Janey asked Molly.

"You need to wash that blood off yourself," Heather said, looking down at the sodden scarf Molly was still holding in a twisted wad.

"Let me take that," she said. Holding the scarf by one of the fringes she took the gruesome rag and disposed of it in a large, industrial barrel, left on site since the construction crew had renovated the Grotto courtyard.

"Come on." Janey took Molly by the elbow to usher her towards the cafeteria where lavatories were located. "Lets get you washed up."

Isaac never did come back with his car; no one anticipated that he would. Some other people drove Jacob to the emergency room where the staff on duty stitched the cut on his scalp and joked with him about getting into brawls at church events. All the fawning attention made him feel childish. Afterwards he was left with a host of lurid, chaotic memories that trailed away into inert darkness. His mind was steadfast in retaining one image untouched by the aberrations of memory. The graven image of Molly's anguished face, positioned right in front of his own, full of tortured compassion. The icon was placed at a ready shrine, where one is prompted to say a prayer.

39

Saturday Jacob woke up to lay in his bed like a figure carved on a sarcophagus, staring up into the little cosmos of his abode. His phantasmal dreams of the previous night had not yet completely receded back into the machinery of synapse and fable. He was with Molly, trudging down a winding stairwell into a network of catacombs. There he watched demonic workers closing all the long drawers jutting out from the walls. He began wiping at the enclosures with a cloth, as though to remove the stains, but his hands were only spreading more blood over the surfaces. At the far end of the cave there was an opening leading out to a garden. Molly was slipping out, looking at him over her shoulder . . .

Jacob rolled out of bed and made coffee. He hefted his guitar onto his lap and stared into space. It felt ridiculous to be sitting in this room, alone, on a peaceful day, his dearest hopes, corrupted by too much leaven, running through his fingers. He played music but had no awareness of doing so. The room looked unfamiliar and utterly strange to him. Why was he in this peculiar dwelling? How could it be that all these things were located here? Who had gone to all the trouble of putting everything together in just this way? Not just these physical objects, which he was said to own, but the ideas concerning society, home, the meaning of solitude, of the outside world. This couldn't really be The Joint, could it? That was suddenly an incredible fact for him to ponder. *He* was living in The Joint?

He was able to steady his nerves by playing a few ballads all the way through with deliberate care. Cody came by and shouted up to him and then clumped up the stairs, bringing a box of donuts with him. Downstairs in the kitchen he had poured himself a cup of coffee and now he sat down to eat with Jacob.

"Here, I brought you the paper."

"These things aren't very healthy," Jacob mumbled as he devoured one of the donuts. "Not bad though." He reached for another.

"It's a new place," Cody said. "They just opened, down on Florissant."

After a terse commentary on the fracas that took place the previous night Cody came over to inspect Jacob's bandage. He asked him if he needed anything. He stood there looking confused; then he said he'd check with him later, and fled down the steps again. This visit brought Jacob back to his normal routine. Cody would tell the others he was okay. He walked the grounds, with his usual vigor, and breathed in the fresh, restorative air; but he was feeling weary in his bones.

On Sunday afternoon he dressed in warm clothes, put on a jacket, and pulled a stocking cap over his head. He stepped down Spencer's hill and walked across the yards to Church and then up to Elizabeth, marching by the sycamore trees with a peculiar sense of abandonment. At Cook's house he clattered across the broad covered porch and knocked loudly, not certain if he should have called first; but Isaac answered the door rather quickly and appeared to have been waiting for him. They repaired to the kitchen where Isaac insisted and so he accepted a beer. Isaac topped off his glass of wine. They sat down in the living room. The windows looking out on Elizabeth let one see the house where Molly had been a little girl, and ran around outside while he, Jacob, might have walked past the magical toddler while he was turning the corner on his way to or from St. Margaret's.

For the first time Isaac looked rather old to Jacob. His white hair blazed like desert brush seen in the natural light, the effect was complemented by the growth of whiskers of the same hue matted on his face. His attire was a deft layering of clothing used when it is not deemed necessary to distinguish the hours, neither morning from evening, nor hope from despair.

"These are the things I spoke to you about." The floor was strewn with magazines, curios, photographs, books and old papers, and other things assembled into piles. It was like Christmas morning in a household of deranged antiquarians. Jacob began hefting and examining various items.

"Do you want any of it?"

"I'm not sure." Jacob replied. "What would I do with any of this stuff?"

"That's up to you. I feel like I'm at the end of something. I've held on to these things too long. My sister has taken what she wants." His sister lived in Connecticut, and she had come home frequently in the last months of their mother's life, but, in Isaac's words, "She said emphatically that she's done with this town."

"It's a good town."

"It's a great town. No doubt. It needs more good people. It needs to overcome a sordid past, like the country."

"How about you? You could be one of them. You'd be an eccentric figure of great renown."

Isaac made a wry face. Then he exclaimed, "What would I be, exactly? An idle king, doling out platitudes? My people were a big part of the problem, genteel racists . . ."

"You could be part of the solution."

"Now you sound like Molly. So much seems intractable to me now. Besides, I'm too much of a gypsy. I have so many places where they receive me without reservation. I'm like one of the old fur traders, one of the Chouteau brothers, who roamed over vast regions, comfortable at an Osage chieftain's tent, or in the best dining halls his peers had erected in Montreal. I suppose some people are never really at home anywhere."

"So travel, and make this your home base. I'll be your groundskeeper and we'll throw parties here every Friday in your honor. You will, of course, have to leave us a lot of wine in the cellar so we can drink in your honor."

Isaac laughed. "I would like to see what happens, watch the change, as it occurs. Change is inevitable, and it will be good for Ferdinand." Isaac fell silent abruptly.

"The times, they keep changing. I guess that is always true."

"I'm the last Cook who will inhabit this house, after a hundred years of our line living here, within these walls."

"We'll always refer to it as the house of Cook."

"Yes, you'll have to do that." Isaac wondered what it must be like for a father to have his son as a valued friend. It occurred to him that Jacob was looking at things from a higher vantage; he had gained those heights by striking off alone, leaving behind the superfluous baggage of society, and even himself. It was disconcerting to meet one so terribly balanced in his outlook at this time in his life. Isaac had been rummaging through a storied past, where noxious maggots swarmed forth from the scattered bones and filth of his charnel house. The world had shifted under his feet.

"Let me show you the yard where I was a boy," he said suddenly, as though taking his own pride by the neck; recalling Jacob's enthusiasm for his childhood days. They passed through the kitchen, where Isaac replenished his spirits from a bottle, and Jacob left his barely touched glass of beer on the counter.

Outside there was a spacious suburban plot reduced to natural graces by loving neglect. The mature hardwood trees around the perimeter held themselves as proudly as the Swiss Guard standing outside a palace or papal see. Isaac began talking of the games he had played there, and how some faint tenor of those times had come back to him after he returned.

"Now, it's just about gone. I can feel all that seeping back into the ground again."

"I know exactly what you mean."

"Memory is such a strange contraption." Isaac said. "Nothing is quite real, and yet it remains full of meaning, that suffuses the present." He smiled. "And it all leaves you melancholy. Why can't the past make us happy?"

"I imagine for some it does. I have many good—"

"Oh, I do too. I don't know what I mean. I would not mean what I mean, anyway. I am too far gone, my boy, too far gone."

"Life is like a baby. It wants what it wants, and nothing else matters. But it doesn't know what it ought to want, or what is even possible for it to want. It just reaches for that magic bottle that it knows, the one with the trusty formula. Oh, and it also wants to smash the things it plays with every day." Jacob was surprised at his own fluent ease when speaking his mind to this unlikely and trusted friend. He had noticed Isaac's astonishment as he delivered his speech.

"You have graduated from your trainee position at the C & H Ministry, I'm afraid to say. All we have to offer you now is a post as salesman of footnotes. If you don't want to work for us, you could lead a small sect of Charismatics at living room revivals."

"I don't know where I stand now. I was raised to be a Catholic. But I'm afraid it doesn't fit me."

"Being Catholic, that never took?"

"Never took." Jacob paused a moment and felt compelled to add, "Well, not the part of paying tribute to that nest of bishops and cardinals in Rome. I mean, what the fuck is that about?"

Isaac laughed, greatly amused at his friend's developing style of rendering his thoughts and opinions.

"I will say, that book you gave to Molly, which she loaned to me—"

"So you do still have it?"

"I guess I do, yeah. Why?"

"I see."

"What does that mean?"

"Nothing. It just seems rather interesting, that you won't give it back to her. She told me you hadn't done so."

"I'm going to give it back to her. I'm not going to . . . Wait, she told you I wouldn't give it back to her?"

"No, no. Don't get off track. What were you saying about the book?"

"Well, in reading that book, and some others in that field, it gave me an idea of the soul, that it's made of human material, just like the brain.

In fact, it probably has evolved from higher functions of the brain. I see it as the moral essence of our being. We don't really know how it evolved that way."

"So, it's our conscience?"

"No, not really, that's an active component of consciousness that changes over time. Like you've said, the racists who once lived here and held slaves, they didn't suffer pangs of conscience. Some said it was highly Christian; to hold what they would have called a lesser people, in safe bondage!"

"Not all of them were that way, some were troubled. There were abolitionists—"

"But that's the point, humans keep arguing over what social arrangement is right, and what is wrong; but deeper, in the soul, there is a clean source of energy that powers all our moral inspiration. Maybe the conscience is merely the conscious part of the soul . . ." Jacob laughed. "Well, I'm not saying I have it all worked out, ready to present to you and Hereford at the table. He'd tear it apart pretty quick I suppose."

"Not so sure about that, but I see what you mean. In practical terms, too often, the conscience is like a state attorney arguing a case of eminent domain, brushing aside some old widow who is standing in the way of progress."

"Something like that."

"A device used to control Darwin's herd for the meat packing industry."

"You may need to put a picnic table out here."

"But really, what you're saying is, that it's part of the psyche, a moral faculty we have evolved; derived from a source code we all hold in common."

"I'm not sure of that; it is part of the flesh, of the individual. So maybe it is tainted by all that distinctly human material which forms each personality."

"So, there are defective souls? That makes sense, we surely know Methodists and Hollywood producers have not evolved sufficiently."

"Well, obviously, the Methodists have not, but I don't know any Hollywood producers."

"I do, believe me. So tell me then, do you think the soul is immortal?"

"No."

"No?"

"That's what never made any sense to me, that fairy tale foisted on us by the same forces that are always upholding the hierarchies of this world, both church and state, the evil twins."

"So, no migrations to other realms." Isaac took a hearty gulp of wine.

"I can only believe in the soul as a vital force. Maybe it's the essence of our hope, that lets us overcome the past, and encourages us to brave the future."

"You've given this a lot of thought." Isaac was happy that Jacob had trusted him enough to reveal these feelings. He's been reading, he thought, and quite a lot. "I used to say at parties that the problem with life was, there just weren't enough good ways out of it. I think you may have stolen that from me. So one is immortal only in the work done for the continuation of the species, depositing memories of lasting worth to survive in the whole. You're ready to take on Hereford!"

"I have too much time on my hands." Jacob laughed. He could feel the cool air on his cheeks and the warmth provided under his jacket. They were sitting on the damp boards of two bench seats inside a dilapidated gazebo. Jacob looked up at numerous, tiny streams of sunlight filtering through cracks in the roof.

"Hereford talks as if we're experimental puppets, implanted with a brilliant array of artificial intelligence. We are unable to free ourselves from the longing to know our creators. Philosophy is therefore a quest after the impossible."

"It makes sense." Jacob responded, somewhat leery of the picnic table echoes crowding round.

"Some day we'll throw away the stone dolls made by superstitious hands, and actually face that darkness that scares the hell out of us. Maybe then we'll be ready to begin to assay the true nature of consciousness."

"You should fix this gazebo up, get it ready for the spring." Jacob abruptly changed the subject, fearing Isaac might wish to continue in this vein, talking to him as he did to Hereford. They could go on forever circling the same ground over and over without ever landing on anything that had any true purpose. Isaac smiled at his friend's rude sophistication.

"I've thought of it."

"I have brothers who could do the work. I could help them."

"Can you give me a quote?"

"No, but one of my brothers could. I'd be glad to help, at no charge."

"No, I couldn't do that."

"We're pals, aren't we?"

"Yes."

"Fuck it, then. Besides I'm not in the union. I'm just a scrub carpenter. I'm not going to guarantee my work."

"I would like to leave something for the new owners. They could sit here and make plans for the work that needs to be done in the future."

"Have you done anything with the place since you've been back?"

"Not really." Isaac laughed, putting a hand out and testing the rot on one of the boards.

"All that will have to be replaced."

"It will be like that joke by Steve Martin, when he holds up the ax, and says it belonged to George Washington: except for the handle. And the head."

"It's like our democracy."

They laughed and Isaac sipped his wine. He wore a ragged button down shirt and a sweater vest, with pajama bottoms, and was shod in a pair of ancient slippers. Jacob thought he could easily become a beloved character around here if he only wanted to be such a personage. He must be cold, but he did not show it. Jacob felt comfortably snug under his stocking cap worn to hide his head wound. Feeling the wintry sunshine on his face, and smelling the moldy earth, was invigorating.

"Aren't you afraid you'll catch a chill out here?"

"Let's go inside." Isaac rose with a series of jerky motions that betrayed the fact that there must be a myriad of kinks in his limbs. As they entered the house again Jacob boasted of his trade skills.

"I could help you with the gazebo. I even own a pair of carpenter's overalls now, so you would be a fool not to take me up on my offer. I might be able to do this without my brothers, or at least with only minimal supervision."

"I would like to leave the gazebo in pristine condition for the next owner of the place."

"We can take care of that for you."

"You know, I knew your brother. The oldest, Mark?"

"Yeah."

"We weren't friends or anything, but we knew each other. He was very serious, as I remember."

"He still is. He's like a machine." Jacob felt embarrassed for putting it that way. "He's the tin man with a real heart." Now he felt he had only made it worse. "He helped to keep our family together, after my sister died, and my dad had his accident at work."

"I remember people talking about that, back then. Such a tragedy. As the eldest son he took the burden on his shoulders."

"He did, yes. And without complaint, more or less."

"So, more or less? You could say the same about Renan's hero, no?"

Jacob laughed.

They sat down in the living room again and Isaac immediately went back to the kitchen to fill up his glass one more time. Jacob wondered if he had a serious problem. It had never really occurred to him before that his license at the Fish Fry might be habitual. He had declined another beer, and was already feeling the drowsy effects of the little he had imbibed. Isaac settled himself on the sofa, placed his glass down on the coffee table, and seemed to take up his place as master of ceremonies, as though they were at St. Margaret's.

"I am every bit as learned as Hereford, more so really, in a way. He's read more novels than me, but I was formally trained. I took the gold letter in Latin."

Jacob requested more information on this honor and Isaac explained it to him as his eyes filled with the glow of enriched nostalgia, courtesy of the vintner's craft. He had gone to an expensive prep school after graduating from St. Margaret's. Then he had gone east to study at Princeton, with the intention of joining the diplomatic corps upon graduation. In his senior year he came home on a break and met a woman after a wedding at St. Margaret's.

"She was from the Florissant gentry." He delivered this fact as if it were pregnant with too much meaning to lightly gloss over and he wanted to give Jacob time to register the full import of these facts. Jacob watched Isaac nursing his glass of wine, now held close to his face, as if fondling his memories in an unconscious reverie.

"Do you know where she is now?"

"Probably in Santa Fe. I am certain she is still there. She moved there many years ago and opened an art gallery. She's done quite well. Got married. Divorced. Married again. I'm sure she's still there."

"When did you see her last?"

"Fifteen years ago, briefly. I was there doing work on a movie set. I called her up and we had a very awkward lunch near the far ends of the civilized earth; looking out at a lot of shrunken trees and mountains. Just outside the window an ocean of sunshine was lapping at our shores. She was overly polite the whole time and I was feeling like nothing was real for me anymore."

"Nothing was real?"

"She was happy, and I was feigning happiness, to a miserable degree. It was rather uncomfortable, you know?"

"Yes."

"We were very happy together, once upon a time, in our youth. You talk about fairy tales. We used to hang out on the church steps. We'd sit there during those eternal autumn evenings of our youth, when . . . well, it was right before we got to know one another in the Biblical sense. Then all was sweetness and light for a beautiful month. Then the bitter herbs had to be ingested as well. She said she didn't want to leave St. Louis. She was so provincial at that time!" He looked at Jacob as if he was still surprised by the woman's stubbornness. "Ah, being young! Knowing nothing and feeling like you know everything. Believing life will continue to get better. Why must a person lose that feeling?" He stood up and went to replenish his glass yet again and Jacob worried he was somehow, by his mere presence, encouraging the man's drinking.

"Don't let things pass you by!" He bellowed from the kitchen.

"Say Isaac, you're hitting that stuff pretty hard, aren't you?" He called out to him.

"Time is relative. You'll find out. Just one more. You must know I'm the last man to abuse liquor." His statement was firm and unconvincing. "That's not who I am."

Jacob thought of a riposte, "Is that like the last man to die in a war?"

When Isaac returned to the room he walked with that slow deliberate gait used by one wishing to prove he is not inebriated. Isaac put his drink down very carefully, and made a slow passage to a book case in a little study and brought forth a volume. Once seated again he opened the book and began reading a passage,

"Primus ego in patriam mecum . . . deducam Musas."

"You're throwing more Latin at me? I hardly know English. I'm still trying to learn that language, so if you don't mind."

Isaac laughed, "It's all there in the book, you can read it." He handed over his first edition copy of *My Ántonia*. "My mother, when she was a girl, met the author out west, at Mesa Verde. She cherished this book. I gave it to her."

"Yeah?" Jacob examined the workmanship of the old volume with his eyes and his hands.

"I was going to give it to Molly, but you take it."

"Oh no, give it to her, then." Jacob tried to hand it back but Isaac refused him.

"You take it. Give it to her, if you want, that's up to you two."

"Okay, are you sure?"

Isaac didn't answer but leaned over and began sifting through one of the piles on the floor and placed another volume by the same author in front of him. Take that one too, he instructed. Jacob began leafing through the pages, stopping to read here and there to find out what kind of book he was holding. In that cursory sampling he caught glimpses of the austere beauty of the southwest wrought in very fine prose, by another soul apparently obsessed by the past.

"What is it about us, that we are so intent on keeping the past alive?" Jacob asked. "Why do you suppose that is so important to us?"

"It's a way of ennobling our journey, I guess. The sacred must have origins, ancestor worship, all of that religious—"

"Is that why we falsify it so often?"

"It could be, to preserve the exalted narrative, to nurture the vision of a better future. The dream of the better place. It might be the work of that soul you've conjured. As you say, the conscience is just a puppet of instinct, or ego, but the power of memory to form parables—that imposing question, what might I have done better?—that facility may be what engendered the soul! What do you think?"

"That I would need to drink too much to keep up with you. Isaac grimaced at the derogatory mention of his drinking and Jacob felt a twinge of guilt.

"I wish you were going to say on here." Jacob said quickly.

"I'm sure I'll be coming back. What would Frances think of me if I abandoned the Fish Fry altogether. What would Sistah say?"

"If we still have them, after all that's happened."

"You can hold them right here, a small exclusive party."

Jacob clasped his new books protectively. He was now a nascent bibliophile. He began picking through other volumes strewn about the floor. "You're sure you don't want any of this stuff?"

"No, take anything you want. Take any books you find there, or on the shelves in there." He extended his arm to point towards the study, as if it's location might not be clear to the sober person.

"I would have to rely on your suggestions."

"Good idea. I will make a stack for you to take. Give me a few days. I must spend some time with them first. Say goodbye. You probably think that is too maudlin. Hereford says—"

"No, I don't.

"I want to sell this house to Molly."

"Really? Is she thinking of buying it?"

"Not sure. She might be. She should be."

"She would love this house."

"I know."

"Was she talking about who she might . . ."

"Who?"

Jacob moved his head, as if to shake off something unpleasant. He looked around at the interior of the Cook household with new eyes; imagining Molly as the woman who made it a warm, sumptuous home. He could not bear to think of her being there with another man, and he couldn't quite picture himself being there with her either. The pretty little picture began to fade from his golden perspective. His view retreated from the harsh glare of sunlight seen flashing on broken things in vacant lots, near boarded-up dream factories. How would he ever be able to walk by this place knowing she was inside sharing her splendor with another?

"How long do you think you'll stay here before you sell?"

"Not sure. I want to go to Sante Fe and see if that woman still feels about anything the way I used to feel about her. The ship borne back, right? You know, Hereford and I really are thinking of working on a project together. He is going to write a novel and I am supposed to see to the making of a screenplay."

"Sounds like a good way to keep you two out of trouble. What's it about?"

"We can't agree on that!" He laughed, way too loud, and Jacob's eyes flared open at the spectacle of his friend's lurid self-absorption.

"You'll have fun hashing it out, I'm sure."

"He's leaving soon, going back east."

"Well, I need to get going myself. I'll see you later, Isaac." Jacob hesitated at the doorway, turning to ask a question. "Say, I'm just curious. Do you think Molly is provincial?"

"Molly? Heavens no!"

"But I mean, from your perspective, the way you were talking about—"

"No. I think the stamp of the provincial is that he does not know, is not aware, has no idea, how small his view of the world really is. It has nothing to do with money, or geography, or travel schedules. It's really about values. That's why Molly could never be considered a provincial, not to me. Her heart is too large; it lets her encompass whole realms." He pointed at Jacob's hand. "In that book, Willa talks of her heroine being the mother of peoples . . ."

Jacob was nonplussed by this wild gush of emotion.

"Now, my grandparents, they were exemplars of bourgeois provincials, if you know what I mean." Jacob did not know, precisely, and could not possibly know he had chanced upon one of the major themes Hereford and Cook had discussed for their project.

"I don't think I care if I am a provincial." Jacob said as if bemused by his own construction.

"You can't be. You're already too occupied with eternal questions. You're no provincial, my friend."

"I better be going." Jacob feared he was on the advent of a new course in dialectics. "Be good, be safe."

Isaac followed Jacob onto the porch and watched him take his leave. He raised his glass in an odd gesture when Jacob turned to wave at him, whispering, "Little monk, you have chosen a difficult path."

Jacob took away with him that noble, worn posture of his friend, and his impious smile, and some of his sage observations, as valuable keepsakes. It struck him poignantly that he did not want to have such terrible regrets when he reached that age himself. He clutched the books tightly as he swung his arms and imagined the shelving he would have to design for his embryotic library. He considered the possibility that one might discover a separate existence in the world he already inhabits; in the process becoming a good provincial, devoted to those native ideals that are held sacred by him alone!

40

The world outside looked different; the absence of verdant color was peculiar. On cloudy days Jacob watched as the sun swept across the sky like a solemn flare announcing the advent of something momentous. He stared out the window a great deal. His spirit kept close watch on changes in the weather. He sat listening to music in a listless torpor.

His birthday was on November seventeenth, and his Mother informed him they would not be having a cake for him on Sunday, as everyone was too busy getting ready for Thanksgiving.

"Mom, that's no problem, really." It touched him that she was so devoted to the maintenance of family traditions.

"Well, I just hate to stop doing it, now."

That 'now' had a plangent ring, for it expressed her worry over his unusual retreat from social customs.

"Why don't you and Dad take me to dinner, maybe to the Olive Garden?" He knew how much his parents liked that restaurant.

"That might be something to consider." This was how Madeleine agreed to a proposal before she wanted to admit that her mind had been influenced by someone else unexpectedly. "I'll talk to your father. Now, you're sure—"

"Mom, let's go out to eat, just the three of us."

Indeed, she called him right back and said, "Your father thinks it's a good idea." Ordinarily it would hardly matter what Henry thought on such matters; but when it was politic, she granted him full honors as the titular head of household.

The dinner was quite agreeable, even wonderful at times, as Jacob found himself enjoying his parents in a way he was not sure he ever had before. They were like this strange pair of friends he had known forever, and about whom he was still constantly learning curious things that amused him to no end. They peppered him with perfunctory questions about 'his wound' at the outset, to ensure there was no dire need to be addressed. He could see it troubled his mother that there was no nefarious entity that she could condemn for doing this to her boy. His father appraised it as he might a piece of craftsmanship; his murmurs suggested it was nothing in comparison with several of his own curios.

Soon enough his parents began to talk frankly to each other, and then about each other, in a blatantly critical vein; clearly for his benefit, the sole witness to their sacred grievances. His mother mostly wanted to give him a firsthand account of his father's idiosyncrasies, which were fatal to her complacency. He, on his part, wanted to defend himself in a way that made light of her specious charges, and he wished to go on record, challenging her authority to question his sovereign habits.

At some point, his mother made an abrupt feint to the topic of Frances. Then they were discussing the infamous Fish Fry, and then Molly's name came up. His father turned quickly with a furrowed brow to see his son's response. Jacob suspected his mom knew more about Molly than she was letting on. He wasn't keen on leading them further into this bog.

"Maybe you should bring Molly over to the house for dinner?"

"Mom, we're not a couple. We're not really anything right now."

"Oh?"

"I mean like that, we're not."

"You can still invite her to dinner. Why is that such a big deal?"

"To meet the parents?" He exaggerated the incredulity her suggestion had inspired; determined to make her desist by force of reason. In fact, that highly touted force is quite often unreliable when opposed directly by a burst of maternal energy.

"Well, you could take her someplace like this. Bring her here!"

"Mom." He wanted to halt this recidivistic force. He felt prepubescent again, being prodded out of the nest by his anxious mother.

"Madeleine." Her husband's gentle, scolding intonation irritated her greatly; and caused her to retreat at once. Reason had regrouped and was again a power to be reckoned with by all the fractious parties.

"Henry, how many beers have you had?"

"Just a few." It was a stock answer, known to get a laugh in front of the right audience. The spouses began to skirmish once more. They began to lob critiques at each other, as if Jacob were not there. A lifetime of being wed together gave license for airing petty gripes; there were no statutes of limitation.

"Well, anyway, from what I've heard, she's a fine, young woman, and I wouldn't mind meeting her." His mother spoke in a voice of heroic resignation. "I'm not trying to intrude into your life. I wouldn't do that to you." She did not look at him, but she waited to be given credit for her admirable restraint. He remained silent. How could they know all that was at stake?

"What have I done?" Jacob thought to himself; as if just the act of discussing Molly, in any manner, was a sure way to spoil things between them forever. It made no sense. His mind was in revolt against itself. In a desperate attempt to escape his predicament, he roused an old rebellious spirit. He was tempted to relate to them some of the things she had told him in the confessional. It was funny to contemplate this breach of her confidence; there was no way he would ever do that to her, or them!

His mom and dad hosted the family for Thanksgiving. Jacob organized a touch football game for the little kids, whose parents cheered the comical mayhem with great satisfaction. He acted as player coach for both sides and head referee. He loved hearing the honesty of the kids as they competed. It could be hilarious, especially when contrasted to adults, who so often disguise their thoughts with baroque expressions. At times it was good to feel the sting when the words are flung out fresh by each innocent party in these emotional clashes. He observed that the child at play is equipped to injure, bind, and heal, in one stroke!

Towards the end of the day all the brothers were in the basement playing pool, the oldest pitted against the youngest. Luke and Jacob won two
games in a row; so they taunted their elders. Mark had gotten a little inebriated, which was rare for him, and he seemed to be enjoying himself
more than usual; suddenly they all ganged up on him, mocking him for his
uncanny reserve. They began doing impromptu impressions. Mark's adult
children began to giggle. And just like that, Mark's restraint broke; gales of
laughter rose from his most hallowed depths.

Jacob watched as his oldest brother was overcome by an extravagant
release of emotion. His other two brothers were at either side of the man,
slapping him gently on the back. Jacob was immensely pleased. He knew
that Mark was very proud of what the real imputation was in all this mock-
ery, and what it meant, to the whole family. It recalled the time when he
had become like an auxiliary dad, while Henry was laid up on bed rest,
enduring much pain, and often raging as Lear against his fate. It celebrated
the era when Mark left school and went to work as a laborer on a construction crew. He put his brothers to work about the house, like a sergeant at
arms, and spurred them into getting after-school jobs. The temper of his
august severity was forged in those times, and he had found it incredibly
difficult to relax the grip of that formulation. It was now intrinsic to the
collective molding of their family escutcheon.

Jacob suddenly thought of numerous incidents when he had watched
Molly teasing someone in a way that was actually a means of flattering that
person, in the most winsome fashion. She teased Isaac for having endeared
himself to all the old ladies of St. Margaret's. She knew it was a point of
honor with him, done out of his own family pride; as complicated as that
was. He had witnessed the power of mocking a person for a particular trait
or habit, which was merely the outward manifestation of an actual value,
highly prized, that lies embedded in that person's heart. She often used
humor to shed light on some quality which the person was very proud to
own. That was the artistry of her soul at play in the world. It has nothing
to do with noblesse oblige, or anything of that sort; it is rather the sharing
of one's best nature with another to foster that person's humanity, as a way
of also refreshing one's own.

For Molly it seemed to be almost an instinctual reaction to the needs of other people, divined by her so easily. For those she cared for the most, she possessed marvelous abilities to assay their hearts. Jacob feared to conjecture what base material she found in testing him! For those favored people who came to know her, she was a steady font of moral encouragement. Jacob thought of how individual souls must be able to make contact with other souls to recognize a kindred sense of how to flourish in this realm. The spiritual pursuit of happiness required resonance with higher purposes lying only partially in our ken. In this rather uncertain mutual endeavor one enriched another's life. His longing quaked forcibly in his breast. He could have sworn he was hearing symphonic movements as he stared out at the stars late that night.

———◆———

The carnival atmosphere of the Fish Fry was gone, as it was now held solely inside the cafeteria. There was none of the restrained hysteria that had pervaded the recent bacchanals. Jacob almost didn't go to the next Fish Fry, but he decided it was almost an obligation. However, it was awkward once he showed up and discovered how absolutely the festive spirit had vanished. There was no milling about between the crowds, no flows of people up and down from one terrace to another; all had been replaced by a sedate collection of lethargic people, lodged at their tables like refugees after a hurricane. There was hardly any lingering after eating; whole tables departed en masse, as if they had a better place to go!

Jacob ordered a beer and talked with some people. The plight of Frances was being discussed everywhere. After the incident with Gregory, and the finding that he should not have been working there, certainly not for the amount of money Frances was paying him, the local priests convened a council. They called upon higher ranking prelates to advise and soon the consent decree was handed down. It was decided to bring a halt to the woman's disarray, and forthwith Frances was relieved of her contractual obligations. She did not resist them in the slightest.

Jacob realized most people were coming up to him just to inspect the gash in his head. Many wanted to touch it. They coaxed him to castigate the guilty parties. He swore there was no guilty party, except possibly society at large. This statement made them look at him a little funny. On what grounds might they be accused? He sorely missed the dialogues at the C & H Court, where one could sacrifice decorum, conventional courtesies, or anything else, merely as a ritual, paying homage to something like humility in spite of the ego's glare.

He was about to get a plate of food and sit down, when he saw Molly at a table with Janey and her husband. Heather was also there with her husband. All of them had their children with them. Heather's brother Kenneth was also seated at the table. Seeing that made Jacob step out of line; he abruptly decided to leave the premises. He tried to catch Molly's eye, wishing to proffer some kind of gallant greeting; which couldn't possibly be heartfelt in that moment. She did not look at him and he was glad of that; she would not want to further confuse things just then. He could not stick around any longer. He felt foolish for coming. He assumed that Cook had stayed away for equally good reasons, and was even now using his house spirits to conjure imperishable dreams in his winter quarters. On the way home he might stop by to see him; but on second thought, he had no desire to share his uncorked misery with him at the moment. He had all he could handle of such griefs. He needed to be alone.

In the coming weeks Jacob threw himself into his music. He needed to get ready for the party Beatrice was throwing for Frances. He wasn't sure who had thought of this, or when it had been put together, but he agreed it was a great idea. They were going to use the Spencer House to give Frances a little party in support of her new charity, that several people were helping her establish. The idea was to cultivate a group of people who would keep an eye out for worthy recipients for the funds they would solicit from people they knew. They would work together to dole out the assistance as discreetly as possible. The Spencer House would be used to attract those established, larger charities able to pay rental fees, which would help defray the cost of those infant groups which could not afford such extravagances.

The idea was to graft new vineyards from older ones. Frances held to the theory that one must know how to receive, and how to give, with equal grace. They wanted her to know her charity was the first one chosen for an event to express their trust in her venerable spirit.

"It's not a real recital." Beatrice explained to Jacob. "It's not like what we will be doing in the future. We want to bring in string quartets, that sort of thing. For now, we just want you to give them a taste of how nice this room is going to be, for listening to music. So, just play a few songs, let them see the potential of the room. Oh my, can you imagine? Once we've transformed it into a cozy little auditorium?"

"I understand."

"Make sure you practice for this."

"I will." He smarted a little at the implication he might be a laggard at his musical devotions.

"I've promised them a musical interlude, something to change the mood, the pace of things."

"I understand." Jacob was confident. He knew, if her expectations were very low, then he would likely impress her. If there were any accomplished musicians in attendance they would find him merely adequate; but he wanted to make sure they did find him to be that, at least.

So he set himself the task of putting together a short repertoire. He thought they would want him to play a few songs at most. He considered several ballads by Bob Dylan, the inestimable voice of his era, but instead returned to the font where he had been most inspired during his long apprenticeship. He selected two numbers from *After The Gold Rush*; "Tell Me Why" and "After the Gold Rush." That might be all he would need, depending on how things went. He had an image of everyone standing around, anxiously waiting to go back downstairs for more drinks and cocktail chatter, or to resume touring the house. He had seen plenty of evidence that old women have an insatiable hunger to know about old houses.

When the evening of the party arrived he waited patiently, feeling very relaxed and composed, until he heard Beatrice call out to him through the door at the bottom of the stairs. He clambered down the steps to see her actually wringing her hands. She wore a loud shiny dress and was draped in jewelry that flashed resplendently. Her hair was piled up in a daring arrangement on her head.

"You have to come to the dinner."

"Oh, I didn't think—"

"Frances said she wants you at the dinner."

"She did?"

"Yes, please." She was acting peculiar; he had never seen her so flustered and excited at the same time.

"Okay, I'll get ready."

"Molly's here too."

"Molly's there?"

"Yes. Now, hurry up. Jacob, I'm sorry I didn't think to ask you before. I wasn't sure how many there were going to be."

"Should I come up right now?"

"Yes! Hurry up."

He wanted to ask her about his attire; but she was gone. He watched her from his window. She made her way to the back door with short rapid strides in her tight dress and clacking heels. She wanted this inaugural event to be a triumph. Jacob decided to wear jeans and an Arrow shirt, and work boots. He felt as if this would keep him in solidarity with Neil Young, the émigré who came to Los Angeles in a Pontiac hearse, without legal papers, but having the full blessing of St. Cecilia. Jacob did not want this contingent of elderly philanthropists to think he was trying to crash the party and act as one of them, an equal in their company.

He almost wished Molly were not there, feeling uncertain about the songs he had chosen for the occasion. But he forgot everything else when he found himself sitting next to her, at one end of the table, her cool, violet eyes full of inexhaustible freshets of resplendent life. She smiled at his rapt silence and he was lost again, stranded in an imaginary landscape where his love pushed reason off the stage altogether. His mind no longer worked in a fashion that allowed him to maintain his normal composure when he was around her.

He had decided to cherish any moment to be had with her. He was surprised how comfortable it was to be around her after concluding there was no future for him being with her. What did it matter? He decided not to question anything. Here she was, putting him at ease; making him laugh before she even spoke as she crinkled up her nose. She was wearing a blue dress that was adorned with intricate lacy patterns on the front, made of whorled stitching of a lighter gray-blue coloring, all of which added enormous intensity to the magic in her eyes. The manifold frills of her feminine costume only served to push her face to the fore as the pièce de résistance. He was so entranced he forgot to be self-conscious as he gazed upon her the way an art lover would study one of those stunning masterpieces done by Antonio Canova. She finally shook her head at him, her visage demanding he desist in his utter lack of normal reserve. Her hair was knotted into a bundle atop her head, drawing attention to the structure of her neck. He marveled at how this precious sculptured trunk contained the coursing flow of her very life. He had to bat away Gothic visions of the beast he was feasting on that neck . . .

"Try this." She fed him a piece of succulent pastry dough wrapped around a rich honey and nut filling. "It's my own creation, from my kitchen."

"Oh my god, it's good." He could only stare back in astonishment at her mischievous smile. It was difficult to imagine these hours would come to an end. He could not bear to think about it, and found it easy to not think at all.

"I hear you're going to play something?"

"Yes, I'm afraid so."

"Too bad you're not a real musician." She was chiding him yet again. Once he had tried to deflect her inquiries about his music by affecting a self-deprecating manner. It did not impress her; she understood his passion and she had called him on his false humility. At the time he did not understand this fear he had of opening up about something so precious to him, which had always been like a private trove of his deepest feelings. From the beginning she simply picked up his heart like a child's piggy bank, and turned it over and began shaking out every coin.

He spoke to her of his recent visit to see Isaac. She had just seen him herself. Was she really going to buy his house? They leaned close and spoke in whispers as the rest of the table nearly drowned them out in a roar of cheerful gossip. Most of the people were friends of Beatrice or Frances, and the voices rose into a crescendo after everyone was finished eating. The paid staff cleared the tables and coffee was served. They became embowered in their own quiet shelter, oblivious of the drowsy spell of many mature voices droning on to no end. They exchanged little private quips and were as children taking advantage of the fact the world took no notice of their secret games.

Beatrice stood up, tapped a spoon to her wine glass, and announced the next item on her agenda. They all rose and trooped in a file up the servant's stairwell. The old people moved prodigiously, commenting on things they observed, while being directed through stories of the house as docile creatures, who live on the fat of past experience as much as the scraps of solid food taken at the moment. They entered the auditorium on the third floor where comfortable chairs on rollers had been arranged to face the equipment Jacob had placed by the front windows.

The guests circulated, peering out the windows to see where they were; sampling the last solemn light of the afternoon. Beatrice invited them to imagine other improvements she would be making in the future. Several suggestions were put forth by the attendees. Ideas for future bookings were discussed.

"You might want to install more windows." Frances said to her.

"That would be expensive—"

"Have you ever gone to see the Chartres Cathedral?"

"No."

"Well you have to go."

"Would you come with me?" Beatrice responded, as if to tease her friend.

"Why of course. It seems only natural for us . . ." She turned towards a blank wall. "You could put a rose window right there."

"Let's not get ahead of ourselves." Beatrice said reflexively, and then began to ponder all she did not know, and had yet to learn, about many things. Frances moved closer to a window, in thrall to the incarnation of her own vision appearing now.

"Don't you see? Several tinted grisaille windows would bring that light in here."

There was a collective murmur as everyone noticed Jacob was awaiting their attention. He had been needlessly tuning his instrument, feeling oddly at peace. This was not something he would ever have volunteered to do, but because of who had proposed it to him, he had no choice in the matter.

He played his two Neil Young songs and they seemed to appreciate his performance. The room itself, flooded with late afternoon light, was an ideal place to hear live acoustic music.

"Play another one," Molly called out to him.

The crowd concurred by clapping rather profusely; showing appreciation also for what Beatrice was doing.

He played "Wounded Bird" By Graham Nash; a song he had not thought of until that moment. He played the song better than he ever had before; with nuanced extemporized phrasings that astonished him as they happened.

"One more," one of the old women cried in a happy drawl.

Again, he did not even have to think before playing "Amazing Grace," much as it was rendered by Rod Stewart on his tour de force, *Every Picture Tells A Story*. Why not pander a little to his blessed audience?

When he finished they all applauded warmly. He looked at her and found her beaming at him with an expression he could not remember ever seeing on her face before. She was proud of him for acquitting himself well, he thought, and there was something else. A subtle critique? It made him want to get her alone again, as though he needed to feed off her every thought, even those that were never expressed in words. If he continued to spend time around her he was going to become a very pathetic creature to behold. They crowded around him. He was overcome by this reception to his music. Maybe a man had to learn there was only so much happiness one small heart is able to hold. He had to learn to know when this was so, and not spoil everything by chasing after phantasmal conceits. Maybe she could be *the* friend, who was like the incidental accent that enriches a musical arrangement so extravagantly.

"That was great, Jacob." She purred breathlessly. She had come up to him right away, as everyone was still clapping politely. Her hand grazed his arm. She looked around, out the windows, and exclaimed, "Beatrice, this is just perfect."

"It really is," someone echoed. Beatrice was ecstatic, it had gone better than she had hoped. Everyone was in great spirits. There was talk of looking for old stained glass to install in the auditorium windows.

"This will be a great place for people to play; I mean for those who are a lot better than me, and who can actually sing." Jacob said, feeling bashful all of a sudden.

"I like your singing," Molly exclaimed. A clutch of elderly women, all of them grandmothers, studied Molly's face. There had been a lilting note in her voice that reverberated in all their maternal fibers.

"I didn't know if I should play these old tunes, but some have just gotten embedded in my soul. I can't seem to let go of them." He spoke quietly to her at his side.

"I know." She replied with such assurance that Jacob began to entertain the idea of asking her to come over to his place, which might be thought rather funny, since it only meant a walk across the back yard. He wanted to make a joke of it, and waited for the right moment. He was still thinking this as everyone descended to the first floor and sat down to feast on various pastries. Time began to work against his hopes. She went off with Frances and a few other ladies and he talked to Beatrice briefly, and then she dashed off, leaving him with an old couple preparing for their departure.

They seemed uneasy in his presence, so he tried to ingratiate himself by speaking of his music. They grew less certain, staring past and around him, smiling defensively, as though seeking help from the others who were absent. It appeared they feared he was about to hold out a tin cup to solicit an offering. It wasn't until they moved away and began talking with another group that he heard the phrase 'our beloved Margaret.' Several people looked in his direction. To some he was just now becoming that one who was trying to get close to their Molly. They were not at all certain about that proposition; it was a rich vein for gossip. And then the party was over; the last contingent gathered around Frances at the door and departed with a lot of ceremonial gestures.

"Jacob? I have something for you." Frances called out to them, as he and Molly were walking towards her car in the driveway. She came back outside carrying a long ornate box.

"What's this?" He asked, looking fondly at the taught strings.

"It's an Aeolian harp," Frances said. "That's what the former owner of the house used to build in the basement. I remembered how you were so curious about that, and well, I met his son. One thing led to another, and he gave this to me! I want you to have it."

"Thank you Frances. I don't know what to say."

Molly moved close to inspect the music box. "That is so cool. I remember my first year in college, these intrigued me so much. That first English class, these were mentioned in so many poems. I always wanted to hear one." She reached out and plucked several strings with her finger.

"I think it's in tune," Jacob said with amazement.

"I'm sorry this happened." Frances said, reaching out and lightly touching his forehead. Looking at them facing each other, Molly noticed that Frances and Jacob were the same height.

"Don't worry," she said. "He likes showing his scar to everyone." Her satiric tone melted on his ear like chocolate on the tongue.

"How is Gregory doing?" He asked, smothering his smile.

"He's getting treatments now. He needs a lot of care. We're looking for a place."

There was a pause while they surveyed the grounds, and glanced at the fine glimmering December gloom spreading everywhere around them.

"Frances, everybody appreciates how much you . . . I mean, I think you really did something special up at the Fish Fry." Jacob said. "Something new, and good."

"Oh, I should have been more careful—I'm no good at handling money! All this, I wonder if this shouldn't be in other hands."

"Don't be silly," Molly exclaimed.

"I've made such a mess of my vows."

"What!" Molly was astonished.

"You didn't make your vows to the church, did you?" Jacob asked.

Molly looked very keenly at Jacob. "That's right." She affirmed.

"It was to something higher than that, I suppose." Frances agreed, her face straining to suppress her discomfort.

"You've been promoted, to priestess," Jacob quipped.

"Now, don't be foolish," Frances replied.

Molly pressed close and gave her a warm embrace. They all stood there a moment.

"What you did up there was remarkable. You brought a lot of good people together." Jacob said with much feeling. "They might not have ever met otherwise."

"That's true." Molly said. "Where two or three gather . . ." Her voice trailed off; Frances was clearly moved.

"You have to follow your heart, too, my girl."

Molly appeared to be speechless, smiling weakly, with an effort.

"For me, it was the best of times." Jacob spoke ardently. Molly was still looking at Frances, but she felt his gaze fall upon her countenance. It was palpable, like sunlight.

"It really was." She affirmed. "We had the best times." She looked quickly at Jacob, who was now looking down. "Well, I want to do some work on my olive trees." She was painting a series of water colors, capturing various things growing in her mother-in-law's greenhouse. "Sophie is taking up the brush these days."

"She couldn't find a better teacher," Jacob said.

"So you have told me," she responded as a mother might to a child.

He was still thinking of some magic words he could utter that would cause her to walk around the grounds with him, even as he watched her get into her Honda and drive around the loop, proceed down the driveway, and onto Clay and over to Church Street, where she turned to go down the hill and disappeared from his sight.

"Sometimes I fear the child is becoming a stranger to our world." Frances said, as if to herself.

"She's a spirited woman." Jacob said, and thought to himself, maybe we all need to have a new baptism, now and then.

"She has such a fine spirit." Frances affirmed; and turning to him she said sharply, "And you, aren't there some vows you'd like to take?"

"I don't know what you mean . . ."

"You don't want to end up living alone, with a flock of gargoyles, do you?"

"We'll see you later, Lady Frances." Jacob smiled as if he were appreciative of her humor, but in fact her words had shaken him."

"Oh Jacob, don't leave us."

"What?" He had turned around to look at her.

"Stay in Ferdinand, won't you?"

"I can't leave. Cody would never let me use my truck."

"Come by for lunch this week?"

"Sure."

"Come on Wednesday."

"Sure."

"Bring someone, if you want."

Someone? He wanted to ask her who did she have in mind, but she was striding off to enter again into her own Byzantine world, and he turned to lurch back towards his den, clutching his new wind harp. It was clear that he had nothing much but his music. He was not wearing a jacket and the chill shuddered his body. He noticed that a squirrel in the maple tree, wearing his luxurious fur coat, appeared to be scoffing at his susceptibility to the cold. He wondered what it would be like if the elements did not matter to him, and all the wracking passions only served to tremble his being into song. What if one fashioned his own tailored haircloth out of reason's rough wool?

41

December came in like a lost lamb. A warm front sustained that autumnal feeling of the yield having been put away, as the world made ready for the feasts yet to come. The proud dormant trees were dispensing long sermons on the virtues of endurance. At dusk he loitered in natural chapels staring at the tracery of the devout hardwood trees. He anticipated the holidays, when he would once more be warmed at the family hearth.

His mother had asked him if he would play carols on Christmas Eve, and he decided to go into the house and up to the auditorium to practice. He played "Silent Night" several times and it only made him more restless. It occurred to him that he needed to learn how to feel more at home with himself. He made the rounds of the upper story, looking out from all the windows; taking delight in the superb vantage. He swept his eyes over the wintry mesh of trees. Through these he could see the lay of the neighborhood. He marveled over the strange position of certain houses, that looked closer than normal. Others seemed to be situated in peculiar ways he had never noticed before, as they had been cloaked by summer foliage. One could see further now . . .

There, for instance, how curious; people were walking down Elizabeth, now turning onto Church Street, and passing into the lower area of the lawns. He pasted his forehead against the glass. It was Molly and Sophie! Jacob leaned back, clutching at himself, before scrambling down the stairs, trying to keep a tight hold on his guitar. He raced to get back into his barracks to put his guitar away. He almost kicked over the stand while struggling to put on a sweater. He rushed down the stairs to greet them outside. She was right there, at the bottom of Spencer's hill . . .

Molly looked up at him and stopped. Sophie looked at her mother, who raised one hand, which held a stick and a tiny burlap bundle.

"What's this?" Jacob called, "A Charlie Brown Christmas tree?" He watched them trudge up the hill. For Sophie it was like an exercise in mountain climbing, and Molly stayed close behind her. She cried out when the girl tried to advance too quickly and lost her balance.

"Catch her!" Molly yelled. "Grab her hand."

"Let me help you there," Jacob said, reaching down, grasping both of Sophie's arms above the wrists. He hauled her up and swung her outward so that she became momentarily airborne. He leaned far back to maintain his balance as he twirled her in a half-circle before landing her on the ground. A flush of childish joy broke out on her face and vanished again in another instant. Molly crested the hill and stood there, her face a breathless mixture of rich color and lovely pallor.

"Look." Sophie said, pointing to the object she and her mother had brought him. "It's a lilac bush. We have lots."

"Since the weather is holding out, we thought it might not be too late to plant." Molly held it out to him. Her cheeks had rosy splotches. Her features looked as plain and natural as anything found in nature. She was wearing a heavy woolen cap and her auburn hair swirled out beneath the woven fibers in dense shining waves. The cloud-muted sunlight modeled her face wondrously and put an added brilliance into her lustrous eyes.

"Oh, well thanks. I don't know about the weather, but that's great." He took the bush by the stem.

"I guess we missed your birthday, old man."

"Not by that much. Wait a minute, when is your birthday?"

"Today."

"That's what I thought. So, you bring presents to other people on your birthday?" He forcibly laid aside the terrible significance of this day, December the seventh, for her life.

"She's weird like that," Sophie said, looking up at her mom with a smile of happy betrayal. "You just have to accept it."

"We need to find a good place for it, then." Jacob said, finding himself falling under the child's spell.

"Show us what you have, buddy boy." Molly said in her most playful tone.

"Are you sure it's not too late for planting?" He asked, wondering if there were some way to save the sapling until the spring.

"You're not much of a groundskeeper if you have to ask me that."

"I may have exaggerated some things on my resume. I never did have gardening experience before I came here."

"The part about being a monk, that was an exaggeration, too?"

"A pretty big one, actually."

Sophie was watching them acting weird, and seeing they didn't seem able to make up their minds about what they wanted to do next, she was growing anxious. She tried to wrest the shrub away from her mom, but then she spied Cody walking up the driveway with his his youngest child, a girl one year older than herself. She sprinted forward to join forces with this marvelous new friend she had met recently. Before long they strode together along the leaf-matted trail behind the tennis court.

"Now, Sophie, stay where I can see you." Molly yelled as the children fled from parental oversight.

"I'll keep an eye on them," Cody said, ambling off in the same direction as the children. He looked back at Jacob and fixed him with a suggestive leer. He then turned back to the task of shepherding the children. He talked his daughter into wishing to help him gather wood so they could start a fire. The girl pressed Sophie into service as her junior partner. They began hauling armfuls of kindling; dumping their loads on the ground around the fire pit. Cody directed the children to collect larger pieces stacked by a wall of the sunken garden. They could only carry one piece of cordwood at a time, and it required an inordinate amount of effort.

"Dad," his daughter addressed him, "You should get those. Me and Sophie will get wet leaves for making smoke!"

He assented without a word. After carrying several armfuls of wood to the pit he caught up to Jacob and Molly.

"Come on you two, make up your mind." He went into the garage and retrieved a shovel and came back to where they had dropped the lilacs behind the cottage porch.

They had been strolling around in an aimless fashion, as if unaware of the task at hand, nor any other; just chattering and giggling in turns. Cody found it rather annoying; it was impossible to decipher a fraction of the esoteric language they were forever crafting to perceive the world together. At times it seemed they existed in a separate bower not open to the mundane traffic of ordinary earthlings. Now they were back, standing by the cottage porch, listening to Cody's strident plea.

"What?" Jacob asked innocently. It was happening again. He was too happy; everything was fraught with a quavering trepidation. He felt like nothing ought to be disturbed or interfered with in any way, and Cody was famous for doing both of those things with the tactics of a brilliant saboteur.

"Come on!" Cody brandished the shovel at him.

"Yeah, where are you going to put the lilac bush?" Molly took up the cause; knocking him with her elbow. "Make a decision."

"What about right here," Cody said, indicating the place behind the cottage porch where they had left it while sauntering about the grounds.

"Yes, you would be able to smell the blossoms when you stand on the porch." Molly's voice pitched Jacob into a reverie; he was seeing these grounds burgeoning in the spring!

Cody began to dig a hole. It was amusing to Jacob that Cody was intent on being the one to handle the shovel. She had that effect on many men; they wanted to do things in her presence. He unwrapped the earthy webbing of the root ball.

"It's a perfect spot." Molly said.

"It was a perfect gift." Jacob replied.

"What else would you expect?"

Her smile was full of mysteries that plumb the depths of philosophy and reach down further into the blood's covenant with earthen materials once born in unrecorded stars now extinct.

"How does that poem go? When lilacs last in the dooryard, you know?" Molly was prodding him, wanting him to contribute a portion of the poem.

"I don't remember. I think I told you, I barely graduated from McDermott High."

"Come on, Jacob! You must remember some of it!"

"I remember it was taught to me, I don't remember learning it." He spoke factually, not intending to be ironic. The others laughed at him and then he caught the fatuity of what he'd said and enjoyed their laughter. He was still feeling the shiver which occurred when she used his name in that peremptory way.

She recited; "'The hermit withdrawn to himself, avoiding the settlements, sings by himself a song.'"

They marveled as she recalled other verses in her fluent diction. She knew most of the famous sequence, but with just a few lines she managed to evoke a noble feeling. There was something aesthetically fresh, and intensely pleasing, in this reprise of the great lilac elegy, now an anthem in the public domain. It honored the continual flowering of their nation. Having gone through their Walt Whitman exercises in school, some sort of mystique in shared recollection calls out to almost every American when the profane subject of human liberty is touched upon in the shadow of that saintly colossus, known to us as Abraham Lincoln.

"If the weather holds out, it should be fine." Cody said, tamping the earth around the tender plant.

"Where have they gone?" Molly was looking around for the children.

"I can see them." Cody answered. "They've gone down the trail again." He looked at Jacob with an exaggerated grin. Jacob asked 'what?' with his expression; and Cody answered tacitly, 'You know. Don't mess it up, you derelict.' You could see his merriment in his gait as he departed from their company. They watched him enter among the tall pine trees along the sheltered path.

"I really like him," Molly said.

"Beware, he's a creature of infinite sorrows."

"Who isn't? I like how he's got them calling it the magic path."

"He's just a kid himself."

"Look who's talking."

"It was nice of you to come over like this." Jacob no longer had any idea of what his role ought to be, regarding his behavior around her; everything was up in the air. He suddenly felt completely free. He didn't care if it were impossible. He was going to soak up her spirit whenever he could, and the hell with it. It made no sense and he didn't care! That was his new mantra. Let whatever is at hand and clearly good, be sufficient for this hour . . .

"I wanted to do something for you."

Jacob wondered if she had come to give him a present so that he would have something to remember her by. She watched a cloud of sorrow pass over his face.

"Show me where you live." She looked up at the windows of The Joint.

"Okay, sure."

They trooped up the steps and she went around exploring The Joint with a woman's instinctive aversion for atrocious décor. Her nose wrinkled up but she didn't say anything. Bending over to scrutinize certain objects on a large table she discovered a sheaf of papers.

"What are these?" She had found his handwritten sheets of music.

"Some old school papers."

"This is your handwriting?"

"Yes."

"Well, I can see you used to be a good Catholic boy, right?"

"Yeah, I don't think I can say I am any longer."

He reached down and rummaged through the pages rapidly.

"Here," he said. "Take this one. My gift to you for the lilacs." It was his personal transcription of Bob Dylan's magisterial "Visions of Johanna."

"I remember you telling me about this song. Play it for me."

"Right now?"

"Sure, why not?"

He went to his CD collection and she cried out, "No! I mean on your guitar."

"Oh." He hesitated, wanting to humbly protest; but it wouldn't be sincere. For a long time he had wanted to play this song for her, and many others. *Now* she was asking him to play it for her? He sat down in his chair and hefted the guitar and began playing the song. She continued inspecting the space and he wasn't sure she was even listening. After about a minute he stopped. "It's a pretty long song."

"That's okay. Jacob, that was beautiful."

"I don't play it exactly—"

"Is this her?" She was holding a picture of Jacob and Johanna on the day of their first communion. He came up beside her, his hand went out to grasp the frame of the picture and they were both holding it together.

"She was so sweet looking." Molly took the picture and put it back where it had been. She walked over to a table on which she had seen her book lying.

"Sorry I haven't gotten that back to you. Go on, take it."

"Are you done with it?"

"Yeah, pretty much."

"You're going to be sticking around Ferdinand, aren't you?"

"I'm not going anywhere."

"I can get it later. Let's go back outside."

He watched her roll up the music sheet, holding it like a little wand, and when she passed by him at the top of the stairs she tapped him playfully on the head. They went down the stairs and walked around to where the heavy boulders were ranged in a row at the back of the area behind the stables. Sophie ran up to tell her mom about the fire they were about to start. She wanted to make sure they would be staying. She started hopping from one rock to another. She almost fell once and Jacob put out his arm like a bannister and she grabbed the sleeve of his fisherman sweater in a bunch to steady herself. She made a sport of leaping between the rocks.

Jacob turned to look at Molly as the child remained a gleaming shape floating between them. He saw that Molly was observing him very closely, and as they smiled their faces were mirroring one another. He saw her eyes becoming darker as he looked at her. Sophie released him as she jumped to the ground and ran off while calling back to her mother to not forget about the fire. Jacob sat down and stared into space, his fate seemed as close as the invisible atmosphere he could feel so sharply on his face. The Aeolian harp, which he had placed in the stables near an open window, now began to wail and moan in tonal responses. He had forgotten it was there. This was the first time he heard it play the music for which it was intended.

"What's making that wondrous sound?" Molly asked. He told her.

"Oh, that's lovely. To be out here, feeling this crisp air, and then it just comes out of the breezes like that. Jacob, this is going to be quite the place some day." She was extremely happy and this made him slightly delirious.

"It will be fun helping them put it all together."

"If you stay, you could be an important part of it."

"Yes, for a while, I guess. I have to make plans for myself, too. I received an inheritance recently."

"Really? From your uncle Julius?"

"Yes, from the woman actually; but it was more than I expected. And I'm going to enroll in classes at the university this next semester."

"Well, good for you. If you get a degree, then I'll have to stop looking down on you for being an ignoramus."

"That's the main reason why I'm doing it. What is your degree, again?"

"Accounting."

"Oh, that's right. Makes it harder to cheat the rich widow."

"Impossible."

They both laughed uncertainly. They were looking very closely at each other and looking away very quickly, when suddenly their eyes met. He heaved a great sigh, struggling against his tendency to withdraw.

"I might be able to get my old job back. The ownership has changed hands again. Some of the old managers bought the company. They said the customers were asking them, 'Where's Gates?'—"

"Is that what you want?"

"I don't know. Maybe part time. I'm not sure."

There was tension woven about them and he was compelled to speak his mind. "Molly, I don't think I can be a very good friend, not for a while, at least. I thought I could, I really did, but—"

"No, I know. I can't be yours, either.

They stared at one another for an instant.

"Where does that leave us?" She asked. He felt a murmurous disturbance deep in the chambers of his heart begin to boom like war drums.

"You know what? I don't know what I'm talking about. I don't mean we can't be friends." He was on the verge of losing control of his faculties. Was he really about to drive her away? He had a sick feeling that everything was going wrong because of his incorrigible stupidity.

"Do you want to know why I came here today?"

"Yes."

"Sophie asked me why I was so sad. I told her I missed my friend. 'Why don't you go see him?' she said to me. Just like that; and she knew it was you. She asked me, 'Is it that man you're always talking to at school? Who makes you laugh so much.' So I said to her, why don't we go see him."

The moment arrived like an oncoming weather front that has to discharge a vast amount of energy back into the ground before passing on. Jacob stared at her in wonder. It still did not seem possible that he could have everything he had ever wanted in life. She seemed to be discouraged by his reticence. She sat down on the large flat rock as though on an ancient seat hewn for kings. She dipped a finger into a tiny clear pool of rainwater. She crossed her denim legs and hunched forward a little, looking out over the sunken garden, and up at the windows of The Joint, where only ghosts could look back at her. The harp sobbed almost imperceptibly.

"It would be good to hear you tell me exactly how you feel." She spoke her mind with quiet resolve.

"About what?" He couldn't believe he had just said that to her.

She stood up, laughing, reaching up and touching his forehead with her wet finger. She ran two fingers roughly over the stitch marks.

He flinched, "Don't, that's still sensitive."

She shook her head derisively. "I don't know, boy, you may have suffered some permanent damage up there."

He was no longer conscious of anything else than the fact he could not bear the thought of living without her. It was clear the only way to keep any semblance of his life's share of ecstasy was to share it with her.

"I love you Molly."

"Since when?" She actually fell back a step, as if to retrieve her balance and to get a better look at him. He almost looked as though he had been caught off guard as well.

"I don't know. Since I first met you." He looked in the direction of the fire pit, as if clues might be hidden there. "That's how it seems to me, anyway."

"No way." She was studying his face.

"I almost told you after we'd gone into the confessional that first time."

"Get out of here. We'd just met."

"That's what I couldn't understand." He was groping after words, many past scenes began whirling in his mind.

"What were you thinking?"

"That I'd met the best friend of my life. I couldn't imagine not—"

"You didn't want to lose me?"

"God, no."

"You big idiot!" Molly exclaimed with enormous fervor.

"What?" He was suspended in awe; completely entwined in her emotions.

"You never said one word to me." She leaned closer and her eyes loomed up, enveloping him. There was no more need of words, in fact; her face fell into that penumbra where the intellect falls away and the being plunges into the magnetic coils of passion. One moment her eyes were peering straight into him and then her body was pressed against his and he was suspended above all his fears. The delicious fleshy feel of her lips intoxicated him. It was obvious each had thought to make it a quick, chaste exchange of sebum, but neither could break away so easily once their love had been sealed. It became almost comical by the time Cody yelled at them.

"Hey! What are you two doing?"

He stood off in a cathedral nave of pine trees, selecting and paring pieces of wood to make walking staffs for his labor force; neither of the children had been able to see what he had just witnessed. Jacob and Molly turned and moved to stand side by side, facing in the same direction.

"Mom!" Sophie cried in her high-pitched screech. "We're making the fire!"

"I know!"

"Mom!"

"What?"

"Do you want to see the magic path first?"

"I do!" She shouted back.

She left one arm behind her back as she strolled forward and Jacob reached over and their fingers laced together. They walked along holding lightly to each other.

"Are you ready for this?"

"I'm more than ready."

"Oh yeah. This is going to get interesting." She said. "There's so much we don't even know."

"I think we're going to know really quick."

"Know what?" Her mouth hung open expectantly.

He didn't answer her, he didn't have to; his hand roved down over her taught jeans. There was an abrupt alteration in the balance of personalities; both teetering in equal thrall on the planted rock of the enraptured banns they had just published in their hearts.

"There's so much to look forward to."

"I'm pretty sure you're going to end up in Isaac's house."

"That doesn't make you much of a soothsayer."

"I can see myself as your groundskeeper."

"I bet your can."

"The best part will be finding out about those things we don't know."

"My God! I've never seen *that* smile on your face before." She began laughing in luxurious abandonment.

Visions played out in his mind, as if he possessed a perfect clairvoyant sense. He could see into the future; the two of them riding on waves of passion, venturing forth on the backs of mythological dolphins. It would be in the modern way; they would have an extended honeymoon at the outset, many local adventures, sporting about in the delicious mist. They would become engaged, get married, and take a short exotic ritual honeymoon, having to take their bliss far away for some obscure reason. They would become as that first pair in the garden again, teasing the archangels on duty in that sector of the world. Returning they would love, labor, and struggle to endure as the physical passion subsided. He knew their life would always consist of what they both held most dear. He had to force himself off this train of thought; it was like a touch of madness. He knew how circumstances sometimes weaken, even destroy, the best intentions, and from now on he had to make sure to pay close attention, in every possible way, as he never had before. This would now become his religion.

"One thing . . ."

"Yes?" Her voice flowed out as honey in sunlight.

"I want to go to Midnight Mass with you and Sophie. I want to sing carols with you two. Are heathens allowed to do that?"

"So you want to go to church for the music?"

"Pretty much. And I want to be by your side."

"I don't know about you Gates; but I'm sure something can be arranged."

"I hope we have lots of snow this winter." He imagined whorls of snow laying a blanket over the floor of his mystic globe of Ferdinand.

"Why did you say that?"

"I don't know, I love snow."

"Oh, I do too.

"We'll go sledding on Spencer's Hill."

"We'll go see my sister in Ithaca, New York. We'll bury ourselves in snow. We'll be wise and foolish."

"That sounds wonderful to me."

"And then we'll come back here—"

"Where everything is—"

"Where our lives will take root again. In our house."

"So, we won't ever leave Ferdinand?"

"Not if I can help it."

Jacob began whistling Adeste Fideles and Molly whispered the Latin lyrics in response, changing the word Bethlehem to Ferdinand; which made Jacob burst into laughter.

———

The first time Molly met Jacob's family at his parents' house, Mark was the last one to bid her goodbye at the end of the evening. As she and Jacob were leaving, his last words, looking at Molly, were only, "Have fun." This incited a riot of mock recriminations to pour down upon him afterwards; the jesting from his brothers on that point continued for a long time thereafter. It was said he had gotten too old to remember his most solemn benediction. Those who knew Molly well, upon hearing of the family joke, liked to attest that the issue was quite simple. Mark's usual blessing did not apply to Molly, for there was nothing she was likely to neglect, other than possibly having enough fun for herself, so of course that was the only part that was germane to her situation. Those who knew her best secretly prized the knowledge she would not even need to hear that prayer material. She understood why all those sacred hymns of life were composed in the first place, she had come to hold them as her birthright.

Madeleine embraced her as a true daughter. In no time Molly could be found working at her side in her kitchen before a feast, like she'd grown up there. This was unprecedented, and the other daughters-in-law formed a cabal so they could grouse about her precedence in peace. But no one was safe from her sorcery. Over time the rich joys of her heart possessed them. Henry Gates once mused aloud to his four sons, "She's gone through the fires, and she's come out better than anyone else I've ever known." Even Matthew's wife Judy was intensely fond of Molly; once burbling like a girl,

"The sound of her laughter always makes me happy." She found that being close to Molly brought her closer to Madeleine. It was Luke who ended up being Jacob's best man.

He told Jacob on the day of his nuptials, 'She has an aura about her.'

"She's full of life." Jacob responded without reflection. "She's my Aurora," he thought to himself.

Right before his wedding began, during a pause in the preparatory bustle at St. Margaret's, Jacob broke away from his groomsmen for a moment to greet Isaac. He arrived late with a woman of his age and stature and appeared to be happy and exceedingly sober. They exchanged amenities and partook of easy laughter. Isaac adopted the ironic role of being an emissary from the C & H Company. Jacob clapped him on the shoulder in solidarity. He met his lady friend. They all gushed affection at one another. Isaac spoke to him in character.

"My son, have you given sufficient study to your vows?"

"I'm too happy to think about it."

"Do you have any questions for the board?"

"How do you thank someone for bringing you to your own soul?"

"I'm not sure, but I suppose you take your time."

"I have many arguments to pick with you at a later date, at the Cook Gazebo in our back yard."

"Very good. We will sit down with ancient voices, and vintages, and let them all breathe."

"On which side?" An usher asked them.

"Molly is an older friend." Jacob reminded him graciously.

"She's the friend of all the world." Isaac replied.

Isaac's lady friend had to shush him as they walked down the aisle, his laughter was bubbling upwards into the rafters.

It had been arranged to have the reception later in the evening at the Spencer House; but Molly had been inspired by a certain painting of Jules Breton, showing a procession of women in a distant time and place. She wanted her maidens to go there with her right after the mass to pop the first champagne bottles, while posing for the photographer in the first effervescence. Provisions had been made to change footwear after the ceremony for the short trek. The men transported a load of flimsy shoes, purses, and other loose sundries to the house by car, as the women, wearing running shoes or barefoot, pranced down Elizabeth, sweeping past the sycamores, crossing to Church Street, and tramping indelicately through the yards. Many sisters and daughters assisted with the garments as the procession ascended Spencer's Hill, attended by joyful squeals and boisterous laughter. Sophie held her mother's hem aloft the whole way. The late October sun touched beauteous fires to their soft hair and glinted upon all their irrepressible movements.

Various photographs of Molly's troop, as seen approaching, climbing, and cresting Spencer's hill, are owned by many people who live in Ferdinand, and many other places to be sure. To this day there is fond talk in many circles of the first wedding celebrated at what is now referred to as the reincarnation of the Spencer mansion.

CPSIA information can be obtained
at www.ICGtesting.com
Printed in the USA
LVHW081727221121
703859LV00015BA/27